Paper Children

PAPER CHILDREN

Norma Levinson

CENTURY

LONDON MELBOURNE AUCKLAND JOHANNESBURG

Copyright © Norma Levinson 1986

All rights reserved

First published in Great Britain in 1986 by Century Hutchinson Ltd
Brookmount House, 62–65 Chandos Place, London WC2N 4NW

Century Hutchinson Publishing Group (Australia) Pty Ltd
16–22 Church Street, Hawthorn, Melbourne, Victoria 3122

Century Hutchinson Group (NZ) Ltd
32–34 View Road, PO Box 40–086, Glenfield, Auckland 10

Century Hutchinson Group (SA) Pty Ltd
PO Box 337, Bergvlei 2012, South Africa

British Library Cataloguing in Publication Data
Levinson, Norma
Paper children.
I. Title
823'.914[F]   PR6062.E92/

ISBN 0–7126–0799–4

Typeset by Inforum Ltd, Portsmouth
Printed in Great Britain by
Redwood Burn Ltd, Trowbridge, Wiltshire

For Itke, Chasia and Leo – with love

Part One

Chapter One

Orthodox Jewish marriages are not made in Heaven. They are made in Front Rooms which reproduce from generation unto generation. The texture; the smell; the exact density of the air remains the same; the sanctity of them forever preserved.

Gentile Front Rooms are used for less hallowed occasions. The windows may be gay with net curtains; the armchairs are used for rest and relaxation, and the colour and pattern of the carpet is bright and well-defined. There will be ornaments on the shelves and a vase of flowers on the mantelpiece. It is possible that on the sideboard is a tray covered with a dainty cloth, bearing matching cups and saucers, for the family have their tea there on Sundays, or when entertaining visitors. The sandwiches are made from neat white bread and are cut across into triangles, the fillings perfectly contained. The biscuits and cakes are delicious and rich, and are not humped and deformed, or frilled with dark brown edges. The furniture is capable of being moved by one or two powerfully built men; and the room gleams with sunlight, is warmed by the occasional fire, and echoes with recent laughter.

Rachel and her sisters were not brought up in such a room. Nor was their mother. Her grandchildren would yearn for one as she yearned, and promise themselves that when they grew up and married, their whole house would be used, lived in and sunlit with activity and life. Vain hope! Fruitless longing! They may consume rashers of forbidden bacon without a spasm of guilt; break the thousands of years' embargo on shellfish without their hearts missing a beat; but the Jewish Front Room will be indelibly printed on their hovels or mansions as remorselessly as the genes in their cells.

One hot September Sunday afternoon, Malka set off with her best friend to Euston Station, for Jinny was visiting her newly married brother. Malka collected her from her house and they struggled off to the tram stop together, sharing the weight of the big brown suitcase. They arrived too early, so she rashly invited Jinny into the Station Buffet for a cup of tea and a Fry's chocolate sandwich bar; then unable to leave her friend to find her own way to the train, she bought a penny platform ticket. They hugged each other until a second before the train puffed off towards the unknown city of Manchester. Malka was left on the platform, bereft of her friend, and after dabbing away a few tears, realized that she was several miles from her home in Stepney with nothing in her purse but a torn platform ticket.

She was young and vigorous, but the way was long and her shoes were tight and high-heeled. Two and a half hours later, hot and exhausted, she hobbled up the steps to her door and opened it; but instead of going down the passage into the kitchen, she went into the Front Room. Here it was cool and dark. She kicked off her shoes and threw her hat onto the great polished table. She padded around the perimeter of the drear carpet, her feet cooled by the brown lino, then flung herself onto the cold leather sofa. She knew quite well that her actions were a profanation; the heavy oak sideboard was a place for the silver candlesticks only, not for her bag. The portraits of holy rabbis on the walls stared at her reclining form, unable to avert their disapproving eyes. The shelves, crammed with ancient Hebrew books, commentaries on the prophets and Jewish encyclopaedias, hid behind their dark, dusty covers. She threw her spectacles on the floor and stretched her arms in an ecstasy that only the exhausted understand. 'O, God!' she sighed, 'am I tired! Am I weary! Am I *dead*!' She closed her eyes and felt for the cruel suspenders digging into her thighs and heard a human cough some eight feet away. She froze, and listened. This time it was unmistakable and male. No one ever came into the Front Room except to wipe away dust or replace the candlesticks after use for the Friday night lights. The only time the table was used was for High Holy Days or when men of learning visited to discuss endlessly the wisdom of what was contained in one of the dark volumes. They would drink glasses of lemon tea; soften her mother's burnt biscuits in its

4

hot harshness; or enjoy a finger or two of whisky if one there present had recently been blessed with a grandson.

But now, on this Sunday afternoon, someone was sitting there, alone, in the great carver chair, coughing! Terrified at this sacrilegious intrusion, she leapt from the sofa and made for the door, her left stocking hanging around her ankle, and flew down the passage into the kitchen. She could not see, through her short-sighted eyes, her mother's expression of exasperation and dislike. Her two younger brothers sat at the kitchen table, poring over their studies. 'There's someone in the Front Room!' she gasped. 'There's a man, coughing in the Front Room!'

'Coughing? They told me he was in good health! Why should they tell me stories like that? Look at you!' sneered her mother. 'Look how you look! Where have you been, fool? He's been waiting over an hour. Wash your face and take in biscuits and tea.' She spoke in Yiddish, and although not yet fifty, had long been old. Her daughter often wondered if she had ever skipped or laughed when she was young, but discarded the idea as an impossible fancy.

'I'm not going in there! He saw me pulling my stocking off! He saw . . . God! I'll never go out of this room! Never! Get him out of the house!'

'He's your Shidduch*, ugly face! Father in Heaven, why am I so cursed? To lose my darling Devorah and be left with you! Where are your glasses?'

'I don't know. In there. Danny, go and fetch them for me and tell him I'm ill or dead. Get rid of him!'

'No! Take this tea in this moment! Danny, get her other shoes from the bedroom. He's been waiting for hours already. You won't have another chance. Do you want to be an old maid? Do you want to end my life? Go!' Her mother began to bang her head against the wall – an old trick which horrified all her children. She knew that her mother had won. She fastened her stocking, wiped her face at the scullery sink with a damp flannel and squeezed her swollen feet painfully into her spare pair of shoes. She hobbled blindly down the passage with the tray. Her brother opened the Front Room door and closed it softly behind her.

*match   (Shidduch – 'ch' as in 'loch')

A young man, his face a blur, rose to his feet and stood before her. He took the tray and placed it on the table, then handed her spectacles to her. She put them on, and caught the end of the sweetest smile that anyone had ever blessed her with. He was tall, though not handsome; yet the dark eyes, the large nose and mouth which crowded his face, were assembled with such gentleness and refinement that his beauty astounded and delighted her. His beardless cheeks were as smooth as hers, and his black hat, tilted back, revealed a high forehead crowned with curls.

'Good afternoon. My name is Sacha Sokolovsky and I am from the village of Liubava near Kalvaria. Yanovy, where your parents were born, is not far away. I have been there many times. I am studying now, in England. Your father told me you are a nice, lovely girl and everything he said is true.'

He had learned what to say; had studied the words on the small piece of paper in his pocket all the time he had been waiting for her, yet had been unable to prevent himself digressing. He spoke slowly, in Yiddish, unsure whether she would understand. She smiled back at him, and asked him, in English, if he would like some tea, and he bowed his head, uncomprehending. She repeated the question in Yiddish, and he nodded and thanked her, then clumsily drew a chair for her and would not sit or take refreshment until she was settled.

'I am sorry I startled you. I coughed so that you should know I was here. You were tired and hot and you must have been on a long journey.'

Malka told him how she had been to see her friend off on the train and had walked home because she had spent her tram fare.

'I like to walk,' he said. 'I would like to walk with you next Sunday. I do not know the country, or English or English ways. Would you teach me some English and the ways of England?' They had difficulty understanding one another's Yiddish. 'Would you honour me with your company?'

'Yes,' she said, remembering that she had promised to meet Jinny's train after an interminable week's separation. 'Oh, yes! I'll show you the Tower of London, then we'll walk over Tower Bridge and look at the river. And you must teach me how to speak Yiddish properly!'

They drank their tea. He sucked his through a sugar lump

6

which he kept in his mouth, but the noise did not offend her or embarrass him. It was the custom of men from Eastern Europe. He showed her sepia photographs of his widowed mother, his brothers and sisters; the youngest, Hannah, being no more than three years old. Something about the pride and love with which he showed her his pictures made her soul ache, and she examined them as if they, even now, belonged to her, too. She learned all their names immediately, and their faces became familiar to her the second she looked upon them, and he watched her, affected by her attention. She gave them back to him, almost unwillingly. He returned them to a worn envelope, and as she poured his second glass of tea, she saw him press his lips to its tattered cover. A melancholy, sudden and dreadful, overwhelmed her, and boiling tears misted her spectacles and squeezed beneath the rims, as if, until this moment, she had not known she was unloved.

He turned away in order to allow her to regain her composure. He would find out, when he knew her better, the reason for her sorrow. 'I hope you will meet my family one day,' he said. 'They will like you very much.'

When her father opened the door, they both jumped. He came in, dressed as if for the Sabbath, and greeted Sacha who had risen to his feet. He was offered whisky and a cigarette, and Malka was told to go and make fresh tea – a mere formality to get her out of the room. They no longer looked at each other.

'Well?' her mother said. 'A sick man with a cough! A skinny nobody with consumption! Your father must be mad, bringing a dying dog into the house!'

'He coughed only because he didn't know what else to do. I might have taken the rest of my clothes off!' She laughed so merrily that her brothers, forgetting their mother, joined in, delighted, questioning her about what had happened in the Front Room. The three of them fell about the kitchen table, helpless with mirth, while their mother sneered, addressing the sink.

'She likes him, the fool. She likes a sick man. She'll be nursing an invalid for the rest of her life. Danny! Meir! Get on with your studies! Do you want to be empty-heads like her? Don't fill your ears with her nonsense!'

The boys bent their heads, shaking; stuffing their fingers into their mouths.

'What if he hadn't coughed?' whispered Meir. 'What would you have taken off next? Tell us, Malka!'

'The waistband of this skirt was torture! The elastic in my bloomers was biting like an Alsatian's fangs!'

The boys screamed with joy as their father came into the kitchen, smiling.

'I have invited the young man to join us for supper on Friday night.' He spoke to his wife, ignoring her scowls. 'He is waiting to say goodbye to Malka.'

He winked secretly at his daughter and patted her shoulder awkwardly, and she squeezed past him and ran down the passage, into the Front Room.

Chapter Two

The child knew that if she didn't follow the road which stretched before her, she could avoid the stone people lined up on either side. Once before, she had resisted successfully. But this time her sleep was too dark and deep, and she was inexorably drawn towards it. They were as enormous as tall houses and she was smaller than an insect. They were shaped like clothes-pegs, without arms or proper legs. She ran as fast as she could, but they stretched endlessly ahead. They would bend downwards in a minute, but she wouldn't look up; she wouldn't look at their imbecilic, grinning faces. They crowded in on her, huge and hideous, blocking her path, preparing to do something unknown and terrible. She screamed herself awake and continued to howl and cling to her mother, who lay beside her under the fat feather eiderdown.

'Hannahle, it's a dream — a nasty, silly dream! Look! I'm blowing it away!' Her mother pursed her lips and blew softly, three times, on Hannah's sweating forehead, then held her in her arms and rocked her and sang to her. The utter bliss of her mother's nearness after the suffocating evil of the stone people, enchanted her soul.

'Are you here all the time, even when the stone people are watching me?'

'All the time, little bird.'

'In the road?'

'Which road is it? Tell me, and I will frighten them away.'

'I don't know,' said Hannah Sokolovsky, and she fell asleep and dreamed of being three years old again, and eating dumplings and meat and sweet carrots. Not until morning, when she awoke, would she remember that she was four, and lived on boiled turnips.

Chapter Three

Sacha Sokolovsky fainted in the telephone box when he heard the news. The customers who saw him all swore that there wasn't a drop of blood left in his face and that his lips were blue. He'd been his usual self, five minutes earlier, collecting the shopping; telling everyone that the baby was due at any time. Percy stowed the jars and packets, the bulging paper bags and the newspaper-wrapped eggs into the shopping basket with marvellous skill and respect for both customer and ingredients. Everyone there witnessed the performance and crowded round to wish him and his family well, and then watched him through the wedged-open shop door, as he walked over to the public telephone box to ring the maternity hospital and enquire after Malka's progress. Percy said that the eggs flowed down the pavement like the Yellow River and the jar of herrings crashed its contents into the swimming gutter. He always exaggerated, but one knew better than to contradict him, since he was the only Kosher grocer in the city.

'Rabbi! What's the matter? What's happened?' he called.

Sacha staggered out of the booth and leaned against its green and yellow wall, his hands hanging by his sides. Someone set a stool against the counter and he was helped back into the shop. 'Your wife? How is she? Come and sit down a minute!'

He sat. A bottle of whisky was pulled from under the counter and poured. He took the proffered glass with shaking hands and raised it above his head.

'To Life!' he croaked, and all there gathered, responded, weak with relief. 'My wife and the baby are both well, thank God.'

For a few seconds you could have heard a grain of rice fall onto the sawdust on the floor. Mrs Firman, whose son had been decorated for bravery in 1918, his audacious courage inherited from his mother, straightened her bony shoulders and spoke, breaking the petrified silence.

'Mazeltov, Rabbi! Another little girl? May she bring you and your dear wife joy and pleasure. Sons are only good for heartache and worry with their foolhardy behaviour and thoughtless ways!'

Sacha and Malka Sokolovsky had four daughters. The birth of Rachel was celebrated in Percy's Delicatessen Kosher grocery shop. She did not resemble either of her parents, or the physique and colouring of her sisters. From the age of three or four she was afflicted with fits and occasional spasms of the limbs. At these times, she would fasten her gaze on an invisible and distant terror, then shake her head, puzzled and distraught; then stare again, as if there was something far, far away which she was trying to summon up or recapture, in vain. As she grew older, the exercise increased in its violent isolation, yet remained fruitless. Her sleep was interrupted by fearful dreams and her conscious life by random fantasy and delusions. Her hair turned from almost white to pale, gleaming flaxen, and her eyes were a brilliant, startled blue.

. . . .

Who can tell with absolute assurance, what went on at the time of one's birth? It is an everlasting and universal secret, yet, oddly, I am the exception to the awesome rule. I had no recollection of leaping into life at St Stephen's Maternity Hospital. My star did not rise there! But the story of what happened in the shop on that grey autumn day was reported to me by so many people, that I grew up with the memory of being born there, among the sacks of dried peas and beans and rice; the boot polish and the butter barrel; the pickled fish and the dirty potatoes; the flour and the beigels. Set free by the wire cheese cutter which always fascinated me, and landed onto the marble counter, looking at my father's stricken face; seeing Percy, as if he were the midwife, in his whisky-coloured, whisky-perfumed overall; hearing him say, 'Well, Rabbi Sokolovsky, I'm sorry, but this is all I have in stock today. Maybe

11

next time you call, I'll have what you want.' Then he wrapped me up in a piece of muslin, along with the cheese, and planted me in the basket with clinical neatness and authority.

Once I had a dream – the kind that everyone has when the heart ceases to beat during sleep, then catches up on itself. In mine, I was walking to Percy's with two empty paper carriers with string handles. I did the entire journey from my house to the shop, and all the time my heart was still. As I entered, I mercifully tripped over the two concrete steps, and I awoke, suffocating, clutching and gasping, and thus lived to dream again. I always took extreme care, thereafter, when going on my interminable errands to Percy's, to trip over the steps, just in case I might be dreaming and not realise it. Lots of people and animals returned to their birthplace when the time of death approached. One could never be too careful.

War broke out a month after my fourth birthday, yet I remembered so much of that time before. No one believed me. Forgetful cynics! My family thought that I must have picked up information from their conversations, and that I was misguided in believing I had actual knowledge, but it was they who were deluded. How could I have failed to recollect our Front Room, dark and forbidding? Who but I could remember the pleasure of the variety of occupations with which I busied myself during my formative years? Smacking and bullying my doll; digging to Australia in the back yard; sweeping the pavement with a small fireside brush, and scraping the enamel off the big bowl when Mam's back was turned. I was always happy and busy and optimistic, and never doubted my ability to succeed. While I tussled with an old knife and fork in a particularly juicy crack between the flagstones, I knew that if I laboured long enough, I would reach that underground country where tiny people lived, happily entombed under the earth, carrying on their daily business upside-down. My days were not wasted, for later, when I thought of the Time to Come, the deep slit in the earth which would be my eternal resting-place, I was not unbearably horrified by the prospect. Some friendly Australians would be there waiting to acknowledge the faith I had in their existence, and I would be reincarnated in New South Wales.

The pleasure I derived from these pastimes was only exceeded by the company of my father's youngest sister, who came from the village of Liubava, in the Republic of Lithuania, to visit us. Dad had sent her the fare-money, and her mother let her go, on condition that she helped Mam. No reunion was more joyous; no relative more welcome. Dad spoilt and teased her; Mam loved and relied on her; and my sisters and I doted on her, for we had never had a playmate who was so daring and different and merry. We screamed with laughter when Hannah failed to understand us, and Esther taught her all the rude words she could think of. When men of learning came to study with Dad, in the Front Room, Hannah would take in the glasses of tea and the plate of humpy biscuits, and repeat one of the swear words, pretending innocence, for she was as wild and mischievous as the devil and had the patience and appearance of a saint. We hid in the passage, listening, cramming our fingers in our mouths, until she emerged, her eyes dancing and her finger on her lips. She taught Sybil to juggle with three oranges and Esther to be the champion skipper in the street. Vered became an expert in card tricks and learned amazing variations of Cat's Cradle. She could vault and climb and turn cartwheels better than anyone in the world.

My sisters and all their friends wanted to play with Hannah all the time, but during the day they attended school, and at these times, she and I were constant companions. Strangers took us for sisters, for her hair and eyes were the same colour as mine. I copied everything she did and studied each idiosyncrasy in minute detail, and it was Hannah I ran to for comfort and attention. When she walked up the street, I chased her, calling, 'Hannah! Hannah! *Kuda idyosh? Podozhdi! Ya poidu s toboi!*' And she would shout with laughter and run back to me, swinging me round and jumping me in the air.

Hannah brought me a dark brown fur hat all the way from Liubava, and it was my most cherished possession. I sat on the low wall which bounded our house, looking at it and holding it against my face, and as soon as I saw someone coming, I put it on, fixing the ear-flaps on top and then pulling them down, imagining the envy and admiration which burned in the hearts of those who saw. One terrible day, Dirty Teddy Lambert snatched my hat in a fit of jealous rage, put it on his shaved and scabby head, ran into his house a little way along the street, and slammed his door. The misery, grief and horror which this crime against me caused, was dreadful. I screamed because my

13

heart was broken, and fell off the wall and rolled about on the pavement in an agony of spirit. People ran to my aid but only Hannah understood. Mam said, 'Shush! Listen! We'll buy you a pixie-hat! You can't wear your fur hat any more – not after Teddy . . . If you shut up now, I'll buy you a bunny hat as well!' I held my breath for a full minute on digesting this crass remark, and only let go when I heard Hannah tell me that we would retrieve it at once, for she knew, had always known the priorities, and that justice must be seen to be done.

We hurried off to the Lamberts' and didn't waste time knocking. Hannah merely turned the knob and flung the door open. I followed her down the stinking passage and into the vile kitchen. She pushed aside fat Maggie Lambert with both hands and made for Teddy, who backed into a corner, holding my hat above his head. Hannah leapt into the air like a wild-cat and clung to his neck, dragging him down to the floor, shouting instructions to me in Russian so that they couldn't understand. I bit Maggie's leg and scrambled across the greasy floor, grabbing the hat from Teddy's startled fingers, while Hannah stamped on his hand. Maggie tore it away from me, ripping one of the ear flaps; but Hannah was there, slapping, scratching and shouting, and in less than three minutes we were flying down the passage with the hat in possession. Thereafter, Mam used it to shine up the stove after she had black-leaded it, but the disappointment of not being able to wear it again was submerged by the excitement of battle. When Hannah told Dad about the stolen hat, he said, 'She shows off too much. If she hadn't been showing off, Teddy wouldn't have taken it from her. She does it with the knitting and reading, pretending she can do everything, and the more you laugh and encourage her, the more she shows off.'

This humiliation was too hard for me to bear. No one realized how much I longed to be able to read; to discover the secret which all about me knew, and in which I was unable to share. I had never asked Mam to teach me to knit; for people to believe I could, was enough. In any case, I could move those needles even faster than she or Hannah. I could point at words and turn the page at exactly the right time, as long as I knew the story well; but when a strange book or comic came my way, I could only gabble wildly and point and turn the pages haphazardly, while my sisters sat, engrossed, magnificent in

their knowledge, managing, without a single picture, to understand what the words said. My ego reached its lowest ebb. My
only hope of salvation was to kick Dad and scream, and thus
disperse the shame which I thought must clog the air for ever.
'Show me how to read without pictures!' I screamed. 'Without
pictures!'

I was glad when Hannah shouted at Dad and pushed him
with the broom until he fell onto the sofa, laughing, and said
he was sorry for his insulting remarks.

'She's bored!' said Mam, with her usual ignorance. 'She
drives Hannah and me mad all day! She spends hours poking
in the dirt, jabbing needles in her eyes, scraping at the laundry
bowl, putting that hat on her head and off her head as if she
can't stop, and chasing Hannah wherever she goes. How
would you like to look after her all day? She's more trouble
than all the kids were, put together! I could never manage
without Hannah; not in a million years! God knows who she
takes after!'

I saw Dad look first at Mam, then at Hannah and back to
Mam again, as if he was thinking very hard.

'Teach me to read English,' said Hannah, 'then Rachel will
learn too. She can learn anything I teach her! See how she
understands Lithuanian and Russian and Yiddish! She knows
all the songs that Mummy sang to me when I was a baby, just
because I sing them to her every night. And do you know what
else, Sacha? After showing her my photographs just once, and
telling her everyone's name, she remembered them all! Every
day, she lays out the pictures on the mat, and I tell her about
Liubava, and she looks at my drawings. She knows who lives
in which house and who I play with, and she knows the way to
the school and the bridge, the forest and the station. She can
point to the blacksmith's and the church and the synagogue.
She knows our village better than you do! Show him, Rachel!
Show your dad how clever you are!'

And so Hannah taught me to read. It was as if my fur hat had
been muffling my powers, and as soon as it became a duster,
they were released. In the midst of my swaggering joy at this
glorious achievement, the worst trauma of my life occurred.
On 15 August 1939, Hannah's fourteenth birthday, she went
away. I thought that the trip to the station was part of her
birthday celebrations, and that Sybil, Esther and Vered were

crying because they were jealous of Hannah and me going on a train. I had never been on one before, and was overcome with excitement. But when Hannah hugged me, I could feel her tears. I remembered the taste of them when, after she had had a bad dream, I would cuddle up to her in her bed, my head in her neck, and we would sing lullabies and chase it away. But this wasn't a dream! She was going to Liubava without me! There had been a colossal misunderstanding! Mam pulled me onto the platform as the 1.59 for King's Cross slid away.

'Hannah! *Podozhdi! Ya poidu s toboi!*' I screamed. 'Wait for me! I want to come with you!' At two o'clock I had my first fit, and three weeks later I was discharged from the children's hospital and war was declared.

Chapter Four

Pineduggy isn't on the map. I don't know why, for it has existed for hundreds of years. How did anyone know how to get there? How did the postmen in the sorting offices find the pigeon-hole for us? Where did we live, then, for the duration of the war? How was it that there was a village hall, a church and a school called Pineduggy Council School? Where was the location of the farms – Wetherby's and Brocklebank's? Where was Mrs Long born; Miss Frith; Flat-Faced Mug and Mucky Mutts? Nowhere, because Pineduggy was not on the map, and yet they and their forebears had never lived anywhere else. When the soldiers camped in the playing-fields and knocked on doors in the evenings to spend a few desperate hours in their temporary billets, we understood. Pineduggy, they said, was the only village in England without a pub. It never occurred to the residents that this was odd or unusual, for they had never lived in a place with one; but to the soldiers, it was one of the most unpleasant wonders of the world. Maybe the cartographers only marked down villages with pubs, and so they didn't know about Pineduggy. But I did, I and my family and neighbours all knew. Pineduggy was the village to which I was evacuated, eleven miles from the city of Hull. For centuries there had been no pub or inn. And no Jews.

But Liubava was on the map. It nestled in the province of Kovno on the edge of a great forest. A stream ran through the village, spanned by a little wooden bridge. The German cavalry had requisitioned the house where Hannah and her family lived and taken their fine horse and cart, but Hannah had no recollection of it. They lived in a converted barn which had been divided into two rooms, with an extra one up the ladder

17

in the roof. But when she came home, a new house had been built. The forest was unsupervised, and the neighbours had joined together with her brothers, cut trees down and accumulated enough timber to build a beautiful house with four rooms in it.

Sacha and Malka sent the money for a stove. Hannah's mother could cook inside, now, and it would be so cosy during the coming winter; but now it was summer, and as most summers in that part of the world, was beautiful, warm, and with bright sunshine every day. They ate their supper at the table set under the cherry trees, while friends ran over to greet the young traveller with flowers and gifts and questions, wondering at the way she had grown; listening with delighted pride to the English words she repeated for them. What was it like in England? Was there really going to be a terrible war? Were Sacha, Malka and the children safe? Thank God that Sacha had been able to send her home beforehand! Half the village went to the synagogue that Friday night and prayed for Sacha and his family, and the friendly neighbours crossed themselves, and prayed too.

Hannah's mother placed the photographs of her son, daughter-in-law and her four English grandchildren in a frame next to those of her less far-flung kin.

'*Papereneh kinderlech* – Paper Children! One day I shall embrace you!' She kissed their faces, looked at her son and his wife intently, then examined the pictures of the four little girls, exclaiming with pleasure. 'Sybil is the image of Sacha, and Esther and Vered have the same face as their mother.' She turned to Hannah who was emptying her box of gifts and clothes onto the bed. 'The baby, Rachel, is exactly as you were when you were three!'

'She tried to follow me onto the train. Sacha told her that he could only travel as far as London with me, and that no one but me could go to Liubava, but she wouldn't listen! I looked after her all the time and she couldn't understand that I was leaving without her. Malka said that she belonged to me and when the trouble is over in England, she'll bring her to visit us. 'They'll all come!' she shouted, snatching up the photograph and dancing her mother around the bed. 'They promised, Mummy! They'll all come to Liubava!'

There was an inn in the village of Liubava, then. Jews too. It was on the map, in the province of Kovno, between the towns of Kalvaria and Vilnius, not far from the East Prussian border. But it isn't on the map any more.

Chapter Five

Hannah always went to the forest to pick raspberries. Laden with jars and basins, they set out early on a holiday morning, meeting a group of friends. Some of the mothers went too, but hers was always too busy. They collected so much from the forest: mushrooms, nuts, wild flowers or wood for the stove. But today it was raspberries. They would make wine and jam and puddings and juice. The younger children played most of the time, but not Hannah. She had a job to do. She found a stick almost as tall as herself, and even more sturdy, and pushing the prickly brambles aside, crept in amongst them, and found clusters of beautiful, ripe raspberries. She filled her jar which she carried on a loop around her wrist, and when it was full, emptied it into the big pot which held the contents of twenty jars. She wasn't afraid of a few scratches. How her mother would smile when she saw the amount and quality of her collection! Backwards and forwards she went with her jar, listening to the shouts and laughter of the others, who were playing nearby. Her brother Yosef and their friends Laz and Yuri were building a den in the branches of a huge tree, pretending it was a tree-house for Sora and Olga, but Hannah knew that the great lads were having just as much fun as the little girls, unconcerned with the job in hand. She shouted out to them, for this bush was the most abundant she had ever seen. She wanted to hear Yuri's mother exclaim and scold the boys into helping to clear the bush.

'Where are you, Hannah? Where are you?'

'Come and find me, you idlers! I'm in the best bushes in the whole forest!' She filled her jar and scrambled out into the clearing to find her basin. A man was standing there – a farmer who had always been friendly and cheerful when she and her mother were buying and selling in the Market Square. She shouted greetings to him and told him she had picked the raspberries single-handed.

'Who gave you permission?' he asked coldly.

'We come here all the time,' said Hannah, suddenly afraid. 'All of us from Liubava pick the raspberries. My mother – you know her – Mrs Sokolovsky, makes wine and jam, and she bottles so much that we eat them right through the winter.'

'I asked you who gave you permission?'

'No one. The forest doesn't belong to anyone. Yosef! Yuri! Laz!' she called, wanting them near her.

'This forest belongs to the People. Not to you. Empty this basin!'

'No!' she shouted bravely. 'Why should I leave them on the ground for the slugs? I'll pick as many as I like and take them home!'

'For slugs of Jews? No you won't!' He overturned the basin with his foot and kicked it away, then trampled the raspberries into the ground. She watched the red juice mingle with the grass and some of the squashed fruit remained on his boots. Her brother came running towards her with the others. 'You may gather raspberries,' he said to Yuri and his mother, 'and you may not,' he snarled, pointing his stick at each one of the Jewish children. 'You Jews bleed the country of everything. Get out of here! Get back to your damp holes!' He smiled at Yuri's mother, and she smiled back; but Yuri didn't, for he was Yosef's best friend, and they had sworn to be comrades for ever.

'Why did you do that to Hannah's pot, Tamsta Kutkus? Why did you?'

'Ask your good mother,' he smiled, patting Yuri's shoulder. 'She will tell you. She understands. Now, you bloodsuckers, get out before I have to use my stick on you.'

Olga pressed her face against Yuri's mother, who moved away from her. Sora tried to take her hand, but the woman folded her arms. Hannah saw. She lifted her stick high above her head, and brought it down over Kutkus's shoulder, so that he yelped like a dog, and dropped his stick. Yosef picked up the basin. There was a little red juice at the bottom. With a quick jerk of his hand, he threw it at Kutkus's bulging belly, and Laz scooped up the mush from the ground and pushed it into his face. Then they grabbed the little girls and ran down the forest path, followed by his vile abuse. Hannah remembered where she had seen him; long before they had become acquainted on market days. But this wasn't the road. This wasn't a dream. But he was one of the stone people. Her mother was digging in the patch of earth in front of their home. She always blew the stone people away when they came to Hannah in nightmares. But not this time.

Chapter Six

We were the first invaders since William the Conqueror and probably just as unwelcome. The village hid out of direct reach of any town, surrounded by flat, lonely fields and meadows dotted with woods. The cottages straggled in groups along one side of the lane, and a great high hedge bordered the other. Cattle were driven up the lane every day, to graze in the fields beyond. At the bottom were three shiny black boulders, huddled together since the Ice Age, and not even Brockle-bank's bull could shift them. The pond lay opposite, the day-time residence of Mucky Mutts's ducks; every evening, his old daughter, Flat-Faced Mug, rattled a bucket, and the ducks came squawking out for their supper, waddling all by themselves into the muddy yard. Beyond the pond stood the village school, flanked by the churchyard and the village green. Behind the school were the playing-fields and the bowling-green, and on a still evening, you could hear the click of the bowls and the conversation of the old men who were playing, while you sat on one of the black boulders.

The hedge opposite the front window of our cottage bounded Mr Cameron-Spurling's garden. None of the people I asked had ever been in it, but I had an idea that it was crammed with dolls' houses and prams; swings and bikes. Tea was served on the velvet lawn every day. There were small cups and saucers for the dolls, teddy-bears and fairies, and rainbow-coloured cakes, the size of buttons, were piled high on plates with doilies. Isobel Cameron-Spurling could eat as many as she liked. She ate them instead of lumpy porridge and bread and jam, and drank red lemonade instead of water. Some-times, Princess Elizabeth and Princess Margaret Rose came to

23

tea, but the hedge was thicker and taller than a house, and I never saw them. Isobel went to a special school for rich children, but occasionally she would be observed in the lane, riding on a pony. Her father, like God, was rarely seen, though almighty and all powerful. Mr Cameron-Spurling owned the whole village and nearly all its inhabitants. I wished that my mam and dad worked at the Big House, like the other people in our row, and when I suggested that they should try to get a job there, Mam said she would, on condition that Mrs Cameron-Spurling cleaned our smoky chimney, which had nothing to do with anything. Everyone was kind and friendly to Spot Cameron-Spurling, even when he barked all night and growled at the children, but Mam was always nasty and unkind, and threw a tussock of grass at him, because he got on her nerves. My sisters didn't try to smile at Isobel, even though she was best friends with Princess Margaret Rose, and once, to my horror and shame, Esther called her a snob, very loudly on purpose. I realized that I would have no chance in life, dragged down as I was by family ties, unless I strenuously tried to free myself of them. Nobody liked my dad because he had a horrible, curly black beard, and spoke with a foreign accent, and was a spy for the Germans. I heard my friend Carol telling the others that he never took his hat off because he had secret messages under it, and that's why England wasn't winning the war. I wished that he would work as a groom or a gardener for Mr Cameron-Spurling, and wear a flat cap and wellington boots. I wanted a grandma with pink cheeks, white hair and blue eyes, who always smiled and who never groaned or looked ill-tempered or said muttery prayers and 'Oy Oy Oy', like my London grandma.

But Mam was the person who gave me most trouble and was ultimately responsible for causing me to lose my battle in separating myself from my family and becoming a Christian. Dad was away most of the time, but she was always there, in Pineduggy, shaming me and spoiling everything. She spoke English, but not properly, like other people's mams. She didn't have a Pineduggy voice, but instead she talked like someone from London, where horrible rabble came from. London people were dirty and went to the lav in the street and spent all their money on beer and going to the pictures. When they had spent all their savings, they expected us in Pineduggy to give

24

them their food. I longed for my mam and dad to learn to speak and behave properly, and run a home like Carol's mam. When I went to her house after school, she always had tea ready on the table. There were flowered cups and saucers and a little rabbit to eat, made out of jelly, and everywhere was neat and tidy. There were no books or newspapers on the chairs and no washing on the fender. Carol was lucky because she had no brothers or sisters, and she had a room all to herself with a bedspread and curtains to match. Mrs Wright asked me if Jews drank blood for their tea, and I told her we only had it on Tuesdays and Wednesdays, but on other days we ate carrots and potatoes and cabbage with dead caterpillars on. Jews were supposed to eat fat which God made Mam believe was meat, but I always put the fat in my pocket when neither of them was looking. We never had jelly rabbits like the one Carol was eating.

I liked going to Mrs Wright's house because she was so kind and attentive, and always asked me questions and listened carefully to everything I told her. One day, her friend Mrs Tuttle was in her Front Room. They sat at the pretty little table, drinking tea from the flowery cups, and I was invited to sit down and have a cup of tea, too. I felt so happy and so important, especially when she began to ask me questions. No. Jews didn't eat ham or bacon or pork chops, but they did partake of fish, crammed with bones. Rye bread, I informed them, was ordinary bread with rye mixed up in it and poppy seeds sprinkled on top. Yes. Mam might put squashed flies in, but I didn't think the poppy seeds were really mouse dirt, because Mam was frightened of mice. Black bread was baked with specially dirty flour. There were always crumbs on our kitchen table and papers under the chair cushions and Jews had no new toys or games; just raggy old books and news-papers all over the place, and Father Christmas never gave them anything. Mrs Tuttle burst out laughing, and said to Mrs Wright that Father Christmas must be very mean with his money; Mrs Wright nearly spilt her tea, she laughed that much, and she made me laugh, too. Mrs Tuttle enquired most courteously whether my dad had little horns under his hat, and I told her that he had, so that she wouldn't think he hid secret messages for the Germans instead. The ladies and Carol ate delicious cake and a new jelly rabbit, but they didn't give me

25

any, because they said Jews weren't allowed to eat their food.

Then I said it. Thus I separated myself from my family; my brethren; my race; my glorious, ancient heritage. 'If I eat a small slice of your cake and the tiny back leg of your jelly rabbit, I wouldn't be Jewish any more, Mrs Wright. I'd turn into a Christian. Would you let me be a Christian, please?'

'First you'll have to tell us why you Jew people killed Jesus and nailed him to a cross.'

'I don't know, but I'll ask my mam and dad if you give me some rabbit.'

'You'll have to kneel and pray and ask forgiveness every night, and tell God you're sorry for killing his Son.' She scooped up a delicious spoonful and dropped it, shivering, into my saucer, topping it with a dollop of the sponge cake and synthetic cream filling. The jelly collapsed in a paroxysm of joy at my conversion. I dipped my teaspoon into its marvellous texture and felt its heavenly taste slide down my throat.

'I will!' I said, and entered the sunlit world of Christianity. I did not need the beat of drums or the fervent study of the Testament; the confines of the convent and the confessional were for other, more hardened infidels. The message of the Church, spiritual exertion, would all have been to no avail, despite their influence on others. I converted, without conscience or regret, for a spoonful of jelly.

After my enlightenment, Carol and I went up to her room, and we hugged each other delightedly, now that we both embraced the same faith; and she assured me that I could now expect a visit from Father Christmas on Christmas Eve, as long as I remained constant. We spent the next joyous half-hour torturing her doll and talking about the disgusting behaviour in which Germans indulged in order to have babies.

As soon as I entered our cottage, I realized that the effect of the jelly was not permanent and that its power was no longer potent. I needed a constant supply in order to remain incorruptible, and in my untidy, dreadfully Jewish home, none was forthcoming.

'Where have you been, you nasty piece of work?' shouted Mam. 'Do you expect me to do every blinking thing? Go to Ada's this minute, before she shuts up shop and nobbles our rations!'

It was nowhere near closing time, and while I stood in line to be served, Mrs Tuttle came in and stood behind me. I smiled at her and said hello. Had we not recently enjoyed a pleasant tea together with our mutual friend? She looked through me with hard eyes, as if she had no recollection of our closeness. I gave Ada the list and the ration books. 'What are they buying today?' she asked Ada, as if I wasn't there.

'Soap, sugar, tea, flour, dried eggs, cocoa, butter, porridge oats and carrots. They've already used up their fresh eggs and cheese.'

'Don't they ever want anything else?'

'Not from here. We're not dirty enough for them.'

'She ate jelly at Wrights' today. Ask her if she wants gelatine instead of part of the sugar ration. Tell her she can have lard instead of the butter. Go on. There's no harm in asking! See what she says.'

I knew that if Mam or Dad had given the list to Ada, Mrs Tuttle would not have said anything; if Miss Ashdown, our headmistress, had been there, she would have given them both the stick. If certain named individuals in our village had sauntered in, Ada would not have read out the shopping list as if it was full of rude words. I understood, as clearly as anything hitherto known to me, which people, by their presence alone, would have stopped Mrs Tuttle and Ada talking like that to each other – and who would have smilingly allowed them to continue. No one came in, to disperse the shadow which hovered over me, and from which I could not escape or explain. For a moment, I imagined that Hannah was there in the doorway, holding out her arms to me, her eyes shining with the light of battle, ready to blow the dark away; and then I was alone again, and the sombre air remained.

'You like jelly, Rachel,' said Mrs Tuttle. 'Why don't you buy some for your tea tomorrow? Fancy never having jelly for tea! Didn't Doctor Toomie ever tell your mother it was good for your funny fits? And haven't you ever tasted bread and dripping? It's delicious! Your mother could make your dad a lovely packed lunch with a couple of slices of ham. He wouldn't have to bother going to the Jew butcher in Hull, if you buy your ham ration here.'

'Yes,' I said. 'Mam forgot to write them on the list, but she told me to use the coupons from our ration books for jelly, lard and ham.'

'You're not registered with us for your meat ration, but I know a customer who would let you have a slice of her ham in exchange for a quarter of your tea.' She smiled and winked at Mrs Tuttle. 'Would that be all right? We like to do our best for all our Jew customers.'

'Yes. Thank you, Ada,' I said. The shadow enveloped me in the sunlit shop. Mrs Daws, a name not on my list of saviours, came in, and I heard whispers as I watched Ada slice the ham and carefully measure out two ounces of a packet of hard, white lard; then she placed a cellophane packet of soft orange rubber on the counter, and told me it was jelly. I stowed everything, together with the remainder of my shopping, into my bag as Ada cut the coupons out of our ration books. I poked my fingers into Mam's big, squashy purse, and eased out the right number of coins and walked out of the shop, into the empty village street.

But I didn't go home – not straight away. Instead, I lingered among the bushes at the far edge of the pond, and making sure that I was unobserved, I threw the ham and lard into the deep water, and the ducks squawked for joy. I felt the jelly and placed it carefully among the reeds, hoping that by tomorrow it would have turned into a rabbit. Mam would never notice anything was wrong. I'd put everything in the pantry myself. She didn't know how much money was in her purse. I'd often taken pennies out in the hope that I could buy something special for Isobel, but had always succumbed to my own, more pressing needs. Once I'd seen her fishing about under the torn lining, in case there were any sixpences lodged there, and I'd locked myself in the lav, until I'd heard her talking to deaf Mr Crawford, next door, about the German bombers who had killed hundreds of people in Plymouth and smashed nearly all the houses and buildings there. All thoughts of missing money were ousted from her mind, and I was saved from discovery. I was able to pinch two or three more pennies from the purse, until the day when I bought the ham from Ada.

'Come here,' called Mam. 'What are you doing in the pantry?'

'I'm just putting the shopping on the shelf, because you're always so busy doing kind things for me.' I felt deeply moved by this saintly remark, and expected to see tears of gratitude standing in her eyes, but all she did was to look at me suspiciously, and interfere with what I was doing.

'Ada has made some very bad mistakes, not to our advantage, and it isn't the first time,' said Mam, crossly, checking the goods against the ration books. 'I'm going over to give her a short, sharp lesson in addition and subtraction.'

'The shop's closed!' I shouted. 'And anyway, it's not dirty enough for you!' I watched her face change, and wondered at the power of a few innocent words.

'Who said that to you, Rachel?' said Mam, as soft and as cold as snow. 'Was it that vile wretch, Ada?'

'She only said it to Mrs Tuttle because you won't buy the meat ration from her; but she doesn't mind really, and she wasn't being cheeky. She wouldn't have said it to you or Miss Ashdown. She told me to tell you that the rest of the rations will be in the shop next week, and Mrs Tuttle and Ada sent you their love and told each other that you were their best friend, but it's no use going back until next week.' I knew that by then, Mam would have thought some more about the poor dead people in Plymouth, and that she'd forget about the missing tea and butter coupons. But she didn't forget.

Chapter Seven

One afternoon, in the early summer of 1941, my mother went to school to visit our headmistress, Miss Ashdown.

She hadn't forewarned me. If I'd looked through the window and seen her crossing the playground, I would instantly have raised my hand and asked Miss Grundy if I could leave the room. Thus, I would have been able to waylay her and feign death to prevent her from betraying me. Too late, I heard my class-mates whispering that Mrs Sweaty-Socks had just turned in at the door, and straight afterwards, all eyes were turned on me. What did she want? Why had she come? She was not to be trusted. I continued to write out my tables while my heart shrivelled and my face burned. I knew exactly what she would be saying.

'Hello, Miss Ashdown. Rachel told me what you said – that she was the cleverest person in the school, and even better than you at sums. Thank you for lending her all the thimbles after sewing lesson so that she could have a party for her doll. I gave her threepence to bring to school for the Pineduggy War Effort. She only handed in twopence? I don't believe you, Miss Ashdown. Rachel wouldn't steal or tell lies. Do you know, she wet herself last week. Five and three-quarters, and she wet herself! Surely you don't believe that story about Gordon Tuttle pushing her in a puddle! You don't have to call me Mrs Sokolovsky. You may call me Malka. Yes, my first name is Malka. I can't imagine why she tells people it's Shirley. My husband is called Dad or Sacha. Not Christopher. We sometimes speak in Yiddish to each other, and she says her prayers in Hebrew. No. Rachel isn't a Christian. She's a Jew, and her Dad wears a hat, even in the house. We do all sorts of things there, when no one's looking. I light candles on Friday night and cover my face with my hands, and recite a blessing, and we're not allowed to eat ham because we killed Jesus. I can't really say that I know what it feels like to have someone kill my little boy, because I haven't got any boys. I've only got girls. It was most kind of you to give Rachel *The Faraway Tree* by Enid Blyton. She keeps it hidden in her drawer when she's not reading it. Don't you remember, Miss Ashdown? You gave it to her as a prize for winning more stars than the whole school put together. Do you mean to tell me that it's not true? That she pinched it from the cupboard? No. She won't be too poorly to come to school tomorrow. Goodbye, Miss Ashdown.'

One horror after another rose in front of me. Perhaps it was not too late to pray. Maybe a wasp would jump into Mam's mouth and sting her tongue, so that she wouldn't be able to speak. Perhaps a bomb would drop on the school and explode so loudly, that Miss Ashdown would remain deaf for the rest of her life. I did not wish her dead. Fear of her ghost was all that restrained me – equalled only by my fear of humiliation. I tried to pray for a miracle, but my heart was still. There was only one thing left for me to do. I must make a deal with God. I knew, even then, that Jesus wouldn't contemplate a quick bargain. With him, one had to fix up an agreement ahead of time. True, he could make blind people see, and crippled people walk, but I was in need of a sharper, harsher kind of action. God was the boy for the job. He'd turned Lot's wife into a packet of salt; made a road through the sea; transformed Aaron's rod into a snake; brought forth flames out of an unconsumed bush. He was a quick worker and a dramatic performer. I lifted up my desk lid, placed my hands together and closed my eyes. 'God,' I said, 'don't let Mam say the things I am thinking about to Miss Ashdown. Do something to stop her. If you do, I'll do everything you want, and worship you for ever and ever, Amen.' Just in case Jesus was listening, and wanted to help, I rubbed out all the kisses in my multiplication tables and changed them to the sign of the cross. Then I put up my hand to tell Miss Grundy that I had finished and was ready to recite my four times table without looking. She beckoned me over to her desk, and I handed over my exercise book. I could see the temper redden her face and a scribble of pencil run all over my work.

31

'What is four add four?' she screeched.

'Eight, Miss Grundy.' I wouldn't panic. This may all be part of God's Holy Plan. I knew perfectly well that my work was absolutely accurate.

'And what is four times four?'

'Twenty-four.'

'Rubbish! Why have you rubbed out all your multiplication signs, and written in addition signs? Do you ever listen to what I say? Go back to your desk and write out *all* your tables *correctly*!' She was in such a temper about the crosses that her spit flew all over my face and she gave me a hard push. In that moment, I understood where my destiny lay. God, through Miss Grundy and Mam, had shown me that Jesus was out and he was in. He would not forsake me. He had every right to be upset. While he was busy performing miracles for me, I was doubting his total, unshared omnipotence. Never again! I turned over a new page and began to write.

Mam was still talking to Miss Ashdown when the bell rang for home time. While all the children ran out into the playground, I sidled over to the smallest, yet most important of the three classrooms. I pushed up the latch, and gently pulled open the door. If anyone shouted, 'Who's there?' I would run into the cloakroom. No one called out. Cautiously, I peered around the door and into the classroom. The 'Private' door beyond was slightly open, and Mam was sitting by the fire, a cup and saucer in her hand, laughing at something Miss Ashdown was saying to her! No one laughed at Miss Ashdown. No one went into the *private* room except for the teachers. I, who had been a pupil at the school for a year, had never seen the inside of the *private* room; yet there was my mother, sitting in there, drinking tea, as if she was in an ordinary place!

Miss Ashdown saw me creeping towards the door, and she opened it wide and invited me to step inside. The place was a treasure trove! Brand new writing books lay on a desk, and next to them was a box of silver stars, a box of gold stars, and one containing all the colours you could think of. And I had to work so hard just to get one stuck on my book! For a moment, my mind wandered and exerted itself as to how I could obtain a few by foul means. I sat on a stool listening to them talking about the Blackshirts and the Jewish evacuees who were expected to arrive in the village in two weeks' time. They were coming without their parents, and they would live with different families and some would go to Pineduggy Council School. Mam was to be in charge of the evacuees, which meant that she was the only one who was allowed to be nasty to them – she and Miss Ashdown. The Blackshirts I understood to be a horrible family who lived in Pineduggy, and they had to be most careful that none of the children went to live with them. They hadn't been discussing me at all! Miss Ashdown didn't call me a thief or a liar. God had saved me. I would be loyal to him forever and he would never have cause to be jealous of Jesus or mean and spiteful.

'Your mother has been speaking to me about you, Rachel,' said Miss Ashdown, pausing in order to give me time to relish the worst moment of my life. 'There are people in Pineduggy – even grown-ups – who are nasty to you, because they don't like Jews. I want you to tell me every single time this happens. It doesn't matter who it is – or where. It might be in the shop or at a friend's house, or at school. You must always tell me or your mother, and you will be helping us to look after the evacuees who haven't got their parents here, to stick up for them. Would you like to help?'

'Yes, Miss Ashdown,' I said, half-crazed with self-importance, aware that she was giving me power above that of my fellows. I would abuse that power to its fullest capacity. Everyone would have to be best friends with me, otherwise Miss Ashdown would know of it. The pendulum of misery and joy had swung to and fro so violently that afternoon, that my emotions were out of control. 'You didn't tell Miss Ashdown a single bad thing about me, did you, Mam?' I said, as we walked home.

'No,' said Mam. 'Not this time, because you're not going to put your meat in your pocket any more, or take things without asking, or tell fibs every time you open your mouth, are you?' Then she squeezed my hand, and gave me a hop, skip and jump and told me she'd once been a girl of five. I knew this to be untrue, but I let it pass, since she'd been so uncharacteristically benevolent towards me, and I felt a great surge of love and gratitude towards her.

'Who are the Blackshirts? Why won't you let the evacuees live in their house? Have they got dicks in their hair?'

'There are lots of nice people who have dicks in their hair!'

shouted Mam, crossly. I was so shocked and excited by this
heresy, that I was quite unable to dispute with her. 'Blackshirts
have got dicks in their hearts, and that's much worse! Pineduggy is swarming with them. Miss Ashdown knows who
most of them are, but she's not quite sure who is for them and
who is against them. None of those kids are going to be billeted
with Fascists, even if it means taking all the lot myself!'

'Who are they? What are their first names? There isn't a
single person in my class called Blackshirt or Fascist. There
isn't anyone in Pineduggy called Anything Shirt. But it would
be best if all the children stayed with us. We've got thirteen
saucers.'

'And I've got thirteen pairs of hands!' said Mam. Sometimes
she was so daft. 'Blackshirt isn't a name like Sokolovsky. It's
the name of a uniform of a Fascist movement. I can't explain;
I'm too anxious and worn out. Just remember what Miss
Ashdown said. If anyone says or does something to you about
being Jewish that upsets you, tell us. Then you'll know who the
Blackshirts are! Then you'll see how your Mam and Dad and
sisters will go for them!'

Scenes of delicious violence crowded my imagination. I
thought of Dad, who came to visit us from Hull every Thursday. I always met him at the bus-stop and walked up the lane
with him, hand in hand. He smiled and said 'Good Evening' to
everyone; shamefully foreign and different; unaware that
many of those he acknowledged regarded him with a mixture
of contempt and fear. All I had to do now, was to tug his hand
and whisper, 'Blackshirt', as my enemies came towards us, and
thus turn him into a ferocious creature. He'd push his fist into
Mr Swindham's face and throw Gordon Tuttle into the
thistles. I pictured Sybil, my big sister of twelve, smart in her
school uniform, walking along as slow as a snail, reading and
chewing her hair ribbon, and sometimes standing quite still, as
if the excitement of the story had sapped all her energy. 'Sybil!'
I'd shout, 'Joan Garner won't give me a ride on her bike! She's
a Blackshirt!' And Sybil would drop her *Girls' Crystal*, shake
back her plaits and whirl her lumpy satchel above her head,
letting it go with a bash into Joan's face, knocking her down
like a ninepin, while I snatched her bike. A dazzling image of
Esther delighted me even more. She was as wild and rough as
Sybil was gentle, and the worst person in my family, except

34

when she was on my side. From now on, she would be entirely obedient to my commands. Vered too! She would be most useful to me, because we both went to Pineduggy Council School, and although she was in the Juniors, while I languished in the Infants, we shared the same playground, which was crammed with bullies and offensive people who wouldn't let me play with them. Vered was 'in' with a gang of Juniors, who wouldn't dream of mixing with Infants. This unpleasant segregation would be flouted at my behest, and I would be admitted exclusively to the society of the eight-year-olds! As for Mam! Well! She was almost as rough as Esther and even more powerful!

Although my fantasies were more impressive than reality, henceforth I wielded a strange power. Every week I reported various happenings to Miss Ashdown, who had comforted me by saying that my communications could in no way be interpreted as telling tales; so I told tales without conscience or discrimination, and with little concern for the truth. Cardew Brocklebank had thrown gravel at me; Paul Daws had pushed me in a trench and wouldn't let me out until I'd promised I wouldn't tell Miss Ashdown; George Walker had poked me with his pen-nib; Joan Garner wouldn't give me a ride on her bike. My arrogance knew no bounds when, one Friday afternoon, I told Miss Ashdown that Miss Grundy had not chosen me to be library monitor, even though I had sat up straighter than anyone else. Too late, Miss Ashdown realized the error of her ways.

I gave Mam quite different information, all of which was invented. Mrs Walker had thrown a bucket of water at me. Flat-Faced Mug had set her ducks on to me, and they had pecked off all the crust from the loaf I was carrying home. Miss Long said my hair-ribbon was horrible, and I should tell Mam to buy me a new one. I was constantly persecuted because I was Jewish, but always I stood firm, brave and stalwart against my tormentors. Gentle Miss Long! Simple and kindly Flat-Faced Mug! Cardew, with your fists full of gravel! You threw it at all the little girls; you didn't just pick on me. Paul, I betrayed you, after all. George, did I omit to mention that I poked you first? Yet I told no one about old Mr Swindham, who glared at me malevolently with his terrible, pulled-down red eyes, as if invisible fingers were checking the inner lower

35

lids for anaemia. I did not repeat his fearful threats, as he pushed me against the wall of the alley-way, spitting curses into my face. Mr Swindham, who played bowls and looked after the churchyard and smiled at other people, snarled at me and called me names which I did not understand, but knew to be evil; he got away, scot-free! Mrs Tuttle, Mrs Wright, Mrs Daws. You, with your indecent questions, your criminal ignorance, your coldness and calumny! I knew about you in my bones, but could not articulate with my breath. Somehow, you flattered and wooed me, while your eyes slid to and from each other, laughing at your esoteric, crude remarks, insulting, injurious and cowardly. I did not report you either. I often watched you from my favourite lookout position on the ancient black stones, as you walked past the pond on your way to play Beetle or whist, and sometimes a chill of fear would numb my limbs. I remembered the place called Liubava, and saw the rushing stream, the bridge, the wooden houses and the great forest, as familiar as if I belonged there, too, and you were also linked in an indefinable manner, strange and terrible. With your limited lexicon, your clogged minds and degraded personalities, why did you suddenly and inexplicably penetrate my reveries and turn my dreams into dreadful nightmares, which repeated themselves for years, starting from the summer of 1941?

Chapter Eight

At the beginning of June 1941, Hannah prepared to start her new job. She was to be trained as a children's nurse in the Kovno Orphanage, and she was going to stay with her two grandmothers, who lived on the outskirts of the town, in a tiny house which they shared. As well as being her grandmas, they were both cousins, and had played with each other as infants over seventy years ago. Yosef lived with them now, and helped with the garden and the shopping. He was apprenticed to a cabinet maker, and several pieces of the furniture had been made or mended by him. He and his friends were involved with a young Zionist group, and his head and heart seethed with plans and hopes to go to the Promised Land.

Kovno was only thirty miles from Liubava, and Hannah would go home every month, and write to her mother three times a week. Since the bombing of Warsaw, her house was full of Polish refugees. Everyone in the village was taking care of them. They had fled, leaving everything behind, and there was hardly a person who had not lost several members of his family. Hannah wondered, with pity and horror, how these poor, lost people could bear their grief and exile. She packed the suitcase which she'd brought back from England, still decorated with two Union Jacks, and polished her brown leather shoulder-bag, which had been a present from Malka. There was a hand mirror in the pocket of it, together with a matching leather folder in which she kept her photographs. Whenever she felt homesick, she would look at them. Probably that would make her feel more lonely, but she'd have to take that risk. Every letter she had ever received in her life was in a big envelope in her suitcase.

She loved Kovno, and knew so many people there. It was such a beautiful morning on which to start a new, grown-up life. Her mother and Jacob's two children, Sora and Olga, came along with her. Hannah had six nieces and not a single nephew, but Tsivia, her sister-in-law, was pregnant again, and maybe, this time, it would be a boy. 'Perhaps twins!' Hannah said to her, laughing, because Tsivia was complaining about her huge belly; 'Twin girls!' Tsivia chased her with the yard broom and told her to go and curse someone else; but baby or babies, girls or boys — who cared, as long as they were born healthy and right in the head! Hannah wanted two of each when she got married, but first she'd have to find someone and fall in love.

Her mother walked beside her and Sora and Olga ran ahead, clomping with their boots on the wooden bridge. They didn't talk much. Never, never could she imagine loving someone as much as she loved her mother. The worst thoughts she had ever had were regarding her mother's death. How would she ever cope without her! She couldn't bear, even, to see her looking old and tired. But she wouldn't die for ages and ages — not until Hannah herself was an old woman, and that wouldn't be for fifty years. Many people lived until they were over a hundred, and in any case, she thought comfortably, her mother and father still had their mothers. She wished she could remember her dad, but it was no use trying, for he had been drowned five months before she was born. People still talked about him, and she had a picture of him, too, in her bag. For a few moments she allowed her mind to linger on the past; on herself as a baby — demanding and selfish, as all babies are. Her mother having to look after her in the midst of her grief and loss. They were almost at the station when, suddenly and inexplicably, she wanted, quite desperately, to get to know her mother as a person. The urge to do so was overwhelming and completely novel. What had it been like for her to be pregnant and bereaved, and with so many fatherless children to care for? What was it like for her never again to have her husband to talk to and to be with? The train was due just after six and the station clock was striking just now. There was no time to talk any more. She'd speak to Yosef and her grandmas instead, and next month, when she came home, she'd try to be a friend to her mother as well as a child; adjust the relationship without

38

diminishing it. Try not to need her so painfully. Why were tears pouring down her cheeks?

Kovno was the loveliest of towns, famous for its culture and learning; its ancient glorious buildings; churches, synagogues, libraries and theatres. A town steeped in history, romance and turmoil, where she would become one of its citizens. She could hear the train approaching the station, a banner of white steam heralding its arrival, as if it wouldn't dream of stopping at this remote little platform, hemmed in by the mountain range. She bent down and hugged the little girls, who hung on to her neck. Yuri's mother thrust herself into her mind unbidden, stony-faced, arms folded, edging away from them. She clung to them, shaking with ungovernable weeping, and covered them with kisses. Then she held her mother in her arms until the train hissed to a halt.

'What is it, little bird? I am already lonely for you, too. Take care of yourself and your grandmas. Be well and safe and happy. And come soon. Let me see you smile before you go.'

There were no vacant seats on the train, but she liked standing in the corridor and looking out of the window. She wore her shoulder-bag with the strap across her chest, so that her hands were free for her basket and suitcase, and she pushed them carefully into the luggage alcove. The door was slammed by the guard and she barely had time to let the window down before the train moved off. She waved, and blew kisses, until her mother and the children disappeared from view. What a big baby she was! She'd been as merry as a sand-fly when she went to England, and she'd been just a kid of thirteen! Here she was, nearly sixteen, going off to Kovno, less than an hour distant, and acting as if she was going away forever! She smiled to herself, wiped her face and leaned out of the window. Before long she would see the cattle grazing on the other side of the mountain range; then the railway line would cheekily cross the ravine and follow the Shishoopa River, before it fell into the great River Nieman on its way to the Baltic. Even with her powers of uncanny perception, she did not see that soon the river would be clogged with blood, or that the fields would be grey with ashes. She did not know that her next train journey would be one of horror; that she had kissed the little girls for the last time and that she would never see her mother again.

Chapter Nine

Sybil was the nicest person in my family, after me, and although everyone I asked liked me best, I could well understand why they thought she wasn't as horrible as the others, although she was dark, like Dad. She and Esther went to school in Hull, every day, on the early bus, dressed in smart uniforms, each wearing a satchel as well as a gas-mask case. Sybil never forgot her sandwiches and was hardly ever rude or nasty to me. Once, when I was deeply upset over a letter which Vered had received from her pen-friend, Sybil wrote a letter to me and posted it in Hull, so that I would stop feeling jealous and angry. She bought the stamp with her own money, as well as a hair-slide which she put in the envelope together with the letter. She never said she didn't believe in fairies, and pre-tended she wasn't frightened of ghosts. On Thursday nights, my Dad didn't have to be on duty as an air-raid warden, so he came to Pineduggy and slept in the front bedroom with Mam, and I had to sleep in a single bed with Vered. It wasn't fair, because I always slept with Mam, but Sybil explained to me that Dad was too big to share such a narrow bed with Vered, and that if I had to go to the lav in the middle of the night, I shouldn't wake Mam or Dad, but I should wake her instead, and she would come with me and stand outside the door, and sing 'You're Breaking My Heart' without stopping, to scare the ghosts. She'd lean against the coal-shed, waiting and singing, and never grumble, even if it was cold and wet, and then stand with me, shivering, in the dark kitchen, while I washed my hands. The kitchen blackouts were torn, so we never dared put the light on in case a warden or worse, a German plane, saw a chink showing through. At these times, I didn't think my friend Carol Wright was lucky to be an only child. Mam never had to shout at Sybil to do her homework or wash her neck, and the only times she was cross with her were when she chewed the ends of her thick plaits and sucked her hair-ribbons. I tried chewing Sybil's hair, to find out why she liked the taste so much, but it was worse than eating fat, or the skin on hot milk. There was more hair in Sybil's stomach than the hair on her head, Mam said, but Sybil didn't seem to mind, and the hair didn't wind round her brains, because she was top of her class. Yet there was a side to my sister Sybil which I was quite unable to comprehend, and that was her unswerving loyalty and devotion to Esther, and her stubborn blindness to her faults.

I usually stayed in bed until Esther and Sybil had left the house in the morning, reading *The Faraway Tree*. Vered always got up before me, because she had five people in her milk-round, including us, and earned one and threepence a week. I helped Vered once, but we had a fight about carrying the milk cans, and because of her bossiness I spilt the milk all over Mr Crawford's step. Mam had to give him our milk, and blamed me. I got the blame for everything. Vered was saving up to visit her pen-friend in Long Island, America. She kept an account book and counted up her figures every single day, and every week, when she got paid, we would empty the money out of the money-box and count that, too. She had eight and ninepence, and calculated that she would have saved up enough by the time she was nineteen. I told her she was stupid, because no one was supposed to travel while there was a war on, otherwise I would have gone to Liubava. It would be a better idea if she saved up for a bike for us, but Vered never let up once she'd fixed on an idea, although she agreed that if she built up her milk-round, she might be able to buy a bike as well. We wrote forty-two letters and poked one through every single door in Pineduggy, to tell people that Vered and Rachel Sokolovsky would collect milk cans and deliver every morning except Saturday, by courtesy of Wetherby's Dairy Farm. I wrote a special one in red crayon for Mr and Mrs Cameron-Spurling, and drew kisses all the way round the edge of the paper, but we hadn't received any answers yet. I wanted to go to the Big House to knock, but Mam said that they only drank milk from golden cows. Vered and I were waiting for the results of our advertising, and she was going to let me do the deliveries she wouldn't have time for. So I lay in bed contemplating and organizing my round; devising scheme after scheme on how I could acquire pram wheels in order to make a fashionable milk cart for my future customers. Perhaps I would be able to hire it out to Vered.

Esther liked Vered better than me, and always stuck up for her, although I was always right. I complained to everyone about Esther, and told tales of her every day, but I could never make her be on my side. Yet sometimes, when I wasn't trying, she would quite unexpectedly stand up for me with such style and flamboyance that I would temporarily forget that she was the worst person in our house, and be radiant for the whole day.

Once, when I smiled at Isobel, patted Polly, her pony, and offered her a ribbon I had found for Polly's mane, and Isobel, who hadn't heard me, trotted past without answering, Esther took me by the hand and ran after her. We stood in front of Polly, and Esther grabbed the reins and shouted, 'Did you hear my sister Rachel speak to you, you ignorant little fool?' Isobel said yes, and then Esther said, 'Rachel is worth a hundred of you! Repeat that!' And Isobel had to say, 'Rachel is worth a hundred of me,' until Esther was satisfied that she'd said it loud enough. But still she wouldn't let her go, and held on to the stirrup. 'If Rachel is stupid enough to want to speak to you, and she tells me you don't answer her, I'll wrap this stirrup round your neck. Do you understand?' Isobel said that she understood, and after that she always said Hello to me, even though she was usually in a great hurry.

Another time, Esther saw Gordon Tuttle push me into the hedge, and wave a stinging nettle at me. I was crying, and didn't see her creep up behind him. She didn't have her gloves on, but she rammed the nettle in his face so that I could kick him on the leg. Esther's fingers were covered in white stinging nettle spots, but she didn't cry. She laughed! She wrapped dock leaves round her hands, and said they didn't hurt. We could hear Gordon screaming, even after he had run into his house and slammed the door. Mrs Tuttle knocked later that evening to tell Mam that she wasn't having bloody Jews attacking her son, and that he was ill in bed; and Mam shouted that the bloody Jews would attack her if she didn't get her feet off our step. I was so overjoyed by this drama, that I nearly fell out of the bedroom window.

Most of the time, Esther was a great burden to me. She was always forgetting her gas-mask or her fare money, and I would have to get out of bed and chase after her, a coat over my nightie, before the bus came. I told her that she forgot things on purpose, because she was jealous of me being able to stay in bed, but you couldn't tell her anything, without her answering back. Usually, when I thought of Esther, I wished that I was an only child.

It was only with Vered that I changed my mind every day. She was only two years older than me, and would usually play with me if there was no one else outside, and when we slept in the same bed, she would tell me stories and answer all my questions with confidence and wisdom. Vered was dark and her hair was black and curly, and nobody believed we were real sisters, because my hair was yellow and straight and much prettier. Esther told me she found me in a tree, living with a monkey, when she was four, and now she wished she'd left me where I was. I knew she was telling fibs. I remembered being born in Percy's shop.

No matter how important and privileged my sisters were, or thought they were, I was the only one who went to Hull on Monday, 23 June 1941, with my mother, to collect the evacuees.

She had spent the whole of the previous day making poppy-seed rolls, and they were tied up in a white cloth in the pantry. She had used all the sugar ration and half a tin of cocoa to make cornflake chocolates, and they were lined up on the shelf. I'd never seen so many all at once, and this abundance agitated me. Mam gave me one – the smallest and most ill-formed – for they had been specially made for the children who were going to live here, in Pineduggy, without their parents. They were all coming to our cottage first, and different people from Pineduggy were going to pick out which ones they wanted to live with them.

Sybil and Esther went to school on the early morning bus as usual, just as if nothing remarkable was happening. Vered went on her milk-round, but I didn't lie in bed, because I felt Mam needed me to help her bring the evacuees to Pineduggy, and I told her to write a letter to Miss Grundy, explaining my absence; but she wouldn't, even though I screamed for half an hour. Her behaviour became so loud, outlandish and threatening, that I went to lie down on the stairs.

'You're not coming with me to Hull and that's that, so *shut up* or I'll write another sort of letter to school!'

I left the house and hid in the bushes near the pond until I heard Miss Ashdown blow the whistle and saw all the children file into school, leaving the playground empty. Then I sat on my gas-mask case and ate the poppy-seed roll Mam had given me for playtime, watching for her to appear round the bend in the lane. I wouldn't have long to wait. Three buses a day went to Hull; Sybil's and Esther's at half-past seven; the 'shopping bus' at ten o'clock, and the 'pictures and pub bus' at five o'clock There she was, running; knowing she was late. I reached the bus-stop and was hiding behind the shelter before she turned the corner. She leaned against the wall, gasping and holding her chest, as the dark blue and yellow 'shopping bus', also known as East Yorkshire Motor Services, burst into view, roaring like a wild animal; and when it stopped to pick up Mam, Mr Corlett and the post-office sack, it seemed to strain at an invisible chain, irritable and dangerous. Mr Corlett politely allowed Mam to board first, and then I jumped on to the platform, thrusting myself in front of him and behind her, with perfect timing. It was almost empty. The next stop was Brocklebank's isolated farm, two and a half miles away. The bus growled with ill-temper and stormed off. She could not desert me now. She wouldn't tell me to get off at the next stop, in the middle of the lonely fields and woods, and no power on earth that I knew of could halt the bus before then. She sat down near the front, and placed her bag on the space beside her. I chose the seat directly behind. 'Mam, I've got an earache,' I whined, as the bus conductor approached. Sybil, Esther and Vered were in school, as if nothing special was happening. But I was on my way to meet the evacuees, while the Germans invaded Russia, crossed the River Bug in Eastern Poland and took Lithuania in two days.

She couldn't shout at me on the bus and I knew that she would have to pass herself off as a loving and patient person when she was introduced to the children. It wasn't in her nature to control herself unless there were outside pressures to assist her. So her show of temper soon resolved itself into spasmodic bouts which held no peril, and all was well.

I so rarely rode on a bus that the journey alone was spiced with daring sophistication. I assumed a bored, urbane demeanour, as if I was used to all this dashing off to Hull, but I was unprepared for the devastation and ruin as we turned into Alban Road, and my composure deserted me. 'Did the Germans do it? Why? Were the people in that house killed?' Houses were sliced in half. The colour of the bathroom walls; the bannisters down the smashed staircases; sculleries; bedrooms, were exposed to the world. A front door lay in the rubble of a back yard; ragged curtains flapped in windowless holes, as if trying to protect the pride and privacy of the erstwhile occupants. Someone here had painted the fireplace blue. Over there, a plain, distempered wall had been decorated with green dots. How pretty it must have seemed! How pathetic it was now!

We got off at the terminus. Where the grandest shop in Hull used to be, was a great pit filled with broken lumps of concrete and surrounded by a field of debris. We stood staring through the chicken wire which surrounded the bomb-site, watching the helmeted men clearing up, and when I looked at Mam's face, I knew that she had forgotten about being cross with me. We hurried to the house where Dad stayed by himself and where we all used to live before the war. I wanted to go straight to the place where we were meeting the evacuees, but Mam said not to be so daft, as they weren't due to arrive until half-past three. I ran ahead of her, down the half-remembered street, as if I were returning home after a long exile. Yet when I got there, I was afraid. The gate and railings had gone. The two coloured glass panels in the door and the Front Room window were missing, and patched with dirty brown paper. Did my Dad stay in this horrible, broken house, all by himself, at night-time? Was he there now? Maybe the kitchen looked like those I had seen in Alban Road, and he would be lying under lumps of wall. Could the people living in Beelby Street, which backed onto our yard, see our lav and bath? I turned, and ran back to Mam. She was standing quite still, staring ahead, her face blank and frozen, looking for something that should have been there, and wasn't. I looked too. The Dirty Lamberts' house had gone. It wasn't sliced in half, but had been mashed with a giant fork. Four of the houses next to it were squashed

45

up too, but I'd forgotten who lived there. Were Teddy and Maggie in bed when the bomb dropped? For a moment, I thought of Hannah, reclaiming my hat; of Maggie's fat leg and Teddy's hand crushed under the broken bricks. A wave of unprecedented horror engulfed me, shocking and terrible.

'Teddy and Maggie are under the dead house!' I screamed. 'Where's Hannah? Something is wrong with Hannah!'

'No!' said Mam. 'Hannah is safe with Grandma and all the family in Lithuania, and Teddy and Maggie would have heard the sirens and run to the shelter. No one is under the house.'

I could feel her arm shaking. Mam sometimes told worse lies than me. I put her empty shopping bag over my head, still distraught. She turned our door-knob, and shoved me along the dusty passage. Dad had lit a tiny fire and the black kettle was hissing softly on the swivel hob. He was wearing a tin-hat instead of a skull-cap, and his dirty shirt sleeves were rolled up above his elbows. There was soot all over the lino and chairs and table, and dusty, splintered boards had been thrown on the stairs. He said 'Hello' and smiled without gladness, and Mam spoke to him in Yiddish, thinking that I would not understand. I stopped wailing, and busied myself with three grimy cups, so that I should not be noticed. Fifteen people were dead in the street and Dad had helped to find them. Maggie was the only one of the Lamberts who'd had time to run away. Our house had been shaken by the bomb and the water and electricity had been cut off. The chimney was broken, and when I wanted to go upstairs to look at the hole in the ceiling, Dad said it wasn't safe. Every time he wanted a kettle of water or to go to the lav, he had to go through the back yard, across Beelby Street and into the Sailors' Orphanage. There was a drinking fountain and some toilets in the orphanage playground, and the Matron had told Dad to come there whenever he wanted. I'd never been to the toilets there, and told Mam that I needed to go. She came with me, carrying the enamel laundry bowl so that she could fetch water to wipe some of the soot away. Beelby Street had been smashed up, the remains of the tiny houses hanging against each other like broken cobwebs. A familiar figure sat on a seat in the playground, wearing a huge bandage on her arm.

'Look, Mam!' I hissed. 'There's Maggie! Why is she crying? Isn't she a big baby?' I remembered the smell of her house and

46

how she had ripped my hat. 'She should be happy that she doesn't have to live in a house full of dicks and creepy crawlies. Why doesn't she wipe her nose? Doesn't she look horrible? God's punishing her for spoiling my hat!'

Mam gave me a spiteful push as if she didn't want me near her, then I watched her walk over to Maggie and put her arms around her, not caring that Maggie's nose was running. She sat down on the bench next to her as if they were best friends. They were deep in conversation when I approached them. 'You fill the bowl at the fountain,' she said. 'Wait for me here. Maggie and I are going to see Matron. I won't be long.' Whenever she said that, I knew she would be. I must have filled the bowl twenty times over and watered all the soil before she emerged, followed by Maggie, who had stopped blubbing. I wondered if Mam had promised to give her all the cornflake chocolates, but it wasn't anything as dramatic or impulsive as that. All that had happened was that Maggie was coming to live in Pineduggy, when her arm was better, and meanwhile, Mam was going to find her a job as a maid.

'In Cameron-Spurlings'?' I gasped. If so, I'd suck up to Maggie and overcome all my objections to her.

'Over my dead body!' Mam snapped. 'You upset me, Rachel. One minute you're so sad, you have to wear the bag over your face, and the next minute you're selfish and hard and cruel. No wonder you drive Esther mad.' I didn't know what she was on about. We carried the bowl of water back to the house, my mind so fevered by all the excitement that I was unable to digest the intelligence of Maggie's future immediately. We wiped away some of the soot from the table, while Dad swept the floor. Right in the middle of our work, Mam put down the cloth and took the broom out of Dad's hand. She held his face and I could see that it had the same expression on it as when I was born. I waited, silent and breathless, for a baby to jump out of the smoky air and land on top of them, but instead, to my dismay, I saw wavy lines of tears running into Dad's beard. Mam spoke to him so softly and sweetly, that I wondered if I was dreaming.

'Oh, Sacha,' she said, 'would we have let her go back if we'd known this would happen? Do we know whether it will be better here than there? Maybe they will be safe in Liubava. Perhaps Mama and the family are in the forest, or being looked after by friends. And you can't stay here alone, darling.' Vered would never believe me, when I told her about this. 'Percy and Rose have a spare room above the shop. I'm going there, now, to enquire. If you blame yourself, then you must blame me, too! Hannah is as dear to me as my own child. You understand that, don't you? May God Almighty protect them all.'

Dad said 'Amen' and so did I. Mam wiped his face, and then she took my hand and we went to Percy's, leaving Dad in the dirty room, drinking his tea through a sugar lump.

We bought two bags full of groceries. All the people in the shop made a fuss of us, and Percy said he and his wife would be honoured and delighted to have Rabbi Sokolovsky as their guest. I got a cinnamon stick and two barley sugars for nothing, and then everyone went very quiet as Percy turned on the wireless for the one o'clock news. We stayed to listen and that's when I heard that the Germans had invaded Russia and were smashing all the aeroplanes up. Nobody spoke while the news was on; nobody bought anything; nobody pinched my cheek or stroked my hair or told me not to eat both my barley sugars before I had my dinner. The sun shone carelessly on that lovely June day, and light and warmth penetrated the dusty windows and a sunbeam danced on the counter, defying me to trap it. Would the Germans find Hannah and burn her house? I slid off the high stool, ran out of the door and leaned against the telephone box until the shaking fit stopped. Mam stayed for a few minutes in the crowded shop, discussing the latest news and arrangements for Dad to have his breakfast and supper with Rose and Percy when he was on fire-duty. We walked back to the dilapidated house.

'What's the matter, Rachel?' asked Mam, unnerved by my silence. 'Are you tired? You feel so cold. Have you had the shakes? I'll give you your dinner, and then you can lie on the sofa for a bit.'

'No,' I said. 'I don't want to lie down.' If I fell asleep, she might sneak off to fetch the evacuees without me.

'What is it? What's wrong? Tell me!' I wanted to tell her that I was sad about the people who had painted green dots on the broken walls; about Maggie in the Orphanage, with a bandage on her arm. About Teddy. I wanted to ask her why Dad was crying and why it was worse, much worse, than when I cried. I nearly told her that I knew that we shouldn't have let Hannah

48

go, but I didn't know why or how I knew.

'I'm hungry for an apple ring,' I said.

We were to meet the evacuees in a disused schoolroom in the same street as our house. During the following few weeks, the children became so familiar to me that the recollection of that first strangeness was almost impossible to summon up. For reasons peculiar to childhood, I had assumed that they would all be the same age as me, but none were younger than eight. Stuart was fat, freckled and ginger, and wore a dark red and black cap and blazer, showing that he attended the same school as Sybil and Esther. Iris wore those colours too; I'd seen her before, because she was Esther's best friend, and her younger sister Daisy wore pretty hair-ribbons and a smart satchel. Helen, an only child, hung onto her mother's hand, crying as if she was a baby, with plenty of spit. I thought that they would all be sitting behind the desks with their fingers on their lips, and wondered what Miss Ashdown would say if I told her that Iris and Stuart were standing on top of the desks, and Stuart's ginger mother was sitting on one, with her feet on a chair. Brown suitcases with labels tied on had been set down near the door. The atmosphere was fraught with excitement and fearful anticipation. Mam sat at one of the desks, opened her bag and brought out a pencil, a list and a tin of cornflake goodies and told me to hand them round to everybody. She had made a mistake with one of the sweets. It was bigger than two of them put together; beautiful, round and perfect. Mothers and children were clamouring for her attention, and I knew that I could take it for myself, without her seeing. But the two boys, standing away from the others against the peeling wall, were watching me. The little one wore his gas-mask case round his neck, like a drum, and huddled up to his brother as if he was cold, even though he wore a navy-blue jacket buttoned up to the collar. His trousers were made of leather and were very short and I could see a dirty bruise on his knee and a scab on the other one. I picked out the huge sweet and placed it on top of his gas-mask, the first unselfish act of my life, then handed the tin to the big boy, who wore long trousers and was nearly as tall as my dad.

'My mam made these. They are called cornflake chocolates.'

He took one, not bothering to grope for the best of the selection.

'What's his name?'

'Rudi.'

'Is he cold?'

'No.'

'Is he shy?'

'Yes, he is shy. He does not speak English so well, like me.'

'Did he cry when he fell over and bust his knees?'

'Maybe he cry for a little time. I don't know.'

'Did his mam kiss them better? Did she press marge on his knee with the back of a cold spoon?'

'My mother is not here.'

'Tell him to eat the cornflake goody.'

He said something to him, and Rudi bit into the sweet, looking at me with eyes as big as saucers. I liked him better than anyone else. 'How old is he?'

'Eight years.'

'Why is he so little?'

'I was so little like him when I was eight years. He is more bigger than you.'

'Where's your mam and dad?'

'They are in Vienna. They cannot be with us. That's why I look after him. You tell your mother that he cannot be in a place without me. We have to be in a house together. Go and tell your mother.'

'I'll tell her you've both got to come and live with us, then I can help you to look after Rudi and teach him how to talk.' He smiled, and spoke quietly to Rudi in a strange language.

'We want to come to stay with you. Have you got a big house?'

'Yes. It's the biggest house in Pineduggy.'

'Have you brothers and sisters?'

'Only a few sisters. What's your name? How old are you? Why did your mam and dad let you come here by yourselves? Is Vienna near London?'

Mam was calling me, telling me to hurry up and give everyone a sweet. She came over to the two boys and spoke to them so kindly that I knew it would be all right for them to live in our house. I left the tin on a desk so that everyone could help themselves, and stuck close to make sure my plans would be carried out.

'Hello, Felix! Hello, Rudi!' she called, smiling; 'Has Rachel

50

been telling you about Pineduggy? Mr and Mrs Wilson would like to look after you, Felix. They are very nice people, and don't have any children of their own. Miss Long and Mrs Long will take Rudi. Rachel will tell you about them, because she's very friendly with the old lady. You'll be living quite close to one another – only about ten minutes' walk. We have Shabbos School at our house for all the Jewish children every Saturday morning. Until now, my four daughters have been the only pupils, but from now on, there'll be ten of us. I always make a special treat for Shabbos School, but you may visit our house any time you want. At first, you'll both go to Pineduggy Council School, and Miss Ashdown wants to give you special lessons in English. We've been looking forward to having you in Pineduggy, especially Rachel, and your parents will be so pleased to know that you're in a safe place while the war is on.'

Felix looked at me, waiting for me to say something. Even Rudi seemed to understand that Mam had got it all wrong, for he was watching me, too, a tiny piece of cornflake sweet held between his finger and thumb, as if he had forgotten to eat it, what with all the excitement. I felt very embarrassed about the way Mam was speaking, and felt it necessary to interrupt her so that she wouldn't go on making a fool of herself.

'Mam,' I said, 'Rudi and Felix want to live in our house. They don't want to go to sleep, one at Wilsons' and one at Longs'. Felix wants me to look after Rudi and I can't if he doesn't sleep in our house. Miss Long smacks children,' I lied, 'and Mrs Wilson's daughter's ghost chases anybody who sleeps in her bed. I'd rather live with mucky Miss Frith or the nasty, loony Trowbridges, than live at Wilsons' or Longs'!'

'Shut up!' hissed Mam. 'Shut up this minute!' I knew that Miss Frith was taking one evacuee and that Iris and Daisy were destined for the Trowbridge sisters, who hated all the male species. 'Don't you *dare* say anything out loud so that they can hear!'

'Alpha and Beattie Trowbridge aren't nasty; they're very nice Blackshirts,' I said, as if I was reciting a poem in front of the class. 'And Miss Frith isn't *very* dirty.' Mothers and children listened to what I had to say with gratifying attention. I knew everyone in Pineduggy: they knew no one. Mam was fully aware that our armchair flattened out into a tiny bed and that it was easy for a child to lie on our settee. I'd slept on it

51

when I had mumps and wouldn't stay upstairs by myself. It was more comfortable than sharing the bed with Vered.

'I have to be with my brother,' said Felix. 'It is not good for us to be in different place. He is not happy without me. The woman and man he was with were not kind to him. I must be with him, Missis. He cries when he is not with me. My mother and father are sad if they knew this. We like to stay with you. We will not be trouble for you. My parents would be glad we are staying with you.'

'I have no room,' said Mam. 'I'm sorry. There are only three bedrooms, and one is the size of a cupboard, and I have four children. I haven't even got a Front Room downstairs – just a tiny kitchen, with a bath in it, and a poky Everything Room.'

'The settee and the chair, Mam! You must have forgotten! If you don't want to clear the newspapers from the settee, Felix or Rudi could sleep with Vered. I don't mind sharing your bed every night, even on Thursdays, when Dad comes. I won't kick or take up much space. I'll sleep on the lump in the middle and not move all night long!' I felt quite desperate, yet I knew that sailing close to the wind was ever my style and the source of my inspiration. 'Please, Mam. *Please!* I won't say anything out loud,' I shouted, 'if you let Felix and Rudi stay with us!'

She tried to make mad eyes at me, but I pretended not to see. 'Just for the first few days, then. I can't say anything else just now. We've got to leave,' she said to everybody. 'Can everyone manage to carry a case each? I've arranged for the Pineduggy bus to stop at the top of the street for us. It's due in ten minutes.' She turned away to comfort the screaming Helen and her sobbing mother. 'If Helen isn't happy in her billet, I'll move her straight away. Don't worry, Mrs Adler. You'll be coming to see her on Sunday, and I'll have my eye on her all the time. Yes, I've got her ration book and I promise you she won't be hungry.'

I took Rudi by the hand and led him to the door, where everyone had to line up. Felix was in charge of the luggage and Rudi and I held his case between us as we walked up the street. When the bus approached, we ran up the stairs, leaving Stuart and Felix to push the luggage under the platform alcove. Now that her mother wasn't there to see, Helen was laughing and talking with the others, and seemed perfectly composed. Sybil and Esther jumped on the bus at a later stop, on their way

52

home from school, and pretended not to be surprised to see me. I felt a great surge of pride, because they were so stylish and competent. They used words like 'Physics' and talked about their French teacher, whom they called Lizzie. Sybil swung her school-bag carelessly and Esther took her hat off, although she wasn't supposed to, and I was too busy to tell Mam of her. Iris and Stuart asked them about the events of the day, because they'd had to miss school to be evacuated. From now on, all four would catch the bus from Pineduggy each morning, and return together, every evening. I envied them their esoteric, mysterious and sophisticated world; to find out what Geometry meant and to discover how it could be that a different teacher taught you for each lesson. Some of the teachers were actually men, and playtime was called 'break'. These girls were my sisters!

Mam sat at the back of the bus, sorting out her papers and all the ration books. Vered would be home by now, setting the table for everyone, and Dad wouldn't be sad any more, and come home, as usual, with a big smile for Felix and Rudi. All my family would look after the evacuees, and make them welcome and happy. I whispered to Rudi that he could stay with me until the war was over and his mother and father came for him, and that he wouldn't have to go anywhere else, but still he didn't smile or speak to me. But Felix did. He was sitting on the seat behind us, and he leaned forward and said, 'Thank you, Rachel. Thank you for speaking to your mother about us. You are my friend. You will be always my friend and the friend of my brother.' He touched my shoulder awkwardly, in a gesture of affection.

I sat on top of the bus, important and knowledgeable – that, alone, sufficed for pure bliss, notwithstanding all the trimmings; but this added embellishment caused too much gladness, so that I floundered in its overwhelming power, as if I had suddenly and unexpectedly fallen in love.

Chapter Ten

The instinct for self-preservation kept me well away from my mother. If physical proximity became necessary, I made quite sure that I didn't come face to face with her in isolation. As long as I surrounded myself with the other children for the next few hours, the danger would pass and disperse. The bus rocketed angrily down Main Street at ten miles an hour, while I pointed out the landmarks, the places of interest and the houses, giving a commentary on the occupants.

'That's Brocklebank's Farm,' I announced to everyone, but in particular to Felix and Rudi. 'Cardew Brocklebank copies off me at school, and they keep their cows in their Front Room. Mr Gibson lives over there with a rude parrot and a spiteful tortoise. He sets his parrot on to anybody who knocks on his door. He's horrible. Paul and Janet Daws live in that house. My sisters know why it's called Janpa, but I've forgotten. They have a lawn mower that makes lines on the grass and their dad won't let them play on it and they can't go in the house unless they wear slippers. Guess who lives there! Mr and Mrs Wilson, and Gladys Wilson, who's dead! Tell Rudi! Tell him that's where my Mam wanted you to live! Gladys Wilson died when she was twenty or forty. She used to lie in a big white bed in the downstairs Front Room. My Mam and Sybil were best friends with Gladys. They still go to see her ghost and her mam and dad, but I don't. Mam didn't mean to be nasty about sending you there. She thought you liked ghosts. It's a long, long way from Longs'. This is the pond. A horse and cart fell in it last week and never came out again. The ducks go into Flat-Faced Mug's house when the ice comes. They sleep in her bed and lay eggs in her pillow. She sets her ducks on to Jews. Look! Look!

That's Isobel Cameron-Spurling, leading her pony Polly Cameron-Spurling. She asked me yesterday if I'd be best friends with her. She's teaching me how to curtsey, so that I know how to say "Hello" to Princess Elizabeth and Princess Margaret Rose, when they come to her house to tea next week. That's our school. I'm library monitor sometimes. I'll choose the most exciting books for you and Rudi. Have you read *The Faraway Tree*? I've read it more than a thousand times. I can read it without looking. Do you want to be a Brownie? Shall I ask Brown Owl if boys are allowed? I go to Brownies on Shabbos afternoon and do a good deed every day. Mam's buying me my Brownie hat next time she goes to Hull. Brown Owl likes me best. She'll let you both come if I ask her. Did you do a good deed today? I helped Mam to look after you. What did you do, Rudi? Felix, ask Rudi what he did? Go on! Ask him!'

'I don't know what you talk,' he said. I didn't care. I would teach them both everything I knew. Throughout my discourse, the older children had been calling over to him, trying to involve him in their conversation; not listening to what I was saying. Daisy and Helen were sitting on the seat in front of me, their arms round each other, telling secrets. But Rudi's attention never wavered from my monologue; his great, luminous, dark eyes didn't even move to where I pointed; and although Felix acknowledged my sisters and their friends with kindly gestures, he stayed by me with unswerving loyalty and condescension. The bus ground to a halt and exhaled a great gasp of asthmatic breath.

'Sybil and Esther ride on a bus every day,' I boasted. 'They are my big sisters. Vered goes to Pineduggy Council School with me and she's top of the class and is blackboard monitor.'

Everyone was pushing past us. He must have observed that I was of no moment to them. He was a boy of thirteen in a strange land, without a friend, the responsibility of his brother heavy on his shoulders; the picture of his distraught parents ever in his mind; having to listen to the incessant, unintelligible babble of a five-year-old girl; and listening with such grace that even I, self-absorbed as I was, was aware of it. There are people who hear a child showing off how he can count to ten with grinding impatience. Let him count to a hundred and the child will be lucky to escape with his life. But what of a thousand? Strong men succumb from lesser agonies. Felix heard me out as I counted to a million.

I forgot about all of them, and the luggage, as we jumped off the bus. To be the portentous bearer of news to the neighbours in general, and Vered in particular, to be the first to confront them all, sent me racing away, ahead of them, up the lane, towards my cottage. 'The evacuees are coming!' I shouted. 'They're coming! They're coming! Vered!' I gasped, 'I went to Hull with Mam! I followed her onto the bus! You can go with us *next* time,' I comforted her. 'Two of them are coming to live with us! Can I have my biscuit now?'

'No!' she snapped, enraged that she'd missed out on all the excitement. 'You'll spoil the pattern I made. Go and fill the kettle. Miss Grundy asked me if you were away poorly from school. I told her you were screaming on the stairs.'

Never had so many people squashed into our house before. The children were now strangely silent. The tension increased as the time approached for them to meet the people who were to look after them. There weren't enough cups to go round; some of us were eating, while others were drinking tea.

'Listen,' said Mam, 'I want to tell you something, before the grown-ups get here. When you go to your billets, which is what we call the houses you live in, you might feel sad and lonely. Maybe you'll miss being in your own house. You might not like the food you're given to eat, or the people who are looking after you. Whatever it is; *whatever* it is, you must tell me. I want to know about the good things, too. Every single week, we have Shabbos School here, and the people all know that you have to attend. They know that I will ask you questions to find out whether you are being well-treated, but if anything wrong happens during the week, come straight here. I don't care what time it is, or even if you have to pretend you're going to school or out to play, in order to visit me. If I'm not in the house, just walk in and wait for me or tell Sybil or Esther or Vered. Even Rachel will know where I am, or take a message from you. In any case, you can come here whenever you like. Now then, who hasn't had a cup of tea? I want all the rolls and biscuits gobbled up very fast. Does anyone want to ask a question or say something?'

Daisy put her hand up as if she was in school. It made me

56

laugh to see her doing that in our house, to my mam. 'Please may I leave the room?'

'Of course,' said Mam. I could tell that she was trying not to smile. 'It's through the kitchen, past the coal-shed. Rachel, take Daisy, and show her where to wash her hands.'

Stuart was talking when we came back. 'What if they give me bacon to eat? What if they want me to say Christian prayers?'

'They won't give you any meat at all.' I wished I could be evacuated to somebody else, so that I would never have to eat meat. 'I buy those rations for you, and we all have it here, together, for Shabbos dinner. If there's any left, you can have a sandwich when you feel hungry. All your ladies know you're Jewish, and I've told them about Jewish people, but if they make mistakes, tell them or me.'

Helen was crying again. Sybil cuddled her and then Mam sat her on her lap. 'I don't want to go to a horrible house, all by myself,' she wept. 'My mother lets me have bacon! I want my mother! I want my mother! Why can they have their mother here, and I can't?' She meant me and my sisters. 'It isn't fair!'

'You've got to try to be a big brave girl,' said Mam, softly and kindly. I disliked Helen more than anyone else. 'I'm allowed to be with my children, because Rachel was under school-age when the war started. I wish all your mothers could be here, but it isn't possible just yet. Miss Trowbridge and her sister are the only people who can take two evacuees. They specially asked for girls, and as Daisy and Iris are sisters, too, and used to being together, they're going there. If I had a big house, you could all stay with me, but I can't squash any more children in here.' She was rocking the blubbering Helen as if she was a baby. I looked at Vered. She was counting her cigarette cards, not in the least offended by Mam's perform-ance. I went over to Rudi and put my arm round him.

'Rudi isn't crying, and his mam isn't even in Hull! He's not being a big baby and he can't even talk properly!'

'Why is he going to live here? I heard what you said in that school. It's not fair! It's not fair!' she screamed. 'Why should those two stay in your house and not me?' Vered stopped counting her cigarette cards.

'They're staying just for a few days, Helen. No longer. Their mother can't come to visit them, and they don't speak or understand English very well, which makes it much harder and lonelier. Shush now! Come and see me tomorrow. Look! Here comes Miss Frith and Alpha and Beattie! Esther! Quick! Wash out a few cups! Rachel! Take Rudi and Felix upstairs for a few minutes, and close the bedroom door. Don't make a sound; pretend you're not there,' she hissed at me. 'Don't come down until they've gone!' She gabbled something in Yiddish to Felix.

I wanted to stay where I was, so that I could witness Helen's distress when she encountered weird old Miss Frith for the first time, but I was hustled up the stairs with miraculous speed by Felix, and shunted into the front bedroom. He closed the door and stood against it, inhibiting my escape; talking to Rudi, who was answering him, but I couldn't understand.

'I'll just see if Helen's stopped crying,' I said. 'Mam wants me to take down a hanky for her.'

'Your mother tell me to stay in the room with you and Rudi. You are not a good girl. Your mother say not for you to go down the stairs and to not make no noise.'

'Helen is making a noise. Do you like Helen?'

'I like or I don't like. I don't know her good.'

'Is she your friend?'

'Maybe she is my friend one day. I don't know.'

'Am I your friend?'

'Always you are my friend, and the friend of my brother. You help us to stay together. You do good for us. But if those people see us, that we stay here, it will not be good. Your mother know this thing. I know this thing, so we must be quiet.'

'Will you and Rudi have to stay in the bedroom for always?'

'No. Just for now. Just for one hour.' Rudi was looking at the photographs on the dressing-table and mantelpiece. Each one stood in a cardboard frame.

'Do you want to know their names? That's Jacob and Tsivia and Sora and Olga. That's Yosef and David and Zalman and Kohath, and that's Frieda and Hannah. My dad's called Sacha and they are his five brothers and two sisters and his sister-in-law and nieces. This is me with my sisters, and these are my mam's brothers. This is a picture of my mam's Mam and Dad, and this is my other grandma. She lives with all those people on the mantelpiece, in Liubava. It's in a place called Lithuania, but it flitted into Russia. That's me with Hannah. She came to see

58

us when I was little. I remember her. She's my dad's little sister. I like this one of me and Hannah best. My Grandma Sokolovsky has never seen us. She calls us "*Papereneh Kinderlech*". Hannah told me it means "Paper Children". She thinks we're made of paper! Isn't she daft?'

Felix laughed so much, but quietly, so that only Rudi and I heard him. 'She don't thinks you are made from paper. She don't ever see you; she know you only from pictures and letters from you. She cry "Paper Children" because she don't see you really, to touch you or hear you. She only have paper things to see. All these photographs from your Papa's country – did you see them; these people?'

'I saw Hannah.'

'I know you see Hannah. She is with you on this picture. But the others? You don't feel their hands and hair and faces or hear their voices never. So they are *your* Paper Children. All people in a family that you don't never see, except on a picture, are Paper Children.'

'When I go to see them, will they be made of paper?' He burst out laughing again, then spoke to Rudi, smiling, telling him what I'd said. And then Rudi laughed! It was the merriest sound in the world! He lay on the bed and squashed Mam's pillow on top of his head, then rolled over and over with it, kicking his legs. 'Tell him again!' I shouted. 'Make him laugh again!'

'Don't make so noise,' he whispered. 'I tell him once is enough.' He picked up the picture of Hannah and me. 'You have the same face like your aunt.'

'The shoe-box is full of photos. I'll teach you all their names tomorrow. We're going to see their skin and their voices when the war's over, on a ship and a train. You can come with us if you want. Have you ever been on a train? Let's look out of the window. We might see Helen holding Miss Frith's hand. Miss Frith once chased me when I knocked at her door and ran away. She's horrible.'

Rudi and I leaned out of the open window, while Felix stood behind. 'Look!' I said, but soft, remembering that Felix wanted us to be quiet. 'There's Iris and Daisy with Alpha and Beattie Trowbridge. They don't want boys. There's Helen with Miss Long! Why isn't she crying? I wish she had to go with Miss Frith. That's her with Stuart! I'd rather be dead than live with Miss Frith all by myself. You'll have to stay with us until your mam and dad come to look after you. I wonder who she'll give to Mrs Wilson. There's no one left. You'd better hide under the blanket. Maybe Mam will give Esther to her. I'll watch all the time, to see who she takes back to her haunted house. There she is! I'll go downstairs and tell Mam about my good idea!'

Felix wouldn't let me go, but still Mrs Wilson didn't emerge from the house. I knew she was best friends with Mam, so maybe she was giving her all the biscuits that were left on the plate. I grew anxious. Perhaps she would make Felix go there after all. I needed to find out what was happening, and told Felix I wanted to go to the lav. He said I could go, but that I should come back straight away, and not say anything. But when I entered the room, the atmosphere was so fraught that I was in danger of keeping my promise. Mrs Wilson was weeping, not loud, like Helen, but softly and terribly. For a moment, I thought she was laughing, until I saw Mam's face. No one else was there. Even my sisters had disappeared. I crept through to the kitchen. Sybil was sitting on the porch step, doing her homework. 'Mrs Wilson is crying, Sybil. Is it because Mam won't give Felix to her? He doesn't want to go there. He's frightened of Gladys. He told me.'

'You're the one who's frightened; that's why you're so unkind.' Sybil was so clever at school, but she often said silly things to me. 'She's crying because she's got a broken heart.' A vivid picture of a shattered, bright red, symmetrical object, poking its splinters painfully into Mrs Wilson's chest, rose before me. 'No one can comfort her – not even Mr Wilson.'

'I heard her saying she wanted to be with Gladys. What does she mean, Sybil? Does she want to be with a ghost? Isn't she scared?'

'No, she isn't scared. She means that she wants to die so that she can meet Gladys in heaven. Gladys isn't a ghost, she's an angel; but even if she was a ghost, Mrs Wilson wouldn't be scared. Not everyone is like you. Maggie Lambert is going to live at Wilsons'; not Felix. Mam has got to find a billet for two boys together; that's why they've got to stay here for the time being.'

Poor Mrs Wilson! I felt so sorry for her! The mere thought of anyone having Maggie to live with them made my blood run cold. Of course, she hadn't seen her yet. What if Mam persuaded her to take Maggie, then when she saw her, she mighr change her mind, and Maggie would have to come and live with us! That state of affairs was too ghastly to contemplate. I would apply myself to the problem when my head felt clearer. 'Are you glad that Rudi and Felix are staying with us? Are you glad, Sybil?'

'I'm more sad than glad.' How clever she was! 'They had to leave Vienna without their parents. They aren't allowed to live in their own house. Their mam and dad sent them to England very quickly, because it's so dangerous and horrible there. Felix and Rudi weren't allowed to go to school any more. Their dad lost his job and may go to prison. Their mam is a doctor, too, but nobody wants her to look after them. People were nasty to them in the street. They won't even let their mam and dad run away.'

'Why? Did they steal money from someone's purse?'

'No. You don't get treated like that for being a thief.'

'Did they knock on doors and run away? Did they throw stones? Did they tell lies?' The eldest, kindest, most patient of all my sisters lifted her eyes to the porch roof. 'Test me,' she said, thrusting a book into my hands. 'They hate Jews in Austria. *Amavero, amaveras, amaverat, amaveramis, amaveratis, amav . . . amav . . .*'

'I've got to go back now. Rudi will be crying for me.' I hated Latin. It was worse than Hebrew. I ran through the Everything Room. Mrs Wilson's face was blotched and red, and I smiled at her, although I was afraid. She was the second grown-up I'd seen crying that day.

I ran upstairs. Felix and Rudi were chatting to each other quietly, looking through the photographs in the shoe-box. I told them what was happening, and that Mrs Wilson was still there, but it would be all right. She couldn't take two boys. Mam was going to give Maggie to her. I wanted to ask them what had happened in Austria, but I caught sight of Gordon Tuttle walking past our house and I had to lean out of the window and spit and stick out my tongue and remind him not to wet the sheets. The boys watched me in amazement, and I explained that you had to do that each time you saw him, otherwise Esther would be cross. He'd shouted at us when he was with some friends, 'Jews don't wash the sheets!' and

Esther had screamed back, 'Jews don't wet the sheets!' He was the worst boy in Pineduggy, and I was going to tell Miss Ashdown of him tomorrow. He'd once pushed me into some prickles, and waved a nettle at me and said that Jews killed Jesus, and I'd had to wait for a week before I could shout out from the window that I was glad I'd killed Jesus. I never spoke to him when I was by myself, but always ran away as fast as I could. Now that Felix and Rudi were my friends, we would be able to call names and even hit him. We began to clear up the photographs. 'Are these Paper Children, Felix?' I asked, pointing to Sora and Olga. He nodded. 'Will they shrivel up and burn and turn into grey feathers? I'm frightened. What if someone strikes a match and throws it at them? What will happen?'

'No one will do that. Nothing bad will happen.'

'What will they do to Hannah?' It was so cold in the room. I started to shake, and my head wobbled that much that the air turned grey, black and red and I couldn't breathe properly, except to scream her name over and over. Felix pulled the blanket off the bed, and wrapped it round me. Some of the pictures fell on the floor. I pulled my arms free and held my breath, trying to reach them. Rudi scrambled around on the mat, picking them up, and thrust them into my hands. I held the picture of her and me in front of my eyes, but Felix pressed my head against his jacket, while Rudi ran downstairs to fetch Mam.

'No one will do nothing bad to her.' He didn't know.

'She'll be all by herself. No one will look after her!' I gasped. There was a pocket in his jacket with nothing in. I slid the picture inside, and stopped shaking.

'I will look after her,' he said, smiling, putting his hand over it. 'Now you don't cry any more, Rachel. There is nothing for to cry.'

Mam ran into the bedroom with Rudi. I sat on her knee until I was warm again, while Rudi and Felix put the Paper Children back in the shoe-box, and replaced the framed ones on the mantelpiece and dressing-table. I could hear Sybil saying 'Goodbye' to Mrs Wilson. Mam spoke to the boys in Yiddish, but I understood some of it. She said that I had been poorly when Hannah went away, and had very bad fits. Now I had little fits, but only sometimes, and if I rested for a minute or two, I got quite better. Mam was so friendly to Felix and Rudi. Rudi stood right next to her, helping her to stroke my hair. I'd never seen her being so nice to anyone before, except Helen, who didn't count, because that was only because she was making a noise and other people were there, so she couldn't smack her. But I didn't want Mam gabbling in Yiddish all the time, because it wasn't as easy as English.

'I talk Latin, Mam, but I wouldn't talk it to Felix and Rudi. I only talk to them in English, so that when they go to school, they'll understand what Miss Ashdown and Miss Grundy are saying.'

'She never says anything worth listening to – Miss Grundy, I mean,' added Mam, quickly. 'You boys understand and speak more languages than this whole village put together – Polish; German; Yiddish . . .'

'Do they speak Latin?' I hoped they didn't.

'We'll find out when Julius Caesar invades Pineduggy.' She seemed tired and cross, but not when she spoke to them. 'I think Rachel's right, though. Rudi might feel confused for a time, but he'll pick English up very quickly, and yours is very good, Felix. We'll try, shall we? Now then, I'll show you where you can put your things. Hang your clothes on the hooks on the bedroom doors and Rachel will clear the window-sill in Sybil's little back room, for your personal things. I think I've worked out how you can sleep there. And don't worry too much. My husband will make sure that your family knows this address. He'll go to the Red Cross and find out as much as he can about your mother and father. He will try to find some people who can help them to send letters to you. He knows exactly how you feel and how anxious you are. You see, he's worried about his own family, too. He's coming here on Thursday and will discuss everything with you. Will you try to think of us as your second family? Your English family? Will you do that, Felix? Will you, Rudi?'

'Yes. We do that, Missis. We are both happy to be here and we say thank you.' He spoke quickly to Rudi, who said, 'Thank you, Missis,' as well. 'We will be tidy and not make no noise.'

'It's important that you feel this is your home; not how you behave.' I couldn't believe my ears.

The sleeping arrangements I made for Felix and Rudi were

not respected. Instead of one of them sleeping downstairs and the other one sharing the bed with Vered, Sybil and the boys pushed Sybil's bed into the back room where Esther and Vered slept. It was so crowded that you could cross the room without touching the floor, because it was entirely covered by the three beds, with a tiny place for the stool, and we had to keep the cupboard door open all the time, otherwise we would never be able to use our clothes. I wondered what Esther would say about this, when she came in. She'd be as cross as two sticks. But she told Felix and Rudi that she didn't mind at all! All my sisters went with them to fetch Mrs Wilson's spare mattress, and they brought it back on Mr Wilson's wheelbarrow, with Vered sitting on top. Vered was spoilt, just because she hadn't been to Hull. I had to stay at home and wash and wipe the pots. They always had nice times while I was having to do horrible jobs. Felix carried the mattress upstairs and squeezed it into Sybil's tiny room. It fitted the floor like a carpet, and only a tiny strip of lino showed, near the window. Mam tacked two sheets together to cover the mattress, and wrapped another sheet round two chair cushions, until she picked feathers from Flat-Faced Mug's ducks, for pillows. On top of that went the very best thing we had in the house. The perrineh!

We were the only people in Pineduggy who owned a perrineh. Even Miss Grundy didn't know what it was, until I told her. I couldn't credit her stupidity and ignorance. Carol's mam thought the perrineh was Jewish, because she said it wasn't an English word, and English people wouldn't cover themselves up with anything but clean sheets and blankets. I told her how my dad had brought it all the way from Liubava, and that he slept on the deck of the ship rolled up in it, and never felt cold. It was like a giant's pillow, puffed out with goose feathers, and sometimes we pulled it into the yard and played acrobats on it. I wished I could sleep on the floor with Felix and Rudi on the nights I had to share with Vered. I didn't ask Mam, because if she said 'No' in front of Felix, he might not let me share on Thursday nights. I'd keep my plans a secret.

Mam told me I needed a rest, if I wanted to play out later. She wouldn't let me stay upstairs while the boys were emptying their suitcases. Vered and Esther went out to visit Iris and Daisy in their billet. They arranged to meet them and Stuart in the playing-fields, for a game of eggety-budge, at half-past seven, and to start a Secret Club. Esther said I couldn't join, because I always blabbed and would spread it and break the code of secrecy, but I could make my own club with Helen. I told Mam that Esther hadn't done her homework, and then everybody started shouting, while Felix spoke to Rudi. And then Rudi spoke in English, so softly and firmly that everyone went quiet, and I held my breath. 'I want Rachel to come to Club,' he said. 'I like her better from everybody.'

Chapter Eleven

Papa and Mama Dorfman were doctors who had studied in the city of Lemburg in southern Poland, and had set up their lives together, their practice and their family, in Vienna. Felix drew the Leopoldstadt to show me where it was. On top of the page, he drew the River Danube, and at the bottom, in the same blue crayon, the Dounai Kanal. I'd never seen an apartment in my life, so Rudi showed me what it was like. He drew so many windows, counting in German all the time, as if he knew exactly how many there were. At four of these, the second row from the top, he drew four faces looking out onto a road, and in the road there were even more soldiers than windows. He gave every single soldier a horrible, ugly face, quite different from the people at the windows. I could see that the apartment was much bigger than Cameron-Spurlings', except that in Leopoldstadt, they didn't have a chimney or a garden.

Dad told us that Papa and Mama were Galiziane Jews and that we were Litvaks, and that's why Rudi spit out Mam's boiled fish, and why Felix swallowed it without chewing. Their mama cooked fish with sugar, not with salt, and so it wasn't just the language which was different. Their apartment had much bigger rooms in it and a room just for having a bath, with hot water inside the tap. They never had to boil water in a black kettle or a copper. Everything was different, except that we were all Jews, and all the Jews in Europe were being attacked. The others listened to Dad when he talked, but I never took any notice of him, except for what he said about the fish and the tap.

After they had been in our house for two weeks, Felix and Rudi received a letter with an empty, addressed envelope inside. The address was different from the Leopoldstadt, as Mama and Papa had flitted from there. They couldn't say where they were. They were somewhere different every day, but the address they gave was of some friends in the country. The boys wrote a letter each, and Mam and Dad wrote one, too, telling them all about Felix and Rudi and that they were safe and well. Mam wrote the Cameron-Spurlings' telephone number in her letter, but best of all, when she read it out, she'd told Mama and Papa that our house was their home for as long as they wanted, and they would not be separated. 'They will be as our own children, until you are reunited with your beloved sons.' I didn't think Mama and Papa Dorfman would be happy about that, if they knew how nasty Mam and Dad were to me, sometimes. I wondered why Rudi didn't cross out the faces he drew at the windows of the apartment, because they didn't live there any more, but he took no notice.

No more letters came, but one day Ethel Crawford, who worked as a cook at Cameron-Spurlings', rushed over to our house to tell us that there was a phone call, and the boys must come over at once. I ran past Mam, and followed Rudi and Felix, who were already flying along the hedge. They vaulted over the great white back gate, and sprinted across the gravel. Rudi was in his socks, but he didn't feel the stones sticking in his feet. By the time I had squeezed under the gate and dashed after them through the back door, Felix was holding the telephone and shouting into it, 'Mama! Papa! Hello! Hello!' over and over again, but there was no one there. He never cried again – not after that.

Some people said that their papa was Hitler's doctor and friend, because he was Austrian. Mam went to church with Dad, who'd come to Pineduggy specially on Sunday morning to speak to Reverend Daws about the wicked rumours which were circulating the village. Dad took his hat off when he went in, because it was rude to wear one inside church. I was glad that everyone would see that he didn't have horns or keep secret messages on his head. While they were singing 'Onward Christian Soldiers', Vered and I crept into the church and sat down on the back pew, behind Mam and Dad. Then everyone knelt down and prayed, and I looked at Vered and stuffed my collar into my mouth, so that no one could hear me laughing. It was so quiet. I could feel Vered shaking and trying not to laugh, too. Then Reverend Daws stood up and smiled at us, and said, 'Other sheep I have, which are not of this fold! Welcome, Children of Israel! May you find peace and forgiveness in Christ!' When the people turned round to stare at us, Vered's laugh burst out with a big explosion, and we had to run out of church before I made a puddle on the floor.

We leaned against the church wall until Reverend Daws came out. He stood at the door, shaking hands with everyone, and even tried to shake hands with Mam and Dad; then for the first time in my life, I heard Dad shout louder than Mam. He moved his arms a lot, when he was upset, and Ada and Brown Owl copied him from behind the churchyard wall.

'We asked you,' shouted Dad, 'to speak to your congregation about the lies and ignorance which corrupt this community, with particular reference to the two innocent boys who have come to this country for refuge and justice, from a country which knows none; their parents are not Nazis, but equally innocent victims of wicked persecution. If you do not understand this, how will the people in this village understand! There is nothing for you or them to forgive. Nothing! Your sermon is an offence to them! You have done worse than waste our time!'

Then Dad put his hat on and ran to the bus-stop to catch the bus back to Hull. There was only one bus on Sunday. Vered and I ran home as fast as we could, to tell what had happened, and Mam went straight to Miss Ashdown's house.

The next morning, at school, Miss Ashdown blew the whistle, but we didn't file into the class-rooms. Instead, she waited until everyone was quiet and still, then called Rudi and Felix out. She said that Rudi and Felix wanted us to win the war more than anyone else and that their mam and dad hated Hitler and were on Mr Churchill's side, too. If she heard about anyone saying something else, she would give that person the stick in front of the whole school. Suddenly, she pointed to me to come out, with a terrible look on her face. I shivered with terror, and stepped out of line. 'No. Not you, Rachel. Gordon Tuttle knows who I'm looking at. You made a face, just now, Gordon Tuttle. A face of disbelief and rudeness. Walk up here. Fetch my stick.' The whole school froze like statues stuck together. 'Now then, do you want it on your bare behind or your bare hand?' Gordon Tuttle said he wanted it on his hand.

'The next person will have no choice,' said Miss Ashdown, with fearful quietness. I closed my eyes as the stick came down on Gordon's hand, and counted four smacks. He walked quickly back to his place, sucking his fingers, and stood behind me. The appalling tension did not ease. Miss Grundy then handed a letter to every single person which was to be given to their parents that evening. All we could hear were Miss Grundy's footsteps, and each child whispering, 'Thank you, Miss Grundy.' Then Miss Ashdown blew the whistle again, making everyone jump, and we walked, in deathly silence, into our class-rooms. The horror of someone having to pull their trousers or knickers down in front of the whole school, subdued and filled my mind the whole day. Mam and Dad went to the school meeting on Thursday night, and Dad said that Miss Ashdown was a brave and righteous lady. After that, no one said that Papa Dorfman was Hitler's doctor. Not out loud.

I taught Rudi to speak properly straight away, and his voice was almost as shrill as mine, and his accent as broad.

Felix spent nearly all day in the 'Private' room with Miss Ashdown, having special lessons. He was jealous because he couldn't say R as well as Rudi, and sometimes he would get cross with Rudi for forgetting his German. Rudi did everything I told him to do. He threw gravel at people I didn't like, and took Joan Garner's bike while she was lying in Gypsy Wood with a soldier, so that he could teach me how to ride it. He wasn't afraid of anything or anyone, except me. Not even of ghosts or the dark or of Miss Ashdown's stick. If anyone hit me or pushed me, I would tell Rudi what to do to them, and he obeyed me without pause or question. The big boys in my school teased him about being my friend, but I let him play with them as long as I had someone else to play with. Felix had a lot of homework to do, for Miss Ashdown hoped he would be able to go to the Grammar School in Hull with my sisters, and all the other clever people, after the holidays, and he studied Hebrew with my Dad, so I had to take care of Rudi most of the time. But I told Felix everything Rudi did which I considered reprehensible, even though his actions were on my behalf; even though my reports were not always blighted by the truth.

One day, I threatened Rudi that if he went out to play

football with his friends, and didn't turn the skipping-rope with Vered for me. I would tell my Mam and Dad to send him back to the transit camp in Dover, and he would have to stay there until the war was over. Why do I remember the look he gave me, and not the fall of France? Why are there great yawning gaps in my memory, swallowing the most grievous happenings of the war, during my early childhood? Why had I no perception of the anguish of those who understood; who lived in my house and spoke of world events constantly, their words never reaching my ears or heart? Why do I remember now that though Felix sometimes smiled, he laughed only once: in the bedroom, amongst the Paper Children? If my mind did not cloud over and reject from itself the threat I used against Rudi, and his reaction to it, what other shameful utterances are clogged and forgotten by me, but recalled by others? He dropped his gaze at last, and fixed it on to the toe of his boot, which poked desperately into the gravel, while he actually wrung his hands. I didn't know that Esther had come out of our back door; that she was watching him, too, and had heard what I said. She had my mother's quick temper and my father's melancholy insight. She grabbed my shoulders and shook me until my teeth rattled and my brains swam round in my head. 'NEVER, NEVER, NEVER SAY THAT TO RUDI! NEVER DARE TO DO THAT TO HIM! I'LL BLOODY KILL YOU, YOU LITTLE DEVIL! YOU CRUEL, ROTTEN DEVIL!' I fought for breath, in order to scream, but her face was inches away, and white and furious and terrible. 'Go on! Blub! And everyone will know what you said. Felix will never forgive you!'

I remained silent, and Rudi stood rooted to the spot. Esther pushed me out of the way. 'Don't ever listen to her,' she said. 'There isn't a Dover camp any more. You'll never go anywhere, ever, unless you want to. You'll stay here, with us, in dreary old Pineduggy, until we find your Mama and Papa.'

'Mama and Papa are dead,' he said.

'Did Rachel say that to you? Did she tell you that lie?'

He shook his head. 'I remember the soldiers in Vienna. And the policemen. The people chasing us and calling us names. They pulled my Papa down in the street and threw his hat and bag away and hit him with a stick. They drove Mama out of the hospital because they said she was making the patients poorly instead of better. They hated us. They said they'd kill us. That's why we came on the *Kindertransport* to Dover. Mama and Papa waved to us at the station, but they couldn't come with us. The camp was so cold. I couldn't eat the soup and I cried all the time because I thought of what might be happening to Mama and Papa. Felix didn't cry. He told me that Carl and Catherine would hide them. But they don't write letters to us. They don't ring up on the telephone. They don't send a message through the Red Cross. There aren't any Jews left in Austria. Some of them jumped from the windows in our apartment building.' I shivered, thinking of all the windows he'd drawn, and the horrible faces in the street.

'Mama and Papa *are* hiding!' said Esther. 'Their friends are keeping them safe. Nobody can get letters from Austria now – you know that! They're alive and waiting for the war to be over, so that they can come to England to live – with you and Felix.'

'What if England doesn't win the war? The Germans are in Belgium and Holland and France and Denmark. Maybe they will come here. I hear about them on the wireless. When I was little, I remember them saying they will kill all the Jews first. Sacha goes to the Red Cross all the time. He tries to find out about his mama too, and about his brothers and sisters. He told me that they live in a little village and maybe the Germans couldn't find the village, or if they did, his family may be in the forest with the Partisans. He said lots of people in Austria could be hiding too, and that their friends would save them.'

'There you are, then!' said Esther, smiling. She looked as if she was going to give him a cuddle, but she didn't. 'Dad always tells the truth. Even if the truth is rotten, he never tells lies. Not like her.'

'But he doesn't know what the truth is. If the soldiers don't find the people they want to kill, there will be friends of theirs who'll tell them where to look!'

'What a lot of old rubbish you talk!' I saw Rudi look at her hopefully from where I was standing behind the dustbin. 'Imagine if Germans came to Pineduggy to kill Felix and you and our family, and we hid in Gypsy Wood, would anyone tell them where to look? The Wilsons? The Longs? Miss Ashdown? There are people like them all over the world. Hundreds! Millions!' She pushed him, and he nearly smiled.

71

The boys were calling out from beyond the back fence, for him to come to football. He ran off, and Esther went in.

I didn't make a face behind her back, because I was thinking of us hiding in Gypsy Wood, and Mr Swindham chopping the grass with his scythe; Mrs Tuttle and Mrs Wright holding lighted papers; setting fire to the branches and leaves, and Brown Owl and Ada holding rocks in their hands. They looked like the black stones at the corner of Main Street and Green Bank Lane, but they were moving and smiling. When they found us, they would chop at us, throw the rocks and set fire to us. Then I saw that it wasn't Gypsy Wood, because Olga and Sora were hiding, too, and all the Paper Children on the mantelpiece, except for Hannah and Yosef, who were somewhere else. I shivered so much that I pulled the dustbin on top of me. Suddenly, I saw lots of stone people standing in two lines along a road. Olga was screaming, because her nightie was burning. I could smell it, and the wet, cold, heavy earth, which got stronger and stronger, as if there was a deep pit at the end of the road. Kohath tried to run back to Olga, but Mr Swindham came at him with the scythe. I screamed and screamed, because Olga was turning into grey feathers and Mr Swindham was coming again. He didn't find me, but Mam did. She pulled me out of the dirt, holding me and kissing me and calling me sweet names, and asking me what was the matter, in baby language. When my legs and arms melted, and my head had stopped shaking, I sat on her knee on the settee, wrapped in Dad's cardigan, while Esther filled the stone hot-water bottle. Sybil poured some of Mam's home-made raspberry wine in a cup, and mixed it with hot water. After I had swallowed it, I started screaming and shaking again, because I didn't like the smell of the earth, so Sybil put some cloves in the muslin bag, and I held it against my nose. I wanted to hold the shoe-box with all the Paper Children inside, so Felix ran upstairs and fetched them for me. I told Mam how I had seen Mr Swindham, Mrs Wright and Mrs Tuttle looking for us in Gypsy Wood, and then I had seen them in Liubava.

Esther gave me two goodies and was very pale and quiet, because she thought she'd shaken something out of my brains. Mam said that she'd bet her bottom dollar that the furthest those blinking Fascists had gone was to a Blackshirt meeting two miles away, let alone to Liubava. Vered came in and

72

assured me that she'd seen Carol's mam and Mrs Tuttle going towards the church vestry for the Beetle Drive, and they always played Beetle until nine o'clock on Tuesdays. I stayed on Mam's knee, holding the bag of cloves and the shoe-box, even after Rudi came from football. He sat next to Mam on the settee, and twiddled my hair.

'Mr Swindham was cutting the long grass at the edge of the bowling-green, all the time we were playing, Rachel,' he said. 'You ask George and Cardew. Our ball went on his mouldy bowling-green and he chased *us*!'

'He wasn't there!' I shrieked. 'He was in Liubava! I saw him!'

I slept in Mam's bed every night; even on Thursday, when Dad slept in it as well. I kept the cloves on the pillow, and the shoe-box next to me, and wouldn't go out unless someone came with me. Mam had to write a letter to school, pretending I was poorly. On Shabbos, all the evacuees came to our house as usual, and Vered and Daisy and Helen went to Brownies without me, even though I had my new Brownie hat, because I was frightened of Brown Owl. On Monday morning we went to Barrowby to see Doctor Toomie. The bus only went there once a week, so we walked. It was three miles away. The Humber Estuary crept right up to the doorstep of the pub, so it was built on a kind of table, and if you sat outside on it, you thought you were on a ship. It was called the Black Swan. Doctor Toomie lived next door to it, although people said that no one would know the difference, because he was more on or under the table of the Black Swan than in his surgery. I hoped he would be on the table when we arrived in Barrowby, so we could sit there with him.

It was the loveliest morning in the world; one that I knew, even then, that I would always remember – a preview of nostalgia. I had my mother all to myself; there were no other demands on her attention, and this rare and marvellous luxury made me heady and careless. The road was narrow and gravelly, blotched with dark patches of melting tar, and wound through a green wilderness. We could hear the birds fidgeting, let alone singing; squirrels, hedgehogs, rabbits, frogs, all listening to our shoes making my favourite sounds – Mam's and mine together, and no one else's. I knew that if I clapped my hands and shouted, I could temporarily disturb a thousand creatures. A stoat ran across our path, with an egg-shell over its head. Mam said it would soon bump into a stump or a root and the egg-shell would break and he'd be pinching eggs again, before he got over the fright. It was the way of such creatures. Then Mam asked me to tell her all about Liubava and who I'd seen there. It was easy to talk as we walked along, hand in hand; easy not to tell lies for a change. We sat down on the grass next to the mile-stone, so that we could look at the pictures in the shoe-box I carried with me. I handed them to her, one after the other. 'What about Hannah and Yosef?' asked Mam, trying to help me to find them.

'Hannah wasn't there,' I said, exasperated. 'She was somewhere else, with Yosef. But she was watching from the place where she was, just like I was watching from under the dustbin.'

'Hannah doesn't know Mr Swindham or Mrs Wright or Mrs Tuttle.'

'Or Brown Owl or Ada,' I added.

'Hell and high water!' said Mam. 'Brown Owl as well! I've always hated that permanent smile of hers! How did they get to Liubava when they were in Pineduggy all the time?' I was nonplussed for a second or two.

'It was Hannah's dream and my dream stuck together.'

'You weren't asleep, Rachel,' said Mam, softly. 'People only dream like that when they're asleep. Nightmares. Everyone has them, sometimes. You had a fit. You shook so much, that you pulled the bin over on top of you. I ran out straight away. Your eyes were wide open all the time.' Mam shivered as if she was cold. 'Wide, wide open and staring, even after you stopped shaking. You never blinked once.'

'Sometimes I have dreams when I'm awake as well as when I'm asleep. I dream about riding my own bike, and having tea with Isobel in her garden and winning more stars than anyone else, and diving into the pond and saving Miss Grundy from drowning.'

We ate a jam sandwich each, and I leaned my head on her chest and we listened to the birds and the insects. The mile-stone pointed one mile to Barrowby. Mam could carry the shoe-box the rest of the way, and I'd skip. After I'd turned my rope a thousand times, we'd be there. I skipped on ahead of her, so that she could see how I never stood on the rope. I didn't look round, except to remind her to watch. I wasn't

74

afraid any more. The air was soft and sweet again, for the bonfires had gone out, in my vision; the earth was replaced and the decay buried. Doctor Toomie gave me a big bottle of brown medicine and then bought Mam and me a sarsaparilla. We sat on the table outside the Black Swan, looking down at the water. I should have been so happy.

Chapter Twelve

Hannah Sokolovsky celebrated her sixteenth birthday on 15 August 1941, and on that day she became a rat. She was driven into a sewer, crowded with all the other vermin of her kind, and it was called the Ghetto. Barbed wire surrounded it and police with lethal weapons and ferocious dogs were stationed everywhere, and at all times, to protect the outside world from being contaminated by these loathsome creatures. But the authorities were indulgent. Starvation rations were allowed – one hundred and eighty-three calories per day, per rat – and they were given an edict to perish by.

'Do physical work! Degrade the spirit! Deafen the soul! You are nameless; known only as male rats and female rats or Israels and Sarahs. Some of you will survive the Ghetto sewers and will reap certain benefits from the meticulous, cultured and superior German race. Your paltry existence will enhance our knowledge. We will study the extent of your sufferings before you succumb. How long does it take to freeze, roast, starve and torture you before you are totally destroyed? What noises deafen the soul? What sights blind it? If you attempt to disrupt our Plan, and smuggle extra food into the sewers, you will be killed immediately, along with every tenth member of your Slave Labour Unit. We, the German people, understand that your subhuman behaviour and your diseased minds and bodies must be contained. Contamination is forbidden. Our brilliant technology will overcome!'

But all work and no play makes Fritz a dull boy. It was fun to shoot at those who tried to prolong their lives, or to give the dogs a feast; a merry diversion to hang a few every evening and to smash to pulp the heads of those babies and children of the parent rats who were impertinent enough to strive for their survival. One must have a few laughs to allay the tedium of guarding scurrying vermin. Fry a few lice and watch them jump; cut off the tails of the rats and see how they run!

Shimon Weinstein was one of these obnoxious pests. He was once a quiet, intelligent, refined man, the Director of Kovno's Central Bank and the Principal of the Jewish Orphanage, where Hannah had started to work. His daughter, Tsillinky, was Yosef's sweetheart and Hannah's best friend. When Shimon came into the Ghetto, his personal calamity was neutralized by the hilarity of his captors. He tried to make a formal protest, for the idea that there was no longer justice failed to penetrate his thick skull, so it was smashed in, and his orphans and family sent to Estonia, from where there was no return. Yosef was working with a Slave Labour Unit as an ant, running at the double, backwards and forwards, in front of the jeering, fun-loving, firing-squad, a paper sack of cement balanced on each shoulder. His head was not thinking of Hannah or Tsillinky; it only thought of legs not caving in, so that it would not be blown off its concrete shoulders. With luck, it might still be in place for another thirty seconds . . . and another . . . and another. How his audience laughed at his puerile optimism, as they deafened his right ear with a blow from a shovel, and adjusted the shape of the irrelevant head and watched, with scrupulous care, for a tremor in the legs. Another thirty seconds.

It was an act of Providence that he was deaf; otherwise Yosef might have heard his friend stumble behind him, and drop his bags of cement, and perhaps the rhythm of his clockwork system might have been disturbed. But his mechanical legs continued to move; one, two, one, two. Count to two. That's all. Nothing else. The bag of skin and bones behind him tried to right itself, and was kicked out of the way by half a dozen polished boots. It was hauled into a vertical position and the sacks replaced on the exposed, bleeding shoulders. Yosef saw him on his return journey. His name had once been Laz; a friend from school, with whom he had wrestled and fished. They had built a hideout in the forest, and carried every log together, for he was as strong and as sturdy as Yosef. Don't remember, unless you want to die now. Stifle everything. Count to two. Run, Laz, run. Why did you allow

77

yourself to think, Laz? Dead, Laz, dead. Forget him. One, two, one, two. Another thirty seconds.

Tsillinky and Hannah left the Ghetto every morning at half-past four for roll call and then for slave labour at the aerodrome. They were in a brigade of a hundred women, five to a row, and to every row there was a German with a rifle which was always pointing at them. It was impossible to try to escape, and live. The Germans were assisted by the locals, who looked on with satisfaction at the way they marched the two miles to their uplifting work. How filthy they were, these Jews; the festering sore of the world! At intervals, they would be ordered to run, and the joy of the onlookers knew no bounds, as they helped the stragglers on with sticks, copying the German conquerors with enthusiasm. The soldiers beat those at the ends of the rows with the butts of their rifles; but a spade, a shovel or a club was also a help.

One freezing night, they returned to discover that Shimon had been killed, and his family and orphans transported to their deaths. One of Hannah's grandmothers had been commandeered to make up the number, since Tsillinky had been unavailable, and only one old grandmother was left, dazed and dumb, in the hole in the streaming wall. Tsillinky screamed, just once. It was enough, for a thousand would have been too few. She didn't weep, like Hannah, or Yosef, when he returned to them. A few minutes after she had uttered that fearful scream, several muscles in her face and neck froze permanently, but for Yosef her beauty was undiminished. Her life ceased to have any value for her, and because of this, she became a saviour; a creature of the night. Every day, the Germans searched the Ghetto dwellers for anything they could lay their elegantly gloved hands on, and to prevent smuggling or hiding, people were shot at random, and the slaves who worked outside were stripped and searched for jewellery or bread. The irresponsibility of attempting to secrete anything of personal value, resulted in horrifying acts of murder. Tsillinky became the keeper of valuables; a genius of cunning. She would disappear, while others swooned from hunger and exhaustion, and weave her way along the barbed wire, and talk to a dog or a Lithuanian Fascist, who had a prior arrangement with her to exchange a loaf of bread or a bottle of medicine for a diamond ring. Those who had nothing for

Tsillinky to hoard or trade for them, were helped to survive a little longer through her careless courage. Grandma Sokolovsky had a blanket and an extra crust every day, and when one of the dogs dropped a rat at her feet, Yosef cleaned it and Hannah cooked it over a tiny fire.

One night, this frail creature, who now weighed less than seventy pounds, told Yosef to meet her at an arranged place at the wire. He arrived there as she approached from the other side, carrying a sack of potatoes. No one ever discovered how she had previously cut the wire, or how or from where she had carried the potatoes, which were double her weight. A hundred people could die for this crime, but in the freezing darkness of this hell, the dogs were quiet; the police at least ten yards away. Yosef pulled the sack through, and held the wire while she slithered under it. Blood from the barbs stained her rags, as they fastened the wire and then fled through the stinking alleys, the sack on Yosef's shoulders, to that night's hiding-place. Hannah and Yosef nursed her uselessly through the rest of the night, but she caused no one else's death. Yosef ran, at the double, carrying his bags of cement, just as he had done the day before. One, two, Tsillinky, Tsillinky. And Hannah ran too, through the lines of stone-faced, grinning imbeciles, without Tsillinky Weinstein and without her mother to wake her up.

Chapter Thirteen

I hated being by myself, and I never grumbled too much if that was the only alternative to sharing a single bed with Vered. We went to bed earlier than anyone else. She had to be up very early for her milk-round, so she came upstairs at the same time as me. We made a crease in the sheet, so that I kept to my side and she was supposed to keep to hers, but she always had part of her over the line. If her toe came over, I put my finger on her side, and quite often we had a fight. Mam went to bed hours and hours after me, but usually I woke up in the night, and went to see where she was. I didn't have to trample over Sybil and Esther, because I was next to the door, but they often disturbed me. If I found Mam in bed, I got in with her, because there was so much more room; but when the siren went in the middle of the night, all of us ran downstairs. I would hear it, while I was dreaming, and feel my heart beating in my throat before I had woken up. Then Vered would jump in her sleep and we would cuddle each other, forgetting the crease in the sheet, and chant, 'We will win the war' ten times. Then we'd sit up, each put a pillow on our heads, and say, 'Ready . . . set . . . go!' The lino was so cold on the landing. If Mam and the others were still downstairs, one of them would run up the stairs to meet us, but if everyone was asleep, I'd rush straight into Mam's room, and she'd shout, 'Run downstairs! Quick!' We didn't have blackouts on the windows upstairs, and the moon lit up the rooms. There were no bulbs hanging from the ceiling, so that we couldn't accidentally switch on a light, and get put in prison by the blackout warden.

I hated and feared the air-raid sirens more than anything else. I'd run downstairs with my pillow on my head, and stand in the black Everything Room, waiting for someone to come with the torch, shivering; thinking about Dad, running about in the street with the bombs dropping like rain, looking for dead people. Felix and Rudi pulled the perrineh downstairs and stuffed it into the gas-cupboard, while Mam spread the spare blanket under the table. Then Felix held the torch while Vered, Rudi, Sybil and I squeezed into the cupboard and hid in the perrineh. Esther said she would rather get killed by a bomb than die of suffocation, and although Felix didn't say anything, he never came into the gas cupboard, either, except that one time. They sat under the table, talking to Mam instead. When Felix turned off the torch, the blackness frightened me. I could feel Sybil shivering next to me, and even though she was singing or telling a story, I knew she was frightened, too. I could hear the guns so clearly, although Felix said that they were miles away, and when I heard planes roaring overhead, he said that they were British, and that it was a good noise. Sometimes there were terrible crashes and explosions; loud, obscene and hideous. Night after night it went on. Rudi told me to pretend it was thunder and lightning, but I was frightened of that, too. Sometimes hours would pass by before the All Clear signal, usually when the Germans were trying to bomb the Hull docks. They were always doing that, because they thought that ships were going to Russia from there, full of ammunition. The bombing went on right through the night and we didn't hear the All Clear until morning. I thought that every house and building in Hull must have fallen down. After the bad nights, we didn't go to school. Dad talked to Mam about sending us all to Australia, but they were nervous of the ship being sunk.

The worst night was towards the end of that year. We were in the cupboard, waiting for the All Clear, when the loudest noise I have ever heard rushed towards us. Apart from the unknown danger it bore, the noise alone was enough to kill. I held the perrineh against my ears, knowing that I was screaming, but hearing nothing else. I felt Mam, Felix and Esther leap on top of us, as the hellish roar passed over, reaching a crescendo for a split second, and then fading away. There was a great explosion that shook the blackout from the windows, followed by dead silence, almost as terrible as the noise. We crawled out as the All Clear sounded, and although it was only about three o'clock, the sky was glowing, orange and dark red, and nobody knew what had happened, except that people must have been killed for sure. We ran upstairs and looked out of the window. Green Bank Lane was blocked with branches, and the trees behind Cameron-Spurlings' hedge had been sliced through, their tops shorn flat. We watched the soldiers who were encamped in the playing fields run up the lane, tearing at the branches, clearing them out of the way so that the army lorries could get past; but some of them just burrowed their way through and ran on. No one was allowed to follow them, or come out of their houses, except for the AFS. I'd often watched the AFS practising with their huge hoses; shooting water into the pond. Mam said they were just about as useful as a shovel of slack, and if your house was on fire, God forbid, you had to shout, 'Anyone for a snooze?' and they would turn up next week to poke about in the ashes. As the sky grew redder and redder, an enormous fire-engine roared past the house, the helmeted man inside ringing a brass bell. It had come all the way from Hull, where the roads were grand and spacious; it had never had to push through a road as narrow as ours. The wheels scrunched over the little fence which separated our cottage from the lane. Cameron-Spurlings' hedge shook. More engines followed. There had never been a night like it in Pineduggy.

Nobody went back to bed. Sybil and Esther mended the blackout and fixed it up against the window, so that we could switch the light on and make the fire. There were only two shovels of coal left, but Mam said, to hell with it; after a shock like that, you had to feel a bit of warmth; you had to boil a kettle for a cup of tea or cocoa, didn't you? I'd forgotten to collect sticks, but she didn't bother to shout at me because there weren't any. We made paper sticks. Rudi and Vered were quicker than me at it, but I made them tighter than anyone, and they were almost as good as firewood. Nobody else in Pineduggy knew about them, just as they didn't know what a perrineh was, and for years I thought it was a ritual peculiar to Jews, and not merely a necessary invention to cope with a lack of firewood. All you needed was a long steel knitting needle and some sheets of newspaper. We rolled the newspaper over the needle to make a tight tube, then shook the needle out and tied the paper tube into knots. The trouble was, you couldn't

82

use slack or coke or big lumps of coal with paper sticks – you had to have small knobs of coal, and Felix was the only person in our house who could make a fire with paper sticks and not lose his temper. I was glad he was making the fire tonight. We piled them onto the grate and Felix held a large sheet of newspaper over it, to draw the flames out. The coal caught at last, and we put the kettle on, and the cocoa in the cups, cut some bread and jam, and talked about the terrible event of the night.

Felix said it was a British plane that must have caught fire and crashed, missing our roof by no more than a few yards. It couldn't have kept in the air long enough to miss the village. Mam said that she thought our last moment had come, and if she didn't end up in a lunatic asylum, it would be another miracle. Had the poor devils managed to bail out before the crash? Who had copped it? God! Which house was burning? We kept running upstairs to look out of the window, to see whether the glow in the sky had grown less, but it hadn't, although we didn't know whether it was the sun trying to rise as well. I kept thinking of the wooden house in Liubava; of the whole village burning, like the aeroplane; like our paper sticks; of the wooden bridge, burning and drowned in the stream. Of Olga. Of Kohath. My head swam and my teeth chopped and my cup of cocoa shook and spilt. The knock on the door frightened me so much, that I jumped in the air, thinking it was Mr Swindham. Three soldiers came in. Their faces were black from the smoke, and their uniforms were wet and torn. Mam told them to sit down and we gave them a cup of tea each, and all the bread and jam. One of the soldiers was called Jock. He lived in Scotland before he went into the army, and spoke in a strange accent. Jock had often been to our house. Every soldier had a billet, and our house was Jock's. He'd brought his friends because they were suffering from shock and exhaustion, and their billets were at the other end of Main Street. They just drank their tea, and sat, looking at the wall. Dad kept a bottle of whisky for when Jock came, and Mam took it out of a secret place and told the soldiers to finish it up.

Jock told us what had happened. The aeroplane had been seen to catch fire as it flew over the Humber. The men inside could have bailed out on their parachutes, Jock said. They could have saved their lives; but they must have seen Pineduggy, in spite of the blackouts, because the flames from the plane would have lit up the village, so the pilot and his friends must have decided to die, rather than risk killing anyone else. He must have been burning all the time he was driving the plane. It crashed in Wetherby's field, but no one in Pineduggy was killed, except for a thousand chickens and the three airmen. Jock's friends had found the bodies and the dog-tags, and that's why they were so upset. The fire would burn itself out, he said.

Esther had been listening to every word, sitting on the fender. Suddenly she stood up, straight and tall, as if the king had walked into the room. 'Pineduggy has been saved by three heroes!' she said, and Jock and his friends stood up too, and saluted; then all of us stood up straight, and Vered and I gave the Brownie salute, even though we weren't wearing our hats. Felix and Rudi put on their caps, while Felix recited the Prayer for the Dead in Hebrew. One of the soldiers started to cry.

'Three heroes are in this house, too,' Mam said, softly. 'May this terrible war soon be over and may you return to your families safely.' She told Jock that she would heat the copper so that they could wash themselves, and maybe she could dry their clothes over the fender, but they said they had to go back.

I lay down on the perrineh with Rudi, so that we could talk about everything all over again and play Mothers at the same time. I rolled him up in the blanket and smacked him if he opened his eyes. I tied bits of string in his hair and told him to spell aeroplane and soldier backwards, and to sing, 'Run, Rabbit; Run, Rabbit; Run, Run, Run,' in German. 'Were you frightened of the noise?' I asked. 'Did you put your fingers in your ears?'

'I wasn't as scared as you! You were crying and screaming even louder than the aeroplane!' I pulled his hair sharply to register my displeasure. He never told tales of me.

'Why do you draw soldiers with ugly faces? Jock and Phil and Tony aren't ugly.'

'The others – the ones in Vienna are ugly.'

'Did anything worse than this happen in Vienna? Can you remember anything worse than tonight?'

'Much worse,' he said, not opening his eyes.

'Tell me!' I ordered. He was silent, pretending to be asleep. I snapped my piece of elastic on his chin. 'Tell me! Tell me!'

'The soldiers made Papa scrub the pavement, while they laughed and poked him with their rifles. They pulled his braces off. They broke our dishes and tore our books and threw the instruments out of Mama's bag. They called us dirty names. Your soldiers save people, even if they're Jews, but Austrian soldiers and German soldiers say that Jews aren't people.'

'They must be daft. They must be dafter than Flat-Faced Mug.'

'*Nisht Menschen* . . .' I didn't know what he was talking about. I put my arms round him, pretending to be his mother in a good mood.

'We're going to shoot all those soldiers. Jock told me, but next time I see him, I'll tell him to leave the worst ones so that your Mama and Papa can make them scrub the pavement, and poke them. We'll watch, and throw gravel in their eyes and make them shovel up dog-dirt and hit them with sticks, then Jock and Phil will shoot them. You and Felix will take me to Vienna with you when the war's over and we'll go to the café and eat ice-cream, and I'll say "Hello" to your Mama and Papa and look out of the windows of your apartment, and you can tell them how I helped Felix to look after you. Answer me, Rudi! Open your eyes and answer me!'

But he kept them closed, although I knew he wasn't asleep, and said nothing.

Chapter Fourteen

Shabbos School was probably the most exclusive school in the country. Everyone had to be Jewish, an evacuee or refugee, and billeted in Pineduggy. No writing was allowed, and there was only one class. Its premises were variable, depending on the weather. On hot, sunny Saturday mornings, we'd push the perrineh out of the small, back bedroom window onto the porch roof, which was flat. It covered our porch, coal-shed and toilet, and continued without a break to cover similar offices next door. The pupils had to climb out of the window and jump onto the perrineh. It didn't matter if you came early or late; you just ran upstairs and jumped out of the window. The perrineh covers got quite dirty, but on Saturday night Mam pulled them off and put them in the copper. We sang Hebrew songs and at least two people would tell a bible story, and sometimes we would learn a new blessing or a psalm off by heart. Helen didn't know a single Hebrew letter when she first came. She didn't even know that you read Hebrew backwards, and actually opened her book upside down, so that I had to laugh, and nudge everyone.

I often asked Mam if I could sleep on the roof, wrapped in the perrineh, but she told me not to be so daft. What if the sirens went and I woke up and forgot I was on the roof, and fell off? What if I had a bad dream? How would Felix and Rudi manage without the perrineh? There was always a good reason why I never slept on the roof, to my relief, but nobody ever stopped Felix going there at night. He made a telescope out of all sorts of broken things, and the headmaster of the Grammar School, Doctor Hunter, was an astronomer, and helped him to make it work. Felix could spot planes and stars better than anyone else. He lay on the blanket we used for under the table during air-raids, and gazed at the sky for hours. Mam never nagged him, the way she nagged and shouted at me, and I wondered a thousand times at her forbearance and patience and good temper. She never brought a cup of cocoa upstairs for me, but I sometimes heard her creeping past Rudi in the little back bedroom, and handing Felix a cup of cocoa through the window.

Once, during Shabbos School, Felix gave us all a fright by climbing onto the roof from the ground. He stood on the coal-shed, then leapt onto the lavatory door and balanced on the top edge, grabbed the edge of the roof and swung himself up. I was right in the middle of reciting Psalm 24 off by heart, when I saw his hands and then his head and shoulders come up, and was so surprised that I said, 'And the King of Glory shall come in,' twice, and forgot the next line. No one else could climb up from the ground. He sometimes did his home-work on the roof, while Sybil did hers on the porch. Esther never did her homework anywhere, except on the bus going to school. There was no room in our cottage, which meant that Maggie couldn't come to live with us, even if Mr and Mrs Wilson didn't like her. Never, not in my most horrid dreams, did it ever occur to me that she would be allowed to come to Shabbos School.

I had just jumped onto the perrineh when I saw Sybil walking through the back way with Maggie, who was wearing a green checked dress and a matching green scarf on her head. I shuddered, hoping Mam wouldn't let her in the house, in case her dicks ran out from under her scarf, and made nests. I'd never seen a dick, but had heard tell of them, and imagined that it was similar to a huge and repulsive beetle, whose sole longing was to embed itself in my hair and clothes, and there multiply with horrific speed. I climbed back through the window, to warn Mam not to let her in, but she told me that Maggie had been specially invited, and if I didn't want to mix with her, I could mix by myself, as far away from her and Shabbos School as possible.

Had Mam forgotten how horrible she was! That she'd torn my hat; that Teddy had not only pinched it, but had snatched Vered's biscuit too, and it was rumoured that before the war, Maggie went into the street without any knickers on! She obviously had, for she waved to Maggie, and ran into the back yard to greet her. I was amazed and not a little disgusted to observe how polite and pleasant Esther was to her. She, who had been so rude to Isobel, was acting as if Maggie was her best friend, and even Vered shouted 'Hello' from the roof. Something had to be done immediately.

'She's not Jewish! She's not Jewish! She's not allowed to come to Shabbos School!' I told everyone who was assembled on the roof. 'She used to live in a dirty house and an orphanage! Nobody wanted to look after her, not even her Mam and Dad, before they got killed! Her brother Teddy stole my best hat! He's still in hospital because no one likes him!' Helen and Daisy were the only ones on my side; watching Maggie approach with satisfactory distaste. Esther, Sybil, Mam and Iris were still in the yard, chatting with Maggie, and weren't paying attention to what I was saying. Stuart, Vered and Rudi stopped playing Fish, and stared at me as if I was Maggie. Stuart said, 'Vered, why don't you bop your sister? She thinks she's better and prettier than you, because she's got yellow hair and blue eyes, but her mouth is big and ugly. No one likes her.' Vered stood up, but before we had a chance to fight, Rudi got in the way, and Felix stood behind me, to stop me falling off the roof. Rudi didn't hit me, but he drew his black eyebrows together, and screwed up his face, so that he looked like one of his ugly drawings.

'I like Gordon Tuttle better than you,' he said. I hated Rudi and Stuart more than Hitler. Helen and Daisy stopped being on my side, and said they would never be friends with me again. I turned round to Felix, but he hated me, too. He didn't say he did, but I could tell. He said that I reminded him of the kids in Vienna. If I missed out a couple of 'nots' and shouted, 'She's Jewish' instead, I'd have it just right. His irony was lost to me, but before I could begin to unravel why everyone was being so mean, he had slithered off the roof and down the drain-pipe – an act of the most astounding daring – and was making more fuss of Maggie than he'd ever made of me. He sat next to her all morning, showing her the Hebrew alphabet, and smiling and chatting to her. I hadn't told a bible story in Shabbos School for ages, and although I told Mam it was my turn, Stuart told one instead. It was about a stinging fly landing on Abner's leg. David was hiding from Abner and

88

King Saul, and Abner fell asleep with his leg on top of David. David didn't know what to do, and stayed very still. Suddenly, the fly stung Abner's leg, and he moved away from David without waking up. David said 'Thank you' to the fly and to God, and blessed all God's creatures, who were there for a purpose; even spiders, wasps and dicks. Then he got up and crept away from Abner, still blessing the fly for saving his life. I thought it was the most stupid story I'd ever heard, and said so. Stuart said that the fly was called Rachel, because I did useful things too, but only God knew what they were. Daisy and Helen laughed louder than anyone, and Rudi didn't fight them. Felix went on smiling and talking to Maggie. I felt tears in my eyes. I understood that his kind attention to Maggie was the result, in part, of my scorn and repulsion of her, and in order to dilute his interest, I must make myself be friendly to her, too. Nobody else seemed to be frightened of her dicks. Perhaps they had all died of cleanliness. The Wilsons' house was a million times cleaner than ours.

Mr and Mrs Wilson pretended that Maggie was Gladys's sister, and although she helped with the housework and worked in their market gardens, she wasn't a servant in the way she would have been at Cameron-Spurlings'. She started calling herself Maggie Wilson, and earned more pocket-money than anyone I knew. Maggie was rich, and should therefore be acceptable. I knew in my bones that this could never be, yet here she was, being treated as someone special, and I found it quite intolerable, immoral and hateful to have to witness such a spectacle. Then I found something out about Maggie. She couldn't read English properly, let alone Hebrew. She was sixteen years old, and a bigger dunce than Janet Daws.

One afternoon, months later, I was resting at home because of a sudden earache, brought on by a discovered felony at school, when Maggie knocked. Thinking it was the police or Miss Ashdown, I hid in the gas-cupboard. Mam had forgotten about Maggie's appointment due to the hullabaloo she'd created regarding my misdemeanour, but now the cat was out of the bag. Mam had been teaching Maggie to read and had kept it a secret. I listened from my hiding-place, and then stealthily emerged, in order to observe. There was an atmosphere in the room more startling than that which I merely beheld. Maggie was sitting on the armchair beside the fire, and

Mam was sitting on the floor, leaning against the arm. They were reading a story called 'The Three Horrid Men' – one that I knew by heart and which was one of the best stories I had ever read; yet it was as if I was listening to it for the first time and was unsure of the ending, and that when I read it subsequently, I would always associate it with these minutes of harmony and peace. She read haltingly, Mam helping her with a word here and there. When she reached the end, Mam lied. 'Maggie, that was marvellous! I'll put the kettle on, while you write the difficult words in your book.' That's when Mam looked round and remembered me. She said nothing, but for a few moments held my gaze, as if she was trying to teach *me* something, too, and was unable to tell me what it was, not only because Maggie was there, but because the telling of it would defeat the purpose. Then she walked past me, into the kitchen. I wanted to tell everyone the secret that Mam and Maggie had kept so well, and to read 'The Three Horrid Men' to her; to destroy her newfound confidence; help her with the words she didn't know; casually; cruelly. I sat on the arm of her chair as Mam came back with the kettle. I remembered how Maggie had torn my hat. I would show her what a great dunce she was! But I couldn't. Abner's leg lay heavily across my throat, preventing me from saying what I wanted.

'Maggie,' I said, 'before you write the words down, will you read the story to me all over again? I can't read it myself, and it's my favourite story, next to *The Faraway Tree*.' I could hear Mam letting her breath go. 'Once upon a time . . .' Maggie began, and she read it right through to the end, and I never corrected her. After she had gone, Mam said. 'You're not a daft baby any more. You're growing up! I thought I'd have to wait until you were twenty at least, until you learnt how to behave properly. It was kind to pretend you couldn't read. Wait till I tell the others how nice you can be, and how well you can keep a secret. Esther will let you join the Secret Club as a full member, and Felix will be proud of you!'

'I hate pretending and being kind and keeping secrets! I don't want to be nice when I'm twenty! It makes me sad! I can't! I can't! It's too hard!'

Chapter Fifteen

The climate is never temperate when you are starving. It adjusts to extremes, as if to exacerbate the agony. Fry in the burning desert of thirst or freeze in the snowy waste of hunger. So it was in Shobodko, the slum area of Kovno which was called the Ghetto, where Hannah spent three years. The summers were lush with flies and lice, and hot with fever, but it was the winters that were everlasting. When she slept, her hair froze to the ground; her feet and fingers were lumps of raw flesh, craggy with chilblains that never healed. Every morning she put on huge, old, broken shoes, and for twelve hours she shovelled and dug sand and stones onto her barrow which she then pulled to a specific point, unloaded, and repeated the exercise interminably. When her mind wandered, wild and alone, forgetful of the body, it recalled warmth and coolness; colour and blossom; her home; her family; her mother. And when her body reclaimed its mind, this moment was the worst of all, for that was when despair battled with the will to live.

After the death of Tsillinky, 'Aktions' took place without prior warning. Old people and children were driven out of the Ghetto and into a large square, and transported to death camps. Her grandma, who they loved and tended so carefully, was one of the old, useless cattle who was dislodged from her dark corner into the icy air. Hannah found the door bashed in and the room empty, when she staggered back, breathless and frantic, from work. The blanket was stuffed under a rotting floor-board, along with her shawl, and within its folds Hannah found her grandma's watch, which she had managed to hold on to, until the last few minutes of her life.

Rumours ran wild that the next night all the men were to be

91

shot. She trembled in every limb for her brother, for his life was far more precious to her than her own. After they had intoned the Prayer for the Dead, they discussed how Yosef must try to escape from his unit and stay outside the Ghetto all night. She knew that this was impossible, even as she implored him to try. But miracles happen, even in hell. He hid himself under a hill, and covered himself with snow and lumps of wood, until he heard the unit running back, at the double, towards the Ghetto. His comrades must have assumed that he was lying dead somewhere, but the dead were counted. It was the coldest night in memory, and even the fat, warmly-clad Germans were careless. When all was dark and still, he turned his jacket inside out, to hide the yellow star, and hid in an empty pig-sty all night.

Hannah hung the blanket over the gaping hole of their home and propped a piece of the door against it. At two o'clock in the morning, it was knocked down, and a guard shone a powerful torch into the gloom, demanding that any man who lived there, should stand before him. She told him there was no one. She lived here with her grandmother, who had been taken away the previous night. He shone his torch into her face and saw the brilliant blue eyes staring at him, unblinking, despite the beam. He tugged back her hair, white with frost, but undeniably as fair as pure Aryan. He leered at her. His orders were to collect someone from this place. She offered him the watch, a capital crime, and as he took it, he promised that he would be back. He would try to forget that she was a filthy Jew for five minutes.

Everyone but a select few were required that night. Where could she hide? There was no door; no window; no place of refuge! She listened to the gun-fire hoping that her grandma had died quickly. Should she get ready for work? She would be shot if she didn't go, and probably shot if she showed herself. The alleys were full of screams and shouts; silences; laughter. She went to join the work unit. Only half the usual number were present for roll-call. Was it the most robust or the most tenacious to life; the luckiest or the most unfortunate, who stood there? Yosef; grandma; mother; *mother*. One, two; one two. You don't freeze when you're dead; you don't think about those you love; you don't starve; have dysentery, feel your stomach shrinking; witness the suffering of your fellow-

92

men. You don't care that you don't care. You don't feel ashamed for the name of Man.

Yosef returned with his decimated unit, after mingling with them that morning. He was almost frozen to death, and the tops of his fingers and toes were soft and rotten. But their joy was boundless when they found each other alive. Had they ever known such happiness? As she embraced him, she vowed to herself that as long as she had him, she could bear the hunger, the cold and the fear. Her nerves would be taut, but never unstrung, and she would try to cheer and help those who had no one, because nothing was worse than that. Thereafter, on Sundays, when there was no work, the tiny room became a meeting-place; a refuge for those who were bereaved and alone. They shared what they had – a comb, water, dead rats, frozen potatoes. Even laughter. Elijah did not point to righteous men, scholars or wise men; nor to the poor, meek or benevolent, when he preached of the World to Come. He pointed to two jesters. Hannah and Yosef were known as the Jesters of Shobodko. On 8 July 1944, a month before her nineteenth birthday, the decree came that the Kovno Ghetto was to be liquidated, and on that day the SS surrounded it, and drove Hannah and Yosef, along with all the living inhabitants, into the square.

Chapter Sixteen

Dogs, Germans and Jews stood in place, obeying orders. Hannah and Yosef were stuffed into the same cattle-truck. It was standing room only; body squeezed against body, so that the lungs could not expand properly. Rifles were pushed into the bodies which stuck out untidily, until they were flush with the opening, which was then closed and barred. They were fortunate, these two, the brother and the sister. They could suffocate together. It was some time before all the wagons were filled, for some of the more important officials were enjoying a leisurely breakfast, and it couldn't be helped if the contents of the trucks had to be kept waiting. Somehow, this knowledge made the food taste more delicious and the spirits merrier. One had to hold on to small pleasures in these tough and challenging times. Those who died while the wagons were yet stationary, stood where they were, and those pressed against the corpses did not know that they were dead. The train moved; lurched; banged. On top of each wagon was a horizontal ladder, stretching from one end to the other, and on each squatted two armed soldiers, delighted by the surging, gasping madness beneath them. Sometimes, these riders were silent, their eyes glazed, and then for sport, they would shout obscenities and bang the metal roof with their rifles, to craze and deafen the occupants. The train stopped every hour so that the guards could have rest and refreshment, but the wagons remained sealed. No food or water or air was allowed in, and no dead or alive were allowed out. The temperature rose, along with the stench, as the sun beat down on the metal containers. After forty-five hours, the train stopped at Stutthof and the door was unbarred. The tremendous force of space

94

sent Hannah hurtling to the ground outside. She gobbled at the air, shoved others away from her and scrambled to her feet, staggering about, looking for Yosef. A boot broke her nose. A dog leapt at her throat. Blood dripped off her chin. Stutthof was for female rats only. The wagon door was sealed again; the bar slammed home. Hannah had reached her destination, but Yosef was still inside the unspeakable prison, for he had only travelled one-third of his journey to Dachau. She was alone.

Chapter Seventeen

Felix and Rudi knew how to speak Polish as well as German when they came to live with us, but by the time he was eleven, Rudi had forgotten all his Polish, and spoke German like a foreigner. I scolded him about this, telling him how upset he made Felix, and what would happen when Mama and Papa came for him. They didn't understand English, did they? They wouldn't be able to talk to him properly, and how would he manage to tell them about me? They would like Felix better than him.

Felix could talk in any language you could think of, and he never forgot anything. Even Dad, who never praised anyone, except God, said that he was the best student he had ever come across. He could read Hebrew without stopping between the words, and was top of his class at the Grammar School and won the prize for foreign languages, as well as the prize for being top. He never boasted, and I wondered why. Was he shy? I told everyone I was top, even though I never was, and could never come to terms with his reticence. Mam stuck Felix's report on a piece of card, cut out of the side of a cornflake box, to save carefully for when Mama and Papa wanted it. She kept Rudi's drawings in the pages of a newspaper. He still went to Pineduggy Council School and Miss Ashdown told Mam that he would pass his scholarship easily, although he was wild and naughty. Nobody had reports in Pineduggy Council School, so I could lie about my excellence with impunity.

'That boy is a sponge – a born sponge!' Mam said, every time Sybil came home with a story about how clever Felix was, and then she would sigh and look sad, as if it was a bitter thing, to be born a sponge. She should be happy that he could learn so quickly and easily. I knew it was no use asking her why she wasn't. She'd tell me it was something to do with me not being kind and helpful. Sybil was the one who understood everything. I cornered her on the back step where she was doing her biology homework. She was drawing a lop-sided pear, divided into quarters, with red and blue pipes sprouting out of it. She had written 'The Heart' at the top of the page. I wondered at her silliness, but understood that in spite of these gaps in her intellect, she was enormously wise.

'Is Felix as clever as you, Sybil?'

'Much cleverer.'

'Is he cleverer than the teachers?' I knew this to be a stupid question, but let it ride. No one was.

'Yes. He's a genius.'

'Why does Mam call him a sponge? Is it the same as a genius?'

'No. A sponge is a sea animal. Posh people use a sponge instead of a flannel. It soaks up water the way Felix soaks up knowledge.' The confusion which this imagery caused occupied my mind for some months. 'A genius is a person who is brilliantly clever.'

'Why is Mam upset because he's clever? Is she jealous?'

'Her heart is heavy with sorrow because his parents aren't with him to be proud of their son.' You could never have a conversation with Sybil without her bringing hearts into it. I looked down at her drawing. It didn't look anything like the red ones on the playing-cards, but I didn't want to change the subject and tell her I thought it a poor effort. 'Of course she's not jealous! Nobody with any feelings could be jealous of Felix.'

'Why? Why couldn't anyone be jealous of him?'

'Because he's so unhappy; so alone, and no matter how hard we try, no matter how much Mam and Dad like him and take an interest in him, it doesn't make any difference. He wants his real parents. His heart aches for them. He doesn't know where they are. He doesn't know whether he'll ever see them again. Think how you'd feel if you thought Mam and Dad were dead.'

I remembered the time when I'd seen Dad in his tin hat and imagined him being hit by a bomb. Then only the other day,

Esther had pretended she wanted to whisper something to Mam, but instead, had blown down her ear. Mam had screamed, '*I'm dying! I'm dying!*' They had been the worst moments of my life that I could think of. Nobody could possibly have been jealous of me, then. Did Felix live in this dreadful agony all the time? Did Rudi? Did . . .? I held on to the lid of the coal-shed, and Sybil wrapped her arms around me, until I was warm again. Her book fell on the ground, but she didn't bother to pick it up. The unthinkable dissolved into the remote future. 'I couldn't play ball or skipping if I thought Mam and Dad were dead. I couldn't take notice of anything or anybody, the way Felix does. I'd cry all the time, until I was dead too. But Felix and Rudi don't cry.'

'Just because they don't cry in front of you, doesn't mean that they don't when they're in bed, or alone. Felix cries all the time.'

I stared at Sybil in amazement. She bent down and picked up her biology book, and looked at the lop-sided pear she'd drawn. 'His heart weeps,' she said, 'and none of us can get close enough to comfort him.'

'Just like Mrs Wilson?'

'Yes. But worse. Mrs Wilson cries with her eyes as well, and that makes it easier. Felix doesn't. He keeps everything to himself, as if he was all alone.'

Even Sybil wouldn't understand, if I told her he wasn't. If I told her he'd got me.

One day, while we were at school, Mam received a message through Cameron-Spurlings' telephone that my dad was in hospital. She was too late to catch the ten o'clock bus, and Mr Wilson took her on the back of his motor-bike. When Rudi, Vered and I came out of the playground, Maggie and Mrs Wilson were waiting for us at the gates, to tell us. Vered's rosy cheeks turned as white as paper, until Mrs Wilson smiled and said he would soon be better, and that maybe it was a good thing he was in hospital, because at least he would have a rest. His face had been burnt, but not badly, and his arm was broken. Dad was the Sheriff's Chaplain and looked after the Jewish soldiers, as well as being a rabbi for the congregation and a warden at night. A bomb had exploded in Lily Street, and when Dad crawled into a house, some rocks and burning timber had fallen on top of him. Sybil, Felix and Esther were going to see Dad and wouldn't be home until half-past nine, and Mam was going to stay in Hull for a few days. Mrs Wilson and Maggie took us to their house for tea – a much nicer one than we ate at home. Condensed milk was my favourite food after liquorice all-sorts, and there was a whole tin on the table. After tea, I began to sulk, because I wanted to go to Hull to see Dad, too. It wasn't fair. But Mrs Wilson said I couldn't and I daren't argue with her. She gave us paper and an envelope and a stamp, and we all wrote a letter each, instead. Maggie and I ran to post them before the five o'clock bus left with the sack. She bought me two comics with her own money, and was so friendly that I thought she must have forgotten how she tore my hat and that I bit her leg. We sat on the black stones for a few minutes, and Maggie said, 'Look, Rachel! Look!' She held out her hand and I saw the ring on her finger. 'Guess who gave it to me!'

'Mrs Wilson or Mr Wilson.'

'Guess again.'

I guessed and guessed, but was wrong each time. 'Jock!' she said. 'Jock and I are engaged to be married!' I was so surprised that for a moment I was lost for words. 'He's being posted abroad, so we decided to get engaged first. After the war, I'm going with him to see his Mam and Dad in Scotland. When we get married, we're going up there to live.'

'Does Jock love you, Maggie?'

'Course he does! We wouldn't be engaged if we didn't love each other.'

I was glad that I had such exciting news to tell Vered and Rudi. I told Maggie that I'd always wanted to go to Scotland, but I had no one to stay with, and she said that I could stay with her and Jock. 'I'm getting engaged as soon as I'm old enough,' I said.

'Who to?'

'Guess.' She guessed and guessed, but was wrong each time. On the way back to meet Vered and Rudi, people asked after Dad, and I felt proud and important. Even Mrs Tuttle enquired politely about his beard.

'I hope it hasn't been burnt off,' she said, with satisfying concern. 'A rabbi without a beard! Well!'

The three of us went to meet the half-past nine bus. I liked the way Esther smiled and said it would take more than a lump of concrete and a piece of rotten old timber to finish off our Dad. He had his arm in a sling and a bandage round his head. His hair and beard were singed, but you couldn't see, because of the bandage. When he was better, he was coming to stay in Pineduggy for a few days.

It was strange, being in the house at night without Mam. Vered was asleep before I had my nightie on. I got under the perrineh with Rudi, because Mam wasn't there to nag, and I wanted to find out if he and Felix cried in the night. I told Rudi I wanted to sleep with him, in case I had a bad dream. We talked about Dad, and I must have fallen asleep, because when I woke up, Felix was lying down, too. I kept as still as a mouse, and listened to them whispering to each other. That night, I understood what Sybil meant.

'I never said GOODBYE,' said Rudi.

'Yes, you did. Don't you remember?'

'I remember that I didn't say GOODBYE. I hugged and kissed them and said it for going away for a short time; for an adventure, the way I would when I was going to stay with Victor. Mama would stand at the elevator, and we would hear each other calling until the third floor. Then we were too far away. But I'd run out of the lobby and into the street and look up at the window, and she would be there, waving. I could hear her shouting Goodbye even if a tram was running past. I knew that I would say Hello to her the next evening. That's the sort of Goodbye I said, when we went on the Kinder Transport. Goodbye! See you soon! Not GOODBYE. Not GOODBYE for ever.'

'The war won't go on for ever, Rudi. A few years *seems* like for ever to you, but not to me. That's because I'm older. Mama and Papa are probably thinking about us this minute, hoping that we're not worrying about them. They'll be hiding somewhere safe; maybe Catherine and Carl are looking after them. They've been friends with them ever since they were students. You told me what Esther said to you about that. There are so many people who like Mama and Papa! Don't cry any more.'

'What about Victor? Mama looked after him when he had measles. She helped to make him better. They were friends with his parents. Papa took out Herr Biehl's appendix, but they laughed at him when he was cleaning the street. He said he'd been ill ever since Papa put his Jew hands on him. Victor's gang kicked my ears and tore my books and Frau Voegele was in the playground and didn't clap her hands to stop them. And what about Gunther? Gunther, from your school? Do you remember how we heard his Mama screaming, even after she jumped from the window?'

'If I remember, I don't think about it. It's better that way.'

'How do you do that? How do you not think about it?'

'I build rooms in my mind. In one at the back, I keep the things that I am going to do to the boys who kicked you and who blinded Gunther. I keep a list of names and a row of pictures there. The neighbours who stole our books and broke our doors and furniture, and who made mockery of Mama and Papa. I keep a record of their lies and the notices they wrote and what they did to the old people outside Greenspan's and how they smashed the shops and the synagogue.'

'What do you keep in the other rooms?'

'Happy memories. My Bar-Mitzvah party. The weekends in the country with Carl and Catherine. Playing football in the park; the camping trip with Gunther when we tried to ride a cow; eating ice-cream at Greenspan's; going for picnics on our bikes. Being at home with Mama and Papa; listening to them playing the piano and singing silly songs and then Mama laughing so much and falling onto the chair, holding her chest. I like that room.'

'Have you a room for what's happening now?'

'Of course! That's where I spend most of my time. That's what you should do; think about what you're doing now; in England. But you shouldn't ever call Malka and Sacha, Mama and Papa. They've only borrowed you from them. The girls can be sisters because we haven't any, but you can't have their parents as your Mama and Papa when you've got your own. Even if they're not living with you, it doesn't mean they're not anywhere.'

'What if they're dead?' I stopped breathing, but I could feel my heart bumping in my throat. For a moment, I thought Rudi and Felix were dead, because they'd stopped breathing too. It was Rudi who spoke next, although he waited for ages for Felix to answer. 'You spend nearly all your time in the back room of your mind. I don't want a room like that. I want to close it up. I want to pretend that this is my family now.'

101

'No! You can't!' Felix whispered it so loudly, that it sounded like a shout.

'They pretend we belong to them – except for Rachel. She never pretends we're her brothers, like Sybil does. Like Vered and Esther. She wants to marry you when she's grown up. Maggie told me.'

'She's a kid. She doesn't know what she wants. She changes her mind twenty times a day and spends her life in fairyland. Why has she taken it into her head to spend the night here?'

'She has horrible dreams, and Malka's not here. Some nights I hear her shouting and screaming in her sleep. Vered shakes her so she'll wake up, then Malka has to sing to her so she'll go to sleep again. She's a much worse baby than I was at her age. She has dreams when she's awake as well. Do you remember that time she pulled the dustbin over herself? She'd been teasing me, and Esther thumped her. Do you know what she shouted out while Esther and I were talking? 'Einsatzgruppe 3''! Rachel doesn't know that word. She doesn't know any German except for words she copies from you. When she was better, I asked her what it meant, and she didn't know, then I asked her what she'd seen. She said she'd seen people made of stone in Liubava, mixed up with some from Pineduggy. They burnt up Hannah's house and Tsivia's and Jacob's and they had to run to some deep pits at the edge of a field. Olga's nightie was burning and Kohath tried to put out the fire, but someone chased him with a scythe. They had to take their clothes off and jump into the pits and the stone men stood on the edge and looked down. The people in the pits were Paper Children. She means those on the photographs. They were smaller than insects and the stone people were taller than houses. When she has a dream in the night, she cuddles the shoe-box instead of a doll. I've seen her! The other night, Malka was out with you on the roof, and I heard Rachel shout out, so I went to look at her in Malka's bed. The shoe-box was sticking into her cheek, so I moved it. She jumped up in bed and shouted, 'Save me! Save me!' I think she thought I was you. All the Paper Children fell on the floor, and she grabbed me round the neck and stared at me without blinking. She pulled me down, onto the pillow, and then fell asleep again, so I picked up all the photos and put them back in the box, and put them next to her. I think she might be a witch, but she doesn't look like one. She looks like a fairy. Did she see the soldiers in Leopoldstadt when she said "Einsatzgruppe"? Their faces were grinning, just like Rachel's stone men. Do you think she knows about Mama and Papa?'

'You mustn't take any notice of Rachel's dreams'

'How does she know about the Action Groups?'

'She doesn't. She must have heard the word on the wireless, and taken a fancy to it. She copies from people all the time. She doesn't know anything about Mama and Papa. Or the people in the photographs. She's never met any of them, except the girl called Hannah.'

'Why does she go on looking at the photographs as if she can't stop?'

'Is she asleep?' asked Felix, softly.

'Yes. She fell asleep talking about Sacha. She hasn't moved since.'

'There's something wrong with her. She's obsessional. Do you know what that means?'

'Yes.' I felt angry with Rudi. I remembered the word, so I could ask Vered tomorrow. 'Is she obsessional about you?'

'She's always been this way; ever since she was a baby. Sybil told me. Do you remember the first day we came here, and she made us laugh about Paper Children? Hannah used to call the girls *Paperene Kinderlech*, because her mother called them that, whenever she received letters about them, or photographs. It stuck in Rachel's mind, and became an obsession. Hannah used to tell her all about her mother and brothers and sisters, and about her brother's children, and the village where they lived. They became more real to her than the people she knew. She actually believed she'd met them all and knew Liubava. Malka said she used to follow Hannah everywhere and slept in her bed. Then Hannah had to go back, because of the outbreak of the war. Even Vered remembers what happened when Hannah went home. Rachel went mad on the platform and spent weeks and weeks in hospital and had seizures every day. Her nerves and mind were damaged by the separation, and she feels better when she looks at the Paper Children in the shoe-box. Malka and Sacha think she'll get better, once the war is over, and she'll be able to see Hannah again.'

'Did she say Goodbye to Hannah?'

'I don't know. I suppose she did.'

'I said Goodbye to Mama and Papa. But I didn't say GOODBYE.'

Chapter Eighteen

The Red Army, led by General Zhukov, captured Warsaw on January 17th and twelve days later they encircled a huge German garrison in Poznan, a hundred miles from Berlin. Soviet troops approached Konigsberg. SS guards obeyed orders and evacuated their prisoners. Three thousand, seven hundred female rats had been working in one of the branches of the Stutthof camp, within Konigsberg itself, so the SS had their work cut out for a hurried removal of these vermin.

Some of the death marches lasted for six weeks, but the Stutthoff-Konigsberg branch was fortunate. It scuttled along with the heavily-armed, crazed Pied Pipers towards Palm-nicken, a small Baltic fishing village, only about a hundred miles away – the shortest march on record. The creatures were told that they were to be removed by boat. Some of the stragglers had their journey curtailed. They seemed not to be able to withstand the fury of the weather or the whim of the guards and seven hundred fell by the wayside. Nevertheless, three thousand managed to catch a glimpse of the sea. They could hear the waves pounding like the heart-beat of the wind, and approached the shore in order to board the boat which did not await them. As the guards sprayed them with machine-gun fire, they attempted to run for cover.

Hannah dived over a snowdrift and dragged lumps of it on top of her, clawing and burrowing until she was entirely hidden. A few seconds later, she forced her arm through the surface, made a breathing tube, and lay on her side, with her mouth against it. She could feel them trampling on either side of her; on top of her, huge and hideous, pressing her into cosy hibernation; solidifying and camouflaging her burrow. She remained where she was, until snow and ice clogged the tiny air-hole. Her friend Tsillinky had carried a sack of potatoes once, over twice her weight. Hannah heaved against the weight of the white blackness, biting and scraping her way out. She slithered on her stomach towards a group of trees which lined the blood-soaked lane and crawled under branches which had been snapped off by the weight of the snow. The Soviet soldiers found sixty women still alive. They knew what to do with rigid, frozen bones, as long as life still fluttered there. Hannah was taken to a fisherman's cottage, and her emaciated limbs were submerged in a tin bath of cold water. The frost splintered and crackled on her fingers and toes, and the snow which crammed her ears and crowned her shaven head, melted and rolled into her eyes and down her sunken cheeks, like tears. Warm water would have killed her. Her inability to eat saved her life, for food would have killed her too. Hannah Sokolovsky was born under a lucky star. There was no other explanation for her great fortune.

Chapter Nineteen

I walked down Lily Street the other day, just to see whether the house would remind me of my early childhood and whether I could recall anything of those days before the war; but it had gone; demolished, with the rubble still uncleared. Rudi came with me. He tagged along, because he said he wanted to be reminded of his childhood, too, even though he'd never set foot inside our old house. But it was the deserted schoolroom he was interested in; the place where he'd first met Mam and me, when he was a little refugee of eight. The school had gone, though Rudi could remember it exactly as it was, or so he said, and he could taste the cornflake sweet I'd given him, just thinking about that day. I reckoned it must have tasted a bit mouldy after eight long years. He sucked in his spit and laughed, and assured me it was absolutely delicious.

I showed him the exact spot where our house used to stand. That rusty, cock-eyed lump of iron was our old black stove, which Mam polished with an old fur hat. All that cleaning seemed to be for nothing now; a waste of time. This blue lump of crumbling plaster; was it part of our bathroom wall? The scraps of half-buried, rotting, brown lino must have lain on our Front Room floor, but I couldn't quite recollect. Pretty prefabricated houses stood at the end of the street, and the huge mechanical shovels were encroaching on my particular devastated area at last. If I'd left it for a few more weeks, I wouldn't have been able to find the place where our house used to stand.

I'd not been down Lily Street since the war was over. I don't know why, because we didn't live that far away. Paradise Street – not more than two miles away. It didn't quite live up to its name. The pavement was wider, though, and lined with a few sooty trees. The railway line crossed the main road a few yards beyond the T-junction. You could go mad with temper when the gates closed to let three goods trains crawl past, while you were sitting on the bus, late for school; but sometimes it was a blessing when you were flying up Paradise Street, and then finding the bus waiting for you at the crossing gates. At first, our house seemed huge and grand, after living in the overcrowded cottage in Pineduggy, but when I come to think of it, the only extra room, apart from a bathroom and an inside toilet, was the Front Room which nobody used, anyway, for *living* in. The back garden was big enough for a chicken-run and a bit of grass, and sometimes I dragged a kitchen chair out and did my homework there, resting my book on my knee. I hardly went to school at all, during the last year of the war. The fits seemed to cluster around the whole year, and Mam taught me at home. All the children taught me, even Esther, so I managed to pass my scholarship to the Grammar School, but I knew that there was something wrong with my brains. I couldn't learn or concentrate. There were great gaps in my head, and although I longed to be clever like the others, it was as if there was a faulty circuit somewhere, and I knew that I never would be.

Felix and Rudi had a bed each in the house in Paradise Street – and the middle room downstairs. It was a wonder that their growth wasn't stunted, what with having to sleep in that tiny back room in Pineduggy, but they grew tall, just to spite it. Felix was well over six feet when we left, and Rudi looked as if he would catch up with him, but I never once heard them grumble about being squashed up. The middle room was horrible, but it must have seemed like pure luxury to them, with two sagging beds, a bookcase and a wardrobe, to spread themselves.

The Front Room was worse – as dark and as gloomy as a tomb for the hell-bound, and crammed with the furniture my mother had inherited from her parents. I felt in my bones that it was practically identical to the Front Room she'd known as a girl, where she'd first met my father. Dad and Mam were so old-fashioned; they made me sick and tired when I argued with them about it. They thought it was fit for Royalty. Why the hell had it got to be so grim and cheerless? The only times I ever

108

went in were when it was so hot outside, that to lie on the leather couch there for a few minutes was as efficacious as climbing into a mausoleum, but somewhat more oppressive; so I'd usually land up suffocating and sulking in the kitchen, or sharing the back-yard with the chickens. The Front Room was my last resort. Sometimes, Dad went in there to study the ancient, incomprehensible books that lined the sombre walls, or to talk to a member of the congregation who wanted to discuss a private matter with him; a personal problem or the arrangements for a wedding or a funeral. I'm damned if I could discuss anything there with anybody, except my own funeral. Once, just once, I stayed in that room for a whole day when we heard about Sybil. Mam and Dad joined me there. It seemed as if it was their last resort, too.

There were three bedrooms upstairs as well as the bathroom and toilet, and that was a definite improvement on the cottage, where the bath was in the kitchen, doubling up as a table. If you were caught short in the night, it was infinitely preferable to slip across the freezing landing, instead of the freezing porch, without the risk of spiders and ghosts greeting you behind the door. The rooms were much bigger, but I liked the smallest one best, because the window looked over the garden, such as it was, and the sill was wide enough to sit on. I wanted to share it with Sybil, because I hated sleeping by myself, but Esther interfered and spoilt my plans. Since someone *had* to share with me and suffer, we should toss up for the luxury of privacy. The back room was for one person only, and the two unlucky ones would stick it out with me in the big room, which overlooked the street. Mam and Dad took the middle-sized one. Vered wanted the chance of a room to herself, as well, because she was fed up with me waking her up in the night, yelling in my sleep. I wanted to join in the dip for the room to myself. Esther said that it would be a waste of the room, because I'd be running into the big one every night. They each tossed a penny after it was agreed that the two who got the same would have to share with me. I hoped Esther wouldn't win, although part of me wished she would, so that she'd be out of my way. Sybil got tails and Esther and Vered got heads. The little back room became Sybil's and there was no further argument.

She made it so pretty. A man who Dad knew, let him have

109

some flowered material without coupons, and he gave it to Sybil. She made curtains and a bed cover to match, and with the bit that was left, she padded the top of an old wooden trunk with rags, and covered it so that it made a stool, and she made a cushion for the window-seat. She put her books on the shelf, and a few photographs round the edges of a mirror she stuck to the wall. She and Rudi washed it all over in yellow distemper – even the ceiling, because you couldn't buy white paint then. They worked on it every night after school, wearing old pillow cases on their heads. I helped a bit, too, until Rudi started throwing his weight about and showing me how horrible my piece of wall looked, compared to his. He got on my nerves so much, that I threw my brush in his face and ran downstairs and out of the house before he could catch me. I never got on with Rudi after Felix left. He changed into a pompous pain in the neck when Felix wasn't there to keep him in check. If only he could have pushed off instead – with Esther.

After the last All Clear, when we'd only been back in Hull for a few weeks, Felix went away to London, to live at my Uncle Danny's and Aunt Aliza's house. He won a place at university there, to study Modern Languages. I passed my scholarship to the Grammar School the year he left, so we never went to school there together. I sat on the bed in the middle room, watching him packing, and already the house seemed bleak and empty. I put his pillow over my head, so that he wouldn't see what a big baby I was, but he took it away. 'You don't need that! Bombs and blackouts are a thing of the past!' He hugged me and stroked my hair. He could see that I'd been crying. 'You're starting a new school and a new life, just like me. Aren't you happy about that?'

'No,' I said. 'I'm miserable. I can hardly remember a time when you haven't lived with us. I don't want you to go. London's so far away. I wish I could live with Danny and Aliza, and go to school there.' He didn't answer me.

'Don't you think I'll miss you too? I'll be back for the Easter holidays. We'll have so much to tell one another. It's only six months away.'

'What about Christmas? Doesn't the university go on holiday for Christmas?'

'Yes. I'm going to Austria. You're not the only family I have,

Rachel. I need to know what happened to the other one – to mine. I have a share in yours, and I'll never cease to be grateful for that, but it's not the same; it never will be. Rudi doesn't feel the same way; he belongs to you more than he does to me, somehow. I sometimes wonder if he remembers his parents. Perhaps it was because he was so young when we left them behind, and he was able to make the adjustment. I wish I was more like Rudi – balanced and reasonable.' He seemed to have forgotten that I was there; sitting next to him on the bed.

'I don't. I'd hate it if you were like him. I wish you were staying here instead of him. Sometimes he's so mean to me; cold and mean. He's always telling me not to be so bossy and that it's time I learnt that he's three years older than me. He never does what I tell him; he never listens to me when I tell him what's best for him. He's not grateful, so why should you be? He'll be worse when you live in London. He's so vain. He's always combing his hair, and when I stuck chewing-gum in his comb to teach him a lesson, he chased me right to the end of Paradise Street. He'd have hit me if I hadn't threatened to tell you. I said, "Don't you dare hit me! I'll tell Felix! Don't hit your sister!" I called myself his sister, so that he'd feel good, but you know what he did? He mimicked me. "I'll tell Felix! I'll tell Felix! Your darling Felix won't be here next week for you to run to with your tattle and rubbish, and you're not my bloody sister! The others are, but you're not! Do you understand that? You're not my sister and you never will be! I don't want *you* for a sister!" He gripped my arms so tight, that I've got two bruises. Look. He's always being nasty to me behind your back. I thought he'd change after he had his Bar-Mitzvah, but he hasn't, except that he's worse. I wish I hadn't given him a present. He's got nicer things than any of us. I've never had a ring or a bike. He's spoilt.'

Mam and Dad had given Rudi ten pounds for a Bar-Mitzvah present. It was more than Dad earned in a week. Vered gave him a pound from her savings for going to America, and Esther and Sybil bought him a paintbox and gave him a pound each, too. I made him a card and gave him a tiny black and white kitten which I'd found in the park, called Lucky. He spent all his money on a bike, which he bought at Halfords. Vered, Esther and I went with him. He was so happy that day, and I was nicer to him than I'd ever been, while we were looking at the bikes. He said the bike was for everybody, and when I suggested that he bought a girl's, because there were more girls than boys, Esther interfered as usual, and insisted that Rudi choose one with a cross-bar. Esther was the bossiest person in Hull. Everyone was able to ride it except me, because the seat was too high and the cross-bar got in the way. Once he took me to school on the cross-bar, without telling Mam, but Doctor Hunter saw us wobbling along Ferry Road, and we got into trouble. He took Vered to see her friends whenever she asked him to, just because she'd given him a pound. I told Vered that she was in love with Rudi, and we had a fight about it. He liked the bike better than Lucky; better than the beautiful gold ring which Felix gave him. It was engraved with the Star of David and his initials, RD, were twined around it. He wore it on his little finger.

'Would you like a ring?' said Felix. 'Would you feel better, if you had a ring, too?' I nodded. 'Which finger?' I remembered Maggie, holding her hand out to me; showing me the ring which Jock gave her. They were married now, and living in Aberdeen. I pointed to the second finger. He took a piece of string from his top drawer, and wound it round, then measured it with his ruler. 'First thing tomorrow, I'm going to Samuels to buy one for you, on condition you give me a smile in return.' That was easy. It was so easy, that it wasn't really a fair exchange. Before Felix went away, he placed the ring on my finger. It had a tiny opal in the centre, my birthstone, he said. For friendship. For remembrance. Mam was cross with Felix for spending his money on me, but I didn't care. I became secretly engaged to him shortly after my tenth birthday. When I was sixteen, he bought me a thin gold chain. My hands had grown in the intervening years, and I wore his ring on my little finger. But when I was sixteen, I threaded it onto the gold chain, and wore it round my neck.

Sybil was sixteen when she ran away. I never said Goodbye to her, because I didn't know she was going until it was too late. Perhaps she thought I'd tell Mam and Dad about her plans and the Emigration Office would have been informed that her parents' signatures were forgeries. They would never willingly have given their permission. Sybil knew that, because I was there when she discussed it with them. 'First the university;

112

then we'll see. We can't let you throw yourself away! You're not seventeen!' Mam always said things that we knew already. 'If we knew what the Movement was ramming down your throat, we'd never have let you go to the Training Farm during the holidays. Let the others go, if they want. They've nothing to lose – no family; no home; refugees without any ties left. But you've got everything, and the chance of a good education. What you do when you're twenty, is your business, but now it's ours. A Jewish homeland is a dream for those who have nothing but dreams. I wish them luck!' shouted Mam, when Sybil tried to argue the point. 'But you're not going, and that's that! There's nothing wrong with living in England! Build your homeland here!'

Dad was much more gentle. He never raised his voice, and that made Mam yell even louder, as if she was doing it for both of them. 'I am proud and happy that you want to go, but the time is not ripe. Go, but equipped with a trained mind and a practical attitude. Idealism isn't enough. Wait a little – if not for your sake, then for ours.'

That evening I took the chair out into the yard and tried to concentrate on my Latin verbs. The hens were asleep, and it was warm and quiet. Esther and Sybil were talking in her bedroom, but so softly that I couldn't hear what they were saying, although the window was open, and they were sitting on the window seat. She told Esther, but she didn't tell me. She knew I couldn't keep a secret. Esther always said it was a mistake to tell me anything, unless you particularly wanted to spread a piece of news over half the world. But I wish she'd have given me just one more chance, so that I could have said Goodbye to Sybil – or stopped her from going. Afterwards, Esther said that Rudi and Vered didn't know either, and that I shouldn't be upset, because Sybil wanted it that way. She didn't want to involve us, so that we'd be blamed. Knowing Mam, she'd blame anyone who happened to be standing nearby. I never imagined that Esther and I could ever be really close, but we were, after Sybil went away. Vered and Rudi were closer than twins, as if they shared a boat together, without oars or a rudder, so that it drifted away from me whenever I came near.

Felix knew about Sybil's plans, because he met her in London and went with her as far as Dover. Mam and Dad thought she was spending half-term with Danny and Aliza, but by the time they found out that she wasn't there, she was already on the ship that left Marseilles for Haifa, and it was too late to do anything about it. Sybil posted a letter to Mam and Dad in Marseilles, explaining why she had run away, and that it was her own decision. Felix and Esther had tried to dissuade her, so no one else was to blame.

I don't think Sybil would have gone if she'd had any idea of the trouble she caused. I discussed this later with Esther, who disagreed. Sybil was like iron, she said. She wouldn't bend, like wire or steel. I thought iron bent, if you made it white-hot and bashed it with a hammer, but Esther assured me that it broke; it couldn't change its shape or direction. Sybil was obsessed by an ideal, and was immovable. Something clicked in my mind, and I tried to remember what Felix said about me once, when I pretended to be asleep, but I couldn't, what with Mam crying and screaming at Esther. When she took her glasses off, her eyes were red and swollen, and although Dad did his best to comfort her, and remind her that it wasn't Esther's fault, she took no notice. Couldn't Mam see that he was sad, too? That we all were. Felix came home, but only for a day, and I hardly saw him. Mam started off at him, too. I heard her, when I came in from school. She said she'd never forgive Felix as long as she lived. She'd always trusted him, and he had betrayed her and Sacha.

'Sybil trusted me too, Malka,' he said.

'Don't patronize me! There's going to be a war there, and you know Sybil as well as I do. We discussed her often enough. She was terrified of the bombing, but tried not to let on. Her sort of courage is being ashamed of being frightened. She'll go to any lengths to hide her fear. Don't you think she deserves to be carefree and enjoy her young life? A future? That's what Sacha and I wanted for her. Is that too much to ask?'

Dad tried to make peace between Mam and Felix, but it took years before they were easy with each other again. Dad wrote to the Jewish Agency, to ask them to send Sybil home and he would pay the fare, and that she had gone to Palestine without his permission. Once she had finished her course of education, he would be happy to let her return. A few weeks later, Sybil wrote another letter, without an address, saying that if Mam and Dad tried to engineer her return, she would stop writing to them. Sybil stayed and the War of Independence for Israel began in 1948.

Looking back, I think Sybil decided to run away the night she and Esther were talking on the window-seat, and I was trying to learn my Latin verbs, and couldn't. She came down into the yard and offered to test me, but I couldn't remember any of them.

'I wish I was clever like you, Sybil. If only I could remember the things I need as clearly as the stuff I don't need, and sort them out in my mind so that I wouldn't always be bottom of the class.'

'What is the stuff you don't need?' I thought for a few moments.

'The psalms I learned for Shabbos School. I know forty-nine off by heart. The names of every single person in Pineduggy and Liubava and where each one lived; and books that I read when I was a kid. I can recite them from memory. But ever since I was poorly, I seem to have come to a full-stop. My brain's seized up. I don't know how I passed my scholarship. They must have muddled up my paper with somebody else's. Miss Delroy said that when she gave me back my maths homework. She put a red line through it, and said I wasn't anything like as bright and quick as my sisters. I hate Delroy.'

'Everyone hates her, but no one takes any notice, because she's stupid as well as being nasty. Geometry is the beginning and the end with her. She can't see anything beyond triangles and circles. You can see a million miles further than that. And as for sorting things out in your mind, nobody finds that easy, unless they are great philosophers, or people who haven't got a lot in their minds to sort.'

'Why can't I learn, Sybil? Why won't my mind fix on anything? Why am I such a dunce?' Sybil was the only person in the world with whom I never dissembled; to whom I could admit such a question. She reminded me of Hannah. There I was again, diverted; veering off the subject as if there was a loose wire unhooked from its terminal. 'I can't even understand why you want to go to Palestine so much. You've always wanted to go to university. You love school and you find all the subjects so easy – even Latin. Even geometry. Miss Delroy says you're the best student she ever –'

'To hell with Miss Delroy!' I felt quite shocked by Sybil's

attitude. 'She can keep her A pluses and remarks to herself. I hate it when teachers make comparisons between students, especially when they're sisters, like us. What you and I share is something deep and secret, that she would never understand.' I was just as dense about this matter as Miss Delroy, and hoped Sybil would enlighten me. 'An obsession. You've had yours ever since you were little, and that's why it's so difficult for you to concentrate on other things, but mine came later; quite recently, in fact. Ever since I saw the pictures.' The pictures! What was she talking about? The photographs in the shoe-box? Sybil hardly ever looked at them, while I sorted through them every day. 'The pictures of the survivors; the refugees who have nowhere to go to rebuild their lives. Everyone should have a place to live; where they're wanted. For them it's got to be Palestine, so they can build their own land; and I want to go with them, to help. I've got to go. Everything else is meaningless. Mam and Dad don't understand. It's not their fault. They might even think that I don't love them. But you understand. Pictures aren't enough for you, either. One day you're going to have to get out of the shoe-box and discover who they are. Where they lived. Then they won't be Paper Children any more, and you won't be oppressed by the dreams and the fits. And when you go to Liubava to look for them, I'll be glad, the way you'll be glad for me when I go to Palestine.'

'I won't be glad. If you go there, you'll turn into a photograph, too. Someone like Hannah, who I know and see and feel and hear, sometimes, but always miss. I won't mind if you go to university in another town, because you'll be able to come home during the holidays and maybe I'll be able to come and see you; skip school for a week. But I wouldn't be able to go to Palestine for years and years. It costs too much money. How will you save up for the fare? You won't be able to earn any money while you're studying. It'll be ages before you'll be able to go.'

'The Movement has offered me a scholarship. It would pay my fare. I don't want to go to university any more. When I go to Palestine, I'll miss you, too. I'll miss you all. I'll remember sitting here in the yard, talking to you, and I'll be homesick. I'm homesick now, for Palestine.' It must have turned cold, for I shivered. I wished I didn't know what she meant.

We used to write to Sybil at a Post Office Box Number in

Galilee. She was helping to build a kibbutz there with some other people from the Movement, but most of them were German refugees, survivors who had no families to leave behind. She fought in the War of Independence and sent us a photograph of herself, dressed in uniform and carrying a rifle. It was the happiest photograph I had ever seen. Much later, I had a copy made and put it in the shoe-box, but the original stood in a wooden frame on the kitchen mantelpiece, covered with a bit of glass. After that, we didn't receive any news from her directly, but the Jewish Agency wrote to say she was alive and well, and that's all. It wasn't until afterwards that we found out that Sybil had been working for the Secret Service and wasn't allowed to send letters or even a message. She wasn't like me at all – not really. I've never been able to keep a secret.

Chapter Twenty

I remembered my sixteenth birthday with a shudder. That year I'd kept a journal, using an outsize exercise-book stolen from the school store-room, and wrote 'European History' on the front cover to preserve it from prying eyes. The first page was devoted to a list of curses which would befall those who dared to read it. Nevertheless, when I entered the classroom during the lunch hour, the boys were assembled there, reading the choicest morsels; the privacy of my most shameful thoughts raucously revealed, interspersed with shouts of laughter. I tried to grab the book, but they chucked it from one to the other like a rugby football. Fred Fielding read the next portion and passed it along, the second before I attacked him. I had admitted that he resembled Felix and confessed, in salacious detail, my physical attraction for this ungrateful, jeering lout. They barred my exit, and the hellish merry-go-round whirled on.

My screams were such that the noise disturbed Doctor Hunter's after-lunch snooze, and he stormed in, his gown flying, his eyes ablaze, to witness all the boys sitting at their desks demurely, and me in a state of great distress. I had no scruples about telling tales. His word, his everlastingly honourable word, was law. Each boy apologized abjectly to me. Then he asked what punishment I decreed.

'They have committed a capital offence!' I howled. 'They have destroyed my life! I want them all expelled so that I never have to set eyes on them again! I want *their* lives ruined! I'm going home,' I screamed, 'and I'm not coming back to school until they've gone!' I rushed towards the door, tearing up my diary as I did so, but he snatched it from me before its destruction had barely started. He was smiling. They were all in it together. This was anarchy.

'You're not going home, Rachel. You're sixteen, and a young woman now, not a child; and you've got to face this out. One day you'll be able to read this, and be glad that you didn't destroy it, and smile too. Let's compromise.' He turned to my despicable class-mates. 'If it ever reaches my ears that you betray Rachel further by discussing the contents of this diary, I'll whack the lot of you in front of her.' He put his arm round me and ushered me down the stairs and into his study, and we drank whisky and water to celebrate my birthday. My diary was returned to me.

Dear Doctor Hunter! Benevolent and kindly ruler of the school! Your precepts were ever just! The wicked were punished; the righteous rewarded and the wronged comforted. 'Today I am sixteen,' I had written that morning. 'My favourite writer is Daphne du Maurier, although I tell everyone it's Tolstoy. My favourite poem is *The Rubáiyát of Omar Khayyám*. My favourite composer is Tchaikovsky and my favourite singers are Paul Robeson and Guy Mitchell. My aim in life is to seek the Truth and to stand by what I believe to be Right, even though I am alone in my beliefs. I have serious weaknesses: a craving for popularity and fame; lack of physical and mental courage, and I am often envious of others and behave spitefully. I am ambivalent, easily influenced and not always honest. I get depressed because my glasses hide my eyes, which are my best feature, and I look horrible in them. Now that I am sixteen, the fits will cease completely. I feel confident about this. I would like to go to Stage Six with Fred Fielding . . . Stage Seven, really, but I'd be much too scared. Nevertheless, I belong, body, heart and soul, to Felix Dorfman, and he belongs to me. He is the Love and Passion of my life and the reason for my existence.

'Today and henceforth I will follow my star and journey towards my destiny. Yesterday, I was young and foolish – a shallow, silly child. Today I have become a woman.'

We always called the small back bedroom Sybil's Room, even after it became Esther's and then Vered's. Even after it became mine. Even after we knew for certain that Sybil would never sleep there again. Rudi bought the wallpaper I liked, gay and

119

bright, for my sixteenth birthday, and on the following Sunday, while I spent the day at the seaside with my friends, he painted the ceiling white and hung the paper for a surprise. Mam and Dad gave me a beautiful dressing-table and a mat, and when I arrived home, late, wind-burnt and dead beat after a round trip of forty miles, I could smell the paint as I pushed my bike into the passage, as fresh and as lovely as the sea and the damp, autumn air. Mam and Dad were in the kitchen, listening to the wireless, and called, but I ran upstairs shouting to Rudi, knowing that he had done this for me. He was rehanging Sybil's curtains at the open window, standing on a kitchen chair. I pulled him down, and we danced a fandango in the beautiful room. All this long day, while I'd been out enjoying myself, he'd been doing this, non-stop. For me.

'I had to do it while you were out of the way; you'd only have wanted to give me directions, and you'd have ended up eating knuckle sandwiches. What do you think?'

'I love it.' I hugged him. 'Look at your beard, you old fool; it's got as much paint in it as what's on the ceiling.' I pushed him in front of my dressing-table mirror, then sat him on Sybil's stool and cleaned up his whiskers. 'I thought I'd hate this birthday. Something horrible happened at school which made me distrust and despise all boys, and then you go and give me this lovely surprise and make me doubt my opinion about you loathsome creatures.'

'What happened?'

'I can't tell you. They pinched my diary and read it out loud. I've never been so upset and humiliated in my life. I wish I went to an all girls' school. Girls would never be mean and cruel, the way boys are.'

'Don't you believe it!' He spoke vehemently; almost bitterly.

'You've been jilted, Rudi Dorfman! Tell me who it is or I'll pull every hair out of your chin!' I grabbed his beard, but he got hold of my pony-tail at the same time, so I let go.

'If there's any jilting to be done, Dorfman will be there first, and if you want a bit of wise advice, don't let the boys know you're upset. Act as if their behaviour is beneath your notice. You'll get over it. You get over everything.'

'No I don't! I cried all night! You don't understand how sensitive I am. You must try to realize that some people have profound, delicately balanced emotions, even if you don't. It's very important for you to recognize this, if you want to be a good doctor.' I was glad to hear Mam yelling for us to come down because the supper was going mouldy. I didn't want to have a row with him on the day he'd done the room. I couldn't spend five minutes with Rudi without him starting an unpleasant argument. He could see that one of the curtains wasn't fixed up, but he didn't bother to get on the chair again. He picked up the chair and took it downstairs. He could go to hell. I'd put the curtain up myself; tomorrow. Felix was the only boy I'd ever had a decent conversation with, and he had to be the one to go away to study, while Rudi had to be the one to stay behind. It wasn't fair. Rudi would always be childish. His beard and attempts at manliness were pathetic trappings to cover up his immaturity. Felix was already a man when he was nineteen. I twirled the exquisite gold chain, his present, round my fingers.

'Well? Hasn't Rudi done a beautiful job?' Mam always liked giving him a boost. It was quite embarrassing. 'Don't take your socks off in here! You're dropping sand all over the place and I've just swept up.'

'The room's a treat. The perfect setting for my mat and dressing-table. I'll be able to admire my ugly face in comfort, and the mat is exactly what I need for when I take my socks off.' I told them about my bike-ride, and what fun we'd had in Withernsea, and that I'd done my homework on the beach.

'Where is it?'

'In my saddle-bag. I only had a bit of algebra and a couple of pages of Maupassant to translate. I wish you wouldn't treat me like an untrustworthy child. I'm sixteen, for God's sake!'

'You left your books behind the armchair. I found them when I was tidying up. You're a liar. You haven't done a stroke of work!'

'You're a snooper. Don't start nagging. I can't go out for once in my life without coming back to nags and insults!'

'Don't speak to your mother like that! I won't have it!'

Thus, my sixteenth birthday came and went – and I became a woman.

121

Part Two

Chapter Twenty-One

When Hannah Sokolovsky was released from prison in 1951, she was twenty-six. She found a job in a furniture warehouse in Vilnius, and a room, and trained herself with single-minded effort not to think about the past or wonder about the future. She was not entirely successful in her endeavours. She lived day by day with caution; watchful and defensive. Minute by minute she built up a protective wall thick enough to dismay her neighbours and discourage any attempts at friendly overtures. If they thought her strange, and wondered at the mystery which surrounded her, she was, on the whole, unworthy of gossip, except on the occasions when her behaviour appeared particularly odd. But everyone had their own problems: food; housing; work; family. She seemed quite obliging and brought shopping for the old woman who lived next door to her; a loaf of bread or a bottle of milk. She smiled at the children and nodded to the parents, but no one asked her to mind the kids for a few hours. There were more approachable people than her around, and a person who muttered to herself in the way she did, was probably not quite right in the head. She never slowed down to chat, unless it was to a cat or a dog. She preferred dumb animals to human beings. Like to like.

Although she was obviously still quite young, and could run for a bus faster than a boy, she often appeared wizened; almost grey. Yet with an effort of imagination you could see that she'd once been beautiful, but something about her made her vaguely repellent. There was no light, no warmth in her expression. All her energy was turned inwards; an unsettling, wild energy attached to a chain of doubtful strength. It devoured her and made her ill, as if she succoured some grievous secret. One summer evening, her neighbour Algirdas, from the floor above, saw her doubled up on the stairway, as if in great pain. Should he call a doctor? Or Tanya, the trained nurse, who lived on Hannah's floor? 'I'll be perfectly all right in a minute or two. It's just something I've eaten, which disagrees with me. Please leave me alone.' There wasn't much you could do for a person like that. Whatever it was that ailed her, she'd never missed a day at work during the four years she'd been living in the building. Her habits were regular to the point of obsession, and she never intruded on anyone. Sokolovsky was the kind of neighbour who was ideal if you were busy or preoccupied with your own troubles, and who wasn't, these days.

The pain. The terrible, agonizing pain. It drowned her in remorseless waves, catching her off guard, tearing at the wall which surrounded her. That morning, Zhivile, the fore-woman, asked her if the rumours were true: that she'd once tried to leave the Soviet Union illegally, and caused the arrest of an innocent man. They were in the works canteen for the fifteen-minute break. Hannah didn't answer her, but she persisted with her detestable curiosity. 'I know more than you think. You hoarded your money like the rest of your kind, and lied and cheated, and lived for nothing, like a rat, in your last place of work, while people like us have to pay rent to live.'

'Do you have a family?' What had she said that for? She must get up; walk away. The pain; something else kept her doubled up on the stool.

'Yes. Even a sister who isn't a figment of my imagination. There isn't much about you that I don't know!' It was wise to laugh when Zhivile was trying to be amusing. Hannah wasn't wise, but the others showed their appreciation.

'Do you visit members of your family?'

'No. Never. I only live with them. What about you?'

'Unfortunately, I do not live with my family. As for the period to which you are referring, the rumour is true. I stayed in a freezing dirty store-room for two years in order to save up to visit them. They live in England, and someone betrayed me, so I visited a labour camp instead.'

'If you have any plans for moving into our store-room, you'll know who the "someone" is this time. Jews don't live in England. Don't try to be clever with me.'

'Jews and rats live everywhere, Zhivile. Don't you know that? Some of them don't even desert sinking ships.' Everyone in the canteen was listening. The days were usually so tedious and an argument relieved the boredom. The bell rang. The grinning faces of her work-mates swam in front of her; on all sides of her. She walked back to her bench, concentrating only on keeping herself upright, so that they wouldn't see. Wouldn't know. She wouldn't give them the satisfaction of watching her wall crumbling to ashes. One, two; one, two. Just push each second away. Each minute. Each hour. Until she was safely alone.

Algirdas had spoken to her so kindly that she was tempted to ask him for help, but somehow she managed to crawl to her room and swallow some of the chalky medicine which she collected from the pharmacy every week. It was something she'd eaten – not yesterday, but a long time ago; at Stutthof, in fact, for breakfast. Wild grass and thistles, floating in muddy water, watched by a grinning devil with a truncheon, until every morsel was swallowed. Those who tried to spill it away were disposed of. Hannah's mouth was dripping blood, but she chewed and chewed, and swallowed, pretending she enjoyed it, so that he wouldn't have the satisfaction of knowing what torture it was. The prickles flayed her throat and guts, and she pretended to be a donkey, fighting for its life. She was a pig too. She discovered a barn filled with discarded, frozen pig-swill and managed quite a number of banquets of frozen potatoes mixed with chopped straw. But now the pain lurched forward to disarm her. The medicine helped her to live with the damage it caused to her digestive system, but she'd lost the knack of living like a starving beast. Perhaps it would have helped her to talk about that time to someone. But she couldn't. She could only talk to herself. She'd lived like a robot for so long, not understanding that a robot sometimes runs amok. As long as she didn't disintegrate in public, her machinery could resolve itself and carry on. As long as the clockwork system resisted the temptation of being curious about its workings; of revealing that it was often in disorder and chaos, it could rattle on for another day, threatened only by moments of unexpected vulnerability and solitude. If Algirdas had insisted on staying with her, no matter how finally she rejected him, she might have been able to explain that once she was a girl surrounded by family and friends, who hated being alone; that the faulty mechanism was not always devoid of personality and love. 'Leave me alone, please.'

She made a terrible mistake. After Stutthof, she returned to look for Yosef; for remnants of the family, but there was no one left. No one who knew her when she was a girl. Before she turned into this. She wondered whether her family in England had survived the war, but by then she was not allowed to leave the country legally. She learnt how to be cunning and to survive without help, and got a job in a factory in Kovno, making boxes. She worked harder than anyone else, and was always the first to arrive and the last to leave. After a few weeks, the supervisor gave her the keys, and Hannah opened up in the morning and locked up at night. She assumed that Hannah shared a room with her sister's family and invented reasons for having to be out of the room before five-thirty in the morning, and that's why she was always early for work. She had no room, and no sister. Once she had the keys, she moved into the factory and lived there for two years, undiscovered. She slept in a disused store-room on two chairs, wrapped up in a blanket, and hid her kettle and personal belongings under a floor-board. She learnt to sleep, move and see in the dark, like a stray cat. The hole in the floor became her pantry, her wardrobe and her money-box.

At last, Hannah found a man, a Pole who made deliveries across the border, and bribed him with every rouble she possessed to hide her in his truck. They arranged their meeting place for the following month. She didn't tell a soul about her plan, but perhaps something of her excitement and apprehension showed in her behaviour, for she wasn't as clever, then, at hiding her feelings. She lay on the two chairs, planning; mad with joy, thinking of her brother Sacha, and Malka and her four nieces. She could see them so clearly. They were so bright in the darkness! Rachel, the baby, would be fourteen – the same age as she was when they'd last been together! She would see herself again! Rachel would know that she wasn't dead! She met the driver at the appointed place with the remainder of his fee, and hid in the back of his truck under the tarpaulin. The border guards were waiting for them. The driver raged and cursed her, and denied any knowledge of her, but they found all Hannah's money on him and took him away, too. She never discovered who betrayed them. She received eighteen months' hard labour, making roads and covering them with tar. The heat in Siberia was worse than the cold. The tar stuck to her skin and the insect bites festered and bubbled on her body. But Hannah survived.

On the day of her release, the prison officials disinfected her and burned her rags. A peasant gave her a sack, and she wore it like a dress, and left. It took her three months to beg and work her way to Vilnius, the nearest town to the place that had once been Liubava, where she was allowed to reside. She was lucky. She found a room and the job at the warehouse. Every evening, she wrote a letter to the address in England, and each letter was returned by the censor. In 1953, a month after Stalin died, she received the first letter from her brother Sacha. The family in England was alive! And Yosef was alive too, and living in America! At last she had a family who knew she existed. She had to be very careful what she wrote, and sometimes one of the letters got through, because Sacha and Yosef were answering them. There must have been a censor who was kind. Her brothers numbered the letters, and one out of eight arrived at her address. No one knew which day she received a letter, because she was so clever and careful at hiding her feelings. She read them over and over again and drank her medicine and talked to herself, calling them her Paper Children.

She opened her eyes and tried to move, wondering how long she had bent over the table. It was then that she noticed the letter stuck under the door. She crawled towards it cautiously, feeling the robot threaten to run amok. The pain diminished, barely troubling her, and she felt as if she had said Goodbye to it for ever. Perhaps this attack was savage because it was the last! 'I'll read my letter to you,' she said to the empty room. 'Then I'll put the kettle on and make tea. I've got two glasses, though I've never entertained anyone in my room before. It will be like having a party to celebrate my marvellous news! I wish I hadn't told you to leave me alone. I never meant to be rude or ungracious. But you weren't to know that I needed someone to talk to, instead of to myself. I'll drink both glasses of tea; one hot and one cool. And read my letter to myself again. It's better this way! The trouble is that I don't seem to be able to trust myself any more. I hate being alone! I didn't realize how much I hated it, until today.'

When Tanya came home from her shift at the hospital, Algirdas stopped her on the balcony and asked her to knock at Sokolovsky's door to see how she was.

'She's ranting and raving in there! She looked as if she was dying, but she wouldn't let me help her. She slammed the door in my face. I daren't insist on staying with her. Remember how she tried to tear the telephone engineer to pieces? We'd better invade the witch's den together.'

Tanya didn't waste time. She could hear her shouting and laughing from ten metres away. She dropped her shopping bag outside her door, ran to Hannah's and banged on it. Algirdas hovered behind her, and a few curious neighbours stood around, watching and listening. They often thought that she belonged to the asylum, although, as a rule, she seemed harmless enough.

'Hannah!' Tanya called. 'I've run out of salt! Could you let me have a spoonful?'

Hannah opened the door. Tanya was an experienced nurse of the mentally sick, and could sniff out a crackpot within seconds. Hannah pulled the door wide open and stood there, smiling, welcoming her and Algirdas into the little room. The scarf she always wore round her head had slipped onto her shoulders, and her hair had escaped from its austere elastic band and hung down on either side of her thin face like golden waterfalls. Algirdas closed the door behind him, stunned by the change in her, and Tanya sat down at the table.

'This idiot told me you were ill, Hannah, but I've never seen you look better. How's the pain? Where is it? Sit down for a moment, and let me check your pulse at least! Is this your medicine?' She was obviously agitated and needed a few minutes to calm down. Algirdas poured a generous measure of vodka from the small bottle he always carried in his pocket into one of the empty glasses on the table. He grinned at Hannah. 'This is the best medicine! It cures everything!'

Hannah thanked him, but shook her head. 'I have no more pain. I'm not ill now.' Her eyes were clear, blue and steady. She looked about fourteen with her cheeks flushed like that. Algirdas swallowed the vodka. 'I talked to myself because I was lonely, but I'm not lonely any more. This is my medicine!' She waved a letter at them. 'Rachel, my niece, is coming to visit me with her friend! From England!'

Chapter Twenty-Two

I was having a serious nervous attack in the Front Room when Rudi arrived. Three of the cases were pre-war, leaden weights even when empty, the hasps broken and rusted and worse than useless. Mam had borrowed an enormous tin contraption, studded with twisted hinges, from one of her eccentric friends. I had exhausted my patience and energy, cramming it to capacity. I closed it securely and dragged it out of the way as the base burst without warning and everything fell into a hateful heap onto the floor again. Mam started shouting at me for overloading it and breaking other people's property. I lost my temper, and threw everything all over.

'Nothing in this damned house works!' I screamed at her. 'Even the string is full of hairy knots! Why the hell did you borrow this old tin can from that Rag-Bag down the street? She ties up her hair with a moth-eaten belt; she's worn the same mucky old coat in the house and out of the house for the last twenty years, and you go and borrow a case from her and expect it to be better than a dented dustbin! Am I supposed to go to Russia with this? Is it so that her ancestors will recognize it as something they threw on the rubbish tip? And what am I supposed to do with this haversack? Did you borrow it from a midget? One dried prune, and that'll burst at the seams, too! Why did you let Vered pinch the only decent suitcase? Why do I always end up with the leavings? Everything and everyone in this house makes me sick! This damned gloom room turns my guts inside out! Why isn't he here? Why is he never here when I need him?'

'Go to Willerby!' screamed Mam, directing me to our local mental hospital. 'I can't take any more aggravation from you.

131

Someone's been banging at the door for the last ten minutes. You borrowed his key. Just *shut up!*'

I was so relieved to see him, but felt angry and resentful that he had not come earlier. He knew better than anyone what a flap I'd be in and how Mam would be driving me mad. He'd brought two huge, soft-topped cases, and he showed me how they folded flat, when empty. Inside the smaller one was a bundle of straps to tie up the most untrustworthy pieces of luggage, and a packet of tie-on labels. God, he got on my nerves with his mother-hen ways and that maddening habit of being sensible and prepared. How could two brothers be so different? Why should one have all the flair and style? I needed this extra luggage and the straps, but why should he have assumed that I would? What was it about him that irritated me so? For a painful moment I wished that he was little again, so that I could take care of him and mould him into the person I wanted him to be. I'd always thought of him as smaller than me; younger. Fifteen years ago, I was looking after him, washing his face, tying bows in his hair, making him turn the skipping-rope; filling his head with wildly inaccurate facts, fantastic lies, while he looked at me with mournful eyes. Fifteen years. Fifteen minutes. He'd grown up behind my back. If I spoke his name, he'd look up from where he was kneeling over the case – the one I once helped him to carry – but his gaze would be different; more knowing. I had things to do; my handbag to sort out. I didn't want to take worn-out batteries, broken pencils or dried apricots covered in fluff, all the way to Russia. I'd got quite enough to drag along. Why was I standing here, leaning against this ugly old table, my hands hanging by my sides, digging up the past, when I should be poised in flight, on the threshold of a great adventure? What was I waiting for? Why were tears standing in my eyes? I got fluff in my contact lenses every five minutes, but I'd rather suffer the torments of hell than go back to wearing glasses.

'Rudi, do you remember how I used to fill your head with all sorts of rubbish and boss you about?'

'Do I remember! Why are you using the past imperfect? You've never stopped. When you're a grandmother, I'll be your bewhiskered, doddery grandchild. You're stuck with the habit.'

'Are you?'

132

'Am I what?'

'Stuck with the habit; with the role I've thrust upon you?'

'No.' He was busy testing the weight and security of the bags, easily and effortlessly, as if they were crammed with ping-pong balls. I thought of our first meeting when I'd shared the weight of his bag and fussed over him, questioning Felix about him. I wanted to remind him of it, but he had answered 'No' too sharply, and I felt strange and uneasy and sad. Why had I taken such little notice of his development into man-hood? He'd always be the child on whom I'd lavish uncompli-cated pride and indulgence. It had been thus from the very beginning – Felix and I caring for him together; but all of a sudden the indulgence was marred by peevish impatience. Mam was calling me from the kitchen, telling me she'd poured the tea an hour since, which meant that she was just putting the kettle on. She came in, fretting and fussing me as usual. 'I hope you haven't packed the Persianelle coat in the same case as the pens. If just one of those biros leaks, the coat will be ruined, and it cost a small fortune.' I'd bought a gross of biros from Woolworth's at ninepence each, and created a minor disturb-ance by clearing out their stock. Hannah could get a rouble each for them – nine shillings and elevenpence in English currency. The coat, when sold, could pay for a month's holiday at a Black Sea resort.

'Don't drive me crazy, Mam,' I snapped. 'If you think I'm about to open up these bags again and start rooting around for the pens . . . Anyway, there's only a one-in-eight chance they're packed together,' I lied, knowing that I'd dispersed them carefully among the eight cases and that at least a dozen were in each of the coat pockets. 'A Russian roulette chance. Rudi, hurry up! The taxi's coming in thirty-five minutes!' He picked up his cup and drank his tea with maddening deliberation, as if I was due to go to Westly Park Library to change an Enid Blyton book.

'Did you tell them you'd got all this luggage?'

'Yes. No. Will you stop fussing! Taxis are supposed to know about luggage.'

'They don't know about this. We'll have to order another car.'

'Do what you like!' I mustn't behave like this. I'd have my whole trip ruined; seeing those great, dark, mournful eyes in my mind; enduring the damned guilt which blighted my life like a curse, as if jealous of my impeccable soul; Rudi almost invariably at the centre of the dreary spiral which entwined it. I wished I knew why. If I'd been mean to him when he was a kid, a defenceless stranger – I'd understand. But I'd been good to him; kind; a friend. Vered and Esther hadn't taken half the interest in him that I had, but I bet they didn't feel dismal about him, when they left home. So why did everything concerned with him make me feel answerable for non-existent offences? He did this on purpose. He manipulated me so skilfully that my self-esteem seemed forever threatened. I watched his receding back through the window, as he ran up Paradise Street to the telephone-box, trying to erase my melancholy with a burst of ill-temper, but nothing was working out today as I'd planned. 'Mam!' She was tying labels on the cases. 'To think that by the time we meet up again, I'll have seen Hannah! Aren't you jealous? I'm sorry I lost my temper. It's just today that I'm insane and overwrought.'

'I've never in my life known you to be anything else. It beats me, who you take after; but do me one favour. Stop behaving like a pig to Rudi. He's got a heart of gold, and you just take him for granted. No one else would put up with the way you treat him. I long for him to turn round and slap your face. Don't you dare tell him what I've said,' she hissed, as we heard him come back; 'he'll be even more hurt and humiliated. Try to behave like a human being – at least for the next few minutes.'

'You bring out the worst in me; you and him. I'm fine with everyone else.' I didn't give a damn whether he heard or not, but I didn't want to leave Mam in a bad mood. I smiled at Rudi and dragged up something particularly generous and kindly to say to him. 'I wish you were coming too, Rudi. I'm so frightened and edgy, as if I can't look after myself from Paragon Station to King's Cross. After all, I say to myself, people understand English in places other than East Yorkshire. My heart's lurching all over the place, and my stomach feels as if it's been badly darned. I'll be OK once I'm with Felix. I'm always OK with him. Perhaps you'll be able to get a visa for your summer holiday next year.' I knew that it was impossible; that it would be his final year and he'd probably be working for twenty-two hours a day at the vile infirmary.

'You don't wish I was coming; nevertheless, thank you for

the lie, but I'd prefer it if you wouldn't patronize me. The taxis are here. Let's get you to the station.'

I didn't answer him. Let him be cold and hostile, so long as it was in front of Mam, so she could see who was the pig. He was jealous of me going away, while he was staying in boring old Hull. He'd slapped my face all right, but it hadn't hurt at all. I'd a good mind to talk to Felix about him, but we'd have far more important matters to discuss.

Mam and I climbed into one taxi and Rudi threw half the luggage on top of us, and he and the rest of it followed in the other one, each driver grumbling in turn about the unusual amount they had to handle, as if they were doing it for nothing. I felt like telling ours that we'd expect better service from the conductor on the 69 trolley-bus, but I had just about enough of confronting touchy and irrational people, and held my tongue, and avoided being flummoxed. What did they want from my life? You couldn't go to Vilnius empty-handed.

The station porter ran to fetch an extra large barrow when we emerged, and examined the luggage labels curiously, before loading up. Even so, he asked us where we were going, for he was unable to read the strange Cyrillic script which Dad had written for us to copy out, and unable to believe his eyes when he read the other, English side. 'I'm the only one who's travelling,' I said, pushing myself forward. I couldn't help being amused by his insular attitude. 'The one fifty-nine to King's Cross.' I wondered why they couldn't call it the two o'clock, like all the passengers who'd missed it in the past.

'Are you emigrating to there?'

'No. Just visiting.'

'Well, I'll be buggered! You need all this for a visit? I never helped anyone who was flitting to Russia before. When you come back, ask for Tommy. I'll be interested to know how you get on. Hey! Come and give me a hand with this lot!' he shouted to his colleague. 'She's going to Russia with eight bloody bags!'

They went off to the guard's van, and I found a seat near the window in an empty compartment, and put my sandwiches, coat and book on it, and then jumped down onto the platform to say Goodbye to Mam and Rudi. I was glad that the guard was closing the doors further down the train, and that Dad hadn't made it to the station to bid me his gloomy farewell. I

135

hated all this hanging about, and couldn't wait to be shot of them, but I wasn't going to be let off the hook so easily. I could see Dad running up the platform, waving his paper, ungainly and forlorn. I felt that everyone was staring at him; impatient because the train would be delayed. The guard stilled his flag, and shouted, 'All right, Rabbi! We'll give you a minute!' Under normal circumstances, I wouldn't be speaking to Rudi, but I kissed him, and Mam, and hugged my Dad, who dropped his paper. Rudi stepped on it before it blew under the train, and picked it up. 'It's the anniversary of the outbreak of war. You've picked an auspicious day for your journey.'

'Be careful,' said Dad. 'Don't lose the luggage. Tell them – tell Hannah I'll try to come next year. Tell her . . .' The train hissed and drowned his voice, and he turned away. I waved and waved until they disappeared from view. I had four and a half uninterrupted hours to think about Felix. I loved trains; loved to watch the town lose its hold to the flat, green, unspectacular countryside, so familiar and beloved to me. Hannah would be thinking about me now, starting my journey towards her; back to her. Seeing me on the train in her mind's eye, the small window open, within the large, closed one, admitting the rush of air which blew through my hair. I wasn't nervous. I'd grown out of all those childish terrors; gasping nightmares which followed me into my waking hours. She'd be so excited at the prospect of seeing me again, trying to imagine what sort of person I'd turned out to be. And she? She'd been a kid; a girl of thirteen, and now she was thirty; yet I could summon up her image in the swaying green scenery more easily than any other living soul. But I'd send her away, now, and think of Felix – as if there was ever a time in my life when I hadn't thought about him! Now it was quite a different activity. We'd meet as two adults – strangers – because there would be no one else; only us. We would not be cluttered by Rudi or my intolerable family. Rudi *or* my family? Why not just 'my family'? How could Sybil, who was twelve when he came to live with us, so easily have accepted him as her brother, right from the beginning – even before the time when we all knew that Mama and Papa Dorfman were dead, and would never reclaim him? It was the same with Esther and Vered, wasn't it? And it wasn't just Rudi. It was Felix too. Their brothers; yet I, although younger than my sisters, had never been able to adapt to that idea. If only I had Sybil to talk to about the subjects which puzzled me. She was so clever and understood so much about the workings of the heart. Did she feel once, what I felt now, on her journey to Palestine? Sybil. Sybil. Would you have been glad for me? Lumps of soot flew into both my contact lenses and my eyes began to pour with water. I was relieved that I had the compartment all to myself. She'd been younger than I was now, when she died. My eldest sister. My youngest. Did Mam still blame Felix in her heart? That, too, was a question for Sybil, if only she'd been here to answer it. Was that why my parents doted on Rudi, now, because they couldn't love Felix any more? When Rudi was a child, he'd sometimes called them Mama and Papa, but mostly he'd used their first names, and always did now.

Felix had never talked to them as if they were his parents. He remembered his own too well. They were ever clear in his memory – too precious for my parents to take over. And I was special too. He'd always loved me more than my sisters; singled me out; treated me differently. It was completely out of keeping to think of either of them as brothers. Affected and somehow embarrassing. Yet I'd always wanted them to belong to us; from the beginning I'd wanted them to share my family, even those I had never met. To share my roots; my nimbus; my Paper Children. I carried a selection of them now in a folder in my 'organizer bag', and the rest were in one of the suitcases. Hannah would want to see them all again, especially since she didn't have a single personal thing from her childhood. I'd sent copies of them, and us, but they'd been lost in the post, like everything else we'd tried to send.

Felix had promised to bring an old picture of Hannah which he'd acquired, one that I hadn't seen for ages, yet had missed and looked for. He'd assured me that he hadn't pinched it; that I'd given it to him, but I didn't understand why, nor could I remember the occasion. Would Hannah be at the railway station in Vilnius to meet us? Would she look at me without recognition? Even though she was unable to write English, would she remember a few words? Would she remember me; like me? Just because it was so easy for me, it didn't necessarily follow that she'd be able to bring me to mind separately from my sisters, with all the horrible intervening years. How strange that she was going to meet Felix too. Felix . . . waiting for me

137

at King's Cross . . . Hannah, waiting for me at Vilnius . . . Felix and Hannah, both together. Both together, with me in the middle acting as the connecting thread.

We were already at Grantham, and a new traveller came over to the window and asked if I minded if he closed it. I nodded and smiled and took my brown paper bag of sandwiches out into the corridor. I liked standing in the corridor best of all, like a kid embarking on her first journey. I didn't need anyone to talk to, as long as I could lean against the wall and look and listen; conjure up Hannah and me and Felix, but it was singularly difficult. I was losing the knack. Maybe it was part of growing up; the loss of childhood and girlhood and the fading of the visual imagination. I'd try Hannah and me! All right then, Felix and me! But all I could get was Hannah and Felix . . . Hannah and Felix . . . Hannah and Felix, as if I hadn't lost the knack at all. As if the only thing I'd lost was me. I wondered why the train was slowing down. It stopped with an impudent, wheezy chuckle in the middle of nowhere, for a sly smoke. It was so quiet; so peaceful, that I could hear the birds and the intermittent tick-tock of the sleepers contracting. The long, wild rye grass and old man's beard crowded the cutting and moved like a pale green sea. I wasn't all alone. There were hundreds of friendly people around me; reading; sitting very still, like statues, shy of talking or even fidgeting; uneasy during the sudden, strange hush. I wouldn't be frightened by dream goblins or haunted by nightmare journeys that I'd travelled long ago with wild-eyed, terrified people. This was real, pleasant and happy. No horror awaited me out there. Once the train started up again, I'd be able to move, look at my watch and find out that I was only an hour away from London – King's Cross – Felix. The train jerked playfully, reminding me to breathe and take another bite of my sandwich and to hand the friendly guard my ticket to clip.

Felix should have been the doctor – not Rudi. He was the one who said I'd get better if I could see Hannah again. Mam and Dad had agreed, as if I wasn't capable of making up my own mind. I wondered what kind of illness they thought I suffered from, but I hadn't argued or tried to pin them down. I knew that it was something to do with my nerves and the fits and that I didn't have some dreadful, terminal disease. I'd always been jumpy as a kid, but who wouldn't be, with the sort

138

of family and upbringing I'd had! Anyway, if my 'cure' or my convalescence depended on my going to Russia with Felix to see Hannah, what did I care? I'd go along with anything they said, like a lamb. He'd insisted on paying my fare and, as it happened, I didn't have the ready money. Dad had argued with him, but Felix had just gone and arranged for the visa and tickets before anyone had time to think straight. 'Why should you talk about money now?' he'd written. 'Did you talk about it when you took us in and you didn't have two halfpennies to knock together? You treated us like your own children. Am I not allowed to treat you like my family? Doesn't it work both ways? I want to do this. I want to take Rachel with me. I'm sure it will do her good.'

'I want to take Rachel with me!' I, who had never been out of the country in my life, was going across Europe with Felix! I'd only been to London twice; the first time was for my Uncle Danny's wedding and three years ago Vered and I had hitch-hiked there, after telling everyone we were going on the coach. We'd stayed with Danny and Aliza for a week; a glorious, mad, sleepless week. How did anyone who lived there cope with its great size; its history, squalor and grandeur, in an everyday way? The train had been rushing through its suburbs for half an hour and at last it was showing signs of slowing down. I put on my coat and went to stand by a window near the guard's van. The railway lines were twisting over one another, multiplying like an arena of fertile snakes. What if he wasn't here? What would I do with all the luggage? Should I engage a porter or wait for him?

But he was there, right on the spot, with a porter and a barrow; waving; calling my name; smiling. He jumped me down onto the platform, kissing me on both cheeks like a Frenchman, and then on the forehead. 'Rudi phoned me to forewarn me about the eight suitcases. We want all this taken to the "Left Luggage", please,' he told the porter. 'Have you got everything you need for tonight in your shoulder bag?' I nodded and patted it and watched him pass everything out of the luggage van; not helping; dumb and immobile, and over-whelmed with shyness. I walked a step behind them as they pushed the barrow down the platform and he half turned, holding his arm out for me to draw near. 'Come on, Slouch! What's keeping you?' I ran up to him and he rested his hand on my nearest shoulder. 'We'll pick this lot up on our way to Liverpool Street, tomorrow. I told Danny and Aliza not to expect us until eleven, because we're going out to wine and dine this evening. Just the two of us. I can't wait to hear all the news. Yes, I know everyone writes everything, but it always sounds so different when you tell it. But what's going on? Your train arrived six minutes ago, and you haven't chewed my ear off yet!'

'It takes me seven minutes to get into my London stride. I've come all the way from up North, remember, but I'm teetering on the verge of complete adjustment.' I'd been here, with Vered, three years ago, and he'd visited us in Hull quite recently. He was instantly recognizable. Nothing about him had changed. I've loved you ever since I first beheld you. As a child; as a girl. But now it's as if I've fallen in love for the first time, and nothing will ever be the same again, whether I want it to be or not. I don't know whether I'm sad or madly happy. I'm both. I'm everything. You're everything. I love you.

Chapter Twenty-Three

'I love London,' I said to Felix. We walked down Regent Street, looking at the gorgeous window displays; the hurrying people and the everlasting stream of buses and taxis. 'I love the great, curved sweep of these buildings. Hull's so provincial. The Blue Lagoon is practically the only place where you can buy a cup of coffee after ten o'clock. It's time I moved on.' One of the shops had oddly angled mirrors in its window, and for a few seconds I didn't recognize the couple walking towards us as being Felix and me. How well we looked together! How sophisticated and attractive! My new dark green suit, white blouse and black shoes were so elegant. I slowed down in order to preen myself, cunningly pretending that I was quite interested in the price of a fox fur displayed in the centre of the pleasing scene. Felix smiled at my reflection and said, 'What's she doing with that ugly toad?'

'She grabbed the first man she saw. She's down in London from the sticks, and doesn't have the know-how. Once she reaches Piccadilly, she'll probably drop him for a handsome prince.' One kiss, I thought, and he'd make fairy-tales come true; but he was my prince already, although he wasn't aware of it yet. Once we sat down to eat, I'd twiddle my chain round my fingers and give him ample opportunity to comment on the little opal ring he'd given me ten years ago. He was as dark as I was fair and even taller than Rudi. And a thousand times more handsome. Poor Rudi! He must feel quite jealous of Felix sometimes. If I lived in London I'd see him every day and make myself indispensable.

'After our trip, I'm going to hand in my notice at work. With my experience, I'd have no trouble finding a job here, perhaps as a supervisor training staff in an exclusive tea-shop or a night-club favoured by tourists. Did you know that the manageress of the Station Hotel wanted me to work in the new buffet there? I declined, because the Lagoon would go under without me. Apparently two of our regular customers had recommended me; friends of hers. They pay top whack wages at the Station Hotel. One meets a more interesting class of person there. You know, you can't imagine what it's like for me living at home. Mam and Dad treat me like a child. It's terrible. I think there's something wrong with them. They can't get it into their heads that I'm an adult, no matter how often I try to ram the fact at them. It's difficult for them at their time of life, to have to acknowledge that all birds fly the nest. Except for darling Rudi, of course. Just because Esther's clever and got the scholarship to Oxford, it's all right that she left home at eighteen. And Vered was younger than I am now when she went to Israel to work on the kibbutz with that Henry she's engaged to. It seems that it's OK to leave dingy old Paradise Street as long as it's for Learning or Love. You and Sybil were both younger than me, too, when you left; yet they cling on to me, stifling me to death, and I'm twenty! What do you think of my coming to London?'

'You're not quite twenty, but we won't split hairs. It would be a mistake for you to live here. Don't leave home, Rachel. Not yet. You need Malka and Sacha as much as they need you. You enjoy your job and have all your friends around you. It isn't good for you to be alone.'

We reached Piccadilly Circus and stood on the island, next to Eros. The lights and the bustle made me feverish and heady. 'I wouldn't be lonely,' I said. 'I'd have you.' He held my hand as we crossed the road, and I kept hold of him, even when we were on the pavement again. He obviously wanted me to live here, but didn't want to encourage me without my parents' agreement. He was probably thinking of Sybil, and how they'd tried to lay the blame on him for helping *her* to do what she wanted. We jostled through the crowds and went into an Italian restaurant, where he'd booked a table for two. There were flowers on the table, and a candle, and iced water and bread sticks were brought to us immediately. I made a mental note for suggested improvements at the Blue Lagoon. I lit a cigarette from the candle, while Felix ordered for me. He must earn a fortune to be able to bring me to a place like this.

'What's the matter, Felix? What is it? You're not happy.'

'I'm all right!' He smiled.

'No,' I said. 'No, you're not. There's something wrong. What is it? You tell me I'll be lonely because you are. If *you* were happy, you wouldn't say that.'

'I didn't say you'd be lonely. I said "alone", but in fact, I think for you, that means the same. But it doesn't for me. And if you lived here we'd hardly ever meet, because I'm not in London for most of the time, and I'd feel anxious about you. But I'm content enough. The World Health Organisation takes me all over Europe and my job as interpreter is interesting and challenging. I listen in to fascinating discussions and meet hundreds of people. I have a comfortable flat in Aliza's and Danny's house and they are my close friends. I work on translations with Danny at the Institute. I go to theatres and galleries when time permits. I have books and music, an adopted family and a brother. My health is good and the majority of people aren't horrified at the sight of me. I'm aware that millions of people are enslaved, suffer and starve and die before their time, and that we are surrounded by madness and turmoil. Nevertheless, I have little reason to complain about being miserable.' He filled our glasses. 'I'm looking forward to our trip tomorrow. Let's drink to that. To your reunion with Hannah and to your complete and permanent recovery!'

'And to yours,' I said bravely. Perhaps I'd gone too far. 'I don't have fits now; I can't remember when I had the last one. And as for the nightmares and daymares – they hardly bother me.' Our journey was safely arranged and admitting to good health wasn't likely to have any effect on the plans. 'But I've been waiting to visit Hannah for as long as I can remember. And you've made it possible.' I raised my glass towards him and guzzled the contents, and began fiddling with my ring on the end of the chain, but his attention seemed elsewhere. He was much more interested to hear about the family and my new philosophy of life. He didn't want to talk about himself, but it was easy to be patient. Tomorrow we were starting on our journey together, and there'd be ample opportunity to draw him out. The sumptuous meal arrived, and Felix refilled my glass. My head swam dizzily and delightfully, and it didn't worry me in the slightest that I found the spaghetti unmanageable. I only had to watch Felix for a few seconds, and soon learnt the knack. Actually, I'd never tasted it before. When I had sucked in the last strand, I quaffed my wine and gave him an account of everyone.

'Mam's going through a particularly bad patch. Of course she's always been neurotic and excitable, but you'd think that at the age of forty-six she'd mellow, calm down and acquire some wisdom and self-control. There's no sign of that happening. I try to excuse her irrational behaviour, because of her time of life. Many women have a difficult time when they approach middle age. I've got a theory that she feels a failure because she never gave birth to a son. She dotes on Rudi, you know. Frankly, it's quite sickening. Thank goodness she's started going to work and has enrolled at evening classes. I'm hoping she'll get off my back as she becomes more involved. She misses Esther and Vered, of course. Her maternal instinct is very strong, and sometimes I feel quite sorry for Dad, because she's far from being the ideal of a rabbi's wife. She doesn't involve herself in communal affairs, and I think she resents him being so busy. The other day, I heard her tell him that he put the congregation before his family. He immediately started to nag me, which is really what she wanted him to do. They can't come to terms with Sybil's death. I can't, either, but I try. I often come home to find her sitting on the armchair in the Front Room. The last time I went in to try to comfort her, I had a funny feeling that she wished it had been me and not Sybil, who'd died. I asked her as gently as possible if that was the case, and she didn't deny it. She just became hysterical. She's such a trial to me. And Dad's no easier. He doesn't talk about Sybil, or what happened to the family in Liubava. You'd think he'd have been happy after visiting Yosef in California. Yosef's a linguist, too. He stayed in Germany, after the war, as an interpreter for the survivors; helping the government there to resettle them, and he searched and searched for Hannah, then went away thinking she was dead. All Dad could say when he came back from seeing Yosef was that his little "Katsap" had to walk with a stick and was very deaf. Why couldn't he rejoice that he had survived and was happily married? I bet Dad's more of a broken man than Yosef. Sometimes, I think he feels guilty about being alive, and so he

144

refuses to enjoy life to the full. I wouldn't talk to anyone else like this, about them, except to you, Felix. I think Dad's frightened of going to visit Hannah.'

'You forget that he couldn't get a visa,' said Felix. 'Also, that he felt it was more important for you to go. Family parties aren't encouraged. You misunderstand him.'

'Can you fathom him out, then?' I felt hurt and aggrieved, but didn't show it.

'Don't be so touchy, Rachel. I feel more akin to Sacha than anyone else in the family. I always have. Unlike Malka, he keeps a tight rein on his emotions. It doesn't mean that he feels less deeply, of course. His attitude helps him to be just and fair. As a lad, I tried to model myself on him. It never occurred to him to blame Sybil's leaving home on me. I'm never uneasy with him, as I am with Malka, who has graduated into blaming me for her death, although she's never actually come right out with it.'

'You've got it all wrong, Felix! She's much more polite to you than she is to me.'

'Yes,' he said. 'Yes, I know. O, Rachel!' he burst out. 'What happiness if I had your problems! Parents who cling to me and stifle me and love me, in spite of everything. Malka doesn't blame Esther about Sybil, and it's not because I'm older.' He was drinking far too much. 'What's happening with her?'

'You see her more often than you see me! Did she tell you who she's going out with? She didn't tell me, but I found out. I think it's a secret. Do you remember that horrible boy Stuart? He's still friends with Rudi, even though he's rude and boorish. I don't mix with him if I can avoid it, and when he comes round, they generally spend the evening talking in the middle-room, or go out drinking to that low-down dive on the fish docks. They've been into the Blue Lagoon a couple of times. I actually had to serve them when I was working late shift. He's a skipper on one of the rusty old boats that go to Sweden or Finland. He gave Mam a box of mackerel last time he came round. We were eating it for two weeks, non-stop. He tries to crawl round our family, because of Esther, but Mam and Dad are so gullible, they don't realize it. It doesn't work for me, though. He complained to me that the cheese roll was stale, and was there a pickle shortage in this café. He tried to insult me by calling the restaurant a café. If Mr Levy hadn't been around, I would have kicked them both out. He's not the kind of friend I like for Rudi. He's got a bad influence on him – and as for Esther fancying him! It's just like Esther, though, to be contrary. I hope she's leading him by the nose, but I don't think so. She spent a whole weekend with Stuart on his boat. She was actually in Hull, and never came to see us! She preferred to spend her time with him. When I say "a whole weekend" I mean a whole weekend, which includes two nights, and I wouldn't be surprised if they spent them together; I mean, in the same cabin. Dad's beard would turn white, if he suspected. I hope Esther doesn't get pregnant, and then have to marry that creep. If there was a tax on charm, he'd get a rebate from the government. Do you think Esther is attractive? I mean more attractive than Sybil was, or Vered?'

'Or you, you mean!' For a moment, I thought he was going to laugh, but he only smiled. 'Beauty is a subjective attribute, and attraction even more so. All the Sokolovskys are beautiful to me, whether their eyes are brown or blue; whether they're skinny, fat, spotty, dark or fair. And whether they wear glasses or contact lenses. They are particularly delicious when they're eating and drinking. What about trifle drowned in cream and sherry, and some brandy with your coffee?'

'Yes, please.' I felt offended, but couldn't define exactly why. He'd never remotely reminded me of Rudi before.

'On the subject of sharing cabins, we'll be sharing one tomorrow night, on the Harwich to The Hook of Holland crossing; but if this offends your moral sensibilities, I don't mind sitting it out in the public room, or on deck.'

'I wouldn't dream of allowing you to do that!' O God, I thought, how good you are to me! I must endeavour to watch what I say. Perhaps he's planning . . . I mustn't blush; I could ruin everything. If only I'd known, hot pokers wouldn't have made me blab on about Esther and Stuart. Felix and I, all alone, in a cabin to ourselves, all night! If only I was more experienced. My nightie was an old, raggy, cotton shirt that Dad discarded two years ago, totally unsuitable for a seduction scene. What should I do? Who could I turn to for help and advice? First thing in the morning, I'd ask Aliza, casually, if she could show me the nearest department store, as I'd forgotten to pack any night clothes.

146

'Then don't look so worried. The cabin has six berths and every one will be occupied. Do you approve of Vered's engagement? She sounded so happy in her last letter to me. I gather her fiancé's a Hungarian refugee. Another lost boy for Malka and Sacha, but a son-in-law this time.' Whatever happened, I mustn't show my disappointment and wretchedness. They'd have two refugee sons-in-law pretty soon, if I kept a poker face and held my cards close to my chest. I was quite good at keeping important facts to myself these days; at least, for a limited time.

'I haven't met her fiancé, so I'm not in a position to approve or disapprove,' I said primly. 'She sent us a photograph. He's quite a lot older than Vered; about eight or nine years. I think that's an advantage in marriage,' I added quickly. 'Women are so much more mature than men. They seem to suit each other. They're both dressed in raggy shorts and shirts, in the picture, but Vered looks *gorgeous*. I wish I had black curls and big dark eyes and eyelashes that touch my eyebrows.' I waited for Felix to tell me that he preferred my colouring, but he was busy with his trifle. I fiddled with my ring and chain. 'They don't believe in long engagements. I think they'll live on the kibbutz for the rest of their lives. She must be really hooked on the life, because when she was a kid, she was always mad about money. Mam and Dad are planning to be in Israel in February, for the wedding. It's high time they enjoyed a happy trip together. They'll visit Sybil's grave, too.' I shuddered. A brilliant picture of my sister Sybil, coming to a stand-still in the lane, weighed down by her bulging satchel and gas-mask, crowded my vision and obliterated the elegance of the restaurant. Felix and the candle flame blurred into insignificance against the dazzling brightness of her. She was reading, unaware of the weight round her shoulders, chewing her ribbon, so engrossed that she didn't see me running towards her, or hear me calling. Sybil! Sybil!

'Drink your brandy.' I was shaking so much that I spilt most of it over the tablecloth. He held my hand while I tried again, then took the glass away. 'There's a good girl! Now take ten deep breaths and concentrate on nothing else. One . . . two . . .' He counted softly, deliberately, and by the time we reached ten, I was in control of myself, and I swallowed what was left in his glass.

147

'Vered and I used to count when we heard the sirens. It helped us not to be frightened.'

'We all have our own ways of coping, Rachel. Different little tricks to help us along. You do so well. Malka and Sacha try, too, but they haven't found one that works yet. Don't be too hard on them.' He squeezed my hand and we drank our coffee.

'Have you found a trick that works, Felix?' I wished I hadn't said that. He shook his head and looked round for the waiter.

'Not yet, but I'm still looking. You haven't told me about Rudi. Is *he* happy, do you think?' If he wasn't so keen on attracting attention to get the bill, he'd see the best trick; the only trick for him right in front of him. Rachel Sokolovsky.

'Rudi is a rather insensitive young person. He doesn't know what it's like to plumb the depths, so in his own shallow way, he's happy. I rather thought he might be upset about Vered. They were always as thick as thieves, but he wasn't in the least disturbed. His reaction was quite the opposite. He seemed delighted.'

'So he should be! You aren't very clever at understanding relationships, you sentimental old fool! Do you still fight with him all the time?'

'Certainly not! He tries his best to rile me, but I treat his attempts as a rather silly, childish game. Mam and Dad spoil him to death, of course. That's their business. It doesn't affect me.'

We walked into Leicester Square and sat down on a wall opposite a cinema. How light and lively it was in London! A thousand people sauntered past. I looked at the young couples, their arms twined about one another's shoulders and waists. I wouldn't change places with any of them. 'What's your philosophy of life these days, Rachel?' I looked at him sharply, not sure whether he was taking me seriously, but his expression was calm and still.

'I have done with fantasy and self-delusion which compounded the errors of my youth,' I said, getting into my stride. 'Off with the old and on with the new! Life can be sweet, although most of the time it is bitter, but one must live it to the full; investigate the black cloud and no longer hover at the edge of the mythical silver lining. I am no longer beguiled or misled by hopes based on false evidence.' Platitudes and truisms chased after one another. It was such a pleasure,

148

babbling to Felix. He was far too gallant to expose me. I held his arm as we walked to the number 13 bus-stop. I tried to remember when I had last felt so happy. But I couldn't quite recollect.

Chapter Twenty-Four

It was dark when the train juddered into East Berlin. Three strangely garbed old nuns seemed to be the only people left on it. They were charming and incomprehensible and had probably hidden children in their convent during the war. Felix began dragging the luggage into the corridor, so I left my three friends to look out of the black window at their reflections, while I went to help. I could see at once that he was in a bad mood. Something must have upset him. 'Look, get out of the way and open the door. We're going to miss our connection.' Long train journeys obviously didn't agree with him.

'We wouldn't have been issued tickets in a civilized country which didn't acknowledge that one has to have time to change trains.' I could never understand long negative sentences like the one I'd just uttered, and wondered if he could.

'Let's get the luggage out. Just stop talking for a minute and apply yourself to the job in hand.' The nuns disappeared along the murky platform. I jumped down and he handed out the cases to me. They were too heavy, but I pretended they weren't. He then left me for a full hour, surrounded by the mountain of bags, while he sought the Polish train. I absorbed myself in the fruitless pastime of shouting for a non-existent porter or a wheelbarrow, in English, and had more than enough leisure time to appreciate the difference between this forsaken place and the Western Sector.

'Felix! Where are you? Come back!' I screamed, for the twentieth time. I could hear footsteps running towards me, and wondered what to do if they were helmeted villains about to snatch my biros and Persianelle coat. Two young men and Felix grabbed handfuls of the luggage, leaving me to chase after them with the two heaviest suitcases, and the strain on my shoulders, back and hands was agonizing. After a distance of almost a mile, I saw and heard a growling, impatient, packed train on the point of leaving. Felix ran, empty-handed, towards me, and grabbed the cases as the train began to move. A guard was yelling at us and trying to pull our luggage from the open door of the moving train, and the two young men were inside, battling with him for possession, barricading the door. Others were standing at another open door, nearer to us, their arms outstretched, grabbing at us; hauling us aboard. Nobody would ever believe what was happening here when I told them about it at home. I was glad that Felix was sharing this experience, so they wouldn't think I was exaggerating. The train stopped before the tail end of it left the platform behind, and the dreadful guard came over to us, trying to wrench the door open, but we had made too many friends by now. He refused to examine our tickets which we offered him through the window, and I screeched filthy English swear-words at him. To my horror, I saw him board another part of the train, a moment before it set off again. 'He'll come to find us and start chucking our things out onto the railway line! He's a dangerous lunatic! Why did you leave me standing all by myself for hours?' The Russian students bundled our luggage into a tiny compartment, then thrust us in after it, and slid the door closed. They leaned against it, hiding us while the train gathered speed. 'My arms!' I whined. 'I'll never be able to get them back in their sockets! I must have run at least a mile carrying a hundred and fifty pounds. What happened?'

'The guard's a rogue. He sold our places on this train and tried to tell me that it wasn't running. The students heard me arguing with him, and told me what must have happened. It's a common occurrence, but mostly with English or Dutch travellers. Some visiting students from Leningrad got caught like we nearly did, last month. I can't have left you for longer than twenty minutes and you ran a hundred yards at the most. Don't always exaggerate everything. We're lucky to be here, moving in the right direction, and it's entirely due to them. They're returning from a visit to East Germany; they're English language students from Leningrad. They could have just turned their backs and pretended that they didn't know what was happening and kept out of our trouble. Let's give them some biros and that portable chess set. They've probably never seen anything like it.'

I didn't want to give them the chess set. They were nice people, but not *that* nice. We would have behaved in exactly the same helpful manner if the situation had warranted it, and, after all, we were now safely on our way. The corridor was so blocked up that the guard couldn't possibly get at us. If he tried any funny business, Felix would sock him in the mouth while I gave him a lethal swipe with my bag, and screeched the train and his blood to a standstill. I didn't have to give the elegant little chess set to anyone but Hannah, and I'd had a shameful inner battle about even giving it to her. It was dreary, too-good-to-be-true, Rudi who'd packed it when I was slyly trying to leave it behind. Those brothers had never understood that I was intrinsically and incurably selfish. They'd been disarmed by my generosity over the cornflake sweet. It had seared through my foul nature like a rainbow in a black sky. All they ever saw was the rainbow. I'd spent years cultivating it; touching it up to give it a semblance of permanence and adding bright daubs of colour here and there; dazzling them with my pseudo-sweetness.

'You never learn,' I said severely. 'You, the most generous, the most disinterested of men, don't know how to allow others the pleasure of helping a fellow human being without thought of material reward. Imagine how you'd feel in their place! Honour them by accepting their integrity in the way you would so wish to be honoured. Why demean these excellent people by offering them a few dried-up biros and a cheap chess set? Any road, the white bishop came adrift while Rudi was packing it and I haven't the room or the energy to start searching for it now.' Felix had always been susceptible to my stirring reasoning. Once I got under way, I could babble on endlessly. Indeed, I had occasionally toyed with the notion of embodying my observations in a slim volume entitled *Aphorisms and Adages for All.*

Felix was regarding me with ill favour. This was no time to dream or dally. 'Oh, Rachel,' he said, wearily. 'Isn't it time you honoured me with a little intelligence? Do I have to remind you that I've known you since you were five? Stop patronizing me with your phoney rubbish. The pens are in perfect condition and the chess pieces were all there when we had that game on

152

the boat and your memory is just as reliable as mine. Why not say, "I don't want to give the boys the chess set, because I want it for myself and find it too difficult to part with." No! You don't want to save it for Hannah; you want it for you. Be honest with yourself. You've got little meannesses: so have I. So has everybody. It isn't important enough to lie about, especially to me. I'd never think the less of you.'

Could he see that I was shrivelling up with shame? Would he remember this incident for ever, in the way that I knew I would? I felt my cheeks wobble and burn and covered them with my hands, not knowing what to do or where to look. Should I lie my way out of it and insist that it was only of Hannah I was thinking and how dare he make me out as utterly contemptible? If only I could give the boys fifty pens and the chess set on my own initiative and cancel my awful sermon, I would do so with delight and joy. But it was too late. I put my bag on the floor and bobbed down next to it, my back to him, fumbling with one of the zips, foraging for the few things he required of me, but he pulled me up and turned me round to face him. 'Don't be miserable and embarrassed as if we were strangers to each other. All we've done is puncture each other's self-esteem a bit. It's not so terrible!' He hugged me so tightly and his expression was so sweet and benign that I didn't give a damn for anything else. He'd always love me, no matter what I did or said. Whatever happened, I mustn't be rash, and go against my baser instincts. I'd put the handful of goodies back in my bag as soon as I could decently do so. But he'd seen them and it was too late. 'You do the honours.' He knocked at the door of the compartment in which we were trapped, and one of our friends in the blocked corridor pushed it open a fraction.

'It is better that you stay in for a short time; perhaps until the guard has passed through this coach. He will be here for tickets in a few minutes, so please have them ready. He will leave the train at Poznan and another one will get in at this town. It will be OK. After that, the train is not stopping until Warsaw. We will come in with you when he comes for your ticket. Do not worry. Do not be frightened.' He smiled. 'We are very happy to be able to talk to you and practise our English. We have not met many English people before. After Poznan, we will have some conversations, please!'

153

I felt overwhelmed by their kindness and interest and handed out the pens like Lady Bountiful, thrusting the beautiful chess set at the ringleader with profuse apologies about there being only one. There were plenty of other goodies in the suitcases which I could spare – scented soaps; chocolates; nuts. I'd rummage through them just as soon as we were sorted out. They shook their heads, laughing, thanking us for everything. 'This is not necessary! This is enough!' They closed the door on us and Felix told me to go easy with the gifts and not to forget about Hannah. As if I could! It was on the tip of my tongue to give him another lecture, but we could hear the guard banging and shouting and Felix wanted to listen. He held his finger to his lips. 'What is he saying? What is he saying?' It drove me mad that he and everyone else could understand, and I couldn't. I was missing out on all the excitement. Andrei, our friend, squeezed in and spoke to Felix in Russian. Felix handed him our tickets and told me not to speak to the guard however rude or threatening he seemed to be. On Andrei's advice, he was going to pretend that he didn't understand Polish. The wretched man shouted and raged, but we stood between him and our luggage, crammed like sardines. Andrei showed him our tickets and he examined them and sneered as if they were poor forgeries. Suddenly, he pushed between us and kicked a suitcase which lay at the bottom of the heap.

'He would like to see the contents of this bag,' said Andrei. 'He has the right.' It took us ten minutes to release it and open it and luckily it was one filled with clothes for Hannah, which he assumed belonged to me. The train was extremely long, and he had hundreds of tickets to collect. He pushed past us, rudely, and left. I told Andrei that I would like to report his horrible behaviour to the other guard and that I had never come across such a disgraceful performance in my life. He looked at me curiously, as if I had said something quite outlandish. 'It is better that you do nothing,' he said. 'We will be in the next compartment if you need us.' He squeezed out and left, as if he'd forgotten about the conversations in English.

We had ordered couchettes and paid for them, but there was obviously no point in attempting to remedy this. We must count ourselves lucky to be aboard this crowded, dirty train, and once we'd stacked the luggage into one leaning tower, we'd have enough room to sit down. I was dying for something to eat and drink. Once we were settled, I'd look for a dining-car or a coffee bar and a place to wash my filthy hands. We had the entire night ahead of us; Warsaw at about three in the morning, and five hours after that Grodno, the Polish-Russian border town. I'd ask Andrei where the facilities were, while Felix piled the luggage, since I'd run out of that kind of energy.

The corridor was seething with people – mostly elderly and poorly dressed, wedged against their luggage in shapeless cloth bags. No business executives here; no well-dressed families off to visit relatives in Warsaw. Maybe there was a day-time train for the smart set. Or possibly a couple of first class coaches up in front. No, Andrei told me; there was no food or water on the train. Passengers brought their own refreshment from home. I squeezed back and told Felix the bad news, but he seemed unperturbed, as if he'd known all along. He'd stacked the cases, but had taken a bottle of our duty-free whisky out of one of them, and a bag of nuts. Four elderly people were crammed into the seats. 'I invited them in,' he said, apologetically. 'You can squeeze in here. We can't loll about while they're wedged out there.' I was furious but had the sense to smile agreeably. Hadn't we booked and paid for a whole sleeping compart-ment? Didn't we, at least, have a sole right to this squalid hole? Hadn't we promised to spend some of the night talking to our friends from Leningrad? Gaily, I reminded him of this. 'Don't be naive, Rachel. They can only talk to us in the corridor. It would be far too risky for them to spend time with us in private. They are Russian students remember, no doubt specially privileged to visit East Germany. It's OK for our friends here. They're Poles, travelling in their own country.'

There was no room for both of us to sit down. We would have to take it in turns to stand up all night. He spoke to one of the old people and all four stony faces became animated and almost jovial. I smiled, wishing them in hell. In no time at all, lumpy bags were opened and bottles of water, withered apples, tomatoes, black bread and cucumbers were placed on our suitcase cum dining-table, together with our whisky and nuts. I poured some of the water on my flannel to wipe the dirt off my hands, and using a borrowed cup, filled it with a whisky and water combination. Everyone did likewise. It was bitterly cold. I never thought that a train journey could be so uncomfortable. After our feast, I insisted that Felix took a turn on the seat. The whisky bottle was empty. He and our travelling companions were talking pleasantly and incomprehensibly. There was no room to sit on his knee. I stood, mashed against the luggage, wishing that I hadn't been so good-natured, as the train hurtled through the black night. The unspeakable thoughts poked like stone fingers into my brain, probing; dominating. If I could move, struggle out into the corridor and open a window, I could dislodge them. I had learned, over the years, to quell the waking nightmares, even if I'd had to succumb to those which oppressed and tormented me when I was asleep. I'd think about Hannah as she was now, her heart merry with the anticipation of our visit. Fifteen hours. Only fifteen hours. But the vision beckoned me, horrible and seductive. I would face it. In a minute, I would try. Felix was nearby and I wouldn't be afraid. If you ran from your tormentors they would chase you, as long as you had strength to run. When you could run no further, it was best to turn, snarling and aggressive, and look into their grinning faces. I had allowed dream goblins and painted devils to frighten me all my life. I was an object of scorn to myself; pitiable; ridiculous. No more! I looked at Felix. He was huddled up in the seat, fast asleep. I wouldn't wake him with my nonsense or disturb the old people who were bent over their bags, dozing. He didn't wake up when the train stopped. I helped our companions out of the compartment, and they smiled and whispered their thanks, happy to let him rest. I wished I could sleep like him. Perhaps I could, now that there was so much more space. I closed the door and wedged it with a suitcase. Only a few people were standing in the corridor now, and others were lying down using their luggage as pillows. Perhaps that was why they brought these soft sacks with them, instead of hard, unfriendly suitcases. The dim light on the wall flickered and died and I fumbled in the pitch dark and sat down, waiting for my eyes to get used to it. I could make out his outline hunched and uncomfortable. He'd be as stiff as a board when he woke. I rolled up his raincoat and eased his head onto it, hoping I could rouse him accidentally, so that he could keep me company, but whisky and weariness combined had made him as heavy as a log, and all he did was sigh and adjust his body to

156

a more comfortable position. Somehow I wasn't satisfied. I wanted him to rest his head on my lap, so that I could stroke his hair and look at his face all night, but the luggage overlapped and two unfriendly wooden arm-rests forbade any real comfort. I sat down opposite him and pulled my coat around me. I wouldn't ask Felix about the evil spirits. Only Hannah. She knew who they were. She knew who could drive them away.

Felix woke me. It was daylight and we were approaching a town. I'd slept all through the night, he smiled. Even the ticket collector who came in at Warsaw and spoke in a voice to wake the dead hadn't roused me, because I'd been dead drunk. We were going to change here, for the Russian train. This town was called Grodno. My Dad had told me about this city. He'd been here as a boy and he remembered it as a friendly, beautiful place. If we could buy a cup of coffee here, I'd be willing to believe it. From the platform it appeared very bleak, but that was probably because I felt tired and cold and hungry and there wasn't a porter in sight. But Andrei and his friends appeared again, and helped us with the luggage on our route march along the platform, which was probably the longest in the entire world. We could just make out the train waiting in the distance, and we walked towards it, across the frontier, into Russia.

After long and tedious formalities, we were shown into our compartment by a friendly official. The luxury of it made me gasp. Two berths, covered with snow-white perrinehs, greeted us like a mirage. A strip of carpet covered the floor between them. There was a table, a mirror. This was the Czar's palace. Felix translated everything he said. 'This is a carriage reserved for foreign visitors. No. You are not allowed to bring your luggage in here. It is to be placed in the alcove, there, where each piece will be opened and searched for gold, arms and forbidden literature.' I tried, in vain, to suppress a complex urge to laugh.

'Give him these ten biros, Felix,' I gasped, 'and implore him for something to drink.'

'No. You cannot buy anything on the train.'

'What about over there, in his office?'

'No.' But he smiled when he saw the pens, took them gratefully and told us we could drink the water from the taps.

It was clean water. Tourists were not allowed to travel in any other part of the train. We should remember that, please. We would arrive at Vilnius at one o'clock. He hoped we would be comfortable.

I asked him his name and told him in English that it was the most beautiful train I had ever seen in my life and that in England we didn't have anything like it. Felix was forced to translate what he obviously thought was nonsense, but I knew better. Nicolai appeared delighted, left us and in no time reappeared with two cups of sweet black tea, the like of which I'd never experienced in England, either, but it tasted like nectar and cheered and revived us. He waited while we drank it and told us that he was born here, in Grodno.

'My father visited this town when he was a boy,' I told him. 'He used to go fishing in the river.' Nicolai refused payment, and left the train holding the empty cups in one hand and waving with the other, and as if his farewell was a signal, the train began to move. We stood together at the window. Felix and I had this sumptuous boudoir all to ourselves, but romantic fantasy didn't occupy my thoughts. I wondered why tears were filling my eyes. I felt ashamed, but was powerless to stop them, and mumbled something about my contact lenses. He gave me his big white hanky and cuddled me, pressing my face against his jacket. The edge of the photograph peeped out, as if I had only just put it there, yet I hadn't seen it for fifteen years. He always carried it with him wherever he went. Always. By itself, in the breast pocket of whichever jacket he wore. 'What about Mama and Papa, Felix? And Rudi? Don't you carry pictures of them?'

'Of course. In my wallet. The one of the four of us when I celebrated my Bar-Mitzvah. No, I'm not going to get it out. You've seen it a thousand times. I've never known anyone so crazy about photographs as you. You'll be seeing the real person soon. The real Hannah! Aren't you happy? Aren't you excited? Why are you crying?'

'I'm not,' I said. 'Not so as anyone but you would notice. You and Rudi, you don't have anyone to visit who belongs to you. No Mama and Papa . . . nobody . . .' My voice, wobbly and cracked, tailed off. I leaned against his shoulder, looking at the flying scenery. I had seen it in day-dreams and in my sleep. Breathed it. Felt the texture of it. But Felix had never been with me before. I longed for him to be happy. To belong to me. Just me.

'You belong to me. No one could be closer or dearer. That's why Hannah is my family too.' We sat down on one of the perrinehs. Feathery air, Clean, cool, cotton covers. Felix's arm around my shoulders. I wouldn't mind travelling like this for another three days and nights. If only I had a perrineh like this in my mind, so that I could jump into it, whenever I felt overwrought and anxious and frightened. Maybe that's what people meant when they talked about 'peace of mind'. 'Don't think of the others, Rachel. The dead. Let them go. Let them go in peace so that you can live in peace.' Would *he* ever be able to do that? I wondered. 'Liubava doesn't exist any more; you understand that, don't you? It's a place you've built into your imagination, but it has no reality. And you've got to be prepared for the change in Hannah. The girl you knew doesn't exist either. You may feel like total strangers when you meet.' He didn't understand.

'I'm better already! I've done with weeping and wailing! Don't let's waste the perrinehs. Let's have a nap before they slug us with the gold bars I've smuggled in.' I stretched out, and accidentally rested my head on his lap. There was a knock at the door, and two attendants walked in.

'We will examine your luggage now, sir, madam.' Felix would manage. He always did. I closed my eyes.

Chapter Twenty-Five

Hannah knew that the train wasn't due until one o'clock and that it would probably be late. She had checked its expected time of arrival six times in the last week, both with the receptionist at the Intourist Hotel and with the station. At the second and third enquiry, they had been irritable, and then suspicious. It was unwise to keep on badgering them, but she was quite unable to control herself. To welcome visitors from abroad was in itself an irregular event, but to be eager, impatient and anxious was irresponsible. She wouldn't arrive too early; it would only make matters worse, and arouse further unwanted interest. It was quarter to twelve. The platform was deserted. No one else in Vilnius was waiting for family to arrive from England. To arrive from anywhere. The ticket collector had watched her come into the station, but had not remarked on it. Now he approached her and asked her for what or for whom she was waiting, as if he had forgotten about the numerous enquiries. She knew he hadn't. They didn't smile at each other.

'The train from Grodno.'

'It is not due to arrive until two o'clock.' She did not correct him, and turned as if to go. 'Who are the passengers?'

'Sokolovsky and Dorfman. They are booked at the Intourist Hotel. The Intourist taxi is to meet them.'

'Where are they from?' He had already been supplied with detailed information, but nevertheless, she replied as if he had not.

'England.'

'What is their business here?'

'A holiday.'

'For how long have they been given permission for this holiday?'

'Six days.'

'Why are they coming all this way for so short a holiday?'

'They would have liked to stay longer.' She shouldn't have said that. 'The Tourist Department decided that six days were sufficient.' Why did she come here by herself? She should have followed the suggestion that if it was necessary for her to meet them in, she should accompany the driver who would leave from the hotel at ten minutes to one.

'How do you come to be meeting these people, Sokolovsky and Dorfman?'

'Dorfman is an interpreter for the United Nations. He has worked in Moscow. He applied for permission to visit Vilnius with my niece. They asked if I could meet them.'

The ticket collector walked away. He wore no uniform; just a peaked cap. He was probably from the Police Department. She couldn't make herself worry. She would continue to stand here, alone on the platform, for another hour. Excitement agitated her whole body, so that in spite of herself she had to walk up and down, to try to disperse the merriment which animated her whole face. She wanted to wave her arms; shout; run; laugh out loud; but instead, she walked demurely, holding the bunch of flowers in front of her, so that no one coming up to the platform could see that she was wild with happiness. She didn't care if the train *was* late, for now she could indulge in the pleasure of anticipation, unencumbered by fear. It had a different taste, these last minutes, from the weeks of waiting; of quite unbearable worry and anxiety. They could have changed their minds and not let them come, and she could have done nothing about it, but gone on with her work at the warehouse, having to pretend she had a headache or a heavy cold, so that no one would realize that she was dying of anguish and disappointment. She was terrible at keeping her thoughts to herself now, and everyone knew that her visitors from England were due. She saved up her free days in order that she could meet them and spend some time with them – if the Authorities decided to allow the visit. But no one, no one could possibly know what was in her heart; how it shrivelled one moment, and leapt the next.

She bought an English dictionary, and she tried to study

161

every evening, and recall sounds and meanings that she'd picked up when she was a girl. The letters were so strange and difficult, let alone the words, and her concentration was poor. My baby; my niece; my Rachel, was all that she could think of. Earlier that day, she'd stood like a stone in the middle of her room, waiting for the moment when the train would pull out of Grodno. Then she'd gone quite mad! She'd run along the balcony in her pyjamas and knocked at Tanya's door. She'd die if she didn't talk to someone! 'Tanya! Tanya! My baby's coming! My baby's coming!' Tanya had nearly jumped out of her skin, thinking for a second that Hannah was about to give birth, and then they had both collapsed in hysterics, infecting each other with uncontrollable shrieks of laughter. Tanya had to run like a bat out of hell to catch her bus, but never mind, for she felt strangely light-hearted, having witnessed again that silent, self-contained woman boiling over with joy. They'd been neighbours for about four years. She knew that she was a Jew, but had nevertheless tried to be friendly. She'd always remained separate and aloof until her breakdown a few weeks back. You couldn't discuss boy-friends or family problems with her, because she had none – none that she let on about, anyway. Then, last month, that letter had arrived for her with the news that she was going to have visitors from abroad. Of course, no one could have foreigners to stay. Even if she'd had room, they weren't allowed to stay with her; only at the Intourist Hotel. She hadn't asked Hannah too much about the people who were coming. One didn't do that, but she noticed the difference in her. Who hadn't! The life in her; the animation; the way she rushed to queue in the evenings, if news got around that one of the shops had a consignment of goods. She'd managed to buy some vodka and soft drinks; a piece of curtain material that she'd split with Tanya. She'd shown Tanya the fur pieces which she kept in a paper bag and had asked her to help her to make a hat for her niece. Although Tanya was always running in to borrow or beg a cup of flour or sugar, seeking advice about making the hat was all that Hannah had ever asked of her. How good it was, this morning, when she'd rushed in, laughing and crying; shouting about her baby. The so-called 'baby' was twenty! A relative she'd met years and years ago – before the war, in fact. She'd spoken of her just now as if she'd forgotten about the intervening years.

162

She'd wanted to remind her of them; that her expected visitor was a young woman, and that she was behaving outlandishly, but she couldn't. She daren't. There was somthing odd about Hannah. Something unbalanced? No. Not that, although a lot of the neighbours thought so. Tanya had professional expertise and knew better. There was something about her that you couldn't quite put your finger on. She shuddered, suddenly, remembering that time when she really thought Hannah had gone completely off her head. The neighbours had witnessed the scene, or at least heard the commotion she'd made, and that business of her muttering and jabbering to herself didn't go down well with them, though Tanya realized that was probably just extreme loneliness combined with a private sorrow.

The outburst that gave Tanya the creeps had occurred about a month after Hannah had first moved into the flats, but had remained in the minds of everyone; festering, so that people never quite trusted her, no matter how impeccable her behaviour had been since then. Did you howl like that unless you were possessed? Tanya stood on the bus, with everyone around her, touched by a sort of fear, thinking of that night. The man had appeared harmless enough, in his middle fifties or thereabouts. He worked at the Vilnius Telephone Exchange as an engineer. No one in the block recognized him. He was simply repairing a telephone cable near the back entrance. Nobody she knew cared whether he repaired it or not, since private telephones were nothing to do with them. Hannah had returned home from work and seen him. He hadn't noticed her, let alone spoken to her or assaulted her, but she'd screamed like a wild animal; like a hunted ermine whose tongue had been torn out in a salt trap. They'd all rushed down to see what was the matter, sick with dread and horror, the screams bursting their ear-drums; freezing their blood. Hannah was standing a metre away from the man, making that noise, her half-closed eyes fastened on the poor man's face, her whole body shaking, as if she were suffering from a seizure. The man was transfixed. Tanya had seen with her own eyes the cigarette he was holding burning the flesh of his fingers, but he'd seemed incapable of moving a muscle. 'Murderer! Murderer!' she was shrieking. 'I saw you! I know you! You were one of those grinning devils who clubbed and

163

tormented us! You were in Liubava, too! You helped them there, with their work! You made them dig the pits and buried them!' Then for a few seconds she became perfectly still and quiet, like a wild cat before the pounce. There was no question but that she would have killed him, if they hadn't dragged him away. That's what everyone said. He hadn't informed the police, and no one else bothered. 'She's a mad woman! A filthy Jewess mad woman!' he'd growled, and had quickly picked up his hoops of cable and tools and hurried off. Tanya had turned to help Hannah come to her senses. She was used to handling difficult, even demented patients. Dead ones, too. It was a hot summer evening, but Hannah's bare arms were rigid and icy cold. Like a dead body. She'd taken her stiff and frozen fingers and led her up the stairs, and she'd been quite calm. No. Not calm. As lifeless as a corpse; but after she'd made tea, she appeared to return to normal.

'He was a Nazi collaborator,' she told Tanya. 'He assisted them in acts of sadism and murder.' Tanya had humoured her; asked her how she'd escaped. 'I was in Shobodko, but it was not only from there that I recognized him. He was in Liubava. He helped to kill my family. I saw him first when I was a child. I have seen him a thousand times since. In dreams.' It had not occurred to Tanya at the time that the telephone engineer had called Hannah a Jew. She'd been too engrossed in the recovery of her body heat and reason. But now, she wondered. Hannah didn't look anything like a Jew. What a Jew was supposed to look like, anyway. She herself was amazed when people told her that she was, because her hair was as yellow as corn, her complexion fair and her eyes blue. Another man had returned to finish laying the new cable. She felt quite squeamish, thinking about the episode now. She hoped that Hannah's visitors would make her happy and more forthcoming. She'd be interested to meet them, but right now she had a long day to face on Ward N3. You didn't have to be a dreamer or a visionary to know exactly what and who she'd see there! Some people had all the luck!

The driver from the hotel parked the taxi in the place reserved for him in the station, then joined the ticket collector for a chat and a smoke, since the train was late as usual. When the signal clicked, he climbed up to the platform and waved to the woman who was waiting there, way up at the other end. She ran towards him and he told her where to stand. The coach reserved for foreigners would stop right near the exit; not at the far end. She thanked him, and smiled. He had a weakness for blondes, especially when they smiled at him like that, and this one would be very attractive, but for her broken nose, and she was a bit too thin for comfort. She didn't seem interested in getting into conversation with him, though. He lit another cigarette and opened his paper. The train was just discernible in the distance. He liked English cigarettes and his passengers were usually pretty free-handed when he drove them around on the arranged trips. He'd not had a decent smoke for months.

As the train puffed up to the platform, the students began to sing, 'Should Auld Acquaintance Be Forgot' in English. Rachel and Felix could hear them clearly, but they couldn't poke their heads out of the window to see. Once they came to a halt and could jump out, they'd wave and join in. The guard stood next to them, alongside the luggage. He opened the door and began handing it out to the uniformed man with 'Intourist' written on his cap in English letters. Rachel squeezed past and had jumped down before Felix had checked that they had everything with them. The moment he found his feet on the platform, the door slammed, and the train slid off. The students waved and sang and disappeared. He'd greet Hannah quickly, and then he'd better help the man with the luggage. Move himself. But he couldn't take his eyes off the two of them as they embraced; as if they were meeting their reflections after a long separation; their other selves, and that he was the dreamer, unable to rouse himself. Rachel lifted her head which she'd buried in Hannah's neck, and they both ran, hand in hand, towards him. He held out his arms. The journey was over.

Chapter Twenty-Six

We didn't speak during the journey to the hotel. Felix sat in front, with the driver. Later, after he had composed himself, washed his face and rested for a few minutes, I'd ask him to tell me what had upset him. Perhaps the journey had overtaxed his iron nerves and inexhaustible energy. I couldn't begin to imagine how he would have coped without me. Hannah and I sat at the back of the car. I held her flowers and her hand. I didn't notice the passing scenery or the life of the town outside the window. I'd leave that until tomorrow; for today, just now, I needed to catch up on all the years of seeing her only in visions; check up on their accuracy, and adjust to their full brightness the shadowy recollections of my childhood. There were experiences that I had missed, both with purpose and by accident; dreams from which I roused myself and images that I escaped. I fled them a thousand times, and after the war, as I grew older, I became tougher; stronger; more cunning at avoiding and pretending. Now I had Hannah; the one person who could hear me and understand the uncanny perceptions from which only the fits had given me reprieve. Felix would help us. He'd tell Hannah everything I wanted to say to her, and everything she wanted to say to me. Yet the language barrier between us now was so unimportant. Nevertheless, it would help to include him, not into this unity between us, for that seemed impossible, but to allow him to wander over the edges of our private world, always welcome; yet inevitably excluded from this. He wasn't usually so confused. Fancy shouting 'Goodbye' on the platform instead of 'Hello'! I only saw him cry once before; years and years ago, when he was a boy. He was shouting down the telephone, 'Mama!

Papa! Hello! HELLO!' But they didn't answer. They'd gone. Maybe he was confused then, too. Maybe he meant 'GOOD-BYE.'

I pressed my open left hand against her right. Exactly the same size now, but she was thinner than I'd realized, although her broken nose was no surprise to me. The livid scar cutting through her left eyebrow and the lines on her forehead – I was unprepared for those. What happened when I wasn't looking? The one dimple was still there, despite the hollow cheeks, and her hair was as thick and as bright as mine. And as long. I never cut my hair, either. Not since handfuls of it fell out one week, a year before the war ended. They shaved her head in the camp. I knew that, long before I saw photographs of the inmates after they were liberated. 'How lonely you've been, Hannah,' I thought, 'but you're not lonely now! We've got six whole days, and we'll be so merry! Just looking at you makes me smile. In spite of everything, you can still make me laugh after I've been crying. Do you remember how you stood in the street, laughing and holding out your arms while I ran after you; calling to you? And that Sunday we gave a concert for Sacha's birthday? I'd almost forgotten, but I remember everything now. Those Sundays! Each one was like a birthday party when you were with us. What do you do on Sundays now? I think I've watched you, sometimes. Searching. Going on a bus to Wilkia, Yanovy, Kaisadorys or Liubava. Looking in dead places for dead people. You knew that you wouldn't find them. You've found me. And I've found you. This is what people call, "Peace of Mind".'

The car stopped outside a new brick building and Hannah and the driver exchanged some conversation. He heaved the luggage off the roof-rack and the three of us helped him to carry it into the entrance lobby. Felix showed the man at the desk all our papers. How pale and tired he looked! How peaceful! Hannah stood by his side, guiding him; helping; smiling; utterly at ease. What would I have done if they hadn't liked each other? But I knew they would. They couldn't not. They were the two most important people in my life. I loved them more than anyone else in the world. I was their pivot; the spring of their friendship; their starting-point. I sat on the couch opposite the desk, watching them walk towards me. Hannah, thin, fair and delicate, looking more like a schoolgirl than a woman, in her clumsy sandals and navy-blue skirt and pullover, edged with the white collar of her blouse, her hair tied back loosely with a thin ribbon. No jewellery; no make-up; no vanity. And Felix, a foot taller, and as dark and as handsome as the devil, wearing exactly the same colours, as if they'd planned it all behind my back; when my attention was elsewhere. Hannah and Felix. Hannah and Felix. Hannah and Felix.

The snooty receptionist led us up two flights of stairs, to two identical rooms. We were given a book of vouchers which could only be used in the hotel restaurant, but we were going to Hannah's room for our supper tonight. The bathroom and toilet were at the end of the corridor. I'd never stayed in a hotel before, but had sneered at Rudi when he'd insisted on packing a plug and a bath towel. How clever of him to know that neither necessity was in evidence. I threw open all the suit-cases, looking for soap and clean clothes, showing Hannah all the presents we'd brought for her, piling them in heaps on the two chairs. She started to laugh, even though tears were in her eyes. She had visited the rooms before she came to meet us, for there was a jar of flowers on each window-sill, a flat plate piled high with apples and some little cakes in a tin. I'd forgotten that I was dying of hunger.

Felix stretched out on the bed, enjoying the feast and talking to Hannah in Yiddish. She shoved the pillows under his shoulders, sat on the bed next to him, and began peeling the spotty apples with his pen-knife, pushing the fruit into his mouth, as if *she'd* known him since she was five! I went down the corridor, having decided to use the plug first. The food and rest and attention would revive him. He seemed utterly happy. It occurred to me, while I was lolling in the dirty bath water, that I had never seen him thus. What was it that Sybil had once said about him? I couldn't remember, but now he seemed light-hearted; tired from the journey, but light and free, as if, at last, he'd let go of all the suitcases he'd been carrying around for years, and had come home. I'd been lying in this cold water for years, too. They'd be waiting for me; maybe worrying; thinking I'd drowned. I wiped the bath with my flannel and stuck Rudi's plug back in place. One could set up quite a good business here, importing plugs from England. I'd leave this one behind for Hannah, so that she could rent it out for a rouble a go. I didn't make a very good job of the bath, since there was no Vim, or the equivalent, to be seen. I turned on the huge bath-tap so that the water would act as a cover-up for the grey tide-mark, ready for Felix, and left the soap and bath-towel for him. It wasn't all that wet. I ran down the corridor in my dressing-gown. Felix was still lounging on the bed, leaning on his elbow. Hannah had her legs curled up under her, their bodies touching. They hadn't been wondering where I was. The lid of the cake tin rested next to them, piled with photographs. She was studying them intently; pointing; remembering; and he was watching her face. For a second, I was gripped by a feeling of *déjà vu*; a strange mingling of someone else looking at the faces in the pictures; two people as close to me as my own parents, but younger. The vision evaded me the instant after it appeared.

I pulled out Felix's towel-robe from one of the overflowing suitcases, and threw it over to him. What a mess the room was in! I'd have the other one. 'Get a move on, you lazy thing! The bath is overflowing.' They both turned to me, smiling. I wasn't intruding, after all.

'I've been telling Hannah how I came to know you, Rachel. How your family took us in, and what each sister is like, and how each one of you is entirely different from the other. She knew that already. She's got an even better memory than you! It's unearthly. I keep thinking I'm talking to you. No. Not quite that. It's as if I'm talking to you in a dream, so that you're recognizable, with a dimension of strangeness.' He gabbled to Hannah, repeating what he'd just said, swung his legs off the bed and his robe over his shoulder and left the room. Hannah hadn't looked at any of the presents, and wouldn't let me start looking for what I should wear. She patted the bed, and I took Felix's place beside her. I ate the little cakes and the apple and looked at the Paper Children with her. I didn't want to cry, because I was happy. She touched the tattered photographs with her lips, repeating their names, and boiling tears poured down my face when she came to Sybil. She wiped my eyes and lay down next to me, singing the songs that I hadn't heard since I was a child of three, and wrapped her arms around me. I buried my head against her neck, and fell asleep.

It was dark when I woke up. Hannah was still lying next to me, and Felix must have pulled the curtains together and covered us with the Persianelle coat. How long had we been asleep? Why were we lying here, wasting time? I sat up and Felix switched on the bedside lamp. He looked as fresh as a daisy and very pleased with himself. The room was tidy and my clean clothes were lying neatly over the back of the chair. I thought it was the middle of the night, but we'd been sleeping for less than two hours. He pulled me up to a standing position, and then did the same to Hannah. She must have been as light as a feather, but he pretended she wasn't, and took his time before he set her on her feet. He'd got us muddled up, the old fool! I picked up my clothes and went into the room next door. Felix had already hung most of my things in the cupboard and had set my hairbrush, ribbon and soap next to the sink. Mam had knitted a blue and white stripy jumper for me and one in red and white for Hannah. From now on, Felix would be able to tell the difference between us, unless he was colour-blind or not right in the head. I was glad Hannah put Mam's jumper on, too. The contents of six of the cases were for her, but she was afraid to be seen taking too many things home. We put the kettle and the pretty cups and saucers into her shopping bag; the biros, the frames and the photographs for her in my 'organizer bag', and Felix put the rolled-up mat under his arm, swathed in his raincoat, along with one of the jars of coffee, crammed into the pocket of his trousers. I wore the Persianelle coat, with style and flair.

Hannah told us that her flat was only a fifteen-minute walk. If I stayed in Vilnius for the rest of my life, I would never learn how to reach Hannah's home unaided. Once we left the main road behind; the old, mellow buildings, the wide pavement and the lamp-posts; the single-decker trolley cars and the few strolling people, all modern civilization disappeared. The narrow side streets ended after a few yards in sand-covered rubble, small, uneven hillocks of broken bricks, and no sign of a proper pathway. There were no lights to guide us. We stumbled after Hannah's stripy jumper. If I lost her, I felt I would be lost for ever. No one understood English here, and although I knew six useless words of Russian, I couldn't read any of the signs. This was a badly bombed, poor part of town. Felix turned round, to give me a hand through a crop of thistles. The sight of me traipsing along, my bulging bag hanging round my neck and the huge, thick coat flapping round my ankles, stopped him in his muddy tracks. 'Don't lose me, Felix!' I gasped. 'Hannah! Don't lose us!'

Hannah turned round, too. They were laughing! Felix dropped the mat and they took a hand each and pulled me onto a piece of flat ground. They flopped down onto the roll of carpet, helpless and hysterical, rocking with laughter; clutching at one another like a couple of kids. Like lovers, sharing a private joke from which, for a moment, I was excluded. But only for a moment, because no one could remain immune from this infectious gaiety. As far back as I could remember of Felix, I had never heard him or seen him like this. I had made this happen; and made it happen for Hannah, too. And I was glad, glad, glad! Wasn't I? 'Oh, Rachel!' gasped Felix, 'we couldn't lose you! Not when you look like this! Found. One blonde zebra, dressed up as a black bear, last seen wandering in the vicinity of Hannah Sokolovsky's flat. Do you know what she calls this? The short cut!'

I could see a dim light revealing a dingy, three-storey building in the middle of a sandpit. There was no path up to the stairway. We climbed up, as quietly as possible, so as not to disturb the neighbours, creeping past four unpainted wooden doors on the second landing. Hannah took a big rusty key from the pocket of her skirt, then jostled it around in the key-hole for a long half-minute. I could see that her hand was shaking. She pushed the door open and although it creaked mischievously, no one came to investigate. Later, I understood the reason for her caution, and the 'short cut'. Visits from foreigners to private homes were not encouraged. We stood in the gloom waiting for her to close the door and turn on the light.

The little room was gay, festive and beautiful. The naked bulb lit up a rickety table covered with a white oil-cloth, set in the middle of the bare, broken floor. It was set for three and there was a posy of flowers next to each plate. Three miniature bottles of vodka stood in the middle, together with a candle stuck into a home-made candle-stick: half a potato set into a jar. There was a bowl of tiny fish-balls, some fried, some boiled; beetroot salad; tomatoes and radishes cut into flower shapes and stuffed with grated cheese; bread, jam, apples; three hard-boiled eggs and a cake. I knew that every edible

171

delight that Hannah possessed was on this table, and that Felix and I were the first guests she had ever welcomed to her home.

The walls were sodden and peeling and the light bulb dangled treacherously from the damp, discoloured ceiling. The curtain was too small for the tiny window, and against it was the skinniest bed I'd ever seen. I wondered where Hannah kept her clothes and whether she had a pantry. She flew about like an excited moth, as if the presence of visitors overwhelmed her. She filled the new kettle from a single tap above a tiny, shallow stone sink in the corner, and lit the gas ring, then rinsed out the cups and saucers we'd brought. Felix unrolled the rug and laid it next to the bed, while I looked for a place to put the Persianelle coat. Hannah showed me her wardrobe – a large wooden box covered with a cushion, which also acted as one of the chairs. I folded it and stuffed it inside and lit the candle. I placed the jar of coffee on the shelf above the sink, next to two dented pans and some oddments of crockery. Felix poured out the drinks and we sat down to our banquet, he on the wardrobe, and Hannah and I, opposite, on the chairs. He had his work cut out, for Hannah and I talked non-stop, and he never let a word pass without translating for us.

I wanted to stay here, talking and drinking coffee and vodka for ever and ever. When I asked Hannah to show me the toilet, Felix looked at his watch and nearly jumped out of his skin. It was past one o'clock, and he'd told the hotel receptionist that we would be back by midnight. Hannah guided me along the balcony to a small brick building at the end of it and waited for me, as if I was a baby frightened of the dark, holding my hand all the way back to her door. She seemed to know that I needed her near me, and that I didn't have to explain. Felix had cleared most of the dishes from the table and piled them into the tiny sink, and had put the photographs and frames on her bed.

We didn't have to worry about getting lost on the way back to the hotel, because Hannah came with us. It was pitch dark and no light shone from anywhere, and although we didn't have a torch, the short cut was easy this time, because we didn't have anything to carry, except my bag, and we held hands all the way. We had to ring the door-bell of the hotel and a young man, who obviously acted as a night porter, let us in and spoke angrily to Hannah for bringing us back so late. When Felix told me what he was saying, I wanted to remon-

172

strate with him. He was on duty for the night, wasn't he? We hadn't woken him up! Felix wouldn't translate for me, and told me to shush. He wanted to call a taxi for Hannah, but the man said that there was none available. She kissed us both, told us she would meet us for breakfast and ran off into the darkness. Back to her little room and the Paper Children.

Chapter Twenty-Seven

It was well after two when Hannah returned to her room. She slipped off her heavy sandals so as not to disturb the people below, scooped up the photographs and sat down on her bed, her bare feet luxuriating in the new rug. She didn't even think of her medicine or sleep, neither of which she needed. For the next two hours she examined the pictures of her family which Rachel had given to her, welcoming each one by name, smiling at their beloved faces. Weeping. She allotted each, reverently, to the little pile of cardboard and wooden frames, as if at last they had arrived at their final resting-place. Then she turned to those photographs of the living. There was one of herself as a girl. For a moment she wondered whether it belonged to the dead and put it to one side. Then she knelt down and lined up the ones of Yosef and her English family along the length of the bed. Sybil in her army uniform was in a frame, but Sybil as a child stayed next to her sisters. Felix and his younger brother Rudi gave her pause. Where did they belong? With Sacha, Malka and her nieces, of course. She'd learnt enough from their conversation this evening, to understand that! They were her family, too, then! She shuffled up the pictures, knowing that she was being silly and childish, and spread them out again, as if she were playing a card game called Remembrance which she used to play with the kids. Rachel always won that game, without cheating! Each time she set the photographs in a line, those of herself and Felix lay next to each other. She turned off the light to test herself; to find out whether she was cheating unconsciously, but no! There they were again, together. Why did this odd chance delight her so? She hardly knew him. In a few days, he and Rachel would go back to

England and who could tell when she would ever see him again. If. The thought of that made her shiver. What was happening to her? She had never known a man. Never wanted to. She felt irritated by her new, wild fantasies, collected up the pictures, then put them on her rug, face down. She washed herself at the sink, put on her pyjamas, kissed the photographs in the frames, which she set on the table, and slipped into bed. It was already getting light. She had never felt more wide awake. At last, she reached down, picked up a photograph at random with her eyes closed, put it under her pillow and immediately fell asleep. She awoke at six, completely refreshed, sat up and pulled back her curtain. She drew his likeness from under her pillow, smiled at it and put it to her lips.

My watch had stopped, but I knew it was morning. The sun streamed through the thin curtains, and I stretched myself and thought of the day ahead of me. An Intourist trip of Vilnius was included in our hotel bill, scheduled for today. I wanted to visit Yanovy, too, the place where Mam's parents grew up, and see Kovno — and the place where Liubava used to be. Perhaps we could picnic in the forest or Vingis Park. I hoped Felix didn't want to traipse round museums and art galleries. He could do that every day of his life in London. Tonight we'd go to Hannah's room again, and perhaps she'd tell us about all the years that I'd missed. She'd only wanted to hear about us last night. She just needed a little time. I'd be completely happy if we spent every night in her room. Just the three of us.

Felix must still be asleep. I twiddled the knob of the radio, but couldn't find any English programmes. In fact, there was no choice; just the one, which consisted of unfamiliar music interspersed with snippets of unfamiliar speech. I leaned out of the window and looked down at Lenin's Avenue. The colour and architecture of the buildings opposite reminded me of Oxford, but there was no Esther here, and no young people riding bicycles. Most of those hurrying along the pavement were elderly women wearing dark headscarves and carrying shopping bags, yet there were no shops in sight. Only a stall on the pavement opposite, an old man standing behind, displaying sheets of postage stamps and newspapers. All these people were strange; foreigners; thinking in a different language;

175

separated from me by an unbridgeable gap. Yet my father and grandparents walked amongst them, once. My aunts and uncles. And Hannah still did. The children and young people must be at school or work. It must be quite late – nine o'clock at least. Hannah was on her way to see me! Happiness swamped me. This was the first full day. Then let there be light!

I swapped my glasses for my contact lenses and ran over to the sink to wash my face. There was a note leaning against the tap: 'We're waiting for you in the dining-room. Don't hurry. F.' His concern that I should sleep as long as possible, made me irritable. He was treating me like a child. It was just the sort of insensitive behaviour that Rudi relished. His infuriating 'do-gooding' act! Surely he understood that I wanted to spend every precious, possible second of my time here with Hannah, and that I could sleep my life away in Hull. I turned on the tap. The water hissed and bubbled at boiling point, and the cold tap gave an empty, unproductive cough. There was no plug. Where the hell had he put it? How could I wash myself in running, boiling water? I put on my dressing-gown, and went out into the corridor, and was about to walk into Felix's room to find either the plug or cold water, when the man on duty barred my way, standing in front of Felix's door, gabbling. I told him, slowly and clearly, that there was no cold water, and when he refused to understand, beckoned him into my room, so that he could see for himself, but he shook his head, and his sullen expression changed into an unpleasant leer. I'd bloody kill Felix for this! I slammed my door in a rage, put my flannel in the sink so that it could act as a plug and a sucker up of scalding water, brushed my hair, then held the flannel gingerly by the corner, and hung it out of the window to cool. I enjoyed the way it dripped onto some of the passing headscarves and caps. At intervals of ten seconds, I tested it on my face, until my skin was the colour of cooked beetroot. There was no way that I could clean my teeth. I put on yesterday's clothes and hurried past the grinning wretch in the corridor, and down the stairs. The receptionist understood English, and I complained about the lack of cold water before asking her to direct me to the dining-room.

'You have cold water in your room. Both taps are in good working order.'

176

'I am not in the habit of inventing idiotic stories!' I shouted angrily. 'Perhaps you will go and see for yourself!'

'The hotel restaurant is down the stairs to your left. It will be closed in five minutes. The breakfast vouchers cannot be used after ten o'clock.' She was a cool bitch, this one. She bent down to her writing.

I was in such a temper that I lost my way, and arrived with a minute to spare. Felix and Hannah were the only customers in the semi-basement room. They were sitting at a square, red-topped table against the window, their two heads almost touching. The contrast in their hair colouring was sharp and beautiful and unreal. As if I was looking at a kid's painting book, without the permission of the owner; as if they were whispering secrets for no one else's ears. Not even mine. 'Don't hurry. F.' I hovered in the doorway, my face burning from the hot flannel, as the lady at the food counter closed the shutters. They didn't care about me. I turned away and found my way back to the receptionist, who was having a conversation with the man from the corridor, and asked her to come up to my room with me. She made an impatient gesture and told me to wait. I sat on the couch, dabbing at my swollen cheeks.

Felix and Hannah strolled into the lobby. Perhaps they *were* pleased to see me, after all! Hannah ran to me, hugged me, and shoved two jam sandwiches into my hand, greeting me in a mixture of Yiddish and English which made me laugh. We all went up to my room to look at the cold tap, which worked perfectly. Trickery was afoot. The man spoke to Hannah, who turned white and Felix turned red, but I saw her squeeze his hand, and he said nothing. Then the receptionist spoke to me, coldly.

'We cannot tolerate loose, immoral behaviour in our hotel. If you wish to stay here, kindly keep to your own room, and do not cause embarrassment to male members of our staff. I hope we will have no further "complaints" from you.'

I could see Hannah's face, behind her shoulder. She shook her head slightly, and put her finger on her lips. The three of us walked out into the street and she slid between us, hooking arms into ours; easing away my distress and fury. We went into a café and I washed down my sandwiches with a gallon of lemon tea. I felt important and interesting, for the few customers watched us curiously, and with a touch of envy, I thought.

'Hannah,' I said, 'why did they pretend about my tap? Why did they say those things about me?'

'We'll talk outside, Rachel,' said Felix softly. 'Don't be upset. Hannah says it's OK in Molodezhny – the park.'

Across the road was a public garden and a few benches. This was the old part of the town. The only modern building nearby was the hotel. We found an empty seat.

'Foreigners are always watched, Rachel,' Hannah said, Felix helping me to understand. 'There was probably someone in the café who knew who we were. Incidents are engineered sometimes, specifically to cause annoyance or irritation. I don't know why. It is no use asking or complaining. All rooms occupied by foreigners are wired to a listening device. Never say anything there which is private or detrimental to this country. It is not your fault – what happened there. They only look for reasons to send you home.' I shivered, but she held my hand so tightly that I felt better immediately.

'Felix, ask Hannah about the dining-room. Is that bristling with bugs as well? Do we have to whisper there, or be careful of what we say?'

They both nodded. Suddenly I felt gay and free. They hadn't been whispering to each other for any dark reason. I looked the seat over for secret buttons and peered up into the tree overhead, but I could see nothing peculiar. Suddenly, I thought of something. 'Does anyone listen when we talk in your room? Is it dangerous for you – for us – to spend time with you there? If the neighbours know we've bought you presents, can you get into trouble?'

'Maybe someone listens; maybe . . .' Suddenly she burst out laughing. 'I don't care any more! My friend is here! My family! I will not be a cardboard figure living in a shelter, without being able to stretch and breathe. I've done it for so long; stifled. Suffocated. Now I'm greedy for air and for freedom, and I'll never be able to do without it again. A butterfly can't creep back into the place where she was once a caterpillar. When I woke up this morning, I realized that. I'm too much like you, Rachel. We're not people who can keep our thoughts and feelings hidden behind black walls. It's horrible; self-destructive! I'm going to flap my wings! While you're here, we

178

must be minimally cautious, because I couldn't stand it if they sent you away before six days. After that, there'll be nothing that anyone can take away from me. I shall be Hannah Sokolovsky again – hoping! Waiting!'

'Waiting, Hannah? Waiting for what?'

'For the next visit. For my visit to you. I have found my past and my future. No one can take away my dreams or my plans. I will save those for the empty time. Six weeks ago, I thought I might never see you again. I didn't even know that I had a friend called Felix!' She looked so beautiful. So alive. Felix translated everything Hannah said, but I seemed to understand her without his help. When I was a child, I understood a smattering of Yiddish. I thought I'd forgotten it all. He talked to her. I only had to watch her listening to follow them. Didn't she know that she could never come to England, ever? I knew that. Didn't she? Had she forgotten that she'd been sent to prison for trying to leave? That there was no thaw in the Cold War for people like her, with a criminal record? Would Felix say anything? Would he dash her hopes? He mustn't. He mustn't ever do that. I'd speak to him later about it, when we were on our own. At least I'd still have Felix after these six days and he'd help me to live without Hannah. I'd fold up and die, otherwise. She was winding a strand of hair around her finger – a particular habit of mine. I'd lost the thread of the conversation. It was time to return to the hotel and meet our tour guide.

The taxi in which we had arrived the day before was waiting in the road outside, with the driver and a young woman standing next to it. Irene, our guide, gave Hannah permission to accompany us, and we squashed into the back seat while Irene sat in front, with the driver. She spoke perfect English, pointing out the buildings which had been heavily damaged by the Germans, the Civic Centre, the beautiful onion-domed churches, which she told us were only visited by old people. The younger ones had more education; more sense. Hannah pointed out the synagogue. Before the war, there were a hundred and five in this town. Now, all that remained was this one, a tiny crumbling building; the last, sad memorial of a vanished world. 'It is not a scheduled stop,' said Irene. 'It is of no interest to foreign tourists.'

Hannah touched Felix's arm and we knew that she would

179

take us later. The market square was full of stalls and barrows, and old people waiting in long queues for something to buy. The car stopped for ten minutes. Irene walked with me, and Felix and Hannah followed behind. 'The peasants are allowed to sell some of their produce here. They come from nearby villages. They live very well. They are better off than we who live in the towns. Would you care to buy anything?' All I could find were onions and cabbages, huge, strange-looking radishes, soft tomatoes and apples – and everlasting queues of old women. I told Irene that I would like to buy some fruit, since she told me that I wouldn't have to queue. I felt ashamed afterwards, because Irene pushed to the front, the long-suffering people stood back patiently, and I was served with a kilo of apples. I wondered if they resented and disliked me.

Our next stop was the big department store in the new part of town. There were no luxury goods in the windows. All I saw were a pair of shoes and dozens of identical hats. Certainly nothing gorgeous like the displays in Regent Street, but I couldn't tear myself away from the sight of the shop assistants using the abacus – conkers threaded onto thick wire with which they did additions at the speed of lightning. What a wonderful idea to buy one for the Blue Lagoon, where the till was always getting stuck! I enquired of Irene whether I could buy one, but she said that there were none for sale. There were blocks of new flats, all identical, except that each building had a different coloured stripe of paint across the front, already peeling off. Palaces, compared with Hannah's dingy block. One of the flats was called 'Zags' which was the Registration Office for births, marriages and deaths, and Irene told me that she was getting married there on Saturday. We all congratulated her. She smiled and thanked us politely, and spoke to the driver in Russian. He stopped on Dzerzhinsky Bridge, which she said was very interesting. Irene got out with us, while the driver stayed in the car. We leaned over the wall and looked down at the Neris River. She talked briefly to Hannah, then came and stood next to me. We strolled along the parapet.

'The driver does not understand English, but I prefer to speak to you out here.' I wondered if the car was bugged too. 'Your aunt tells me you are very kind and that you have a pair of stockings in your luggage, but I am not permitted to ask if I may buy them from you. I only ask you, because I am so anxious about my wedding day. I do not have anything special to wear. I have been an Intourist guide for five months and it is a very good job, but I will lose it if they find out that I have asked you for something. I hope that you are not offended, and that you will not tell anyone. I would like to look pretty for Saturday.'

'You *are* pretty,' I said, 'and I have lots of stockings, Irene. Everything we brought is for my aunt, but she will be happy to give you anything you need.'

'Perhaps just to borrow,' said Irene. 'I would be so grateful to you and to her. I would like to be her friend after you have gone. I could help her a little, too. I have never asked any of the foreigners for anything before, but you are young; you under-stand that I would like something frivolous for my wedding; for my honeymoon. There is nothing frivolous in the shops, but please, please do not speak about this!'

'I promise. Trust me.' I took her hand and squeezed it. Felix would be so pleased with my flush of generosity. Irene seemed to have taken a great fancy to me, and wasn't at all interested in Felix and Hannah. 'My job is very important to me too. I'm the manageress of a very exclusive restaurant and when I get married, I shall have my wedding party there. And I'll want to look my best, too. I understand, and Hannah will too. O, Irene!' I burst out, 'she'll be so lonely after we go home! I'll be so happy if you and she could be friends!'

'Yes,' said Irene, glancing towards Felix and Hannah who were leaning over the wall at the other end of the bridge. 'She will be very lonely. Your aunt is a Soviet citizen. Soviet citizens are not allowed to marry foreigners. I am glad that my fiancé is a Soviet citizen. Are you engaged?'

'Yes, but secretly!' I pulled out my chain and showed her my ring. 'That's why I understand how you feel.' She smiled at me so warmly that it was difficult for me to connect the two personalities – the cold, formal guide, and the friendly girl, talking so confidentially to me. She showed me a picture of her boy-friend, Petrov.

'This is your first visit here,' she said, as if reading my thoughts, 'so you do not understand that I could not take you to the synagogue. I am sorry. When we return to the hotel, ask if I may come up to your room, because you need some information about the shops for foreigners. The wedding celebrations for all newly-married couples are arranged in the dining-room of your hotel. I cannot invite you, but I would like you to join our party if you happen to be there after our marriage registration. Petrov and I and our families will have our party at seven o'clock on Saturday.' The driver honked his impatience, and she burst into a descriptive flow of language about the history of the bridge as we walked quickly towards Felix, Hannah and the car. She was staring at Hannah so oddly, that I looked too. Irene had tears in her eyes.

'What's the matter, Irene? Don't be upset about anything! Hannah won't let you down!'

'Poor Hannah,' she said. 'Poor girl. Tell her . . . tell her I will see her after we return from our honeymoon in Memel. We will be there for three days.' I found it difficult to follow her train of thought. Hannah looked radiantly happy. So did Felix. They were still leaning over the bridge. Holding hands.

We climbed back into the taxi, and drove towards Lenin Square and then down Traku Street, Irene advising us to visit the excellent local museum there. The Ethnographical Museum was also extremely interesting and we must be sure to go to the Revolution Museum, too! Not if I could help it! I was glad to note that Felix wasn't showing too much enthusiasm. I preferred walking in the street or talking in Hannah's room. We drove towards the hotel. 'The stop at Dzerzhinsky was unscheduled,' she said to Felix. 'Our driver was kind enough to stop for us, but the tour does not cover it. Please remember that tipping in this country is not allowed.' Felix immediately offered the driver several packets of cigarettes which he locked into his glove compartment. By this, I understood that all presents except roubles were gratefully if secretly, accepted.

The receptionist appeared quite amiable. Irene and I walked upstairs to my room, watched by the loathsome man in the corridor, but she said something to him, and he turned back to his newspaper. There seemed to be no difficulty whatsoever. My room had been tidied and someone had left the radio playing softly. I remembered what Hannah had told me about bugs in the room and turned up the radio to an ear-splitting pitch, but Irene immediately turned it down. I'd noticed that one couldn't turn it off entirely, with a satisfactory click. Why had she done that, knowing that we might be overheard? I shivered, suddenly, wondering whether I'd been tricked, but dismissed the idea immediately. She shyly accepted the gift of stockings, earrings and a silky set of underwear, which she crammed into her bag. In a moment of sublime inspiration, I gave her a dozen biros for Petrov. She hugged me, and whispered in my ear, 'I thank you, my dear, dear friend. I will be so happy on Saturday.'

Hannah was allowed to have lunch with us in the dining-room, as we had so many vouchers to spare. We were so gay, even though we were careful of what we said. A group of three young men sat smoking and drinking at a nearby table, and the man who lived on our corridor was eating bread and cheese at one in the corner. 'Could you take us to Yanovy, and to the place where Liubava used to be, Hannah? We've all been invited out on Saturday evening! I'll tell you about that later.'

'I've already asked permission for a trip. The receptionist will let us know this evening whether you are allowed to leave Vilnius.' I felt suffocated in the dining-room. I swallowed a last bite of black bread, spread with odd-tasting soft cheese, and we went out again into the street and walked towards the synagogue.

It was locked and shuttered, but an old man who lived nearby greeted us in Yiddish, and gave Hannah the key. He told us that he would follow us in five minutes, to show us round. The synagogue consisted of one room, lit and aired by a few broken panes of glass in the ceiling. You would have to use an umbrella here, when it rained, and it must be icy cold in the winter. The old man came in and unlocked the cupboard with another key. Inside were the scrolls and a cloth bag, tied with a knot. He proudly displayed the half-dozen tattered prayer-books and a shelf of memorial candles. Since the rabbi died, he conducted the prayers on Saturday morning. The government would not allow the building to be repaired or a new rabbi to take over. Would we like to buy a candle? Felix gave him a handful of change, and each of us lit a memorial light. The old man pointed towards the East and we recited the Prayer for the Dead. I told Felix to tell him that we would come again, to the service, but the man shook his head. 'There is no service this week.' He followed us out into the sunshine. By coincidence, one of the three men who had been drinking in the hotel was standing nearby. I nudged Felix and Hannah, and told them that he must be a Jew, too. Should we go over and say hello?

Hannah giggled, and shook her head, but Felix didn't smile. We said goodbye to our guide, and returned to the park. Our bench was vacant, but groups of young people sat on the others, watching us kindly and curiously, as if longing to come over to us and talk. Was something wrong? I felt anxious and didn't know why. Was this bench reserved for foreigners too? Hannah held my hand between hers, and spoke to Felix, but I couldn't understand her, this time. Then he spoke to me.

'Rachel, I am anxious too, although Hannah is not. She told me that the three men in the dining-room are KGB officials. They take pictures of us with cameras attached to the inside of their lapels. She doesn't care about herself. She refuses to take these spying activities seriously any more, and says they will never do anything to trouble us. That girl, Irene, what did she say to you? I'm so afraid for her.'

I told him and Hannah nearly everything that Irene and I had discussed and that we were all invited to her wedding party. 'We won't tell anyone of her. I've given her a few pairs of mouldy stockings, a petticoat and some beads to wear for Saturday. Big deal!'

'Don't be naive. I'm not afraid for *her*; only of her. I'm talking about Hannah! All Intourist officials are directly responsible to the KGB for information about foreigners. Do you realize that Hannah could go to prison if that Irene decides she wants it that way? She can say that Hannah plans to sell the gifts; that she tried to sell them to her! That's a criminal activity here, worthy of a nice stiff prison sentence! They'll watch her like a hawk from now on. Maybe they'll search her room. For years she's been afraid to trust anyone. Now we've brought her nothing but trouble! Me, for wanting to see the synagogue, and you, for blabbing out everything to that girl!'

I trembled with fear. 'Why didn't you warn me? What shall we do? What can we do? We've done nothing wrong. Nothing. Irene wants to be Hannah's friend; she told me. But if she makes trouble, I'll say how she asked me for the stockings. She doesn't want to lose her job. All she wants is to look beautiful for her wedding, but you'd never understand that! All *you* see is KGB, KGB, running through her like a stick of rock! You read too many stupid books, and you're just trying to give me the jitters. Hannah isn't scared. She saw you two holding

184

hands,' I added spitefully. 'She thought you were in love with each other, and told me that foreigners weren't allowed to marry Soviets!' This sudden enlightenment of what Irene meant drove me into a blazing temper. 'If Hannah gets into trouble, it'll be because you've been seen flirting with her! But she wouldn't dream of hurting Hannah. She's not spiteful, like you! She cried, because she was sorry for her being lonely after we go home. She asked to be Hannah's friend.'

They gabbled to each other. I was too upset to bother to try to understand. We would go back to England, and Hannah would go back to prison. I wanted to be in Hannah's room, talking and laughing. I remembered how Irene had turned down the radio. I was afraid to tell them, but realized I had to warn Hannah that I might have misplaced my trust; risk Felix's wrath again. I had learnt, by long experience, that if I had to admit to a wrong-doing, it was always wise to do so while in a fury. I turned on him with scorn. 'And you needn't worry about my having said anything upstairs in the hotel room. She turned the radio down, as a sign for me to keep my big mouth shut! And that's all I've got to say on the subject!' He could jabber to Hannah as much as he pleased, without telling me anything. I looked at her. She wasn't taking any notice of us. She was in a private world; one that I recognized from myself. From the expression I remembered when she was a girl. A light of battle in her eyes. The planning of some great mischief concerning impudence and courage. And there was something else shining in her eyes when she looked at Felix, or spoke to him. But I didn't know what it was. I hoped that right now, she was telling him off, and that on no account was he ever to be nasty to me again.

'Hannah says I must apologize to you for making you anxious,' said Felix. I should just bloody think so! 'Apparently she told Irene that it was all right to speak to you. It's a good sign that she turned the radio down. Stupid foreigners like us imagine that the volume drowns sound on the listening bugs, but it does exactly the opposite. Nevertheless,' he added, irritably and rudely, 'the pair of you are irresponsible children.' I told him to tell Hannah what he'd just said, but he ignored me. 'She doesn't consider or value her safety. She refuses to take her position seriously. Maybe you can knock some sense into her head. You're two of a kind. She insists that you are incapable of doing her harm, however innocently. You can only do her good. I hope she knows what she's talking about!' The radiance of her smile silenced him, and we walked back to the hotel, hand in hand. She held my hand just as she held Felix's. It was Hannah's way. I shouldn't have said those things to him about flirting. I hoped he hadn't been silly enough to translate nonsense that I shouted out, in temper.

The receptionist was again her usual sour self. 'No trips can be arranged outside Vilnius. It is sufficient that you see this town.' I felt like throwing a hot flannel in her face, but instead I copied Hannah, and smiled sweetly. 'You are eating at the hotel tonight.' I wasn't sure whether this was a question or an order. We smiled again, and nodded. She spoke to Hannah in Russian, and she sat down on the couch while Felix and I went upstairs. The man in the corridor was sitting on a chair, next to the toilet door, dozing. I went into my room and wrote a note to Felix in which I asked him what the receptionist had said to Hannah and whether we should smuggle some more clothes and desirable articles out of the hotel, then I slipped into his room, before the man could waylay me. Felix was busy writing a note to me, telling me to wear as many of the clothes as possible and that Hannah had been forbidden to accompany us to our rooms. I took the plug from his sink and slipped out, not caring whether the lout in the passage saw me or not. A stream of cold water came out of the hot tap and the cold tap was dead again. Needless to say, I preferred it this way. At least I could brush my teeth and wash my face. I dressed in a swimming-costume, underwear, two skirts, two blouses and two sweaters, and tied a rope of silk scarves round my neck. Compared to me, Felix looked overdressed. It was a mystery to me, why, when we were so obviously taking things to Hannah's, we couldn't just cart a suitcase along, but she assured us that we would be stopped if we did this.

When Hannah saw us emerge into the lobby, she turned her face to the wall, but I could see her shoulders shaking with laughter. The evening meal was exactly the same as the one we ate for lunch. I was sweltering, and glad to get out of the dining-room and into the open air. We took the short cut again, and arrived at Hannah's room gasping. Photographs standing in frames covered the table and another pile lay on her new rug. Two bags of shopping stood near the sink. She

186

must have been occupied with the pictures for hours after we left last night, and risen early to go and queue for food. She busied herself clearing the table of her pictures with Felix, while I undressed and dressed again. Hannah and I packed the wardrobe box with the new things and Felix unravelled himself on the rug. There was a knock at the door. Hannah whispered softly and quickly to him, and went to answer it. He pulled back the blanket and pillow from Hannah's bed, laid the clothes along the mattress and covered them up again, while I pulled down the wardrobe lid, and replaced the cushion. We managed the business in ten seconds, while Hannah stood talking at the open door, blocking us from the visitor's view. I could hear her voice quite clearly; friendly sounding and pleasant. Hannah drew her in and introduced us to her neighbour, Tanya. She knew no English, and I couldn't understand a word she said. She had brought a small bottle of vodka for a present, apparently, but didn't stay to share it. I learned later that she had been kind to Hannah, and looked after her when she felt ill, but that she couldn't stop; she just wanted to say hello to the visitors. She had to rush off to do night-shift at the hospital. I was very disappointed with Felix for not translating a word the woman said. What had come over him? He seemed different. Strange. Confused, as if he'd just stepped off the train and for a minute or two didn't know who or where he was. The knock must have startled him out of his mind. Was he afraid?

'Felix,' I said. 'What's the matter? Were you frightened that someone was coming to take Hannah away?' He bent down, and placed a photograph he was holding under Hannah's pillow. His face was flushed and his eyes were as bright as diamonds. Hannah was singing away, washing out glasses under the tap. He smiled at her back, then turned to me, and for a second held my face between his hands, as if puzzled by what he saw.

'No one,' he whispered, 'is going to take Hannah away. No one but me.'

Chapter Twenty-Eight

The man whom we'd seen outside the synagogue was in the Post Office, the next morning. He stood in line a few feet behind us. He was in the park, where we sat, in the street, where we strolled, in the museum which we visited, and on the bus in which we travelled to look at Hannah's place of work. But eventually we dodged him, and managed to take the remainder of our gifts for Hannah back to her room. I didn't know that this would be our last full day with her, but I think she did. After our tea, she took each photograph and told me again about the Paper Children, as though we were children again, and Felix looked at them, too; as if seeing them for the first time. As if, at last, they belonged to him. Liubava was only one of thousands of villages that had been destroyed, but it was ours, she said, for she could find no one else left to remember it. Yosef's, Sacha's, hers – and mine. Then she pulled out the fur hat she had made for me, my surprise present, from the bottom of her wardrobe, and put it on my head. I wore it all evening with the ear-flaps tied on top. She cried because she had no present for Malka or Sacha, Esther or Vered. And nothing for Felix or Yosef. Only letters. One each, which she would give to us tomorrow.

Felix held her in his arms and I lay down on Hannah's bed, and looked through the pictures again. How peaceful I felt, speaking their names, here, in this room, with Hannah sitting nearby, with Felix. Then she told us about the last time she had seen her mother and the family, and how she had finally been separated from Yosef. Stutthof. Her release. The searching and searching; and finally, her attempt to find us, her English family, and her imprisonment in the labour camp in Siberia.

She had been ill after that; ill in her mind, for criminals were never given permission to travel, especially if they were Jews as well. But since Stalin's death, there had been changes. Two years ago, the idea that we would be able to visit her would have been unthinkable. Maybe other unthinkable events could happen! She was better now. The waiting would be nothing to her, compared to what she had been through before our visit. Her soul was free, for she knew that she could hope to see us again. All of us. Miracles happened, and one day she would come to England; even go to America to see Yosef!

Felix sat at the table, quite still with his eyes closed, holding her hand. Hannah's gaze was fixed on him. She no longer wept, but was smiling and radiant. Then he spoke to Hannah in German, telling her about his parents. He took his Bar-Mitzvah picture out of his wallet and handed it to her. She held it for so long, that, watching her, I almost drifted off to sleep. I couldn't have dozed for longer than half a minute, for when I opened my eyes she was still holding the picture, and she was looking at me, then back to the picture, as if confused by what she saw. Then she stepped over to the bed and kissed the top of my hat and went back to Felix. She, too, seemed totally at peace, and a quietness pervaded the little room, so that I drifted off to sleep again – only for a minute – for I had no dream. They were sitting there, together, as if time had stopped. It was I who jumped when there was a knock at the door. Neither of them seemed to have heard it, and even at the second knock, they appeared unperturbed, as if both of them expected it, and were not surprised or afraid.

It was the man who had been following us all day. We must return to the hotel with him, he said. We would be leaving tomorrow morning on the ten o'clock train. Felix translated for me, and then whispered that I should make no objection. I turned to Hannah. Her cheeks were as white as paper, but she was quite calm. She untied my ear-flaps and put them over my ears, fastening the ribbon under my chin. '*Podozhdi!*' she said. I followed the man out into the night, and looked round for Felix. I saw him kiss her in the doorway.

The receptionist was still on duty when we returned to the hotel. She told us that our rooms were required, and we must be packed and ready to leave with our luggage in the lobby by nine-thirty in the morning. I took no notice of Felix telling me to be quiet. 'We have a visa for six days! We've only used half our visit! The hotel is almost empty! Why can't we stay any longer?'

'You have been here long enough,' she answered, coolly. 'There is no room for you here. Our driver will escort you to the train at nine-thirty.' She spoke like a robot, without sense or feeling. I hated her. I burst into tears and followed Felix up the stairs.

Hannah closed her door, and sat at the table until the colour returned to her cheeks. She did not go to bed. She took a writing pad out of her wardrobe, and a pen from her bag, and began to write. It was six o'clock when she stopped, and beginning to get light. She tucked her letters into her shopping bag, pulled the Persianelle coat out of the bottom of her box, rolled it up and squeezed it into her bag. Then she crept softly to her door, opened it and looked about her. Then she ran as fast as a boy to the bus-stop, and was waiting outside the warehouse where she worked when Zhivile came with the keys. They exchanged a few words with one another, Zhivile smiled and ushered her in to the empty store-room. A few minutes later Hannah emerged with her bag, holding her letters, and made her way towards the station. She bought a return ticket to Grodno.

Chapter Twenty-Nine

Hannah travelled with us almost as far as Grodno, the frontier town, where Felix and I would have to change trains and go through endless formalities, before being shuffled on to the Polish train, a thousand yards beyond the end of this railway line. There was no siding there; no sleepers to bind the rails together for easier connection of passengers and goods. Even the gauges were different, so no train from here could possibly travel there, anyway. During this, our last hour together, Hannah and Felix talked incessantly. Except for one or two lapses, he'd been tireless as an interpreter between us. Yet here they were, talking more animatedly than ever, cutting me out of these last minutes together. I looked from one to the other, but it was as if I wasn't there. I understood nothing. They were speaking quietly. Purposely excluding me.

I wanted to say to Hannah that I would come back. Year after year I would return. I would never do anything again which might jeopardize her well-being or give any cause for my not obtaining a visa. Hannah's history could not be erased. She would never be able to come to us. It would be cruel to discuss such an event; foolhardy to dream. Madness to plan.

The train was travelling so quickly now. I wore the present she had made for me, and she was wearing my personal present to her – an arty, lop-sided Star of David on a thin, overlong chain. I thought of that other necklace she had told us about, last night; the mouldy potato attached to a piece of string which she had tucked into the top of her rags; a postponed feast. It had been stolen by a fellow inmate in the labour camp, while she slept; cut free with a razor. When Hannah had cried on discovering her loss, someone had said she should sing for joy, because all that had been severed was a piece of dirty string – not her jugular vein. I'd been fifteen then, carelessly cramming my mouth with grub; the *News Chronicle* propped up in front of me, unaware of the anguish of my own flesh and blood. Now, I thought, these moments of reprieve from awareness of her sufferings are past. Her vitality has encroached on me again. How like me she was! The resemblance had made Felix gasp. Even our gestures were identical. She twisted the chain around the top button of her cardigan, another familiar habit of mine, then tested the points of the Star between her finger and thumb. I'd known she was going to do that. It was a symptom of agitation. We would be stopping any minute now. When she left the train, two miles before the check-point, she would cross over the bridge and wait for the Grodno-Leningrad train, which would take her back to Vilnius; to her room with its damp walls, bare, splintered floor-boards and ill-fitting cracked window. Though now she had a rug, new dishes and a shiny kettle, and dozens of smiling, paper faces to keep her company. And once she sold the gifts, she might be able to buy an armchair, a cupboard, a piece of lino for the middle of the floor. A radio! Perhaps she could have the stove mended so that it didn't fume so horribly in the winter. The winter! What would she be doing then? I closed my eyes and tried to imagine what it would be like for her; cold; all alone; waiting. For what? Forlorn; remembering. Jabbing the points of the Star between her finger and thumb.

Their tones were so low that the double strain of an alien, as well as an inaudible conversation separated me completely. Other people were in the carriage; perhaps that's why they were talking so quietly. There was no luxurious compartment for foreigners going in this direction; or perhaps we'd been banned from one, because of Hannah's presence. Felix would fill me in on what I was missing. We had so much to say to one another. So much. I wouldn't mind being excluded. How could I? Perhaps they wanted a private conversation, or just felt the need to talk effortlessly to one another. I watched them, happy to witness her animation; looking at her, as if through a mirror; examining my hitherto invisible self with indulgent affection. So this was how I appeared, when totally absorbed . . . surprised . . . delightedly startled . . . enchanted.

How lovely she was! I thought of Tolstoy's two little prin-
cesses; twins. One ugly and one beautiful because of a mole on
her lip. Hannah had the mole. Maturity; lines of suffering
round her mouth, now subtly and wonderfully adapted to joy.
But the beauty remained and shone so brightly that it stung my
eyes and I had to look away.

No! Don't let her love Felix! It would be too cruel; too
terrible for her! Wasn't it enough that she had to say farewell
and cross over to that barren, year-long, lonely platform? I
covered my face with my hands. Don't let her have to pine and
suffer more than what was inevitable. Don't embellish the
barbed wire of her solitude. Don't do that, Felix. Don't do this
to her; to me. I could hear the Soviet guards coming through
the long carriage. I could feel the train slowing down. When it
stopped, the silence would frighten and suffocate me, and any
disturbance would make me jump stupidly. This wasn't Adles-
trop, where no one left, and no one came. Hannah was leaving.
No blackbird sang. Don't make it worse for her!

I forced myself to look at her again. I couldn't look at him.
They had stopped talking. I would say something to cheer her;
to lighten her heart. I'm coming again next year, darling
Hannah! Sacha and Malka too! Think about that! Not about
Felix! He lives in England; you live here. He can't love you
back. It's not allowed. Even if you did live in England, he
couldn't. I live in the same country; I've lived in the same town,
the same village, the same house, and I know the limitation of
his emotions. I've known it all my life. Why can't you understand? You've never let me down before. Why are you so
abstracted and distant? Why have you separated yourself from
me, just because I'm going away? Why are you looking at him
like that?

I wanted to be cheerful and composed; embrace her without
tears and then wave to her gaily until she was out of sight; but
our imminent separation was so painfully shocking to me, that
Felix had to shove me back into the train, for I could not find
my own way. He remained with Hannah on the no-man's land
platform. I could hear the two officials speak to them sharply,
and then there was that venomous hiss again, cutting out
everything else. He leapt onto the train and dragged me to the
window. She was holding a flower; the one that Felix had
worn in his coat. She held it in both her hands, like a bride.

193

We had so little luggage. I kept thinking we had left something behind in the train, as, ten minutes later, we walked along the Great Divide. I scrabbled neurotically through the crammed partitions of my bag, wondering what the hell I was searching for. It was as if I'd put a half-eaten sandwich down, and my appetite could be assuaged only by finding it. Yet I could not. Felix walked ahead of me without looking round. A smiling man checked our passports and tickets, using one of the biros we'd given him a few days ago. He displayed the others in his shirt pocket and recognized us with pleasure. 'Felix! Look! It's Nicolai!' I felt ashamed of his lack of friendly zeal. It wasn't like him to be so distrait and unresponsive. Naturally I overdid the compensation, and felt angry with him for making me behave foolishly. We squeezed into a mucky carriage. Half the citizens were travelling to Warsaw. I left him standing on one leg in the corridor, while I went to check up on the plumbing, but there wasn't even a working toilet. I struggled back, knowing that everyone was making ill-tempered remarks to me, and I responded by swearing at them in English, which baffled and perplexed me. I could see Felix quite clearly although I was several yards away, separated by mounds of lumpy luggage, when the train started. I wanted to mark the occasion in some way; look out of the window – the same one as him – and think about Hannah, and perhaps hold his arm as I did so. His body jerked with the movement of the train, but he didn't turn towards me, or move his eyes to watch the passing platform. I wondered what steady vision his mind beheld. How odd, that though I had met Hannah only twice in my life, I could follow the harmony of her thoughts like a well-known melody, yet with Felix, I was all at sea, though I had known him for so many years. I reached him, and had to jog his elbow, to tell him I was there. He smiled and spoke my name; my island, my safe and secure anchor among this ocean of strangers. For a few seconds, I was able to see him as if I was she. The insight fascinated me but saddened me unutterably. She would be feeling so wretched. I would ask him later, why he had allowed this to happen; he was wise and kindly and totally without vanity. He could have acted in a way which would have prompted a different response; but his lack of conceit went hand in hand with a sort of naivety, which made him irresistible. Was this what Hannah felt, or what I felt?

194

'I love her, Rachel,' he said.

Really, I thought; the pair of them were totally irresponsible and emotionally immature. One didn't fall in love with a dream, otherwise reality became a nightmare. We were tearing through the open countryside now. What a leaden afternoon it was! There was a cottage plonked in the middle of a thousand fields. It was like a picture in a fairy story-book. Smoke spiralled out of the chimney. A girl holding a bucket stood watching the train, together with a story-book pig. I wondered if the pig understood Polish, and whether the girl could read and write. I looked around for a school, but there was no other building. A path from the cottage door wound this way and that, and then stopped nowhere and for no clear reason. I applied myself to considering a cause for this. Maybe the young woman and her pig were both obsessional or suffered from agoraphobia. I bet 'agoraphobia' is Polish for 'agoraphobia'. Words like that were the same the world over. One could have quite a sophisticated conversation with the other passengers if only one knew a few verbs and they had a smattering of Greek. I hadn't seen the cottage on the way out, but next year, I'd make a special point of looking out for it, to see whether they'd extended their boundary. I took note of the time, so that I could measure the distance to the next town. These deliberations temporarily outweighed in importance what Felix had just said, and at least a minute elapsed before I was able to give it my full attention. As a rule, I was patient and understanding, but I found it most difficult to suppress my irritation.

'I know,' I lied. The romantic, stupid fool had mingled us together; he'd worn himself out interpreting, and now was unable to distinguish between who was who. It was me he loved. The night that Tanya had called on Hannah, he'd expressed it clearly enough; holding my face; looking right into it, and telling me he'd take Hannah away, because he knew what she meant to me. He'd known Hannah for a few days, and me for years and years. His intelligence and realism were letting him down badly. The path he was following led nowhere, unless he examined it properly, trampled around a bit, and found that it led to me. Maybe that cottage path meandered a lot further than I'd perceived with my short-sighted eyes, and beyond the horizon lay a village with a friendly farming community, full of schools and dance-halls and potential boy-friends for the girl. The symbolism was getting me into a disturbing muddle. I must erase such nonsense from my thoughts, so that I could guide him tactfully into the direction of true self-knowledge and reason. 'You know that she can never come out, Felix,' I said gently. 'You do understand that, don't you?' What are you going to do?'

'Marry her.'

'Have you and Hannah discussed it?'

'Yes.'

'When?'

'Last night. This morning.'

'You're mad,' I said. 'And cruel. You know it isn't possible. You'll never get permission. I've got to sit down; I'm exhausted. Why the hell aren't there any seats on this vile train? Why do they sell us reserved seats that don't exist? These peasants may be used to this treatment, but I can't take any more. I can't even find a lav or a sink. It's disgusting! It's like being shuffled off to Auschwitz! I must have a drink. Where is our flask? Are you standing on it or is it in my bag? Well get it out then, for God's sake; I can't move my arms. No, I don't know which section it's in. Look in all of them. Why do you think it's called an 'organizer bag'? Organize it, and find me something to drink, before I drop dead!' I elbowed wildly at the people crushed against me, and then sat down on someone else's bag. I didn't give a damn about what they thought of my performance, and flew into a temper when Felix told me to shut up and behave myself.

'Plenty of these people have done their share in betraying three million Jews,' I yelled at him hideously. 'Do you think I give a damn about them, or whether I bring disgrace on the Union Jack? Don't kid yourself, either, that you pass off as the typical English gentleman! You're way out of your depth. They'd be tearing at us like dogs if they knew we were Jews. Do you imagine that if I offered that old hag over there my opal ring for a drop of water, she'd oblige? I can't stand the sight of them! Every time I manage to draw breath, I taste human ashes. What time are we due to arrive at the Bialystok graveyard? I'll shut up when you find me a seat, and not before!'

An elderly lady, wearing a black head-scarf, spoke to me so

196

kindly that I immediately started to cry, and then stopped very suddenly because she was speaking in English and must have understood everything I'd been saying. A cross swung from her scraggy neck. I would have to make it quite clear to her that I'd known all along that she understood English, and that she, of course, was not one of the people I'd been talking about. I must start ranting about righteous Gentiles, or better still, fling myself out of the window.

'You would like to drink something? This is good. Good taste.' She gave Felix a thick white cup to hold and poured some dark liquid from a large medicine bottle. What with the blundering train and her trembly old hands, it was a miracle that the engine driver didn't catch a mouthful, but not a drop was spilt. Her English was obviously very poor and she hadn't understood a word. Felix smiled at her and spoke to her in Polish about me, no doubt excusing and explaining away my behaviour, as if he was blameless and not responsible. They were conspirators. What if the old hag's concoction was seething with poison? Maybe it was Communion wine and after I'd drunk it, I'd have to kiss the cross. Worse still, it might be a most horrid old wives' laxative and that was all I was short of on this primitive locomotive, which nonchalantly ignored the fact that it was carrying people with physical needs. I thanked her most graciously, and took a tiny sip. It savoured of laudanum, a drug I had read about but never actually come across. I handed the cup back to her. 'Finish! Finish!'

'*Ma yesh?*' I said to Felix, hoping she didn't understand Hebrew as well.

'What do you think it is? Poison?' He couldn't possibly hate me as much as I hated him at that moment.

'You shout out the most venomous, scurrilous outrages at innocent travellers, and then get bashful about admitting you know what brandy tastes like. Stop assuming that everyone is as wildly and ignorantly vengeful as you. Drink it and shut up. I'll try to find you somewhere to sit after the next stop, but try to remember that you're not the only person with sensibilities!'

I drank the medicine, and immediately afterwards knew that I'd quaffed a dangerous drug. If I'd had room to wield a pencil, I could have written a sequel to 'Khubla Khan' in fifteen minutes. I understood why my fellow travellers could cope

197

with this mode of transport without complaint; they were full up to the gills with this marvellous stuff. I held out my empty cup to the old girl who had been standing all the time, while I lounged on top of her luggage. She had shoved the cork back into place and didn't seem to understand that I wanted more. Felix was still rattling away quite nonsensically. 'Tell her I want another dram; then give me a notebook and pen; I wish to compose a few verses.'

The scenery was flying past me, green and golden-brown, criss-crossed with red and black bars. I was mesmerized by this bizarre panorama and didn't even notice who took the cup out of my hand. I had never had a worse headache in my life, all hell concentrated in tip-top, classic migraine form, in the left hemisphere. 'Half in love with easeful Death.' The train was actually saying it, in English, over and over again, a second out of step with the words in my head, exacerbating my martyrdom. I fell asleep to escape the horror and woke up when I heard Felix tell me that we'd arrived at Bialystok and there was a couchette reserved for me a little further along the train. The guard would escort us to it as soon as I felt able to move. I'd fainted, he said. I was greatly cheered by this intelligence, having never done anything quite so impressive for years. He was suitably subdued and upset and helped me off the train so that we could walk along the platform to the appropriate carriage. The guard walked ahead of us holding one of our empty suitcases, while Felix carried everything else. I didn't care. I felt like a green jelly that hadn't been properly set, and it took all my energy to keep myself from falling to pieces. I longed to lie down and for someone to massage my left shoulder and temple with ice-cold fingers. We crawled back onto the train. I saw Felix give the guard some pound notes and the suitcase for a present. Perhaps these two narrow little beds were the ones we'd been stung for on our way out here, and which had never materialized. They were the sort of beds that the police used to accommodate unruly overnight visitors. Each was covered by a dirty grey blanket, but the pillow end was bordered by a crisp, white sheet. I hugged Felix, savouring the moment when I could crawl between the sheets and, with luck, faint away again. He extricated himself without hurting my feelings and pulled back the blanket for me, and I sat down while he bent down to take off my shoes.

He saw them before I did. By the expression on his face, I thought I'd dumped myself in the middle of a family of tarantulas and froze with terror. He pulled me quickly to my feet, knowing my phobia, yelling at me that there wasn't a spider in sight, so that I wouldn't swoon again. There were no clean sheets. The torn, stained mattress was alive with little red bed bugs. The top sheet was also non-existent. A six-inch strip, tucked craftily across the top of the dirty rag, was a hateful trick; a parson's collar worn by a vagabond. 'I'm going to find that guard and I'm going to kill him!' I shrieked. 'My head! My head! I'll die if I don't lie down!' The train jumped out of its skin, hurtling us against the window, and continued on its journey to Warsaw. The corridor outside our cubicle was packed with people again.

'Listen,' said Felix, 'we've got space and privacy here, and at least the bed bugs don't have any luggage for us to fall over. The pillows are OK. I'll sit on them, and you sit on my knee. Your neck muscles are in spasm, that's all! Once I've untangled them, you'll be better. Let's try it this way, first.'

He put a pillow on the floor and one on the bed. I knelt down and laid my head on his knees. I could feel his marvellous comforting hands kneading my scalp, neck and shoulders. I listened to the creaks and crackles as he eased the agonizing tension, talking to me as if I was a baby. Within twenty minutes I was ready to sit on his knee and go to sleep. I'd never sat on his knee before, and I was grateful to the guard and the bed bugs for giving me the opportunity.

I awoke from a nightmare which made reality feel like overwhelming luxury, peace and joy. After a gap of years, I had travelled the road which led through hell to an unimaginable horror. 'Save me! Save me!' I screamed.

'It's a dream, Rachel, only a dream! I'm here, holding you. There's my good girl, you're awake and safe. You've only been asleep for a few minutes. Tell me what it was,' he crooned, rocking me in his arms, 'and it will go away and never come back.' He kissed my sweating forehead, penetrating the coating of ghastly terror.

'The road! The stone men!'

'Where is it? Who are the men? Tell me and I'll smash them to pieces. I'll break their damned necks and tear up the road so that you'll never go there again.'

I told him about my dream; how it had blighted my childhood with its undisguised, undiminished evil. 'Hannah knows the place,' I babbled insanely. 'Palmnicken! Palmnicken! I don't want to go there. I want to go home! O, Felix, darling Felix, thank God you're here! I'm so glad to be awake and to be alive and to be with you. Where are we? Do you know?'

'Yes,' he said. 'We're on our way to Warsaw – on our way home. I'll be with you all the time; every minute.' I could feel his knees shaking and wondered why his face had gone so white. 'What do you mean about Hannah knowing the place?'

'I always muddle people up in my dreams – almost as much as you do in reality.' The pain in my neck had gone, along with the agonizing headache and the gruesome dream. 'Sweetness and light is my name from now on. I won't be a pain in the neck any more.' I fell asleep again and woke, completely refreshed, as the train pulled in to Warsaw.

Chapter Thirty

We had three hours to wait for our connection in East Berlin. Arriving there in the early dawn, it was unrecognizable. I found it difficult to believe that this was the same place we'd been at, five days ago. I wondered if the Russian students were playing chess and thinking of us. I hoped Felix wasn't preoccupied with the memory of my behaviour. The few people who had left the train here had all disappeared. They had better things to do than sit on this dreary bench. It was quite chilly and I put on my Russian hat, trying it out with the ear-flaps down, and then with them up, tying them on the top of my head with the black tapes. We only had two suitcases to carry now. Felix had given one away and left the rest for Hannah.

'There's no sense in sitting here,' he said. 'Let's find a "Left Luggage" place and go for a walk. Think of the luxury of stretching our legs and finding a café. We'll gorge ourselves with gallons of coffee and rolls and butter and jam, then see something of the city and the people. Would you like that? Your hat looks extremely chic with the flaps up. Come on!'

'Does it look horrible with the flaps down?'

'No. It looks good like that too.'

'Then why did you say it looked better with them up?'

'I didn't, but it does. Listen, I'm not going to sit here talking about that hat for ever. We've got more important matters to discuss.'

'You're very German in many ways,' I said maliciously. 'Please don't give a thought to anything that is important to me. Naturally, it's of no moment to you how I look. I'm frivolous and shallow and my mind can't embrace weightier matters. Nevertheless, I'm not moving from this place. It's bad enough that we've got to travel through this country, but I am certainly not embarking on any pleasure trips here. And I'd rather starve than eat in one of their beer gardens.' I was dying of hunger and thirst. I fiddled with the tapes of my hat, winding them around my ears, hoping he'd be nice to me and persuade me to promenade with him towards the nearest café.

'You're quite intolerable,' he said. 'If you're determined to sit here, sulking, perhaps you'll keep an eye on these. I'll see you in a couple of hours. Hang on to your own tickets and passport, just in case we get separated.' He shuffled through the pack of rubbish in our travel wallet and handed me a bunch of it, then walked away without a backward glance, leaving me on the deserted platform. He had looked at me with chill distaste; my darling, everlastingly patient, affectionate Felix, not caring whether I was here or not when he returned. Obsessed with Hannah; repelled by me. My life was over. I would die if I considered this personal catastrophe for another moment. But I wouldn't let them shovel up my bones in this forsaken city. Too many of us were crammed in their godless pits. I ran after him, leaving all the paraphernalia on the bench.

'I'm coming! Felix! Felix! Wait for me! Don't leave me all alone! Why are you so nasty to me?' This affecting appeal was bound to disarm him. His heart would melt and he would turn and race back to me; hold me in his arms and cover me with passionate kisses. He'd do it if he was a character in a book, wouldn't he? I wasn't going to be some damned tragedy queen left all alone in the last chapter, dedicating my soft, sloppy heart to good works. My heart was a flea which bounced up and down in a confined space because it couldn't help itself, and it would go on bouncing until it had latched on to Felix. He could scratch for ever, but he'd never be rid of me. He'd catch the plague from no one else. Once I'd written to Hannah about my passion, she'd loosen her hold on him. She loved me too much not to. And I'd make him see sense and acknowledge the error of his ways. I'd wear him out with the energy of my devotion, until he succumbed.

He walked slowly back towards the seat, keeping his head averted, not seeing me hovering by his side. God must have boomed spitefully down his ear that he'd turn into a pillar of salt if he heeded me. I dodged in front of him, forcing him to

202

look at me, so that I could tell him I was sorry and that I loved and needed him with me always. And then I knew. He thought of me as his sister; his favourite, but none the less, his sister. But I wasn't. I'm not. He'd got it all wrong. Why was he so obtuse? If I embraced him; kissed him in an unsisterly way, which was what I longed to do, what would happen? I'd try it and see. And if he recoiled in embarrassment and disgust, I would lose him for ever. He would never meet my incestuous gaze again. Through his blurred vision, I saw her standing on the platform, holding a flower; waiting for a train which was not on the time-table, but with absolute certainty that there had been an official error and that one day it would arrive. He walked towards her, and I gasped because I realized he could not see her as I did. She was singing to herself; I knew the melody, but could not hear it. 'Hannah!' I screamed. 'Darling Hannah! There's no need to be frightened or lonely! He's coming back for you!' I snatched off my hat and waved it at her. 'This winter! I'll give him this to wear! It's all right; it's *all right*! Be happy! Be happy!' I shouted idiotically. Tears were pouring down my face, soaking my neck, as if I was in the throes of some unidentified sorrow. As if I would always be his sister; his accomplice; he, my unrequited love. The sense of *déjà vu* enthralled me, effacing my present self, as the station clock struck. The loose cog in my mind slipped back into place. Felix wiped my face with his handkerchief and put the hat on my head, tying the ear-flaps stylishly on top of it. 'We'll miss the train if we move from here,' I said.

'We've got three hours,' he smiled. '*Three hours*. Since when have you been so frenetically punctual? We hung around in Warsaw long enough and we're not going to repeat the same performance here. We'll dump the bags, just as I said, then we'll walk or take a taxi to the nearest coffee shop. You can close your eyes if you don't want to see anything or anybody. Of course I'm not going to leave you by yourself! But I'm not staying in this miserable, draughty, foodless station for their benefit again. I've done with creeping into cold corners, and it's you I want to walk and talk and eat with. Not them.'

We went out into the street. Grey-faced men and women were already walking towards the factories. It was only in Britain that people rose at a reasonable hour. Here they went to bed with the hens and rose with the cockerel.

'I wonder what Hannah's doing now; what she's thinking about.'

'I'll tell you,' I said. 'She's going back to work this morning. Now that we've left, she's saving up her free days for the next important event. She isn't gloomy or lonely. People are never lonely when they know absolutely that someone they love is thinking about them. She'll be dressed by now, and brewing up the Lyons coffee in that little blue jug. She won't waste a grain. People melt gold the way she makes coffee. She'll sit on the bed with both hands round the new cup, sipping it very slowly; relishing every drop. It's got to last her for months. Now she's put it away on the shelf. She isn't sad – she's just missing you; in fact, she's madly happy. She's wearing her chain; it's tucked into her blouse, but *she* knows it's there. She's putting her stripy jumper on top and now she's having a look at that snapshot of you. She'll wear it out if she looks at it so often. Now she feels composed and comforted. The flower is in a glass on the table. There! Now it's time for her to leave.' I would have put my hand on my heart and sworn that Felix had always listened to me with the maximum of attention, but I knew now that I'd been wrong. My monologues had hitherto been spilling over with wise precepts and pronouncements; jam-packed with penetrating truths and astute observations. And here I was, babbling mawkishly; filling his ears with self-evident commentary, and his focus on me was total; the difference, immeasurable. We were supposed to be looking for a café. I saw it before he did. 'Look! Isn't that a place?' It was a small, dark establishment, with a counter and four wooden tables. 'Do you think she'll take English currency? If we tell her we're Jews, she might ask us for a few shillings for the gas.'

We walked in and he spoke to the woman, who greeted us with courtesy and friendliness. The Blue Lagoon should send their staff here on a training scheme. Sterling would suit perfectly. The café was heated by an oil-stove, and it was warm and clean. We were obviously her first customers of the day. We sat at a table, after Felix had given her the order. I worked hard at smoking a Russian cigarette which was a hollow tube, devoid of tobacco.

'Don't stop talking, Rachel. Please! Go on with what you were saying.' I'd tell him that I was making it all up; trying to impress him, as usual.

Talking a lot of old nonsense, because I didn't want him to feel wretched, like me. His eyes were burning like torches, boring into me, and his hand which covered mine was cold and trembling. He always knew when I was lying – I did it so often. But I couldn't now. I was committed to the straight and narrow with him looking at me like this. I nearly always regretted telling the truth; it invariably did me colossal damage. I chafed his hand between both my own and kissed it, pretending to be his sister; his step-sister. The frau brought a jug of coffee, a basket of rolls, a large jar of beetroot jam and two omelettes. I crammed half a roll into my mouth and followed it with a spoonful of jam for starters. It tasted delicious. The serviette was a tiny square of woody paper which scratched my mouth. I poured us both a cup of coffee and cut into my omelette. It was quite impossible to hold a conversation. It would be too vulgar and outlandish and my manners, greed and discretion kept me silent for five minutes.

'Do you remember when we were on the number 4 bus on Traku Street and Hannah pointed out the building where she works? That huge warehouse? I reckon she'll be clocking in about now. Her job sounded so tedious. She sits at a table writing out coloured labels for each day's delivery; white for Monday, blue for Tuesday, pink for Wednesday, green for Thursday and yellow for Friday. Day after day, week after week, she does the same old thing. It's Green Thursday today. She'll write out hundreds of tickets and then she'll take a great pile to the stapling machine, and she'll sit there, stapling, not having to think about what she's doing, but she won't be bored; she'll welcome the two hours' worth of mindless tedium so that she can indulge herself, thinking about you. She's not hopeless any more. She won't dwell on her horrible past; only on the marvellous future. On you. When we were in the Post Office, lining up for stamps, she said hello to her neighbour and spoke a few words. That was the woman who came shouting and banging at her door, telling her that someone long lost to her had turned up in Yanovy and was alive and well. She was unable to speak or move. Her heart banged into her throat. She thought, a relative; a brother; her niece; her mother. A miracle. Then Mrs. Khusnev told her it was Elizaveta, a girl with whom she'd gone to school. She almost expired from disappointment, but she had to pull

205

herself together and pretend to be glad. But now, if that sensationalist came to Hannah and said, 'Someone you love is here', she'd think, Felix! Felix! and her heart would drum in her ears and she wouldn't be able to utter a word or move a muscle. She wouldn't have to pretend to be glad. Not if it was you! We've got to talk; to plan; to find a way. We can't pretend that it hasn't happened and that she'll come to terms with her life before you. She can't. She's too like me. I can't.'

I stuffed another roll into my mouth. 'Ask Frau Schmidt for some cheese, tomato and cucumber, dear love, and perhaps a further gallon of this liquid; I'm quite dehydrated from listening to you talking. I would also appreciate the recipe for this jam. Perhaps she'll sell us a jar so that I can analyse the contents. It's so singularly delicious.' She wrote it out for me; I knew that I'd never make it. It was full of beetroot and nuts, lemon and complications. I sat there, scraping at my mouth with the wooden table napkin, watching her; smiling; showing interest and friendship. All the signposts in my life that I had thought of as being of consequence were dwarfed into insignificance. There was no way back – no retreat from my miserable commitment. I'd have to wear the sickening smile of suffering and self-sacrifice for the rest of my life; overturn my personality; train as a saint. And no one would see my halo. Only me. When I got home, I'd buy a huge pan and brew up a hundred jars of jam and send them off to friends and enemies, anonymously. It would be excellent practice and help me to prepare for the fifty forthcoming years of unacknowledged generosity and altruism. I wouldn't even write the date on the lid, in case the recipient might recognize my handwriting.

We walked out of the café carrying refreshments for the remainder of the journey. I pretended to close my eyes so that I wouldn't have to look at my surroundings – and so that I would have a reason for holding onto his arm. I was just profound enough to recognize how superficial and shallow I was. He led me into a small park and we sat down on a seat. A group of children came towards us, chattering and calling to one another. The girls wore tiny pleated skirts and the boys, very short leather trousers. One of them was a mongol, but they didn't notice, and nor did she. As they jostled past us, one called out, 'That lady had a funny cat on her lap!'

'It isn't a cat. It's a hat!'

206

They watched carefully as I stroked it and spoke to it softly and affectionately, then they screamed with joy and fright when I suddenly chucked it at them. I longed to squeeze them; they were so adorable. The little mongol girl must attend their school, too; as an equal. Perhaps as an experiment. These kids would never believe in euthanasia. I wouldn't close my eyes again.

'Tell me what you saw on the platform,' he said. 'Tell me how you know her thoughts and the details of her past. The woman in the Post Office greeted Hannah, but she never told us that story. I would have remembered it too. I didn't know about Blue Tuesdays and Green Wednesdays. What language do you understand, that I don't?' His voice was so low; I had to lean against his shoulder in order to hear.

'Green *Thursdays*; Wednesday is *pink*. I saw Hannah on the platform. She was waiting for a train, I think. There were people with her; her mam and the two tiny girls, but they went away and she was left all by herself. Then I saw that she was waiting for you. She was singing a lullaby, the one her mam sang to her after a nightmare. I learned it from her when I was three. If I could hear it again, I'd be happy, like her, but I can't remember the melody. Every time she sees Mrs Khusnev, she feels sick with guilt and grief, but she got over it after she said it to me in the Post Office. She didn't say it out loud – or about the details of her work in the warehouse. But I know. The chairs and tables and dressers that have to be delivered today, have green tickets tied to them. I can see what she does and how she thinks as if I was watching her in the pictures. I understand, without subtitles, but I don't know why. I've never known why. Her mind jumps into mine without warning; without trying; without thinking. As if I'm her.'

'Oh, Rachel, what would I do without you! Where would I be without my interpreter! I felt that closeness between you all the time the three of us were together. It fascinated and delighted me. You, the worst linguist in the world, understood before I'd finished translating; before I'd started. It was all too easy. It was the same for Hannah. Is it reciprocal, then? Does she know about you, the way you know about her? Can she tell what you're thinking sometimes?'

'No.' The idea had never occurred to me before. I sincerely hoped not.

'What's going to happen? You mentioned . . . you . . . she was hopeful about the future.'

'We can't do anything about that while we're idling in this park,' I said prissily. 'What's come over you, Felix? You're so irresponsible suddenly. We're going to miss the train!'

We ran out of the park and along the road towards the station. The train was already standing there. The police and their dogs were pacing up and down, peering under the train for unauthorized passengers. I wondered if they understood the cruel irony of their predicament; perhaps uniforms dulled the sensibilities of their wearers. Our tickets were examined with extreme care and our paltry luggage scrutinized for drugs, guns and secret codes. They could search until they were blue in the face. All my nerve pills had been digested long ago. It took four hours to do the next hundred miles and we were checked up every hour. Would the kids from the park grow up to be policemen? One of the dogs was called Adolf. The train stopped an interminable number of times, often in the middle of nowhere; unscheduled, so that Adolf could sniff out a non-existent stowaway. The image of someone clinging to the underneath of this train; the desperation of such a traveller being tormented into taking this horrifying risk, made my blood run cold. Apparently it was a common occurrence. Each time the train stopped and I heard the dogs barking, I pushed my way into the corridor and opened a window, wondering how I could distract the attention of the meticulous searchers if it proved necessary, and each time I was told to return to my seat. How could one, ever again, enjoy a railway journey? How would we ever be able to get Hannah out? It would have to be by legal means. I wanted to talk to Felix, to ask him about his plans, but I couldn't do it yet; not until we were out of the Eastern Sector. The old woman sitting opposite might have a listening device stuck in her hat and the old man with her had probably stuffed his walking-stick with microfilm. What reason had I to feel melancholy? I was going home to my family and friends and to trains devoid of policemen and aggressive dogs – and to help Felix and Hannah pave the way for their lives together.

Chapter Thirty-One

He had never been like this before – so affectionate, so dependent and so selfish. During the long, miserable train journey through Holland, he talked of her incessantly. As far back as I could remember, I'd longed for someone to talk to me about Hannah; to share my troubled thoughts about her life and to comprehend the strange invasion of it into mine. Now this great feast was laid before me, and though I was greedy for it, it seemed as if every morsel was soaked in a concoction of bitter herbs. And I had fantasized about his need of me; his utter reliance on my strength, wisdom and manifold charms. I had almost everything and had thus been cheated of everything.

He questioned me about every detail of her past life, as if he hadn't heard it all before, on our last night, from her lips. But he wanted more. He wanted to dredge up my insight into her sufferings and character; to go over with me, interminably, their conversations and the extent and depth of his love for her. I tried my best to remind him that he had known her for little more than two days, and that his behaviour was rash; out of character.

'Why do you pretend not to understand one minute, and be so perceptive the next?' he asked. 'It's as if I've known her all my life, but I've been afraid; closed. I'm no longer the man I was last week. Then, I secretly scorned those who allowed their emotions to thrive freely. It's a shameful confession to make, because now I can tell you everything. You're the only one who's known her through and through; who's always known her. What happened to me when I stood on the platform and saw you both running towards me? It's beyond

209

analysis! She looked so radiant; so alive and beautiful; the sight of her broke my heart.' If it's beyond analysis, why bother to try? Let me glare out of the window and ponder on the destruction of my own damned heart, which you've smashed to smithereens. 'Then everything swung into place, as if the laws of gravity were defied. Into exactly the right place!' How's that, then? Explain the mechanics of it to me in detail, so that I can pull one of my painfully jagged remnants from beneath your feet; your stamping, clod-hopping, insensitive feet, so that I might live through the next five minutes. 'Once before in my life, I thought that I might have been in love, but that seems so ridiculous now. So paltry.' So you broke faith with me before, did you, Felix? Couldn't you have told me about that occasion at the time of its conception, development and death, so that I could have prepared myself to withstand this? I could have guided you wisely; steered you clear into a path leading directly to me. 'I understand that, now. One doesn't *think*. If one thinks, then it means you're not. I can't understand my past emptiness and stupidity. How many people, I wonder, settle for the "thinking" instead of the "being"? Who have the misfortune never to know the difference? You never would, Rachel. You're too wise and uncluttered. It's marvellous, talking to you; looking at you. You remind me so much of her. Even if you didn't, I'd love you, because you love her. Why are you looking at me like that? Of course I love you, just as I think, I'm sure, that you love me! O, Rachel! I'm so fortunate; so blessed! Just imagine what it would have been like, if Hannah hadn't been waiting for me, too. Searching, searching, and not quite knowing for what, until you took her hand, and showed her! We experienced the same miracle at the identical moment, and you were our catalyst! I love you for that!'

Maudlin, stupid, cruel, blind Felix! Kiss me, then, as you kissed her! Why had I pretended not to understand? We will be sharing the same cabin tonight. If I woke up and found you next to me, I would turn towards you and hold you in my arms and make you forget about Hannah. I would cancel her out with my equivalent powers. But if I came to you, you would writhe away from me in horrified embarrassment and utter wretchedness. Do you know what happened to me on the platform, this morning, in East Berlin? It's beyond analysis, so

I won't bother to distress you with a drivelling attempt. I would like some advice, though, on what I should do with the rest of my most horrid life, without you. Without Hannah; for she has betrayed me, too. Without even the comfort of confiding in you; of telling you all about it. I've never been able to keep a secret. It's too hard! I can't!

I pretended to fall asleep on his shoulder. He put his arm round me, so that my head could rest more comfortably. I wondered if the other passengers thought we were lovers; if it had occurred to Hannah that she had destroyed every possible chance of happiness for me. Did it work both ways – this burdensome perception? It had never consciously occurred to me that this could be possible, until Felix had asked me about it. It wasn't! She would never have allowed this to happen if she knew me as strangely as I knew her. She was just as painfully ignorant as he was. Lolling on his shoulder, I tried out endless possibilities for them. Letters – censored – love letters, written daily, albeit a fraction of them getting through from the writer to the recipient. Censors were human, lazy and careless. And, perhaps, romantic. Felix would be able to go to Leningrad in his capacity as a freelance interpreter. They could meet up at Pulkova airport. Hannah would risk anything to see him. She hadn't managed to survive by sitting back and wringing her hands. She was now a woman of fortune compared with her position of a mere week ago. She'd find out who to approach with the fine gifts we'd brought. The petty police who trailed after her would report her. Perhaps she'd lose her job. And if they applied for a marriage licence, she'd be bound to, and anyway, Soviets were not permitted to marry foreigners, were they? Irene had told me that. Irene had seen that they were in love. She had a man who loved her, so she could see what had happened, while I looked at them through blinkers.

What if they did get married? What then? The Secret Police wouldn't stand there, smiling and throwing confetti, then push them into a beribboned wedding car, with an old shoe trailing behind, and give her an exit visa as a present. But Hannah could be trusted to do everything possible to get her way. She'd been without someone to love for too long and had nothing else to lose. A few years ago, it was out of the question for people like us to visit a relative. The position had thawed, and the USSR wasn't totally ice-bound. Maybe Felix could defect or whatever one did to be with the person they loved, or to live in a country they loved. I'd spend the rest of my life in an igloo if that was the only way we could be together, and convince everyone that I was mad about igloos. A fat chance I had of proving myself! Hannah wasn't my auntie for nothing. *She'd* prove herself all right! I pictured them living in Hannah's room together, happily ever after, and every two years I'd pay them a visit and dandle their kids on my lap; a smile on my twisted lips. Rudi would want to come too; to visit his brother, and I'd let him trail along with me, getting on my nerves; aggravated and sulky, because he'd have to accept that I knew how to go about these matters better than he did; that I was experienced as a traveller to these parts. Why hadn't I suggested that he came with us on this trip? Hannah might have fallen madly in love with him, and he with her. I would have engineered it and given them both a shove in the right direction. Then Felix would have turned to me. Rudi was quite good-looking, if you liked his type; almost as handsome as Felix, if you tried hard at convincing yourself. What was the use of thinking this way? None of my pictures had any reality. None! Let Felix conjure up a way of getting Hannah out. It was beyond me.

'What's the matter, Rachel? I know you're not asleep. Why are you crying? Tell me! Have I said something to upset you? Don't keep your trouble to yourself. You don't have to keep anything at all from me. You know that!' Tears were bursting out of my closed eyes. I turned my head more towards him so that I could wipe my face against his jacket, and opened my eyes. The photograph was in his top pocket. I could feel it against my cheek. I pulled it out and looked at it. Hannah and me. I wiped my face with his handkerchief. I wouldn't keep my trouble to myself any longer. I couldn't. 'Ever since this photograph was taken, you've been waiting to see Hannah again,' he said. 'It must have been almost as hard for you to leave her as it was for me, and all I've done is think about myself missing her, and not once of how you feel. We'll see her again, soon; I promise you that. I've got so many friends who can advise me at work about what procedures to follow. I'll think of and work at nothing else. We'll get married. With luck on my next but one visit. There have been people who have made it to the West under these circumstances. There's been a

212

lot of easing up recently. Loopholes in the law of forbidden marriages. Maybe this time next year, she'll be travelling back with me.' How could he be so naïve, I wondered. 'O, Rachel! Think of that! Think of that, and be happy!'

We stood up then, for the train had arrived at The Hook of Holland. All that lay ahead of us now was the overnight boat trip to Harwich, then the three-hour journey to London. I'd stay with Danny and Aliza overnight, then Felix would take me to King's Cross. I'd be back at home the day after to-morrow, telling them all about our trip. They'd have been thinking about me all the time; me meeting Hannah at last. They'd hang on my every word. I'd write long letters to Esther and Vered. All the customers and staff at the Blue Lagoon would tell me how lovely and quiet it had been while I was away, and I'd laugh and open the bottle of vodka I'd brought with me, and everyone would get a little drunk, and Mike would play a Russian tune or two on his mouth organ, and then everything would be just as usual. Esther would rush home on the first available weekend, to hear about my adventures, and Vered would write to Mam and Dad asking if I was better, now that I'd seen Hannah again, and weren't we all delighted that Felix had found his true love at last, and could anything be more wonderful than that it should be Hannah! Rachel must be revelling in it all and showing off shamelessly about how she'd planned it and what a marvellous match-maker she was.

'Yes,' I said. 'Yes. I'll think of that, and be happy.'

Chapter Thirty-Two

We didn't sleep on the boat although this time we had the cabin to ourselves. Felix spent practically the whole night writing a letter to Hannah, sitting on the edge of his bunk and resting the paper on a book balanced on his knees. When he left the cabin for a few minutes, it lay there, carelessly available for me to sneak a quick read, but I couldn't understand a word. I wrote to her too; a beautiful and affecting letter, describing our journey home and how we both talked and thought of her constantly. I gave it to Felix to read, so that he could translate it and check that I had said nothing which might cause the censors annoyance. He said that it was a lovely letter and Hannah would think I was right next to her, talking. I thought that he might have had the common courtesy to read his letter out loud, in English, but it must have slipped his mind that he'd said he could tell me everything. It was late before we lay down to rest, but sleep evaded us both. Now that this journey was over, he would stay in London, without me, and from there fly off to all sorts of glamorous places; mix with clever and intellectual friends and acquaintances and think about Hannah. Once I was back in Hull, I'd be outside his orbit. I would only rarely cross his path, let alone his mind. We were lucky if we saw him three times a year. I couldn't bear the thought of the endless weeks and months ahead without him, now that I didn't have our trip to look forward to.

'Will you come home for your next vacation? I feel so worried about Rudi. I think he misses you. He's changed so much, lately. He practically lives in the hospital, thank goodness, but when he does come home, he's so rude and overbearing. Sometimes, I wonder how I put up with him. Mam and

Dad have spoilt him outrageously, of course, and in some ways it's better that Esther and Vered aren't living in Hull, because they dote on him sickeningly. Do you remember how they all started on me, but Rudi was the little blue-eyed boy? Well, it's just the same as it ever was. They've stunted his development. I happened accidentally to see a letter that he'd written to Vered. He signed it, Ever Your Devoted Brother, and he told her I was just as bossy as ever. He's the one who's bossy. He's spoilt rotten. Mam and Dad boast about him to everyone. They're proud of you, too, but they don't go on and on about you, the way they do about him. They get on my nerves. I can't talk to them about him, because they jump down my throat at the faintest hint of criticism. Dad actually said that I was jealous and that I had a short-sighted soul! That I couldn't see what a good and honourable man he was! Can you credit that? They're not in the least proud of me. They're ashamed, because I'm not clever like the others. They don't go around telling everybody that I work at the Blue Lagoon, even though I'm practically the manageress. God knows how they've coped there, while I've been away. It's "Vered's working on a kibbutz now, but she had a place at Jerusalem University. We're very happy about her engagement, of course. and Esther; well, she's still a bit wild, and never did a stroke of work at school. Learning came to her too easily. She won an Exhibition Scholarship. To Oxford, you know. The boys? They're a credit to us, and to their parents, may their souls rest in peace. Felix was always brilliant at languages. He works as a simultaneous interpreter, and goes to important conferences all over Europe. He's always in demand. And Rudi qualifies this year as a doctor. He could hardly speak a word of English when he came to us. Look at him now! He's as dear to us as if he were our own!" They go on and on and on! They can't bring themselves to talk about Sybil. Not to other people, anyway. Only to each other. I pulled out my trump card. "I wish I'd died instead of Sybil." I do wish you'd come home, so that you could put Rudi in his place!' His mind was elsewhere. He'd stopped really listening to me, unless I talked about Hannah.

'You've always been much better at managing Rudi than I have. Can't you see he's . . . Can't you see he's a man now; not a child. Nearly twenty-four. Not eight! And I'm not really that close to him any more. People go their own ways when they're adult. Relationships change; grow cooler or develop. It was different when we were all kids. He's no longer your responsibility and you're grown up, too. Maybe it's time someone should tell you a few home truths, but that's up to Rudi.'

'Up to him? *Him? He* needs telling, not me!'

'Look; perhaps you should think about a career for yourself. You could go to night school. Didn't you once tell me you'd like to be a . . .'

'I've changed my mind. I don't want to study for anything. I haven't got the head for it. I'll stay at the Blue Lagoon. There's nothing wrong with that. It isn't such a terrible hole! Rudi comes in nearly every day for a cup of coffee and an egg-roll, and no one's more fussy or finicky than he is! You've never once been there! Not once! Come back to Hull with me tomorrow, Felix. Just to say hello to everyone. Just for one day!'

'I can't, Rachel. I've so much to do; to plan; to think about. Sacha and Malka will understand that, once you tell them about Hannah and me. You'll be able to give them all the news without my butting in, and exaggerate the horrors of our journey to your heart's content!'

'Why do you talk to me as if *I* was eight? I'm a woman, for God's sake! Can't you get that into your head?'

'One gets hooked on images of the past, Rachel, and yet . . . and yet when I first saw Hannah and you together – just for a fleeting moment – I saw you quite differently, as if you and she were parts of the same person, fusing; she giving you maturity and you giving her youth. I couldn't distinguish between you. The confusion was like a marvellous dream, except that the awakening was even more delightful. When I came to my senses, I recognized two entirely different individuals, each with her own personality and disposition, and although the physical similarities are remarkable, that wasn't what disconcerted me. You both shared a common experience, from which everyone else was excluded. You've been burdened with that all your life, and no one understood – not until now. Now that I know, you can share it with me! I want you to, Rachel! It brings me so close to her!'

'I can't. It's too late. I can't share anything with anybody any more!' He only smiled. Nothing that I could say could hurt him.

216

'It's probably a very good thing that I can't travel to Hull with you tomorrow. We need a rest from each other. I'll try to manage a weekend in a couple of months. By then, I might have seen Hannah again! I think I'll go up on deck for a bit. Why don't you try to sleep for an hour? I'm too restless to lie down. I'll wake you the moment I see land in sight.'

'I'm not sleepy. I'll come with you.'

'No, Rachel. I want to be on my own – to think.' Of whom? Of me? It isn't fair! It isn't fair! I wanted to scream at him. Look at me! Look at *me*! It was nearly me you loved! Why did you have to wake up from your dream? It would have been so much simpler; so much more convenient! Why can't Hannah see how dreadfully unhappy I am? How could she betray me? And why are you so absurdly romantic, with your hopes and careless words? Everything you say hurts me, but I mustn't let on. I've got to pretend, pretend, *pretend*!

He covered me up, and kissed the top of my head, then hovered over me, smiling. I pulled his head towards me, overwhelmed by a physical passion only he could invoke, and he drew away from me without fear. 'If you were my flesh and blood sister, I couldn't care for you more. Are we friends again?'

'Friends,' I said, and turned my attention to suicide.

I'd read in an article in the *Reader's Digest* once that the hour before dawn was the most popular time for dying. That's when pain reaches its zenith and crushes the spirit, and the mortally ill loosen their tenuous hold on life. This gloomy hour is cursed by dread of yet another day full of hopelessness and misery. I recalled the amazing statistics very clearly. The sick turned their faces to the wall and the wretched put the poison to their lips. 'Alone, alone, all, all alone, Alone on a wide wide sea . . .' And then I recalled the stuff we'd bought at the shop called duty-free. I'd pretend it was the cocktail hour. I dragged out a bottle of cherry brandy and filled one of the cone-shaped paper cups and took a good swig, then topped it up with water from the tap. Suicide was a selfish and aggressive act. It would blight the lives of Felix and Hannah and my family. I would be unselfish, and continue to exist for their sakes. I swayed about the tiny cabin, not sure whether the waves or the brandy were causing me to stumble, and veered away from morbid thoughts. A new philosophy of life was on the cards. I'd managed to live without Hannah for years, never knowing for certain when I would see her again. Without Sybil, knowing that I never would. And now I'd have to endure life without Felix. I knew that I would love him for ever and that he would never love me. I drained my paper cone and threw it at the porthole, then sat down with my notebook and pencil. 'Felix will never love me,' I wrote. 'NEVER NEVER NEVER NEVER NEVER.' These few words took me several minutes to set down, for each NEVER blinded me with self-pity. I wrote 'Rachel Dorfman, née Sokolovsky' for the last time – a habit in which I had indulged since childhood, written on the inside cover of every notebook I possessed; then blotted each letter out, slowly and deliberately. I searched for an apt quotation which would compound my new personality and view of the future. Something in Latin, perhaps, which would sound impressive and incomprehensible. I might as well get something out of my years of unproductive studying and failed exams. '*Aequam memento rebus in arduis servare mentem.*' Yes. That would do.

I staggered to the little shower cubicle, and let the hot spray stream onto my face and hair, too lazy and tired to wash myself properly. Each time I burst into tears, I turned it to cold and counted to ten, as a scourge, a foretaste of what I must suffer for evermore. At last, dry-eyed and shivering, I stumbled back to the cabin and pulled on my clothes with difficulty, unable to summon up the energy to rub myself with the towel. Water from my hair dripped down my neck and onto the shoulders of my horrible green jacket. Few people were up and about; just two or three neurotic types looking for bathrooms; getting ready to disembark, although we had miles of knots to go. I decided to go up on deck, so that the wind would dry me out. It would be easy to avoid Felix. I wouldn't dream of interrupting his solitude. Perhaps after he had done thinking, he would go back to the cabin and find me gone, and imagine that I'd thrown myself overboard. I read what I had written in my notebook, put it carefully in my bag, tidied the cabin and climbed the companion-way to the deck. He was leaning against the rail at the stern, not caring or seeing me or wanting me. I walked towards the bow, fighting the wind, and then stood like a figure-head, suffering the icy blast which swept through my sopping hair and freezing bones. NEVER NEVER

218

NEVER NEVER NEVER. I'd read that line before somewhere. It had a ring of tragedy. There was the east coast of England creeping towards us. If we blundered a couple of hundred miles further north, I could jump off at the fish dock in Hull. The thought of returning home made me so miserable that I had to shout out my lines of Latin to the waves several times. Perhaps I would stay in London for the few days left to me before I had to return to work. Would his face light up if I suggested the idea? I'd rattle on about Hannah for all I was worth.

'What are you doing here, freezing to death? Put this on.' Felix had my hat and scarf and his raincoat over his arm. I put on the coat. The sleeves hung down beyond my hands, so he buttoned it up for me, wound the scarf round my neck and combed back my hair with his fingers. He put my fur hat on my head and pulled the ear-flaps down, tying the ribbon under my shivering chin. 'I could hear you shouting from the other end of the boat. I thought you'd be asleep. What brought you out here? Why are you always so perverse? Leave your hat alone. It looks fine with the ear-flaps down.'

'I had things to think about,' I said primly, but my teeth were chattering that much that my dignity was lost. He tried to get me to go back to the cabin with him, but I held on to the rail. 'I want to stay here.'

'May I stay with you?' His coat was so warm. 'What were you shouting about?'

'A quotation from Horace. I just thought of it. It seemed rather apt.' I repeated it for him.

'Do you want me to translate?'

'No thank you. You've done your stint. It's my turn. "Remember when life's path is steep to keep your mind even." '

'Is that your new philosophy?'

'No, Felix. That's for you. You need it more than I do.' I couldn't keep the spite out of my voice, but he didn't notice. He didn't notice anything important about me any more.

'Yes,' he said. 'I believe I do. Can you see our train over there? We're almost at the end of our journey. We're going to travel back to London in style. A first-class carriage and a first-class breakfast.' He turned me towards him. 'And when life's path is steep for me – or for you – we'll think of Hannah coming home to us.'

219

We disembarked, and Felix was as good as his word. We ate our breakfast in a warm dining-car and the service compared favourably with that of the Blue Lagoon. My recent experiences would prove invaluable in the reorganization of our establishment. After about an hour, we returned to our compartment and sat opposite each other at the table. Felix opened his file and dictionary, studying technical words in German for a forthcoming conference on Water Purification. I looked at his upside-down books, then pretended to direct my interest at a large-scale map of Eastern Europe, which was twice as big as the table, when spread out. Part of it covered his book, but he didn't push it away, so I knew he wasn't studying that hard.

'Felix,' I said, 'I think that perhaps I won't go home tomorrow. I'll stay on in London for a few days. I'd like to spend time at the British Museum and maybe go to a concert. Also, I have some shopping to do.' I made my voice casual, as if the idea, not particularly exciting, but practical, had just occurred to me. My map shook all over the place. 'I don't have to be back at work until . . .'

'I'm putting you on the train first thing tomorrow morning. You're not going tramping around London in the state you're in. Danny and Aliza are out at work all day and I've got a ton of preparatory work to do. We won't argue about it or discuss it. What you need is a few days of lounging around at home, taking it easy, so that you're bright-eyed and bushy-tailed for Monday morning.' How dare he order me about as if I was a fractious child! I wasn't asking his permission! I thought of standing up and slapping his face, but instead, I bent my head well over my map, so that my tangled hair covered my face, and said to myself, 'Remember when life's path is steep to keep your mind even.'

'I am *not* in a state. But it was just an idea. A cruel and thoughtless one, though. Mam, and especially Dad, must be on pins and needles to hear all my news about Hannah. I'm not going to keep them waiting a moment longer than necessary. I shall go back to Hull today. I'll take the tube to King's Cross from Liverpool Street and you are not to come with me. You're obviously far too busy and preoccupied. I'll be home in time for supper. No. We won't argue about it or discuss it. I won't interrupt you again.' I pawed through my 'organizer bag', found a pencil, and began drawing wavy lines from Vilnius to the Baltic coast. I was delighted to observe that he wasn't even pretending to study. I affected to be busily engrossed with my map, forestalling any further conversation. I could feel him watching what I was doing.

'Why are you crossing the Baltic? Your Latin is better than your geography.' I took no notice, scorning his humorous endeavours to be friendly. I thought of Hannah, her patience corroding because of this new-found light in her life; her impudence and courage enhanced by it. The lines on the map dazzled my eyes; the frontiers waving at me like great cobwebs. A horrible inescapable maze. I closed my eyes, imagining what I would see if it was as big as a tennis court. The threadlike lines thick and clear. Invisible towns and villages dotted around like children's toys and looming guards on either side of the net in the middle. I looked for a hole in the net, without result. Beyond the northern post was the Baltic, its watery heel digging into the Gulf of Danzig, the length of its sole patrolled by Soviet military installations; its toe pushing towards Denmark and Sweden. There must be a way. There *was* a way. I looked down at my map again, shaking with excitement. I could feel Felix, without seeing him, moving from the seat opposite, and coming to sit next to me. 'Rachel! Come on! You've grown out of all this, remember. Tell me what's the matter. You've been staring at this damned map for too long!'

I took his finger and trailed it along my pencil line. 'I'm planning Hannah's journey,' I told him. 'She's not going to hang about waiting to see whether they'll allow Soviets and foreigners to marry, in ten years' time. She's going to do it this way. She won't go back to Siberia again. If Irene . . . if Stuart . . .' I gabbled on and on. My head was spinning. Felix pulled me towards him and hugged me until I gasped for breath. The train slowed down and stopped.

'O, Rachel, where would I be without you! If this could happen, come the winter, I'd be able to give Hannah the information; and come the spring . . . We could be married, here, in England! I love you! I love you!' NEVER NEVER NEVER NEVER NEVER.

We stepped off the train, and walked together down the platform towards the barrier. The person who had been me

221

less than a week ago had changed into someone else. The metamorphosis would be complete once we reached it, handed in our tickets and emerged at the other side. Goodbye Rachel Dorfman, née Sokolovsky, I said to myself. The words hung in front of me, taunting; teasing; refusing to be erased. I blinked, but they were there still. I'd be rid of them in a day or two. One couldn't break the hopes and habits of years, just in the wink of an eye. Rachel Sokolovsky, here I come! Pledged for ever to silent suffering and good works! Travellers bumped against us as we stood on the station concourse. 'We've travelled a long way together, Felix.' I took my suitcase from him and slung my 'organizer bag' across my chest. 'I can find my own way from here. Goodbye. GOODBYE.'

Part Three

Chapter Thirty-Three

There was no one to meet me, not even the friendly porter who had seen me on to the train a week ago. The few passengers who had stayed the course beyond Doncaster, hunched their shoulders as they walked along the windy platform, waving at familiar faces at the barrier, while others made for the warmth and comfort of the Station Hotel. I pulled down the ear-flaps of my hat against the cold, braced my shoulders against something more formidable and chilling, and lugged my suit-case across the echoing, lonely concourse. I crossed the road and waited at the 69 trolley-bus stop. I was glad to be alone and hoped Mam and Dad would be out so that I could have a little extra time to adjust; prepare for her shriek of surprise and his painful, sweet smile; his inadequate cover-up for melancholy. The bus turned the corner, its antennae flickering and winking at me as they clicked through the junction of overhead electric cables. A blur of rainbow colours dazzled my eyes, and I bent down, ready to heave my luggage aboard.

'Rachel! Rachel!' Rudi was flying across the road, dodging in front of the bus, out of breath from running. He grabbed the case and ushered me onto the bus. 'I ran all the way from the Infirmary and missed you by a whisker! The spiteful train was on time. I'm glad I caught up with you, though!' He pushed the ancient brown suitcase into the alcove, and sat down next to me.

'I'm glad too. That case is bloody heavy. No it isn't. It's horrible not to be met. O, Rudi, I've so much to tell you! I've been away for fifty years.'

'You don't look a day over sixty-five.'

'Is everyone OK? Do you know, they kicked us out after

225

three days. It's so queer being back in Hull. How did you know I was arriving today? Did Felix phone you at the hospital? Did he tell you . . .?'

'Everyone's alive and well and longing to see you and hear all your news. Sacha and Malka are at the City Hall. The Yorkshire Symphony Orchestra are playing there tonight. *They* don't know you're back. Felix left a message for me at Reception and Ethel didn't tell me until I finished in Casualty. I was as mad as hell. Well, Rachel, my torment, was your reunion all you hoped? Tell me! Tell me about Hannah! You can look out of the window at Alban Road tomorrow! I'm on tenterhooks to hear how you got on!'

'This town is so mucky!' I said crossly. 'I've got a dustbin full of dirt in my contact lenses!' He handed me his hanky and turned away slightly, so that I had time to compose myself.

'You must be dead tired. I've waited for fifty years to hear about your travels. Five minutes more, a cup of tea and a little rest won't kill me and will revive you. I remember people telling me, during the war, that they recognized Russian soldiers because of the snow on their boots. It wasn't that at all! It was their magnificent fur hats! There isn't a soul on this bus who doesn't know where you've come from!'

I insisted on helping him to carry the case down Paradise Street, so that, for a minute, we could pretend we were little kids again. We walked past the lamp-post, and once midway between it and the next one, so that it was as dark as possible, I said, 'Guess what, Rudi? You're going to have a sister-in-law!' The idiot stopped so suddenly and let go of the handle, that I wrenched my shoulder with the sudden weight of it and tripped over. 'Clumsy Fool! I said sister-in-law! Not a bullet through your heart!' He pulled me up, but with such a show of temper that once on my feet, I pushed him away. He snatched the case and walked on, ahead of me, so that I had to chase him. 'I'm disappointed in you, Rudi. I thought you'd be so happy about Felix. You can't be the most important person in his life for ever. Unfortunately, he's had to be a sort of father to you, but we've allowed you to be a little boy for too long. You're both grown men, now. Don't imagine that I don't understand how you feel,' I said gently. 'It must be terribly difficult for you to accept the idea of his getting married. You're not losing a brother; you're gaining a sister. And you'll

226

love Hannah, Rudi; you'll love her as much as I do!' I was so puffed out from trying to keep up with him and comfort him at the same time, that I had to stop and lean against the wall. 'O, Rudi,' I gasped, 'you've gained a sister, and I've gained an uncle! It never occurred to me until this moment!'

'What are you blethering about?' His voice was so harsh, that right in the middle of laughing I started to cry, and the tears plopped onto my bag like a rainstorm. 'Uncle Felix! Uncle Felix!' I shouted. Without any warning, he dropped the case, pulled his ugly black eyebrows together, grabbed my wrists in his left hand and swiped me across the face, twice, then pulled me along the pavement and into the house, ignoring my screams and insults.

'Go upstairs and wash yourself. I'll build up the fire and put the kettle on. Get yourself together. Sacha and Malka will be home in less than an hour. They'll catch the fright of their lives if they see you like this. Go on! Get a move on! No more hysterics and certainly no more lectures about my quaint relationship with Felix. Hannah can wait until you've calmed down.' He pushed me all the way up the stairs, then ran down and went into the kitchen.

'You mad, crazy bastard! You need shoving into a cage, you gorilla!' I could hear him drop the kettle and come charging out of the kitchen and along the passage. I locked myself in the bathroom and ran the water, then lay in the bath, listening to him moving about downstairs. I never dreamed that he'd take the news about Felix so badly. He must be very severely disturbed, both mentally and psychologically. I'd write to Felix about him first thing tomorrow. The next minute I heard him whistling and then swearing at Lucky quite cheerfully. He must be quite mad. He called up to me, asking how long I'd be. Of course I didn't answer. He came up the stairs and I watched him through the key-hole as he crossed the landing with my luggage and put it in Sybil's bedroom.

'Are you hungry?' he bawled.

'No.'

'I'll have supper ready. Don't keep it waiting. What do you want in your omelette?'

'I want cheese in it.' I was starving alive and, anyway, it was wise to humour him. 'Go *away*! Let me wash my ears in peace!' I stood on one leg and pushed the other one about in

227

the water, making a loud swish, so he wouldn't suspect he was under observation. He stretched his length along the banister and took the stairs in one leap. He only ever did that when he was in a good mood. He was probably a manic-depressive. I splashed my face with cold water and exchanged my contact lenses for my glasses. My face and eyes felt sore and swollen. I put on my dressing-gown and Dad's slippers, and shuffled into the kitchen and sat down on the fender with my back to him. He busied himself at the stove with the frying-pan.

'Make the toast,' he said, 'and tell me whether my future sister-in-law is as bossy as you. I hope she is. Felix loves to be henpecked.'

'Apologize for slapping my face! It's swollen up like a turnip! Is it impossible to enjoy a private joke without you behaving like a dangerous lunatic?'

'You seemed to be hysterical and overwrought. I'm sorry if I was wrong.'

'You were; and if ever you dare to manhandle me again, you'll see your eyes on the end of this toasting fork. Is that understood?'

'Wouldn't that defeat the purpose? Make the toast, and don't let's quarrel. Please, Rachel.' I took a peep at him. He looked satisfactorily contrite. 'I'm sorry that I didn't show pleasure at your news. For the moment I thought it was a joke in rather poor taste. Felix is a cautious fellow. He doesn't fall in love in five minutes. He isn't made that way. I can't believe that he'd allow his feelings to become so unruly as to form a romantic liaison with a virtual prisoner in a matter of a day or two. When you're ready, I'm all ears. Here. Eat this up like a good girl. I don't mind if you talk with your mouth full.'

'You don't know the first thing about your brother. He's not in the least like you, and you haven't any personal experience of love, otherwise you wouldn't be so thick. Also, you don't know Hannah.' I looked at him with scorn and dislike. His eyes were luminous in the firelight, and for a second, I thought I saw tears in them. It was obvious he was having great difficulty in coming to terms with the fact that he wasn't of prime importance to Felix any more. I decided to go easy on him. The supper was so delicious. 'It was love at first sight for both of them. Perhaps, one of these days, something like that will happen to you, and then you'll understand; not feel so

228

upset. They were terribly confused about it, but thank goodness I was aware of what had happened, and was able to help and guide them into realizing what had occurred between them. She's so lovely, Rudi. Felix loves her so much! I've never seen him like that. And Hannah! I felt as if I'd never been separated from her, despite her horrible sufferings. Felix swept them away for her. And she did the same for him!'

'You did well, Rachel,' he said soberly. 'You have helped to create great happiness.' I looked up quickly, but there was no mockery in his eyes. They were soft; tender. I'd delay writing about him to Felix. With me to talk to and listen to, he might well get over his bizarre jealousy. 'Tell me, does Hannah resemble you as much as she does on the photographs?'

'Felix thought so, but it's really only our colouring that matches. And the mannerisms. It's a strange experience, watching one's own facial expressions and habits being acted out, very precisely, by someone else. But Hannah's beautiful. There's nothing ugly or clumsy or short-sighted about her.' I took my glasses off because they were so steamy. His face was a blur, but I could hear him swallow. He was silent for a few moments.

'And what about the other kind of sight – second sight, for want of better words? You've had that – for Hannah – ever since I've known you. Some people might call it love.'

'She loves me; just as much as I love her. But she doesn't have the other thing.'

'Are you sure?'

'I'm as sure as I've ever been about anything,' I said to the fire. 'I'm ready for another piece of toast.'

'Have you and Felix and Hannah thought about the difficulties in getting her out? Wouldn't Sacha have moved heaven and earth to bring her over here, if there was even the remotest chance? Hasn't Yosef tried, through diplomatic channels?'

'Stop talking for five minutes, and listen to me. I want to discuss this before Mam and Dad come in. I had a fantastic idea while we were on the train coming back to London. I'll tell you all about it tomorrow, when we've more time, but it involves Stuart. The plan can't work without his co-operation, and he hates me. Ever since . . . ever since I tried to make mischief between him and Esther. He won't listen to anything I say, but he will if you or Esther ask him to. Tell him I'll dance

229

at their wedding and I'll try to forget how nasty he's always been to me, if only he'll help Hannah to come home! Will you talk to him, Rudi? Will you?'

'Of course. I'm meeting him for a drink tomorrow evening at the Pier Head. You be there at half-past seven. Don't be so dramatic. He doesn't hate you. Nobody does. and anyway, whatever you want him to do will be for the benefit of my brother and Hannah, and that involves all of us, doesn't it? Well, doesn't it? Would you like to tell me what it's all about now, or do you want to leave it for tomorrow? Sacha and Malka are coming. Tomorrow? OK! Come on! Get that smile back on your face. That's the ticket! Hey, you two! We've got a visitor! A drop of the hard stuff for everyone, I think! I'll fetch a bottle from the Front Room. We have cause for a celebration!'

Mam gave such a screech when she saw me, and cuddled me in her arms as if I was a baby, stroking my back and acting as if she'd thought she would never set eyes on me again. 'Mam, I've so much to tell you! The best thing in the world was seeing Hannah, and the next best thing is being home again! Dad! Don't you recognize your daughter? What have you done to your face?' I wished I hadn't said that. It was so quiet in the kitchen. In the excitement of the moment, I'd forgotten. The scarred tissue which was the result of an accident during the war was mostly covered by his beard, but the faint remains of the burn which stained his forehead had turned as red as the fire which branded him, shamefully betraying his undisclosed sense of loss, from which he was never reprieved. I ran to him and pressed my lips against it. I could feel its hot, throbbing pain.

'I thought, just for a second, that you were Hannah. You have been so close to her. To them.' He smiled; the slow, sweet smile that I had seen so often, and looked beyond me, at Mam. He raised his glass, but I stopped him.

'Dad; Mam; Rudi! To Hannah's homecoming! And to Felix, who is going to make this happen! Tell them, Rudi! Tell them! I've just got to go upstairs for a minute!'

I held the cold flannel to my face, waiting to hear them exclaim for joy. I wasn't disappointed. Mam would forgive Felix for everything that she'd imagined he was guilty of. Tomorrow, I'd try to talk to them about Sybil; get to know them as people; not simply as my parents, but people, separate from myself, with individual hopes and memories. I gave my face ten freezing splashes of water, then, dry-eyed, ran down the stairs, tripping clumsily over the huge slippers. But I didn't go into the kitchen. Instead, I opened the door of the Front Room and closed it softly behind me. The frosty moon peered at me through the window, and I stood quite still, in the middle of the carpet square, as if waiting for someone to find me there, yet puzzled by this singular sense of expectation; of hope. I closed my eyes for a moment, seeing again the smile that my father had bestowed on my mother. It made my heart ache. Boiling tears poured down my icy face. I could hear Rudi calling to me, opening the kitchen door; walking along the passage to find me. God! It was cold in here! I shivered and wiped my face, then slipped out of the Front Room and joined him and my parents to tell them about my journey.

Chapter Thirty-Four

The 'Cod Run' left from Grimsby when weather permitted. Each of the five trawlers carried a crew of six. Stuart talked about his dirty old boats as if they were beautiful and delicate women, and the men who sailed in them were his beloved brothers. He was the skipper of the *Celerity* and Esther was the only female he had ever allowed on board. The trawlers swept through the North Sea like tiny pegs joined by a huge, invisible washing-line, stopping at Malmo on the most southern tip of Sweden for fuel, repairs, provisions, or shelter. Depending on the size of their catch and the state of the weather, they either turned around and went home, or continued eastwards, through the Baltic, towards Gdynia, in the Gulf of Danzig. Here they replenished their ice, the engineers checked the trawlers and equipment, and after their papers were found to be in order, the fishermen were allowed to disembark and join their Polish counterparts for company, refreshment and non-political conversation. Occasionally, their boats would be searched by officials from the Port Authority, for contraband or illegal passengers. The round trip could take as little as three weeks or as long as six. Rachel thought that Stuart looked like a cod, and that names like *Sea Nymph* or *Neptune* were unsuitable for boats that should be called the *Muck Tub* or *Ye Rusty Lump* or the *Filthy Funeral Fish Parlour*. He'd been unforgivably rude about the Blue Lagoon, and she took every opportunity to pay him out. It had become a game; this exchange of insults; for Stuart, anyway, who was merry and jovial, and he delighted in taunting her; recognizing the limitation of her humour and self-mockery, and crashing, like a great tidal wave, beyond it.

Rudi had been his friend since childhood, and each time Stuart docked at Grimsby, he took the ferry across the Humber and they would meet, just the two of them, for a meal and a few drinks. On the many occasions when he had more than a few, he would spend the night at Esther's parents' house. Although her old man was a rabbi, there was a kind of simplicity about him. He never preached or criticized him, even when he'd vomited over the door-step, but had helped Rudi to clean up and get him into bed before the old dragon Mrs Sokolovsky came home. She'd given him hell, more than once, babbling on about him leading her daughter astray, and if it was up to her, she wasn't having Esther getting involved with a drunk and a wastrel. Rabbi Sokolovsky had reminded his wife that the life of a trawlerman was fraught with danger, and that Stuart was a courageous young man, and where would we be if there weren't such people to brave the hostilities of the sea and its anger? Rabbi Sokolovsky always talked like that. He'd lived in Hull for years, but was still unquestionably foreign. Alien. Curiously proud of his British citizenship. A strong supporter of the working man. Stuart knew for a fact that Rachel put her oar in along with her mother, whenever her father tried to say a kind word. But he was thick-skinned, and after all, they were Esther's family – and Rudi's. He could put up with them once in a while.

When Rudi told him that Rachel wished to join them for a drink, he knew that something was afoot. She was a devious, selfish little bitch, and he knew that she'd be after something. So Felix had fallen for the rabbi's sister! That would bring her down a peg or two. She always thought she came first with him. Did she expect him to mix in and ruin their romance, in the way she'd tried to mess up his and Esther's? Rudi assured him that that wasn't the case. Hannah, the girl, was a Soviet citizen; the only survivor of the Sokolovsky family left there after the Holocaust. There was one brother, too, but he was in the States. Felix and Rachel had evolved a plan for getting her out, but he'd not been able to speak to Felix about it yet; or to Rachel, for that matter. They only got back yesterday. It seemed that they thought he could help in some way.

'What? Are they out of their minds? Are you? Am I supposed to fish her out of the sea? Have you any idea of . . .?'

'She's here,' said Rudi. 'Go easy on her. She's had a tough

233

time.' He made as if to stand up and go towards her, but Stuart stopped him with a movement of his hand.

'If she wants to see me, let her find me without your help. And let her ask me a favour without your help. I want to play it my way! I won't keep her on the end of my line for too long before I let her go with a nice cold splash. You can fish her up then. Not before. I'll hear her out on that condition!'

They watched her from their corner beside the fire. She stood in the doorway, looking around, blinking through her contact lenses. She had her hair tucked up under a peculiar fur hat, the ear-flaps standing out like bizarre fins, almost at right-angles. She was wearing a pair of green slacks tucked inside her wellington boots, and a huge fisherman's jersey; the grey one that he'd given to Esther. It hung down practically to her knees. She looked like a little lad. The barmaid thought so, too, and an argument began about under-age customers. 'No kids in here! Go on! Bugger off!'

Rudi stood up, but Stuart was there first. 'Let him in, sweetheart! He's a bit under-developed, but I can vouch for him being past drinking age. He's a friend of mine!' The barmaid waved and smiled, then turned to Rachel and jerked her head towards Stuart. 'Go on, then, if he says so.'

She pushed past the smiling customers, and sat down next to them. 'I've never been so humiliated in all my . . .'

'O, shut up!' said Stuart. 'What are you drinking? Where did you pinch that jumper from?' Suddenly, he saw that she was near to tears. 'It looks almost as good on you as it does on Esther. Rudi, how about a double sherry for the young man? And another pint for me, while you're at it! Now then, to what do I owe the pleasure?' She took off her hat, and placed it on the chair next to her, then shook her head slightly, and combed her hair through with her fingers. It fell, tangled and heavy, beyond her shoulders. She looked like a forsaken mermaid. 'Why, it's Rachel? I didn't realize you were back! Rudi, the dog, never told me? How was your journey with darling Felix?' He looked up at Rudi, who was standing behind her, holding the drinks. Enough was enough. 'I'm only kidding you, Rachel. Rudi did tell me you'd be joining us tonight. Let's cut across the pleasantries and tell me what you're after. You seem subdued. Have they given you the sack at the Blue Lagoon? I could give you a job as a cabin boy, but you'd have

234

to help to behead the fish and sleep with them on a marble slab.'

She took a sip of her drink, and then to his utter astonishment looked straight at him and smiled radiantly. 'Do you have a job, Stuart? I wouldn't mind doing anything for you, like that. I'd give up the Blue Lagoon, if you needed me to, but I know someone who'd help you if you're short-handed. Her name's Hannah. Dad's sister. No. I won't be dishonest. It's she who needs your help. I'd do anything for you, if you could help her. Anything. I'll make it right between you and Mam, about Esther. I'll never, never make trouble for you again, and I'm sorry for being nasty and spiteful. You can tease and torment me for the rest of my life and I'll always be on your side. Please, Stuart. *Please!*'

The settee and the bed chair, Mam. Please, Mam. *Please.* Rudi, the little refugee boy, standing there, against the wall, while a tiny little kid pleaded his cause. He'd never forgotten that. Yes he had, but somewhere or other the memory had lain dormant, as if waiting to jump into focus. Everyone in the schoolroom had heard her shouting; holding her mother by the hand, willing her to agree. He actually recalled the tension of that moment, followed by a peculiar kind of relief. He looked at Rudi, who was watching her; never shifting his eyes from her face. How long had he and Rudi been close friends? Fourteen, fifteen years? He downed his drink, then put down his glass and took her hand. 'Tell me exactly what you want me to do, Rachel. If there's a hope in hell that I can help, I will. You have my hand on it, and Rudi is our witness. But win or lose, I'll want a favour from you in return. Is that agreed?'

'Yes! Yes! What do you want me to do?'

'I'll let you know when I'm good and ready. Fire away!'

'I want you to fetch Hannah home in the *Celerity*. She's been in prison for trying to get over the border, and they'd never let her out of Russia, ever. But this time, it'll be different. We made a friend in Vilnius called Irene. She's nice. She saw straight away that Hannah and Felix were in love, because she was in love herself. She knows people in the KGB who could give Hannah a birth certificate, in exchange for the presents we brought for her. Vilnius used to belong to Poland before the war, although it was disputed by the Lithuanian Republic. But Poland pinched it, anyway. After the war, it belonged to

Russia, but anyone who could prove they'd been born in Vilnius between 1922 and 1939 could go to Poland.'

'Look, Rachel, this is all very interesting and informative, but what's it all got to do with me? Even if she managed to cross into Poland and waited for me in Gdynia, I couldn't take her on board. We'd never move an inch from the dock. The trawlers are searched each time, and our papers examined meticulously. We'd be carted off to the nearest jail and Hannah would be worse off than she is now.'

'Please, Stuart; let me finish. Hannah wasn't born in Vilnius. She was born in Liubava, but it isn't there any more. She lived in Kovno afterwards, and went into the Ghetto. There wasn't a ghetto in Vilnius. All the Jews were taken to Ponary, and murdered. But it's Soviet policy to keep quiet about the Nazi atrocities against Jews. It's known that she's Jewish, but she doesn't look it. If she got a new passport without that information; just saying she was born in Vilnius, she could pretend she was just going for a little trip – cross over at Konigsberg. Show that she was allowed to do that. I know that she can't go wandering about Poland with suspicious papers; that's not your problem; it's hers and Felix's. He'll sort out the best route for her. Then she could hide in a wood and dress up as a Polish peasant. She speaks fluent Polish and can see in the dark and is very brave. And the best actress in the world. She could find her way to a tiny seaside place, and hide there or thereabouts until you flash a message that you're approaching. Then she'll come down to the beach and wait for you; perhaps hide behind a rock. Of course, she couldn't manage it in a big, busy port like Gdynia or Gdansk; but a little place; a nowhere place, even, where there's a cliff or a rock . . .'

'We don't go to cliffs or rocks. We go to Gdynia and there's no way we can crawl up to a mythical, deserted beach!'

'What if someone on board was ill, and you radioed a message that you needed immediate medical help? You couldn't hang about. You'd have to bring the patient to the nearest possible point, and bring him ashore by dinghy. The local people wouldn't know to search your ship. They'd allow your dinghy to beach, and then help you to see to the sick man. Meanwhile, before help comes – you'd have to time this properly – Hannah could jump in the dinghy, and in the confusion she'd be taken onto the trawler.'

236

'And what happens when we report to our harbour? What happens then? Do you think they'll turn a blind eye to a woman on board?'

'She wouldn't be a woman! I forgot to explain. She'd dress up as a peasant boy, and once in the ship, she'd have a sou'wester and oilskins on. They'd count her as one of the crew, and one of your sailors would stay home and you'd be able to use his papers.'

'And what if we have to stop in Malmo, and they check us out there? What happens, for God's sake, when we dock at Grimsby? And what about the poor bugger who we've left behind in your cute little fishing village? Does he have to have his appendix out, when he's as fit as a fiddle?'

'Rudi could lend you a syringe with a nasty injection in it. Your friend would soon recover. Or it might be that he just had food poisoning or too much to drink. You know what big boozers your friends are! Your shipmates would never let you down. Dad says you're always risking your lives for each other. And even if they found that there was something fishy in Sweden or Grimsby, you could handle it, Stuart! You've got so many friends who would turn a blind eye. Especially if you told them about her horrible sufferings and her hopes for a happy future!'

'Is this Hannah anything like you?'

'She is!' said Rudi. He had been listening, his hands round his glass, watching Rachel in absolute silence. 'I've never met her, but I've seen her picture and heard about her. She's brave; she's unquenchable and . . .'

'Probably quite mad,' interrupted Stuart. 'But not half as mad as I am! Tell that idiot brother of yours to come up here immediately. I need to talk to him; I refuse to believe what I'm thinking I'm going to do, without enlightenment from him. Meanwhile, I'll have to take the crew into my confidence and work out all the details with them. You understand that I've got to have their backing. You do realize that, don't you? If they're not prepared to risk trouble, there'll be no rescue.'

'I understand,' she said. He could see that she didn't. She looked so delighted; there were actually tears in her eyes. Of relief? Grief? He'd never fathom her out.

'Every single tiny detail will have to be reported to Hannah. If she isn't in exactly the right place at the right time – that is, if we can work something out – then we'll have to leave her behind. Who's going to give her instructions?'

'Felix will. He's going to Leningrad in December, for a Geneva-based conference on World Health.'

'If it can be managed – please listen to that "if", it's a big, loud word – we would try for next summer. It's impossible to do it any earlier. There are too many difficulties to be sorted out, and the weather's got to be good. Even if there was a dying man on board, we couldn't risk poking around your little old rock in heavy seas. Would she be ready by next summer?'

She nodded. Tried to say something, but changed her mind. She jumped up and ran to the bar and bought them each a drink. Rudi raised his eyebrows at him. His anxiety was almost palpable. 'I'll do my best. Get hold of Felix as soon as you can.' She brought the drinks to the table. 'Rachel, do you know the story of Abner's leg? I told it at Shabbos School, once. I don't think you were listening properly. Do you want me to tell it again?'

'No. I remember it. I thought it was a daft story – at the time.' She raised her glass. 'To you, Stuart! Thank you! Thank you! To the best and bravest of friends!'

'And to the most charming lady in the world! What's her name? You'd better get it right, first time!'

'Esther!'

'That is a foregone conclusion! Who, after Esther? Think before you speak!'

'The gallant ship, the *Celerity*!'

'Well done! And our final toast, ladies and gentlemen. To Operation Abner!'

Chapter Thirty-Five

Hannah knew that she would be under surveillance after Felix and Rachel left. If she was caught selling the gifts, she could go to prison. But she had no intention of selling anything. She would be buying, buying, buying. And you couldn't buy favours with money; only with goods which were unobtainable and highly desirable. All along, she understood that her visitors' stay would probably be cut short, whether or not they did or said anything which might cause annoyance or arouse suspicion. One didn't ask why, because questions caused that, too. But if she held on to her own logic and kept her personal reasoning clear and uncluttered, and was never beguiled into talking to anyone – not even Tanya, who she felt was now her friend – about her wonderful secret, she could hope. No one and nothing could set her back and allow her to despair again. The relief of being able to confide in someone – in him – had been like the final climax of a malignant sickness from which she had miraculously recovered. She thought of his face; his arms closing around her; safe and warm, like her mother's. She had closed her eyes, thinking that he was about to blow gently on her forehead, to disperse the horror. But he hadn't. He had kissed her so wildly and passionately that she had been able to let her mother go, and to crush him to her, relinquishing her childhood and acknowledging her womanhood which she had ignored for so long. He was the first man who had kissed her, and yet she had recognized love the moment she beheld him, for Rachel had been there, showing her what it was; helping her to be the person she had almost forgotten. She had forgotten Rachel, that last evening. She'd been lying on the bed, asleep, as if purposely leaving the two of them alone, so that they could tell each other, joyously, without words, that they were in love.

She drank her coffee from one of the beautiful cups, lingering over it; knowing that this would be the last time she would use her tea-set. She couldn't imagine how much it must have cost Sacha and Malka and Rachel. Rachel. She felt wistful about her. Was it because she, Hannah, had never experienced youth? Was it that? It puzzled her, this ache. When she was twenty, she'd been a diseased, ageless wreck, her head shaved, her rags filthy. She could have looked like Rachel, if things had been different; had a family around her. She looked across at the photographs. She did have them! She could look at them as often as she liked; feel them, almost; remember them without losing her senses. Smile back at them. Her paper family. Paper Children? No. Not really. They were more palpable than that, because she could hear their voices and recall their atmosphere. She had only to adjust her mind slightly and be back with them in Liubava. Felix had told her how Rachel had kept them and looked at them every day; talking to them by name and unable to let them go, as if trying to breathe life into them, he'd said, and being ill and frightened, because of her failure. She hadn't failed. Not entirely. They seemed to breathe life into her, now, giving her back her old self. Her old wildness and courage. While she had them, she could cope without Felix, but she knew only too well that she had a short fuse when it came to patience; sitting about, waiting for something. She'd waited for too long, for nothing. She'd done with all that! But two months wasn't long! Two months was two seconds compared with the mechanical days she'd pushed through before. She couldn't even remember them properly now. She would relive her youth again – with him. And right now, she had things to do.

She washed and dried the new crockery, polishing it until it gleamed, then packed it carefully in the cardboard box she'd picked up from the Post Office. She tied the box, without inserting a message, then wrote a letter.

Dear Irene,
The visitors from England, Felix Dorfman and Rachel Sokolovsky, have had to return home. They wished me to thank you for your great kindness and friendship, and to

240

apologize for being unable to accept your wedding invitation. They left a gift for you. Perhaps you and Petrov will let me know when and where I could deliver it? I take a walk along Rudninku Street every evening at nine o'clock, past the Museum of Folk Art. I am giving you a list of all the other beautiful gifts that my niece and fiancé brought for me. Would you be able to put me in touch with someone who would like them? I do not know many people in Vilnius, although I was born here in 1925. I send you my best wishes for your future happiness together.

Irene would understand exactly what she meant. So would Petrov, who was bound to be a KGB official. Irene was lucky in so far as she had fallen in love with someone who was 'approved of'; that's why she still had her job as an Intourist guide. Hannah had hung around the Intourist Hotel so much when she knew that she was soon to have visitors, that she knew Irene's routine, and Irene had given her her time-table. That was all Rachel's doing! Tonight, she was taking a Finnish couple to the theatre. When she'd escorted them back to the hotel, and the driver went off duty, it would be easy to waylay Irene, once she turned off the main road, call a greeting and hand her the letter. One didn't forget how to trust. It was like swimming or skating. It stayed somewhere, in the blood-stream, for years maybe, without practice, ready to hustle along to the relevant muscles so that you could retrieve your buoyancy and balance. Trust sickened when it was displaced by constant suspicion, but it never died without trace. Rachel trusted Irene. Rachel knew. There was no need to quake or fear betrayal. She had to start sometime to relearn. She ate her supper, put on her coat and scarf, stuffed the letter in her pocket and went out into the chilly night. Ever since she had lived in the store-room, she could see in the dark better than anyone else. No one seemed to be about. She picked her way with the ease and confidence of a cat, over the rubble, through the short cut.

241

Chapter Thirty-Six

Felix leaned against the barrier, watching Rachel as she walked towards the tube station. As she disappeared from view, he was overwhelmed by intolerable loneliness. It had been terrible, leaving Hannah behind, but Rachel's bizarre and irrational behaviour had occupied him, despite himself; her chatter and hysterical outbursts, her dependence, had exasperated yet absorbed him. The suddenness of her going off like this forced him to acknowledge that he was dependent on her. Hannah seemed to be near at hand when she was around. He could see her; talk to her; hear her voice; touch her. Now, the pain of his separation dissolved his ability to contact her and threatened his self-control. All he could see was that lonely figure on the platform, as desolate as he was at this moment. More so. Maybe she would do something rash and dangerous out of desperation. He couldn't stand the worry. The anxiety would drive him mad. Perhaps none of her letters would reach him, and his would not reach her. He had no way of knowing what was happening to her. What she was feeling or thinking. He didn't even have a recent picture of her to look at. They were all undeveloped. The only one was the photograph in his jacket pocket. He sat down on a seat, fumbling clumsily for it; staring at her; trying to see her again. It didn't help. He had nothing and no one to hold on to, to see him through the next few dreaded weeks.

Why had he chased Rachel off like that? Why hadn't he made her stay for a few days? He didn't know what to do. That hare-brained idea of hers; it had seemed such an exciting possibility when she had explained it to him! Now it merely seemed fantastic and fraught with danger. He knew what he had to do. He must check immediately that he was engaged to work at the conference in Leningrad in December. Then discuss with Danny, who was a Professor of Soviet Studies, what the options were. Check out if and when marriages between Soviets and British subjects had been performed. Jewish Soviets with criminal records. He returned the photograph to his pocket and made as if to stand up, but his legs were as weak as water. His spirit withered. He'd always acted as if he was as tough as old leather. He was. But not now. Not without Rachel to hold him up. He'd go after her and beg her to stay for a day or two at least; promise her that he'd help her to look for a job – and face the wrath of Malka – so that she could be nearby and keep him going until he felt better and more optimistic. He'd follow her to Hull if necessary. Someone else would have to stand in for him at the conference in Cardiff. He wasn't up to it. He looked at his watch and realized that he'd been sitting on the seat for hours. Maybe if he rushed to King's Cross, he'd find her. She might have lost the way; gone for a walk; missed the train. Maybe she'd be waiting on the platform, or reading her map in the waiting room there. Strength returned to his limbs. The tube would be quicker than a taxi.

He raced across the concourse at King's Cross and looked up at the departure board, but his eyes wouldn't focus properly, and he had to ask a passing porter to direct him to the appropriate platform. The train had left a few minutes back. Perhaps she wasn't on it! Perhaps she'd decided to wait for a later one and wander around by herself. He lurched into the 'Ladies Only' waiting room, unconcerned by the angry glares levelled at him. She wasn't there. 'I've lost someone!' he shouted to the ticket collector, who was on the point of leaving his booth. 'A very fair girl wearing a brown fur hat. She was supposed to wait for me here. Have you seen her? Did you notice whether she boarded the train?'

'If she didn't, she'll have to wait until four-fifty-five tomorrow morning. If she did, she left at six-one, like a couple of hundred other passengers. My business is to clip their tickets and answer their bloody stupid questions, because they can't be bothered to read the information on the board. Hold on a sec. A fur hat, did you say? Does this girl happen to have a screw loose as well? There was one, hanging about the booth, staring at the clock, until I told her to get a move on. She told me she was waiting for someone, but I'm sure it was for a lady. She said, "She'll be here." I'm sure she said "she". Then she counted every chime out loud, and waved her hat, and burst out laughing – or crying! That's why I noticed her.' He pointed at his forehead, denoting her derangement. 'The little fool ran and wrenched open the door, and left it swinging open. The train was moving and I had to run up and slam it. That's how accidents happen, and the railway has to answer for them. She was still grinning, dragging her suitcase along the corridor. But it wasn't you she was waiting for, sir. It was a female. You've nothing to be cut up about.'

'Thank you! Thank you so very much! Please accept this for your trouble. I can see that I've delayed you.' He shoved a ten-bob note into the ticket collector's hand. The man touched his cap and smiled. He didn't mind if a hundred such lunatics 'troubled' him.

'Any time, sir. Do you need a porter?'

'No. No, thank you. Goodnight!' Good old Rachel! Everything would be OK. Her confidence was infectious. He could rely on her to approach Stuart and he'd get on with the job at his end. He'd always scorned Rudi's theories about her, but it was peculiar how he'd been suddenly sapped of energy. Maybe she'd been practising her witchcraft on him! He felt as fit as a flea, and as strong as a lion! Only nine weeks before he saw his darling Hannah again! He swung his suitcase onto his shoulder and hurried over to the taxi rank. He sat in the back of the taxi, feeling hope and energy flood his whole being. After dumping his luggage in the hall, he knocked at the door of Danny's and Aliza's flat, and they greeted him with surprise and delight. Aliza fetched another plate and glass, while Danny opened a bottle of wine. There was obviously something afoot which called for a celebration, but where was Rachel?

'She's on her way back to Hull. She didn't want to keep Sacha waiting a moment longer than necessary, to give him news about Hannah. You know *her*! And *I* can't wait to give you news about Hannah, either. Charge the glasses while I run upstairs and phone Rudi. I won't be a tick. I want to tell him to meet Rachel's train if he can.'

They had barely a minute to comment to each other about

244

the change in their friend. The wild, almost unbalanced excitement, which was so uncharacteristic of him; as if he had discovered another dimension to his life, which they only now realized had been missing. Aliza felt tears in her eyes. She brushed them away impatiently and surreptitiously. But Danny saw them. He saw most things. He touched Aliza's hand. 'What is it, Danny? Don't dare ask me why I'm crying. I don't know why!' He smiled as Felix burst into the dining-room. For a split second he was a boy again, watching Malka burst into the kitchen one hot Sunday in September.

'I don't know about Hannah yet, but I know about you, Dorfman.'

'What do you know?'

'You've fallen in love with her.'

Felix sat down and turned to Aliza. 'Don't bother to keep your affairs clandestine. Aliza. It's a wasted effort.'

'And are you about to fall out of love?' Felix shook his head. 'In that case, you and your beloved are in one hell of a quagmire. We'd better talk about it when we're drunk. You know as well as we do that the hangover is going to be rough. My head is swimming already, so – begin at the beginning. Go on till you get to the end. Then stop. Stop to think. And drink.'

'Don't you dare let him pull you down, Felix. He's as pleased about it as I am, but you know him; he can't help hiding his light under a bushel. You've got to pity him. He's his mother's son, remember. He can never quite escape her permeating pessimism. Now shut up, Danny. Felix, we're both agog!'

They talked until the early hours. There would perhaps be a time, about ten years ahead, when such marriages would be permitted, but there'd be no guarantee that she could ever join her husband. She'd most certainly lose her job and would become an object of uncomfortable interest. They discussed the political situation; the territory west of what had once been Lithuania, an area which probably contained the most powerful and secretive military zones in the USSR. They pored over Ordnance Survey maps of Poland, west of the border, and of the coastal area in particular.

'Well?' Danny said at last. 'Has your Houdini the courage to risk the consequences of this folly? Have you?' he added, harshly. 'This is your hangover. It will last for a long time, but once she's through, you'll be able to cope with every damn thing – together. She's lived through hell and has survived. Paradoxically, it makes one remarkably tenacious to life. I met her brother, Yosef, on my last trip to the States. He told me about an opera singer, a gifted, successful and popular man, accustomed to luxurious living, who was greatly respected by his fellow-men. He didn't know he was a Jew, until he found himself at Dachau. Many of the inmates recognized him. They tried to encourage him not to give up hope, but he died within two days. His health was good and he didn't have time to starve. The weather was warm. But his well-fed, cosseted body was unable to withstand the shock and horror of his predicament. His soul was unused to privation and degradation. Yosef also told me about a friend of his and Hannah's, who lived in the Ghetto with them. She survived the most horrific dangers in order to perform her final miracle. She stole a huge sack of potatoes from under the noses of the SS. It was impossible, but she did it. He said that this friend was very like his sister Hannah. She's been well-schooled. She can make it, with luck. With help. With love.'

The following day, Felix caught the train and went to Hull to meet Stuart, and two months later he flew to Leningrad for a conference on World Health, which was to be held there for five days.

Chapter Thirty-Seven

The aircraft touched down at Pulkova airport. 'Ladies and Gentlemen. Please remain seated until the indication lights are dimmed. The local time is eighteen-thirty and the temperature is sixteen degrees below zero. Welcome to Leningrad. We hope you will enjoy your stay.'

He staggered down the steps, almost floored by the intense cold. He could feel the hairs of his moustache stiffen with the frost as he breathed, and he was glad of the fur hat which Rachel had insisted he should borrow, so that Hannah would recognize him. As if either of them would have any trouble! In his capacity as official interpreter, he was guided through security without the usual lengthy red-tape, and within an hour of disembarking, he had retrieved his luggage and was boarding the private bus which carried the linguists from the airport to the hotel. He had no idea how, when or where he would see her. If she'd tried to inform him, or the family, by devious remarks in a letter, it hadn't got past the censor. The bus was warm, but nevertheless he shivered, wondering crazily whether she was standing in the open, waiting; freezing to death.

She watched the bus stop outside the hotel and saw him climb out with the others. A couple of youngsters were clearing the pavement outside the entrance, muffled up to the eyebrows. Felix stood at the desk, waiting for his name to be checked, his passport examined and placed in a long metal drawer. Most of his colleagues were from Finland, Sweden and East Germany, their bags and brief-cases piled up in the foyer. One of the snow-clearers pushed his way through, carrying his broom like a crutch, telling the busy receptionist that they'd finished.

Could he help to take up the bags? They were short of staff; kids were short of parents in this city. For a bite of supper and a few kopeks, they came in useful. Felix followed the boy to the first floor where a bald, fat, genial-looking man sat at a table. He greeted him, checked his key and room number and directed him to the end of the bustling corridor.

His porter was obviously amenable to a tip, despite the rules. He walked into the room, dumped the case on the bed, and stood waiting until Felix turned on the light, half-closed the door and fumbled for change. Hannah held up her forefinger, pulled down her muffler and pushed back her cap. He was ready for any contingency, except this. The shock made him useless and stupid.

'Have you forgotten me, my darling?' she whispered in his ear. 'There's no time! Go to the bar on Pozhely Street as soon as you can.' She pulled a waterproof envelope out of the front of her jacket and shoved it into his pocket, then adjusted her cap and scarf and swaggered out of the room. He could actually hear her asking the man at the table if anyone else needed help.

He sat down on the bed. A pulse was banging like a sledge-hammer in his leg, so that it shook like a piece of string in a draught. He closed his eyes, remembering, after half a minute, to breathe again. He knew that he would never forget this moment as long as he lived. She had been in his mind's eye constantly. He had looked at photographs of her umpteen times a day, yet he hadn't recognized her! He lay across the bed convulsed with hysterical laughter, knocking his suitcase to the floor. The bald man knocked; pushed open the door. 'Supper is ready in the dining-room. Please take your seat there in ten minutes. Are you well, sir?'

He sat up, forcing himself to control his features. 'I had far too much to drink on the plane. I dislike air travel. I believe I shall feel better after a meal – and a walk.' His head was spinning, as if from liquor.

The man laughed. 'After a walk of twenty yards, you will be frozen sober. The dining-room is on the lower ground floor.' He left the room. Felix leapt to life, locked the door and pulled open the envelope.

My Darling,

If I could write down everything I wish to say to you, I would use up all the pens and then have to ask for more, but I must be brief. I received only two letters during our separation – one from Sacha and one from Yosef. Your visit obviously alerted the censors! But they didn't understand the significance of my brothers' letters; of what they conveyed to *me*! The code worked. I'm here! I bribed Zhivile with the coat in exchange for the free days owing to me, to use whenever I requested them. Irene and her husband directed me to the Colonel in Vilnius who has prepared my birth certificate. His cousin is a patrol guard at the Konigsberg check-point! KGB is a family business! He has several contacts there, but I must cross only when this particular man is on duty. I must present my certificate to him, so that he can destroy it. My false papers must not be traced back to them, in case I am apprehended. But that will not happen. I have given the Colonel everything that I had left from your gifts, except for fifty of the pens which I will use as bribes if necessary; and the most precious – my photographs. He doesn't need those! If my room is searched, they will find nothing of value. I pretend that the rug is still on the floor, and that I eat and drink from the beautiful tea-set, and that I wear the lovely clothes; but I do not have to pretend that I am bursting with happiness. My problem is that I must pretend otherwise! To pretend that I do not love you! Anything is possible; everything is manageable – except that!

While you read this, I shall be revelling in the joy of having seen your face. The map is to direct you to where I shall see it again! I am staying at the place marked – Vrublyovskovo Street, 90 – the next block from Pozhely. The bar is frequented by foreign visitors. Whether or not your colleagues accompany you, it must appear that we have not previously met. I have known you all my life. Bring a copy of your schedule and anything you have for me for my journey in your coat pockets. I am in Leningrad for three days.

Felix read the letter for fifteen minutes, then tore off his layers of outdoor clothing. He had a list in his head of the items

249

he must give her: compass; torch; batteries; binoculars; money. Detailed instructions which he'd written out dozens of times; checked with Stuart; rewritten, added, amended. But he'd been unable to bring a copy with him, in case his papers were examined. He'd write everything out during the night, then give the notebook to her at their next meeting. If she could wangle this – this impudent admittance to his room under everyone's noses, she could wangle anything! God! It would take him a lifetime to recover from the shock! So Rachel had been right to trust Irene. Hannah had been right. She had her birth certificate. Hannah! Hannah! How could I ever have doubted your optimism? He washed his face, straightened his tie and walked down the corridor. He sat down at the table with his colleagues. The lukewarm onion soup tasted marvellous. His friends were too tired to accompany him for a walk. He must be a lunatic to want to freeze to death. There were drinks a-plenty in this hotel bar.

He left the company as soon as politeness and discretion permitted, walked back up the stairs to his room, and then with lightning speed collected the items for Hannah. He cut the bag containing the wad of money from the inside knee of his long underpants, stuffed the envelope together with his schedule into his huge pockets, distributing everything else in the inside pockets of his greatcoat, and sauntered downstairs to the front door. It was locked; sealed against the freezing air. He asked the receptionist to open it.

'Where do you wish to go?' He longed to shout at the man; tell him to mind his own business. For a moment he felt like a prisoner.

'For a short walk – maybe to the bar on Pozhely.'

'Pozhely is closed. There is everything you need here. Breakfast is served at six-thirty tomorrow morning. You must be tired from your journey. You will want to go to bed early.' Felix felt the temper blaze in his blood, overpowering the claustrophobia that threatened him.

'I know exactly what I want. It is for you to open this door at once! I am the chief interpreter here, and I understand my schedule perfectly. There is no work tonight. Our time is our own. I cannot take a walk in the open air inside this hotel. Unlock the door!'

250

'It will be bolted at eleven o'clock. You will return before that time, please.'

The freezing air; release from panic; relief, made him gasp for breath. He hunched his shoulders, hurried along the road and round the first corner. Pozhely Street. The bar was open! He could see nothing through the heavily curtained door and window. He pushed open the door. The place was hot and smoky and dimly lit. He was directed to an empty table and shown where to leave his coat.

'I am frozen to the bone,' smiled Felix. 'Perhaps I will warm up a little with a bottle of vodka – and a jug of water, please. I have only sterling with me, I'm afraid. I have had no chance to change my currency. Could you change this? I would be very much obliged.' It seemed that the staff were obliged, too. Pounds or dollars were far more welcome than roubles. They had purchasing power at the shops for foreigners.

The pianist struck up 'Auf weidersehn, Sweetheart', probably for the benefit of the Germans at the next table to Felix. He watered his vodka and looked round wildly for Hannah, pretending to survey the scene. Although he was sweltering, he dare not remove his coat, in case the items in the pockets were spotted. A few couples were dancing on the tiny floor space shared by the piano. There she was, leaning against it! He had absolutely no acting talent – only a limited amount of self-control, which diminished dangerously as he watched her, quite unable to direct his gaze elsewhere; to keep his face from breaking into a grin.

She was wearing the red and white striped jumper – the one article of clothing she had felt unable to part with – and her navy skirt. She was smiling and chatting to the pianist. Her hair was parted in the middle, held back loosely by two red hair-slides, her pale face brightened with rouge and lipstick. Her canvas bag slipped down to her elbow from her shoulder, and she adjusted it carelessly. He could hear her laughing uproariously at something the pianist was saying to her, and she rested her hand on his shoulder, flirting with him while he played. She shimmied over to the bar in time to the music, bought herself a drink and exchanged remarks with the men next to her, eyeing them with a kind of amused wantonness. She looked across at Felix for a second, nudged one of the men

251

to draw his attention to him, sitting there, idiotically, in his huge coat. The man turned around on his stool, then touched Hannah's glass with his. She winked at him, then at the pianist, drained her glass and walked over to Felix, smiling.

'Do you dance in your coat, too, or do you just drink in it?'

He stood up and she helped him off with it. He daren't watch her carry it over to the line of hooks visible behind strips of plastic. She returned immediately, swinging her bag from her little finger as if it was still as light as a feather. Had she managed to pick his pockets with all those people watching her? Was the little devil a conjuror as well? But he could tell that her bag was all but empty. She left it on his table and walked with him to the tiny dance floor. They managed two steps before she tripped him and he staggered against the other dancers, trying to regain his balance. She hopped around on one foot, holding her other one, swearing loudly. The scene was a diverting one, especially since the pianist took a break from his duties to laugh and take liquid refreshment.

'You clumsy fool! My ankle! Can you see the mark of your boot, you great bear? Help me to the table!' All eyes were on them. She picked up her bag and limped ostentatiously to the cloakroom, leaning against his coat, her back to her audience, as she removed her shoes. Attention was diverted solely to him. He sat down and called over for an extra glass. She returned, still limping badly, in her stockinged feet. Felix almost fainted with relief. He could see the shape of the binoculars' case in her bag. Her shoes, to everyone else. The pianist executed a skipping rhythm for Hannah's benefit, and a few customers applauded as she hopped around on one leg, smiling and waving, before she sank down on the chair which Felix held for her at his table.

'I'll teach you how to drink vodka, even if I can't teach you English to dance!' she said raucously. 'We'd like some more over here; lemonade, bread and fish! Now. Vodka first. One gulp only, followed by lemonade . . . followed by fish . . . followed by bread! And again! Well done! We'll have you falling over your own clumsy feet in no time!' People laughed. The pianist bashed out a lively drinking song while Hannah and Felix started another round. 'The buffoon and the bitch go well together and are never taken seriously. Keep it up, my darling! You'll be able to escort me home without anyone bothering us. Get drunk for them, but keep a clear head for us. I have everything in my bag. When I put my head on the table, stand up, ready to leave. Be careful; don't look at me like that. Exclude all tenderness. Lust, with a dash of contempt; let your face go slack. Push the bread in your mouth in big lumps; wipe your mouth slowly with the back of your hand. Leer at me. You're a terrible actor, beloved. Keep it going for five more minutes!'

Little interest was shown in them now. Hannah laid her head on her arms and knocked a glass off the table. Felix picked it up and went to fetch his coat. 'Which is yours?' he called over to her. She didn't answer. The man at the bar pointed it out, grinning. Her shoes were in the inside pockets. She took her coat, opened her bag, and with a deftness that made Felix blink, transferred her shoes to the bag under cover of his coat. Then she put them on, slowly and painfully. He helped her to her feet, held her coat for her, and she put it on like a cloak, hiding her bag from view, while he muffled himself up. He offered her his arm, and she leaned on it, shouted her farewells, and hobbled out with him into the dark, freezing night.

'Walk slowly, darling,' she said. 'Remember that you're a foreigner making a drunken fool of yourself and I'm half-crippled. We have forty minutes. I'm staying on the next block.'

'Did you know that you're the most amazing woman I ever had the good fortune to be madly in love with? Is this the kid in my room or the flirt at the piano or the cunning witch who sent me sprawling? I'll have my revenge on you yet! If I could just have a couple of minutes' warning. There was never a duller oaf at improvisation than Dorfman. What are you going to do next?'

'Turn left down this alley and kiss you.' He enveloped her in his arms, feeling, hearing, loving the real Hannah. He tore off his gloves with his teeth, frantic for her nearness, and she felt the warmth of his hands against her flesh; his face in her hair; on her neck. Passion mastered caution. Longing overrode dreary acceptance. Snow was warm when it fell on them both. It melted fear; unleashed the senses. Dazzled her eyes so that she could see no one else but him, even when they closed. Without him, she would perish, for she had survived too much. Life and liberty beckoned her irresistibly, giving her mastery. She forced him to heed her. He wrapped his coat around her and pressed her head against his chest. She could hear his heart pounding; feel him trembling. They had fifteen more minutes before he had to dash back to the hotel. 'Tell me, Felix,' she said.

He explained the plan to her, omitting the details, all of which he would write in the notebook; signals, times, maps; where she must be and what she must look for. To keep as near to the coast as possible, avoiding the towns, following rural lanes and tracks, so that she could avoid all possibility of being asked for identification. Hide in the woods at Ustka if she was early, but be in the fishing village of Chylonia on the last day of May. Stuart would come there at night, but he couldn't be definite as to which, exactly. There were too many considerations which were impossible to foresee, but he wouldn't be later than the second night of June. She must rest by day and watch by night, like an invisible, silent owl.

'I'll be with you every step of the way; watching you on my map; feeding off Rachel's witchcraft to find the wood you're sleeping in; the hedge; the barn; the haystack. Counting the minutes; the hours; the days; the weeks. O, God, Hannah! If only I could be with you in reality instead of in imagination! If only we knew someone along the way who we could trust! A farmer or a fisherman. We've just got to leave all that to you! You'll recognize a friendly face! Someone who'll offer you a night's rest or a lift on a farm cart. There's plenty of Polish currency in the pouch. You've got to make all the decisions which our plans can't cover. It's impossible to anticipate everything. At least the weather will be warm. But the nights may be cold. Take care of your health. There'll be no one to tend you if you fall ill. No one to protect you, if . . . Every moment of your journey will be a risk! O, darling! Take care! Your life is mine!'

'Why have you so little faith? Haven't I impressed you with my cunning? I'll be on your doorstep tomorrow morning, clearing the snow, ready to take the notebook. Nothing can go wrong for me ever again – for us! Nothing!' She looked at his watch. 'I already see myself on the bus taking me across Konigsberg. From then on, I'll be invisible! Tell me where I go after that so that I can dream about it tonight! Felix! You mustn't cry!' She held his face, kissing his tears. He controlled

254

himself for what he had to tell her.

'From Konigsberg you must go to Palmnicken. On foot. On the same road.' His voice was harsh; cruel. He could feel her stiffen as if every bone in her body fused with fear and terror. She shook her head. He held it still, pressing his fingers into her temples. Danny had told him that it must be so. No public transport after she'd crossed the border. It was too risky. This route had to be followed. The snow was dark on the ghastly whiteness of her face. It settled on her hair and brows and lashes, rolling down her cheeks like tears.

'I can't go there!' she gasped. 'I have been down that road a thousand times. Not that way! No! Not that way!' Her terror almost disarmed him.

'Yes! It must be that way! Hannah! Hannah! Listen to me! Look at me! A boat will come for you this time – to Chylonia. It will be your last nightmare! The very last! And I shall be waiting at the end of it – to wake you up!' They had five more minutes. He couldn't leave her. He would be tormented for the rest of his life. Her body relaxed. It seemed to be defrosting; melting. Everywhere was deathly still.

'I shall dream of you,' she said. 'Go, my darling.' She slipped out of his arms and limped away from him through the snow, like an injured bird, towards Vrublyovskovo Street.

Chapter Thirty-Eight

May Day was a National Holiday. Hannah had taken only two short breaks during the years she had worked at the warehouse. Zhivile, her supervisor, gave her an excellent reference with regard to her work and co-operation, and permission had been granted for Hannah to go away for the first two weeks in May. She could not be spared for any longer than that and it was not possible to give her the last two weeks in May instead. She was going to the seaside – to Memel.

As soon as she left work on the eve of the holiday, she hurried home to do her packing. Everything she needed was in her head. In preparation, Tanya had helped her to turn her canvas bag into a back-pack, sewing in extra pockets, as she hoped to do lots of walking and climbing. She had given Tanya so many of her things: a beautiful, multi-coloured scarf, coffee, half a dozen pens, two folding suitcases, the like of which she'd never seen before – but their close friendship was nothing to do with gifts. It developed shortly after the foreign visitors left, as if Hannah could no longer do without friends. The silent, autistic, obsessional creature of this time last year, had changed into a cheerful, pleasant, witty young woman with whom Tanya spent some of her free time. They popped into each other's flats; talked about the past; the difficulties and triumphs at work. Not of their plans for the future, except in a tenuous way, for neither of them were definite. Tanya grumbled ruefully to Hannah about her non-existent love life, and marvelled at her lack of appeal among unmarried men. Of course, she was in great demand on the wards; in her uniform and position of authority, the cheekier, livelier patients found her irresistible – until their wives reclaimed them. She allowed

256

herself a few mild flirtations, but no hanky-panky. She had to be a shining example to the junior staff. Yet those who were unobtainable were those to whom she felt the strongest attraction. That's how it was for the men, too! The minute she went out in her off-duty clothes, looking for love, there was nothing doing! There was someone in a wheelchair – a charming, suffering man, whose bitter humour she delighted in. If only . . . well, you could go on saying 'if only' until you were blue in the face.

'Would you marry someone in a wheelchair, Hannah? Someone you could never enjoy the basics with? Would you, if you loved him?'

'Yes. A thousand times, yes!' Just like that. There were still things about Hannah she couldn't fathom.

She pulled out one of the suitcases that Hannah had given her, thinking that her friend might like to borrow it back for her holiday, and went along the balcony with it, to wish her a happy time and give her a last hug.

'I don't need the case, Tanya. I'm travelling light.'

'What the hell for? There are other things to do on holiday, apart from walking and cliff-climbing and being solitary. Men go on holiday too! They want to see women in pretty dresses, looking fetching and feminine! OK! Agreed! Maybe they do prefer them in uniforms and behaving like dragons, but there might be two or three out of a hundred that aren't kinky! With your looks you could have the pick of the bunch. If you have room to take all your photographs, you've got space for a dress. I'll lend you that yellow and white one of mine. You'll look gorgeous in it. So travel light if you must! Pull out ten photographs and put in my dress. You can live without them for a couple of weeks!'

'I can't go without my family.'

'You went to Leningrad without them.'

'That was just for three days.'

'Two weeks isn't for ever.' There was a silence; a moment of indefinable tension.

'Shut up and stop nagging, Tanya. Drink your coffee instead. I'm taking the pack and nothing else. It's all ready.' It lay on the bed, as plump as a balloon. Her travelling clothes were draped over it ready for the morning – trousers and a striped sweater; walking boots, socks and an elasticated jacket.

'Why don't you tart yourself up a bit – for the journey at least? The bus will be packed, and half of the passengers will be men – in holiday mood.'

'I'm not interested in men.'

'Liar! Selfish cow! I'd have the ones you don't want! Anyway, I'm keeping you up. Don't forget to leave your key under my door. You're sure you don't want to change your mind about the suitcase?'

'No thanks, Tanya. Goodbye. Goodbye, *Podruzhka*!' They embraced, and Tanya returned to her room. She couldn't sleep. She was never one to dismiss troubled thoughts. Often, when she was on night-duty, a patient would jump to mind who'd been more than usually restless; feverish; depressed. And although she might be dropping on her feet, she'd have to go and check up on him, to satisfy herself, before she put her legs up on the chair for a midnight glass of tea. People called her dedicated! If dedicated meant suffering from anxiety neurosis, then dedicated she was! There had been a line of perspiration on Hannah's upper lip, reappearing the moment she wiped it away. Blobs of sweat on her forehead. Yet her hands had been cold when she'd held them. She cursed and groaned, swung her legs out of bed and felt around for her slippers. She pulled on her dressing-gown and tiptoed along the balcony. The light was on. She could tell by the gleam under the door. She knocked softly.

'It's me – Tanya.' Silence. Fraught. Strange.

'What do you want?' The voice was quiet; the response peculiarly abrupt. They had embraced less than two hours ago.

'Let me in.'

'No. I'm tired.'

'Let me in or I'll shout the place down.'

'Give me a few minutes then.'

'No! Open the door *now*! You're not well. Be quick!' she hissed. She could hear Hannah fumbling about, then she unlocked the door and poked her head round it. She was wearing a headscarf and her face was white and taut.

'I'm perfectly well What's wrong with *you*?'

'I want to go to sleep. *I've* got to work tomorrow. Some of us have to give injections, make beds and empty bedpans even if it's May 1st.' She tried to make her voice light, casual, while

Hannah pushed her away. 'Hannah, please! Please let me in, just to satisfy myself that you're OK. I won't stay. Please! O, God!' she gasped. 'What have you done? What . . .?'

The thick, golden braid lay under the table where Hannah had kicked it. 'I cut my hair! Is there a law against that, too?'

'For you, there is a law against it. Your own law. Show me.'

Hannah showed her. She looked like a young man – a youth, already dressed in the trousers, lumber-jacket and boots. Tanya closed the door, turned the key and sat down on the chair. 'Tell me.'

'Tell you what?'

'Tell me why.'

'Of course I'll tell you why! I decided to change my image for my holiday! Stop being so dramatic, Tanya!'

She recognized the expression on Hannah's face. She had seen it a thousand times before. Patients of hers, brave, hopeful ones, joking; smiling at her and the doctors as they approached with the clipboard of notes, as if, by being cheerful and self-mocking, they could somehow alter the diagnosis. The hand, icy cold when she clasped it, belying everything; listening to the doctor's awful prediction. 'I'm afraid the tumour is malignant. I wish we could give you better news. Nurse Tanya will stay with you to explain everything.' She was nearly always disarmed by the courage shown; the continued flippancy, until shock was dispelled and grief and anger took over.

'I'm your friend. You're mine. We've confided in each other. You don't have to pretend to me.' Something clicked in her mind. 'Not this,' she waved the braid at her, 'for two weeks' holiday in Memel. It's for longer than that, isn't it? You're leaving Vilnius for ever.'

Hannah stood as if nailed to the floor, rigid with horror. Tanya moved near to her. 'I'm not the telephone engineer. I'm Tanya!' She held her icy hands. 'Bon voyage, my dearest, dearest Hannah. I think I will never see you again. Let me be sure that you're well, before you go. After two weeks, I'll report to your work that you're sick; sign a certificate for infectious diseases. What about a bad case of measles? How long do you need?' She recognized the expression on Hannah's face; less common in her experience, but one that made her job the happiest in the world. 'The operation was a complete success! The tumour was benign. You can go home next week. Nurse Tanya will tell you when to report to Out-Patients.' No light-hearted remarks after that! Just a moment of disbelief followed by wild, uncontrolled weeping. 'I'm going to live, Nurse Tanya! I'm going to *live*!' 'You've got a friend here – right here – next to you! They don't all live far away. I want nothing from you. Just trust.'

'I don't want to involve you, Tanya. I *do* trust you. What if they come, asking questions? If they find out – find me – and they suspect you of being aware of my plans . . .!'

'I'll take that risk. Will you?'

Hannah told her what she had been living for all these months. The planning; the fear, when she had been refused the last two weeks of May. The part of the journey which frightened her. She told Tanya the route – the boat which was going to pick her up; when and where. It was against her nature to be secretive when faced with love. She could fight most things. She couldn't fight that.

'When are you leaving?'

'Now. O, Tanya! Tanya! Is there anyone else like you in the wide, wide world?'

'Millions!' She held the braid against Hannah's face for a moment, then stuffed it into her dressing-gown pocket. 'I'll get rid of this. You'll have another one in time for your wedding.' She helped Hannah to put on her back-pack, then stuck the cap on her head. 'Love to Felix. Be safe. Be well. Be happy, happy, happy! Try to let me know, one day, that you are!' They closed the door behind them and Tanya took the key. They clung to each other. 'I'll watch for you. Go now!'

She stood quite still against the wall of the balcony as Hannah disappeared into the night, then tiptoed back to her own room. She wondered for the hundredth time how she always managed to control her tears in front of her patients; smiling; comforting; rejoicing. But when she was by herself – that was a different story. One day, when it was all over, she'd tell Alexis what some people could do for love. It might – just might – make him get out of that wheelchair. And if not? Well, she'd see!

On May 1st, at dawn, a fishing fleet left Grimsby for the 'Cod Run'. It was a cold, blustery morning for a landlubber, but fair enough for those who manned the trawlers. High tide was at five-fifteen and the fishermen were already checking their gear. There was little that was odd or unusual about their leave-taking except for the man who stood on the jetty – a stranger to all but one of them. He shook hands with each of the men in turn, before they boarded their creaking, rolling vessels. He remained quite still, watching, oblivious to the wind that tore at his coat, or the spray which blew in his face. The trawlers fanned out and dissolved into the misty horizon, but he continued staring ahead at something in the distance, which had no visible shape. When at last he turned away, the sun was already bright on the water. He walked towards a waiting train, only a hundred yards away, and sat, with his eyes closed, for the short journey to the boarding place for the passenger ferry. He stood against the rail until the boat docked at the Pier, disembarked and walked slowly across the cobbles. He leaned against the plinth which bore the statue of Wilberforce, as if exhausted; then he looked at his watch, smiled to himself and buckled his raincoat. He ran along the narrow cobbled lane lined with warehouses until he reached the town. It seemed as if he had remembered an appointment which in-jected him with sudden, boundless energy. He raced along Alban Road towards the Blue Lagoon. It was still closed, but he could smell coffee and new bread. He banged on the door, then laughed out loud with relief, as through the frosted glass he saw her shadow bobbing towards him.

Chapter Thirty-Nine

The Blue Lagoon closed at seven on Mondays. I was glad when the last customers left and told Mike and Dandy to go off, as I hadn't any plans for the evening and would mop the floor and do the tables. We often did favours like that for one another, when Mr Levy was safely off the premises. I locked the door against the lovely, June evening and turned on the fan. I didn't mind being alone now. In fact, I welcomed it. I put the chairs up and filled the mop bucket, grateful for the half-hour's hard work ahead of me. The activity seemed to ease the dull heaviness of my thoughts and strengthen my resolve. I tried to concentrate on visualizing the new extension; what it would look like on completion; working out colour schemes and table arrangements, but my heart wasn't in it. I wouldn't think about the nightmares, though; the frightful, hideously evil nightmares that had tormented me, non-stop, for a whole week in May, making me afraid to go to sleep. They'd stopped now, but the horror of them still made me wretched. When I saw Hannah again, I'd feel better. If I saw Hannah again. No. Not if. When. I wouldn't think of that horrible little word, either. I fetched the scrubbing-brush and kneeling mat and scoured the area near the door until the perspiration rolled into my eyes. For a whole month I'd lost track of Hannah, and although I seemed to eat as much as usual, I'd lost twelve pounds in weight and looked ugly and skinny. I heard Mam talking to Rudi one night, about me; he told her that I'd be OK once the anxious time was over, but meanwhile he'd make an appointment for me to see a neurologist, in case I didn't improve. If only Felix would bang at the door now, this minute, I wouldn't need a nerve doctor. But he'd only visited the Blue Lagoon once, one morning when I was setting up for breakfast. Holding me so tightly, as if quite suddenly he'd realized that it was me he loved, and then he'd said Hannah's name over and over again. Wild; muddled, strange. Once he'd had coffee and a breakfast, he seemed to be clear again. I spoke to Mr Levy that very day about my plans. Even the scrubbing-brush was saying it. Hannah and Felix. Hannah and Felix.

Someone banged at the door. I jumped up so quickly that my head swam and my heart pounded in my ears. I unlocked the door and flung it open, not caring; not seeing; staggering against Rudi. He put his arm round me to stop me falling, and led me across the wet floor. He pulled a chair off one of the tables, and didn't let go until I was sitting down. He wiped the sweat off my face, dragged down another chair and sat opposite me. He held my wrist for about half a minute and told me not to move until I felt better. The urn was still bubbling, and he brought me a cup of tea, holding it to my lips as if I was too poorly to manage it by myself. 'I've come to finish the floor for you,' he said. 'You sit there and watch that I do it properly. Are you ready to hear some marvellous news?' I nodded. I was shaking so much that I couldn't make my voice work. He held my hand again. 'Hannah's in Malmo, Rachel! Safe on the *Celerity*! The worst is over and you've nothing to worry about.' All the icy tightness that had gripped me for weeks, melted and burst into a torrent of tears. I could hear the noise I was making each time I breathed in and out, and Rudi encouraging me, as if I was doing something clever. 'You can go on for as long as you want,' he said. 'Another gallon of water on the floor won't make a scrap of difference. I'll clear it all up!' He talked as if I'd wet myself, and I started to laugh in the middle of it all, but he didn't slap my face. He didn't dare!

'O, Rudi!' I gasped, wiping my eyes with his sopping handkerchief. 'Tell me everything! *Properly*. Do Mam and Dad know? Has Felix seen her yet? When will she be here?'

'Of course they know! They've been running to the phone-box on the hour, every hour, ringing Felix. He hasn't seen her yet, you dope. She's still on the boat, incognito. It's just a fluke, engineered by Stuart, that he was able to send him a message. "THE FLY BIT ABNER'S LEG STOP DAVID OUT OF THE CAVE STOP." I met Sacha in Paradise Street, leaning against the phone-box. He was . . . he was so overcome that I walked

263

him home and left him with Malka, so they could celebrate together. Then I came straight here.'

'Why didn't you phone me?'

'I don't know. I didn't think. I wanted to see . . .' He jumped up and grabbed the mop, swishing it about and making a mess.

'I'm glad you came.' I slid across the floor and jumped on the mop while he gave me a zig-zag ride, as if we were kids again. 'What do you think Hannah's doing, right this minute? Tell me, Rudi! Tell me!'

'You don't know?' I shook my head. 'Then I'll tell you! She's combing fish-scales out of her hair and dabbing on the perfume which is exclusive to the *Celerity*. She's no doubt dressed in oilskins and trying to understand Stuart's sign language. I hope he remembers that Hannah is a lady. Every time she thinks of you, her face takes on a Cheshire Cat appearance, which disturbs the fish.'

'And every time she thinks of Felix?'

'The ice melts, and the fish ferment. Now get off and let me get on with your work.'

'What will happen when they get to Grimsby? Will she have to stay in a refugee camp?'

'Not if I can help it!' He shuddered. 'Those hell-holes don't exist any longer, do they? Mind you, compared to the places Hannah's stayed in, they'd put Buckingham Palace to shame. She may not be able to come home straight away, because she's an illegal immigrant, but Sacha will speak to the Sheriff, and he'll have her out in no time. Is the floor clean enough? Why not leave your bike here, and I'll give you a lift home. Or do you fancy a little celebration? I know the very place.'

'As long as you don't have more than one,' I said, prissily. 'You'll be with me; not Stuart. That Stuart! I'll have to sing his praises for the rest of my life! I'd like to go out somewhere. I need to talk to you about something. Dad and Mam must be so happy. I don't want to spoil it all for them.'

'Why should you? What do you mean?' He waited until I'd locked up. We walked over to his motor-bike, and I climbed on the pillion.

'I'll tell you when we get to the pub. Where is it? I don't want to go to that disgusting dive on the Pier.'

'I'll tell you where we're going when you tell me what you're talking about.'

'It's about me going away.' He revved up his bike, and it roared like an angry animal along Alban Road.

We rode into Barrowby and climbed up the wooden steps of the Black Swan. We sat on the table listening to the water lapping against the supports; watching the lights of the boats in the distance. 'I think this is the loveliest place in the world. I came here once, long, long ago, when I was a kid. I'd been poorly – I can't remember why, or what it was all about. I sat here with Mam and Doctor Toomie. I knew it was beautiful, even then. Why was I so sad, I wonder?'

'And now – do you feel sad, now?' I didn't answer for a minute, and while he turned away, I managed to wipe my eyes surreptitiously with the back of my hand. 'What is it you want to talk about?'

'I'm ashamed because I should be so happy. Nearly everything I ever hoped for has come to pass. I think I take after Dad. I've inherited his melancholy spirit. I need to go away. Don't ask me why, Rudi. One of these days I'll tell you. When I've sorted myself out. I don't know when that will be.'

'Neither do I.' Whatever happened, I wouldn't rise to his bait. I'd avoid an argument at all costs. I needed him too much, as an ally. 'What are you going to do about the Blue Lagoon? You've been itching to be boss there for years, and now you've landed what you wanted, you're ready to chuck it all up! Walk away from a power fantasy come true. What the hell for? You can't stick to Hannah and . . . to Hannah all your life. Once Felix and she are married, you must leave them to get on with *their* lives. It's different while she's here, in Hull. She'll need you; your support and nearness and love. She might be depressed for a time. Really, Rachel, I mean it! When the novel is finished, the author sinks low, although that's what he aimed for. The artist turns away from the painting after the final stroke, and feels empty and lost. It's the price one pays for success after perseverance. Hannah's never stopped fighting and hoping for liberty and family. She'll need time to come to terms with happiness. She'll need you – but only until she goes to London to live with her husband. You mustn't go after her.' How pompous and patronizing he was, prating on and on without a ray of comprehension about anything; fancying himself as my instructor. Had he forgotten that *I'd* taught him practically everything worth while saying? He must have felt

265

my contempt, for he stared at the water. 'She will be Felix's responsibility after that, and he will be Hannah's. If you think about it logically and unselfishly, you'll realize I'm right.'

'I don't want to go to London, you stupid fool! Who put that idea into your fat head?'

'You've been rabbiting on about going to live in London ever since you left school! What the hell is it you *do* want? I'm going to find a drink. Perhaps you'll enlighten me when I get back. Try not to change your tune in the space of three minutes!'

He got up and went to the bar at the back of the table. I sat by myself, hoping he would stay there for an hour. I loved it here. Loved my job. The Blue Lagoon was expanding. It would be the most exclusive spot in Hull. Mr Levy had heeded all my ideas, and he wanted me in charge of everything, and had refused to accept my notice to leave until he knew of my exact plans. Maybe he'd be able to manage without me. The very thought of such a turn of events was like a blasphemy.

'Well?' Rudi's voice was sharp; ugly. He plonked a half-pint of lager in front of me. I hadn't asked for it and didn't want it. He spilt some on the table, on purpose, but I controlled my temper.

'I'm going to stay in Hull with Hannah, and help her to adjust. I wouldn't dream of going anywhere for the next few months. And I can't just leave the Blue Lagoon in the lurch. I wouldn't be so selfish as to do a thing like that! Anyway, Hannah will need a job until everything's fixed up. She could work with me! Mr Levy would take her on like a shot! You know how thick he is with me. Hannah would give the place a touch of the exotic. We'd have Russian music and . . . Just imagine what she and I could do together! People would come from far and wide to eat and drink and dance! We'd put Hull on the map in big red letters! Once we got it going, it would run by itself. I'll miss it. I'll miss it so much, but it's time I moved on. With my experience, it wouldn't be difficult to find a good job in another place, and the British quota for emigration to America is about a hundred per cent. Yosef writes to Dad in every letter for one of us – all of us, to come for a visit. I wouldn't be a liability to him, and Mam and Dad wouldn't make too many objections because I'd be with family, and broadening my experience. You've got to help me to persuade them that it's the best idea in the world. I'll go anyway, but I want them to be cheerful about it. You can manipulate them without even trying. I can't.'

'I don't believe this, Rachel. You're absolutely mad. Go for a holiday if you must. Yosef will come for the wedding, and you could plan when to go for a few weeks after that. But don't give up this wonderful opportunity at the Blue Lagoon. It's being spiteful to yourself.'

'My mind's set on it. I wish I hadn't told you now. I wrote to the American Embassy, and filled out all the forms. And for your information, I've already written to Yosef to ask him to sponsor me. The letter's in my bag, ready to post. By November, I should have saved up enough money for a one-way trip. It only costs sixty pounds on the *Queen Mary*, from Southampton to New York. From there, I'll catch a train to Los Angeles. I'll find a job immediately. I'll break the news to Mam and Dad myself. Don't bother to help me. I should have known better than to ask you a favour. I wouldn't dream of asking you to help me to paint Sybil's room for when Hannah comes. I'll do it myself. I'd never desert Hannah! You'd desert me, though. You never trouble your head about *my* feelings!'

'What? *Your* feelings! I get lost in a vacuum when I try to consider them! Do your own dirty work. Manipulating is your special talent – not mine! Make sure you have a thousand pounds in your pocket before you sail away to the Land of Plenty and Opportunity. You might have one of your "turns" there. Medical expenses are enough to give you a few more, for good measure!' He was beneath contempt, hitting me below the belt like that. I wouldn't answer him. I turned my back and swallowed nearly all my lager, waiting for him to apologize. He didn't. He was worse than Mam.

'You have deliberately spoilt this place for me. But of course you wouldn't understand that. And I have got feelings! I just don't display them to everyone, the way you do. You're jealous and horrid, because you're staying here, while I've got the chance of leaving this provincial dump. Why can't you pretend to be pleased for me? Ill-tempered envy can be pushed into the background. You never make any effort at controlling yourself.'

'Just *shut up*!' I threw the rest of what was in the glass at him, but the breeze made it fly back into my face. I laid my head on the table and started to cry. He tried to take my hair out of the wet mess, and I pushed his hand away. Usually, Rudi never cared whether people were staring, but he had so much to be ashamed of that perhaps he felt contrite, for his voice was low and soft, and he did the next best thing to saying he was sorry. 'I'll come over on Sunday and paint Sybil's room; and speak to Malka and Sacha about your plans.' I sat up, and wiped my eyes. 'Come on. I've spoilt this place for myself, too.'

After the room was painted, I fixed it up for Hannah. We bought a new lamp and a lamp-shade, and I put my wireless and wind-up gramophone on the shelf. Felix came home with the prettiest, fluffiest rug which covered half the lino, and I waxed and polished my dressing-table until it gleamed like a mirror. The curtains, bedspread and frilly cover looked worn and threadbare against the richness of the rug and the sparkling new paint, but I didn't want them changed. I put my records in the wardrobe, and carried up a rickety table which stood in our passage, so that she would have a place for her photographs. I collected my clothes and notebooks and shoe-box, and moved out of Sybil's room into the one I'd shared with Esther and Vered, before Sybil ran away, and made up the three beds. It would be strange sharing with them again, as if we were still kids. I took a last look at Sybil's room. How beautiful it was! How luxurious! The gramophone; the flowered table-cloth; the rug! I sat on the bed, stroking Lucky. 'Goodbye, Sybil,' I said, out loud. 'GOODBYE!' It was Hannah's room now and I wondered what was missing. I brought back the shoe-box containing all my photographs, and put it on the dressing-table, in case Hannah had to leave hers behind. Everything was as it should be. She wouldn't be lonely now, and I would be nearby, if she had a bad dream.

Esther was planning to spend nearly all the summer holidays in Paradise Street, and Vered was coming all the way from Israel for a special visit. She was having a baby, and wouldn't be able to come for the wedding. She'd be so surprised to hear that I was saving up to go to America now. Vered would be a mother in November, and I'd be an aunt. I hoped it would be a girl. How long would it be, I wondered, before I met my niece? I closed my eyes, trying to summon up a picture of the future, but all I could see was the present. Rudi and Esther talking to my parents in the kitchen. Dad shouting with laughter, as if he'd forgotten that I was going away. As if he knew that Hannah's homecoming would make everything all right. Esther and Stuart set on getting engaged, despite Mam's loud-mouthed objections. Felix, waiting on the jetty all alone, staring at the horizon through his binoculars. Mad with joy and relief. The lights of the *Celerity* winking at him like bits of coloured glass. Hannah flashing her secret message to him. Nobody needed me any more. Nobody. Tears of self-pity poured down my cheeks onto Lucky's startled back. He jumped off my knee and I stood up, trying to remember the line of Latin I'd thought of when I was on the ship, but I couldn't. It had gone, like everything else. I felt my way blindly into the bathroom, and splashed cold water on my face ten times.

Chapter Forty

Rabbi Sokolovsky was summonsed to appear before the magistrates on a charge of harbouring an illegal immigrant. His letter, pleading extenuating circumstances, revealed that it was his sister. For compassionate reasons, it was decided that she could remain for three months from the date of the hearing, on condition that she stayed at her brother's address, was maintained by him, did not attempt to take up paid employment and reported to the Central Police Station every week. Apparently she had stowed away on a fishing vessel and had evaded discovery until it was three miles away from the east coast of England. Her entry into the country was in defiance of the law – the letter of the law – but provided she abided by the conditions laid down by the Court, there seemed to be no reason why Hannah Sokolovsky should not be allowed to reside here permanently, since she was engaged to be married to a British subject. If she married within a week of her temporary permit expiring, she would automatically become a British subject, too.

The next day, she celebrated her birthday in the house in Paradise Street, and Felix took the ring which she wore on a thin gold chain round her neck and put it on her finger, and asked Rachel if they could book the new wing of the Blue Lagoon for the wedding party, in three months' time.

Rachel taught Hannah everything she knew, and Hannah worked with her every day as an unpaid but invaluable member of the staff. At the end of each week, Rachel received double wages in her pay packet. Mr Levy knew when he was on to a good thing and was prepared to pay for it. Hannah went to night school twice a week, and with her quick mind and talent for mimicry, with Rachel talking in English to her all day long, she made tremendous progress. Malka loved and relied on her; Sacha teased her and laughed at her, and the horrible, intervening years of loss and grief, suffering and stolen youth, gave in to the present as if she had been awakened from an intolerable nightmare. Felix came to see her whenever he had a free weekend, and delighted in the way she flourished in her new life. He failed to notice that sometimes she would glance at Rachel, then turn away, puzzled and sad, as if there was something that troubled her; an indefinable sorrow that momentarily clouded her face. But Rudi noticed. He noticed everything.

'What is it about Rachel that makes you unhappy, Hannah? Is it because she won't be at the wedding?'

'I wish that *was* the reason! It's not knowing *what* it is, that drives me mad! She's never stopped worrying that Felix and I will be distressed because her sailing date and job are unalterably fixed, but she'll always be nearby, wherever she goes. She'll *be* at our wedding, wherever she is! And why should I expect you to understand that? Felix can't. He's hurt, and can't believe that I'm not. Rachel could never hurt *me*! O, Rudi, I don't know what it is that disturbs me. A thought; a feeling that I can't trap.' They always spoke in a mixture of German and Yiddish. He'd thought he'd almost forgotten the language of his early childhood, but it was easy to recall it when he spoke with her. 'It's like a dream from which I wake before I've seen the ending. Can't you help me to see what it is? Have you some medicine to show me the way to it?'

'I wish I had. Have you told Rachel about this? She always says she understands you better than anyone. It's her favourite boast. I don't think it's an empty one.'

'We share the same blind spot as well as the same sight.' She looked into his eyes. 'There isn't a thing I don't know about Rachel. It's my favourite boast, too!' She punched her head with her knuckles. How alike they are, he thought. How different! He wouldn't disenchant her. Rachel had managed to keep her secret and he would never betray her.

Chapter Forty-One

Mr Levy, my boss, was the only person outside the family who knew I was going away. He reacted very badly, and although I tried to convince him that no one was indispensable, he was understandably distressed and doubtful as to how he would cope. I shared his anxiety, but kept it to myself. He knew better than to beg Hannah to stay on, since he'd understood all along that she was helping out on a temporary basis, and that she and Felix would live in London. He didn't consider my plans as important and urgent, and I knew that he felt I was letting him down, even though I was staying for the opening night. He wrote out a letter for me, so that I could give it to a future employer. If I'd dictated it to him myself, it couldn't have been more glowing or honest. When I showed it to Mam, she said it was no more than I deserved. I remembered how she'd put Felix's reports away, and gloated over Esther's and Vered's academic successes, but she didn't make a song and dance over my testimonial, or bother to ask for a copy so that she could frame it, and I never showed my disappointment. I bought a plastic folder and placed the letter carefully inside, after learning it off by heart in case I ever mislaid it. I hated long goodbyes and told Hannah and Mr Levy that I would tell the rest of the staff and the regular customers that I was leaving when they were all gathered together for opening night.

Every table was booked in advance. Hannah and I had worked from morning till night and every single item to do with the arrangements for the evening had been checked and rechecked by me, until I was satisfied. Mr Levy and Hannah insisted that I should go home and rest for the afternoon, so that I would be fresh for my busy evening. I *was* tired! Mam lay down on the bed next to me, while I gave her detailed instructions as to how I wanted the menus and flowers displayed for the wedding reception, as I'd be on my way to America by then, and she promised to see that everything was done exactly as I suggested. Then she put her arms round me and sang to me as if I was a little girl again, until I fell asleep.

When the alarm woke me, the house was silent and empty. No one was in, to wish me luck for the first night. The Last Night for me. It wasn't that important to them. It wasn't as if I was taking an exam to show how clever I was. How stupid. They didn't care. Only Hannah cared. Felix would be there, but I knew that was only for Hannah's sake; not for mine. Even Rudi was too busy. I'd cry, if only I had time. I had a bath and washed my hair; stuck my head under the cold tap until I felt better, then sat down by the fire in the kitchen to dry my hair. I put on my new dress which I'd bought specially for the occasion and put the gold chain round my neck. This should be my finest hour! If only . . . I pulled on my coat and went into the Front Room, and looked at the two huge suitcases already fastened and labelled for my long, lonely voyage to the New World. I'd think of this horrible room when I was homesick. I poured out some brandy from one of the bottles in the cardboard box. I didn't need anyone and nobody needed me! I looked at myself in the mirror. "NEVER NEVER NEVER NEVER NEVER". King Lear said that after the death of Cordelia; after he'd been deserted by everyone. I pushed my bike out of the passage and into the cold, bleak street, and pedalled off to the Blue Lagoon.

The whole place was in darkness. Where was Hannah? Mr Levy? Mike and Dandy? Customers would be arriving for supper in half an hour! The band was due in ten minutes! The door was locked! Panic-stricken, I fumbled for my own key, unlocked the door and turned on the lights. Family, friends, favoured customers, Felix – stood there in the flower-bedecked room, shouting my name; smiling; waving! The band must have arrived early, too, for as I stood staring, nailed to the floor, it struck up with 'The Entry of the Queen of Sheba' and every single person in the Blue Lagoon stood up and clapped. Hannah presented me with a huge bouquet, which Vered had particularly requested should be given to me from her. Hannah said this in her speech, which Felix translated, and when she came to the part about what she owed to me and how much she loved me, Felix looked straight into my eyes and repeated it in English, saying that he wanted to say that as well, and so did everyone in this magnificent room. I could hear Stuart shouting, 'Hear, hear!' I was so overcome with emotion that my contact lenses misted over, and while I wiped my eyes, Rudi made a toast and everyone drank my health. There had never been a night like this at the Blue Lagoon.

Mike and Hannah and Dandy wouldn't let me help with the serving but, even so, the supper was perfect. Mr Levy presented me with a hundred pounds and then pointed to a pile of beautifully wrapped gifts from the friendly and grateful customers. Towards the end of the celebrations, Rudi sat down at the piano and Mike grabbed his mouth-organ, and they and the band played 'Wish me luck when you wave me Goodbye' and 'We'll meet again', and tears poured down my cheeks because I didn't want to go away. Esther put her arms round me and guided me into the shining new cloakroom.

'See what you've done, Rachel! Even Dad looks happy; and Mam's being remarkably civil to Stuart. *You* pulled it off. Hannah and Felix were right. They owe so much to you. We all do. Stop crying, and wash your face, for God's sake!'

'I'm sad because it's a farewell party.'

'Then let it just be a party. You don't *have* to go! Nobody wants you to – except Yosef, of course. You're such a success here. I bet you haven't the nerve to say you've changed your mind! You'd get a refund on your ticket. All you've got to do is to go in there, tell Rudi to belt up with his sentimental songs and shout out that you're staying, and everyone will dance for joy, especially Old Man Levy when you hand back that envelope. He'll be so relieved that you're not leaving after all, that he might insist on your keeping it, anyway – if you make it a public gesture. Stuart! Get out of here! This is for ladies only.'

'They're all too far gone to notice. Did you see me dancing with your mother? I want a word with that sly bugger when she stops splashing water over herself. She owes me a favour.' I pressed the towel against my eyes, wishing that I could do what Esther had suggested. She didn't understand. Nobody did. 'I heard what Esther said, and I want you to do just that.

274

Don't go. Cancel your dramatic departure. If I'd have been told that you were buzzing off, I'd have caught up with you sooner. I ask you for a reason; not to tease or torment you. It's tit for tat, except that I had to risk life, limb and liberty and you have to risk a fraction of your pride. What are you shaking your head for? I thought you were a gentleman.'

'Esther will have to take over any favour I promised. I'm going away to start a new life. You're too late.'

'You know what happened after the Mayor broke his promise to the Pied Piper?'

'Do your worst!' I shouted. 'Blow your pipe now, till you burst! I'm going back to the party.' He stood against the door, blocking my way.

'She's not going anywhere,' he said to Esther, 'until you promise me a favour, instead. You never break your word. Not like her.'

'I'll give him his pound of flesh, Rachel. My farewell present to you!' She pushed Stuart away from the door and I ran out, slamming it behind me. I hoped Esther wouldn't do anything rash, like promising to marry him, even though she didn't love him. She couldn't possibly really want to; he was such a big, crude ox. I crept back down the stairs, and pressed my ear to the door.

'Why do you always persecute her, Stu? You know what she's like. Let her enjoy her glory unmolested. She's already humbled herself for you. Asking you to rescue Hannah was the first unselfish act of her life. She doesn't know the meaning of altruism. She reminds me of you.'

'You remind me of your mother. And you're wrong about Fly-Bite. It's the second unselfish act of her life. I never kissed you in a ladies' convenience before. Now shut up for a minute.' Really, they deserved each other. I could hear them playing a polka upstairs. Rudi and I would show them what a polka was!

Stuart and Esther came in when it was almost over. They looked at me rather sheepishly. They obviously felt ashamed of themselves, carrying on in a cloakroom, but I pretended innocence and smiled across at them from over Rudi's shoulder. I wondered what Mam and Dad would think, if they knew. They bumped into us on the dance floor as the music ended. I heard Stuart tell her that he'd set fire to the *Celerity* if she asked him to, and never quarrel with his mother-in-law more than once a week. I poked Rudi and slid my eyes over to them, to see whether he'd heard what Stuart said, but he was busy watching Hannah and Felix, and paid no attention to me.

Chapter Forty-Two

She went into the Front Room, although she knew that the whole house was empty. Here she could revel in her misery. What more did she need? A wet, cold Sunday afternoon in Hull:

> No sun – no moon!
> No morn – no noon
> No dawn – no dusk – no proper time of day.

Why had she always hated this room? Railed at her parents to fix it; modernize it; do something about the vile furniture, the hideous curtains and the dreary carpet. It suited her exactly! It could be used as a tomb for a dead Egyptian; a lesser tribune. This sanctified, sombre air was perfect for both him and her. He could enjoy a good long death here; sit at the polished table that her mother had inherited from her parents; support his crumbling vertebrae against the stiff, high-backed chair, and put his shrunken lips to one of those bottles in the cardboard box in the corner over there. A long pull of brandy every hundred years would keep him going until eternity. He wouldn't mind splitting a bottle with her.

She hadn't eaten anything since last night, except for a sandwich she'd saved from her train journey to Southampton and a couple of murky old dried prunes which she'd found at the bottom of her bag during the frantic search for her passport and ticket. The stones had kept her mouth going while she watched the *Queen Mary* sail away without her – and for hours and hours after that; huddled up on a bench in the station, waiting for nothing. But the flavour needed renewing. She poured herself a triple dose of cherry brandy into one of the glasses from the sideboard. It tasted nutty and old and delicious, and made her quite light-headed. Could be, that after another shot, it might have a similar effect on her heart. One could but try!

'Have a good cry!' she'd heard people say. 'Don't bottle up your trouble and grief. You'll feel much better if you let it all out!' What arrant nonsense that was! What did they know, with their misguided myths and corny old clichés? She'd be damned if she'd follow that advice for another moment. It would take at least a week to get her eyes back to normal. Her contact lenses felt like jagged lumps of frosted glass. She eased them out and one disappeared onto the carpet. She'd have fun searching for it when she was sober. There was some consolation in being unusually myopic; one could concentrate on self-pity without being diverted by sight.

She poured herself another huge brandy, and sat on the leather armchair in her wet mackintosh. At least the pockets were dry. She'd take it off, once she'd defrosted her hands. Her shoes were sodden and she kicked them off. She could feel all five toes of her left foot protruding from a massive hole in her stocking. She leaned back, listening to the clock, feeling a ladder crawling slowly up her leg. Tick, tock; tick, tock; heel, calf; knee, thigh.

> No warmth, no cheerfulness, no healthful ease,
> No comfortable feel in any member –
> No shade, no shine, no butterflies, no bees,
> No fruits, no flowers, no leaves, no birds –
> November!

No resources. No one to tell. No stomach for self-sacrifice. No Felix. No defence against another avalanche of melancholy that descended on her again without warning. She breathed deeply until the crushing weight of it had passed. An obscure memory taunted her. A ghost nudged her without menace, telling her that this had happened before, and would do so again. She drained her glass and waited, but the strange message eluded interpretation. She closed her eyes.

She opened them with difficulty, as if they were stuck down with glue, not knowing how long she'd been asleep. She

278

couldn't remember switching on the electric fire. Its glow illuminated her face, but did not penetrate the gloom. She moved her toes against the hot rubber bottle which lay under her feet, and thought she heard her name whispered and the soft breathing of another soul.

She stretched out her arms and tears rained down her face, filling the hollow of her neck. He knew that she was in a stupor; that she had held out her arms to another. Not to him. But for a few moments he could comfort her, and pretend that he was thus loved. He chafed her frozen hands in his warm, dry ones, then hauled her to her feet and peeled off her wet coat. She was too drunk to stand; too drunk to know or care. He held her on his lap and rocked her, pressing her head against his chest. In two or three minutes he would have to face her disappointment and his own treachery. But not yet. Not yet. She would fall asleep again and have no recollection of his exploitation. All he would have to do would be to ease her back into the chair, then wake her up before she caught pneumonia, and identify himself instantly. They'd go into the kitchen where it was warm, and he'd make something for her to eat, and dilute all that brandy she'd consumed with half a dozen cups of coffee. He'd question her about what had happened, and she'd answer dramatically, waving her arms about like a tragedy queen; and he'd pretend he was blind to her wretchedness. She'd hate it if she discovered he wasn't.

He attempted to extricate himself from his physical predicament, but she wrapped her arms around him, straining him to her. 'Don't go! Don't leave me! I was having a nightmare – a horrible, primeval nightmare. I was running; running, and someone stood at the end of the road and held out his arms and saved me. It was you! All this time and I didn't know it was you! I'm so glad! I've been so cold; so bloody cold and dreary! I'm much better at being miserable on my own; it's quite difficult to wallow in woe with a witness. Guess what happened! My ticket and passport disappeared. Someone stole them! I went quite mad, and searched and searched, and called the police. They wouldn't let me on the ship. I left all my luggage at the station in Southampton. The station master and the policeman were very sympathetic. They wanted to telephone a message through to the City Police, so that Mam and Dad would know what had happened, but I wouldn't let them. I was *so* distraught. They put me on the train this morning. They're looking after my things until . . . How did you know I'd be here? Why aren't you at the wedding?'

Should he tell her? How Hannah, after the ceremony, had abruptly left Felix, the guests and the photographer, and had come to him? She had gripped his hands, shaking; trembling like a leaf; her eyes closed. 'Find Rachel! Find Rachel!' He had smiled uneasily, disconcerted by her intensity and the outlandish request. He had reminded her that she was on the high seas and he wasn't that good a swimmer.

'Please! Go to the house! Now! Quickly! She doesn't need Felix. She never has. I've always known that. But I didn't know who! I didn't know who – until now!'

'Hannah, what is it? What's upsetting you? You mustn't think this way. Rachel would have been here if she could. This is your day; yours and Felix's. Nothing, no one can get in the way of it. But if you need something from home, of course I'll go and fetch it. All you've got to do is to tell me what it is and where to look; but don't ask me to go swimming after Rachel in my best suit in November!'

She'd opened her eyes; looked beyond him; at him, and laughed with such a burst of pure joy that he knew all was well. 'No,' she said. 'You don't have to do that. Just go back to the house and look in the Front Room – on the armchair. *Yes!* On the armchair!' Then she'd put her arms around his neck and smiled and kissed him, and run back to where Felix and the photographer were waiting.

'I *was* at the wedding,' he said. 'Hannah asked me to find you.'

'Hannah asked you? How did *she* know I was here?' He shrugged, and she saw him raise his eyebrows, for his face was close to hers. His eyes crossed, for he was not shortsighted and didn't have her advantage of being able to see someone clearly from a distance of three inches. It made her laugh, and she examined his face, seeing its familiar, beloved lineaments for the first time. How like Felix he was. How different! She looked at his bow-tie and watched it move slightly, every time he swallowed. It performed quite a dance before he said, 'I know about you and Felix. I've always known. Don't be unhappy – I can't bear it. I can't get used to it. There's so much waiting for you; so many people who rely on you and need you. And love you.'

She wouldn't ask him who they were – he just might omit his own name. 'I rely on you to find my contact lens while I wash my face and ravage Hannah's wardrobe for something to wear. I'll be ready in twenty minutes, and you won't have to get accustomed to my being a wet rag. I've discovered I'm not good at it with you around.

She jumped up and ran out of the Front Room. She ran the bath and pulled off her wet clothes. She put her head under the tap and splashed her face with warm water. He listened to her singing – an old Yiddish lullaby that he'd never heard before. It was probably one that Hannah had taught her when she was a baby; one that she'd suddenly remembered. They'd be in time for the wedding feast at the Blue Lagoon, if she hurried. The worn leather cushion had slipped half-way off the chair, revealing the missing passport. He opened it up. There was a note inside. 'This is Stuart's pound of flesh. Love, Esther.' He looked at the photograph. How like Hannah she was. How different! How like Olga . . . Sora . . . Freda . . . the children she had never seen; would never know. *Papereneh Kinderlech*. Paper Children. He pressed the picture to his lips and slipped the passport into his pocket.

He had found the missing lens by the time she returned. She cleaned them with some liquid from a little bottle, leaned over the table away from him, and jammed them into place with a steady, practised hand. First time lucky! Her eyes weren't that swollen. She blinked, and turning to him, she caught the end of the sweetest smile that anyone had ever blessed her with.